Inquisition

ALFREDO COLITTO

Translated
by
Sophie Henderson

sphere

**FT
Pbk**

First published in Great Britain as a paperback original in 2011 by Sphere

Copyright © Alfredo Colitto 2009
This English translation © Sophie Henderson 2011

The moral right of the author has been asserted.

A CIP catalogue record for this book
is available from the British Library.

ISBN 978-1-84744-478-3

Typeset in Sabon by M Rules
Printed and bound in Great Britain by
Clays Ltd, St Ives plc

Sphere
An imprint of
Little, Brown Book Group
100 Victoria Embankment
London EC4Y 0DY

An Hachette UK Company
www.hachette.co.uk

www.littlebrown.co.uk

For my mother, with immense gratitude

Prologue

.

Messer,

On 12 January of the year of our Lord 1305, you and other Knights Templar took part in an act of extreme cruelty against an innocent man, in the hope of obtaining a secret that would make you immortal as well as rich beyond measure.

You were not even certain that he was in possession of the secret. But nonetheless you tortured him and finally killed him, without inducing him to confess. The fact that he was not a Saracen and enemy of the faith, but a Christian like yourselves, did not suffice to hold you back.

Your actions disgust me, but that is not the reason that I am writing to you. The secret you have been searching for is now to be found in the city of Bologna, in Italy. I also desire to possess it, but I need help.

Rather than try to convince accomplices of its existence and find they turn out indecisive and unreliable, I have decided to ask people who, like you, have already killed without hesitation in order to take possession of it.

If my proposal interests you, come to the place that they

call Jerusalem Bononiensis, opposite the Mount of Olives, on Saturday 1 May 1311, after vespers. I will explain what I want from you in return for what I am offering.

Consider the object that you find accompanying this letter as proof of my truthfulness.

In faith,

A friend

In the autumn of 1310, three Knights Templar, in Naples, Cyprus and Toledo, each received a copy of this letter, written in faultless Latin and containing variations with regard to the place and time of meeting.

They were astonished and deeply uneasy. All three knew to which event the mysterious 'friend' referred and were inclined to believe that the letter was genuine. Indeed, in the copper tube that contained the parchment, each of them found, wrapped in a piece of black silk, an object that possessed the repellent fascination of a reptile: an emaciated human finger, with neither skin nor fingernail, covered in a network of blood vessels.

However, the veins of the finger were cold, hard and dark, made of filaments of metal. A skilful artisan could have made the object by covering a human bone with iron. But the incredible precision led the observer to think that it might even have been a real finger transformed into iron, rather than a work of ingenuity.

The knights had no way of knowing that all three of them had received the same letter. Each decided independently that he should find out whether the person was telling the truth. If someone were able to change human blood into iron, it might be possible to change it into gold too.

And blood changed into gold was an essential step in attaining the limitless power over life and death that they wanted. The secret that they had spent years searching for and that had seemed lost for ever had now returned to haunt them. But it was imperative to take precautions. In Bologna, as in most of the cities of Europe, the trial of the Templars initiated by Philip the Fair and endorsed by Pope Clement V was well under way.

Disguised as merchant, pilgrim and mercenary respectively, the knights took to the road. One thing was clear to all three of them: the person who had sent the letter knew too much and would have to be eliminated come what may.

I

Mondino de Liuzzi saw the fire and heard the crackle of the flames and the dull crash of a roof beam collapsing. The street was so full of people that it might have been broad daylight. There were men, women and children everywhere, all half-dressed. And everyone was shouting to make themselves heard above the din. From the wells behind the Church of Sant'Antonino and the neighbouring houses, the women drew one bucket after another, while the men formed a chain up to the top floor of the building where the fire was spreading. The rasping of the well pulleys produced a constant background screech to the shouting.

Mondino did not stop to lend a hand, thus twice neglecting his duty: both as a citizen and as a neighbour. He had other things to do that night. The men he was expecting would be in a hurry to rid themselves of their burden without being seen. They were probably hiding in some courtyard, but couldn't stay there long with all these people about. He hurried on to the School of Medicine, keeping to the arches so as not to be recognised. No one he knew would have risked going abroad at night without an escort. But if they had done, they would use the centre of the street. It wouldn't have entered their minds to walk through the thick pools of shade under the arcades. Mondino was tall and stronger than his narrow frame suggested, but physical readiness would count for little against two or three villains armed with daggers. As often happened when he thought of the dangers that he was forced to undergo for the love of science, he felt a rush of anger and clenched his fists.

He paused behind an arch to let past an entire family running with buckets to give a hand. The husband rushed by without turning, as did the three children, scampering along in bare feet in the mud of the road. The wife, a dark and alluring woman, seemed to sense his presence and turned to stare into the darkness. She spotted him and opened her mouth to shout, so Mondino did the only thing possible: he half-leaned out of the shadows and put a finger to her lips. His high forehead, green eyes and wavy chestnut hair, worn neither long nor short, usually inspired confidence in the opposite sex. He hoped so this time too.

Out of the blue, a short, fat old hag, with her round head wrapped in a grey bonnet, bumped into the woman, murmuring a word that sounded like 'whore', grabbed her by the arm and dragged her away. It must have been her mother or mother-in-law.

Mondino hurried on a bit further, peering ahead into the gloom, then he stopped at a doorway and took a big key from under his tunic, put it into the keyhole and entered, closing the door behind him.

He busied himself in the dark with flint and tinder and lit the candle that he always kept on a shelf near the door. Then he walked between the empty desks, touching the flame to the wicks of the oil lamps on the stands at the four corners of the dissection table. For what he had to do it was important to see well. He went to a cupboard and took the saw and two surgeon's knives, one long and one short. Then he began to sharpen the blade of the long one, forcing himself not to listen to the turmoil outside caused by the fire. He tried to concentrate on the swish of the knife on the strip of well-oiled leather, but couldn't. He only hoped that there would be no deaths or injuries.

All of a sudden he heard three urgent raps at the door. With a sigh of relief, he put down the knife and went to open it.

He stopped short in front of his student Francesco Salimbene who was standing there with head uncovered: wild hair, sweaty face and a slightly mad look in his blue eyes. Even by the uncertain light of the lamps, bloodstains showed on his knee-length tunic and his chausses beneath. Mondino took one look at the man who Francesco held up by the waist and saw that he was dead. Before Mondino had time to react, the young man pushed him aside and entered, quickly closing the door behind him with his free hand.

'I beg you, Magister, don't shout for help,' he said, while he laid the corpse, not without delicacy, on the marble tabletop. 'I can explain everything.'

Mondino took advantage of the moment to go quickly over to the sloping workbench where he had left the knife and pick it up with a decisive gesture. Then he went back to stand between the young man and the door. Glancing at the body on the dissection table, he noticed for the first time the stumps where the man's hands should have been and the fact that his tunic was drenched with blood around his chest.

'I won't shout for help,' he said. 'But I have no intention of covering up a murder. Tell me what my laziest student is doing here with a corpse in train. Then we will call the city guards and sort the thing out according to the law.'

'This man, Angelo da Piczano,' said Francesco, turning round and noticing the knife but not showing the slightest

7

concern, 'was killed in a way that seems to have something to do with the magic arts and trade with the Devil.'

'Did you kill him?'

The young man opened wide his arms in a gesture of entreaty. 'Certainly not. Do you think I'd have come to ask for your help if I had?'

In the flickering light, his eyes seemed more black than blue. Mondino suspected that he was waiting for a moment of inattention to try to disarm him. But he would find to his cost that a doctor knows how to wield a knife even better than a soldier.

'I did not say that I would help you,' Mondino said, in a flat tone. 'Go on.'

'I can't tell you everything, Master,' said the young man. 'I am asking you to trust me and to help me get rid of this man's body. If the Inquisition finds it, many innocent people could suffer.'

Mondino stared at him. 'Do you realise what you are asking? Destroying the evidence of a murder is a serious crime. Harbouring a fugitive is an even greater crime. If you think that I am prepared to help, you are severely mistaken.'

'So you really do think I killed him?'

There was a desolate tone in his voice, but Mondino was unmoved. 'It's the most logical thing to think. To convince me otherwise you'd need to do better than just ask me to trust you.'

Mondino wasn't frightened of him, but there was no sense in running unnecessary risks. The best thing was to play for time. The gravediggers would soon arrive with the corpse he had asked for. He would tell one of them to call the guards and the problem would be solved. He just had to keep the student talking until then.

'I can tell you this,' said the young man, after a moment's indecision. 'My real name is not Francesco Salimbene, but

Gerardo da Castelbretone. And I owed this man help and protection, as he did me. I would never have harmed him.'

'Is he a relation of yours?'

'No. Why?'

The doctor looked at the dead man. He was about forty, with an athletic build and an austere expression on his face that he had not lost even in death. He was dressed in a simple tunic with neither surcoat nor belt.

'Because he resembles you. A resemblance of character, more than looks.'

Gerardo da Castelbretone, if that was really his name, seemed to be deliberating with himself. Then he smiled bitterly and shrugged his shoulders. 'You are very quick, Magister. No, he's not a relation of mine. But we are bound by a tie that is just as strong. I am a Poor Knight of Christ and the Temple of Solomon, as was he. That must account for the resemblance that you notice.'

A silence followed in which Mondino absorbed the information, then he burst out: 'You're a Templar! That's why you use a false name, why you don't study and only come to my lessons to waste time. You are pretending to be a student to avoid arrest in the current trial against your order.' He was so furious that he took half a step towards the young man, brandishing the knife in one hand. 'And now you've decided to come clean because you need my help. But you're mistaken. The Church's quarrels simply do not interest me.'

Gerardo lifted up both his hands in a gesture that invited calm. 'Please, before you decide, listen to me.'

'Go on,' said Mondino, without lowering the knife.

The young man explained that Angelo da Piczano was a confrère who had escaped the wave of arrests ordered by Pope Clement V at the will of Philip the Fair of France, and taken refuge in Naples. They had met one another in Ravenna when Gerardo was preparing to take his vows and they had become friends, despite the difference in age. Four months previously Angelo had written to him to say that he was coming to Bologna on urgent business, naturally travelling incognito, and he asked if he could stay with Gerardo for a few days.

'I answered that my house was at his disposal, and five days ago he arrived.'

'Did he tell you what business brought him to the city?' asked Mondino, interested despite himself. He had not understood the reference to the Devil, but the amputated hands alone were enough to show that the Templar had not been killed in a tavern brawl or a robbery.

'No, and I didn't ask him,' answered Gerardo. 'These are difficult times for us. The less we know about each other, the better.'

Mondino nodded, and the young man rapidly finished his story. That evening Angelo had asked him if he could borrow his room. He had to meet someone and didn't feel safe in any other place in the city because he feared a trap. Gerardo had explained how to escape across the rooftops in case of danger. Then he went out to have supper in a tavern behind the Mercato di Mezzo, doing his best to avoid the offers from prostitutes without letting them know that he was a monk.

'Angelo had told me that the meeting would not take long and that I could come back after compline,' he continued, briefly turning to look at the corpse out of the corner of his eye. 'When I returned to my room I found him lying on my bed, dead. But I hardly had time to register the outrage that had been inflicted on his body because the Inquisition started knocking at the door, obviously notified by the person who had killed him. I thought that it'd be better if they didn't find his body devastated in such a manner. I set fire to the house to distract them and made my escape over the rooftops, taking him with me.'

'And you decided to bring the problem along to me,' said Mondino, having difficulty containing his fury.

It was Gerardo who was responsible for the fire. He would have to answer for that too. The shouting outside had diminished, a sign that the flames had been overcome. The gravediggers would not be long now.

'The fact is that I didn't think I'd find you here at this hour, Master,' said the Templar. 'But I saw the light showing under the door and I thought I'd knock.'

'You're lying! All my students know that I often come here at night to conduct anatomical experiments so as not to attract too much attention.'

The young man nodded, admitting the truth. 'The Inquisitor's men were looking for me and they wouldn't have taken long to find me if I'd stayed out on the streets, hampered by my dead friend here. I needed help.'

Mondino thought of his uncle, Liuzzo, who had been predicting for some time that his habit of coming to their School of Medicine at night to dissect corpses would sooner or later end in disaster. Liuzzo had really been thinking of him being attacked in the street by some miscreant because he insisted on going out alone without wearing his physician's red robe or even taking an attendant as an escort. He would never have imagined anything of this sort.

'Why didn't you leave him where he was when you set the house on fire?' he asked. 'The Inquisitor would only have found a body burned to a cinder that was wholly unrecognisable, and you would not have run enormous risks by taking him with you.'

Gerardo turned away from him, silently staring at the corpse on the table. A current of air fluttered the lamp's flame and for a second, because of the rapid movement of the shadow, it seemed as though Angelo da Piczano's body had moved. Despite himself, Mondino took a step back.

'Answer me, Templar!' he exclaimed, irritated for letting himself be frightened. He was still finding it difficult to address the Templar by the name of Gerardo. The man's face, long hair, blue eyes, athletic and well-proportioned frame, all corresponded in his mind to an image to which he had given the name Francesco Salimbene from Imola. And now he resisted the idea of giving him another.

'Perhaps not all of him would have been burned,' answered Gerardo, without turning round. 'And what remained would have gravely damaged our order. The accusation of adoring the Devil that has been levelled against us would have been well substantiated.'

It was the second time that he had referred to witchcraft, but the corpse spread out on the table had nothing strange about it, apart from the amputated hands. The face conveyed an expression of stupor more than horror. Some dried blood in the short hair at the nape of the neck suggested that he had been attacked from behind.

'So,' said Mondino, 'you found this man murdered and left naked in your house. You dressed him, set fire to the house and fled. How were you thinking of getting rid of his body?'

Gerardo opened his mouth wide, surprised. 'How did you know that he was naked?' Then he nodded. 'Oh, I understand, the tunic.'

The fact that his surprise lasted so short a time slightly annoyed the doctor. But it was not the moment to worry about such nonsense. He had to carry on talking and hope that the gravediggers would be there soon.

'Exactly, the tunic,' said Mondino. 'It is stained with blood and yet there are no holes, a sign that the wound to the chest was inflicted on this man when he was undressed. And perhaps,' he continued, moving to the side to get a better view, 'when he was already dead or had fainted due to the blow to his head.'

'Your perspicacity is worthy of your fame,' said Gerardo. 'You already know everything before you've even examined him.'

Despite himself, Mondino felt pleasure at a compliment that he sensed was sincere and he rebuked himself silently. Vanity was one of his greatest defects.

'You have referred to devilry more than once,' he said. 'What is so strange about that wound?'

Gerardo turned to look at him, with an expression that was both fearful and resolved. 'See for yourself, Magister,' he said.

Quickly but respectfully he lifted up the dead man's chest and pulled the tunic over his head. As soon as Mondino saw the chest wound his interest grew tenfold. He asked Gerardo to step back and stand between the benches of the lecture hall and, without losing sight of the Templar, he approached the table and ran a finger of his free hand along the cold skin at the edge of the wound.

'The person who did this knows how to cut flesh and bone,' he said with assurance. 'It took me months of practice to make such precise incisions.'

Under the livid skin, the sternum had been sawn lengthways and the ribs broken at the sides. To the left, there was a small triangular hole. Having stunned him with the blow to his head, the murderer must have stabbed the heart with an awl or stiletto, then got down to producing his work of art. It looked as though the man's chest had been turned into a small casket and one had only to open the door to see what it contained.

'I closed it,' said Gerardo, confirming his thoughts. 'When I found him, stretched out on my bed, his chest was wide open like an obscene mouth. And inside ...'

He stopped short, won over by an emotion that could have been horror or pain. Mondino was no longer thinking of the gravediggers who were about to arrive, or the fact that

Gerardo might be a dangerous criminal on the loose. Now he only wanted to know the secret of the dead Templar. He rolled his sleeves up to the elbows and put his fingers between the edges of the wound. The idea of a tabernacle came to mind. He banished the thought as sacrilegious, but then it came to him with lightning intuition that perhaps this was the mysterious murderer's very intention. To make a mockery of religion by building a tabernacle out of flesh and bone in the chest of his victim.

However, he couldn't waste any more time. In the room, there fell an unnatural silence in which any tiny movement sounded like the crack of a whip. With the greatest care, he moved the sides of the wound apart and opened the two strips of flesh in the chest.

He instinctively jumped backwards, giving a cry of horror that sounded all the more anguished in the empty hall.

Looking round, he stared at Gerardo, who was standing behind the bench almost as if it were a normal anatomy lesson, but there was no sign of surprise or derision in his blue eyes. Just an attentive look, as though he knew exactly what the other man was feeling.

Mondino wanted to say something but abhorrence silenced him. Taking control of himself, he went back to the table and looked at the tormented breast again, without giving in to the impulse to turn away. What he saw, between the dried blood and the broken bones, took his breath away, but in a certain sense calmed him down somewhat. It was ghastly, yet perfectly explicable.

'Someone wanted to have some cruel fun with this poor fellow,' he said, in a strained tone that was meant to sound relaxed. 'And I agree with you that to desecrate a human body in this way makes one think of trade with the Devil. The murderer wanted to transform the chest into a blasphemous tabernacle, sculpting a heart of iron to substitute the one of flesh and putting it in the place of the holy pyx with the communion wafers.'

'It's not a sculpture,' said Gerardo, in a voice so low that Mondino thought he hadn't heard properly.

'What?'

'The heart. It's not a sculpture. Have a better look.'

Mondino looked again at the man's gaping breast and saw clearly what in reality he had noticed before but had blotted out because he couldn't justify it.

The heart in Angelo da Piczano's breast was a real human heart, transformed into a block of metal.

It couldn't be otherwise, given the precision with which it was welded to the veins and arteries connecting it to the other organs. There was absolute continuity, with no joins to be seen. It was a work of art that reflected a perfection more divine than human, but twisted and oriented towards death rather than life. At that moment Mondino did not doubt that he was contemplating the work of the Evil One.

He turned to Gerardo. All the certainty he had felt before deserted him, leaving a sense of parching thirst that prevented him from speaking. Hurriedly, he brought the four pedestals with the lamps closer to the table. He had to see more clearly. He had to know. To think. He was no longer interested in keeping an eye on Gerardo. He only had eyes for that open thorax, full of dried blood, the now motionless organs devoid of the glimmer of life, and that heart converted into an abomination.

The perpetrator of the revolting spectacle was human, of that Mondino had no doubt. You could see the marks left by the teeth of the saw on the bones of the thorax, and the Devil, as far as he knew, wouldn't use such crude instruments. But the murderer had certainly acted from an evil impulse. Why? What did he hope to accomplish?

All of a sudden he looked up, fearing that Gerardo would

15

take advantage of his inattention to try to overpower him. But the young man hadn't moved. He was staring at him with his hands resting on the sloping surface of the desk where Mondino usually put his study books and the sheets of paper on which he made notes.

'I won't do anything to harm you, Master,' Gerardo said, reading his thoughts. 'If I had wanted to, I would already have disarmed you.'

'Try, and you'll get a surprise,' countered Mondino, but without hostility in his voice.

He was distracted by a thought that made his insides vibrate with curiosity and fear. It was clear to his scientific mind that the transformation of Angelo da Piczano's heart was not the result of the shadowy spell of a witch, but the much more concrete art of alchemy. Although a distorted alchemy, it was true. None of the treatises that he had read during his medical studies had referred to the possibility of converting human blood into metal. At the time, Mondino had even got hold of a copy of *Liber Aneguemis*, the Latin translation of an Arabic manuscript on the dark side of alchemy, but not even that made mention of such a horrible thing.

And yet, if he could only lay his hands on the formula and apply it to a corpse, the entire vascular system passing through the organs and muscles of the human body, which stubbornly escaped his every effort with the dissecting knife, would be revealed with complete clarity, like a map, down to the smallest detail. And he would be able to copy it into the anatomical treatise that he was preparing, for the benefit of medical science and all physicians of the present and future.

He turned to the Templar, who had not moved and was peering at him intensely. Mondino had the distinct sensation that he was in front of another person, someone very different from the absent-minded student whom he had known from the first.

'What would you do if I decided not to denounce you?' he asked.

The young man allowed himself a slight smile. It was clear that he had understood Mondino's interest in the corpse and the secret that it contained, and thought he could turn this to his advantage.

'Magister, help me to get rid of Angelo's body. I will have a mass said for his soul, then I will dedicate myself completely to finding his murderer,' he said, firmly, as if Mondino had already made his decision.

And in a sense, thought the scientist with amazement, that was exactly how it was. He continued to tell himself that it was ignoble and dangerous to conceal a murder, but given that Gerardo meant to catch the perpetrator anyway, justice would be done in the end. He thought of the dangers to which he would be exposing himself and perhaps his family if he were caught. He thought of the office of Magister of the *Studium* that he held, for which he had made so many sacrifices. But every objection melted away like snow before a fire. For the dream had taken possession of his mind.

Suddenly, without thinking about it too much but in the full knowledge that they were rash words that he would later regret, he looked Gerardo in the eye, laid down the knife on the table and said, 'Very well, I'll help you.'

Before he could add anything else there were two loud knocks at the door. A coarse voice shouted, 'Open up, in the name of the Holy Inquisition!'

Gerardo looked at him, afraid but motionless, waiting to see what happened.

Contemplating the man at the other end of the long oak table that almost divided the room in two, Remigio Sensi felt himself transported back into the distant past, to a time when he had not yet returned to Bologna from the Kingdom of Aragon, and was not yet an established banker.

17

He had first met Hugues de Narbonne in the city of Tortosa, on an occasion that he did not like to remember. Then as now, the Knights of the Temple were among his best clients. They often needed money to buy a new horse or a present for a lover, and they certainly couldn't sign a letter of credit to their order for loans of that nature.

Remigio charged them a low rate of interest so as not to provoke the wrath of the Archbishop of Tarragona. In fact any loan with interest was defined usury, but the Church knew that the Templars were necessary to wrench the south of Spain away from the Moors, so closed its eyes to the activities of the moneylenders.

Nonetheless, Hugues de Narbonne had never had need of Remigio's services. He had been Commander of the Vault of Acre, responsible for the Templars' vessels and all the merchandise carried in them, and even after the fall of Acre in 1291, he held important offices within the order. He was not lacking in money, or lovers either it seemed, despite his vow of poverty and chastity. As far as that of obedience was concerned, Remigio suspected that the Frenchman had made the vow to obey himself alone.

On the day that Hugues de Narbonne first came to see Remigio, he made it quite clear that he knew all about the banker and his affairs although they had never set eyes on one another before. Hugues had then asked Remigio in no uncertain terms to violate the confidential agreements on which he based his credibility as a money-changer and moneylender, by revealing to Hugues the names and extent of the debts of some of his clients. Naturally Remigio had refused, and Hugues had shown no scruples about beating him up in his own office and giving him a split lip. After which Hugues had explained that, if Remigio didn't talk, a hired killer would finish him off that very night or perhaps the following. If that happened, the King's soldiers would search his office in an effort to shed light on his death and Hugues would find a way to assist the soldiers in their investigation. So he would find out what he wanted to know in any case, and the banker would have lost his life unnecessarily.

Remigio went to fetch his ledgers and showed them to Hugues.

Soon afterwards it became apparent that Hugues was using the information to reveal the Knights' violation of their vows. Thanks to the evidence, they were found guilty of serious crimes, judged unfit to serve in the order and condemned to years of rowing in Spanish galleys.

It may be that the verdict was correct or that Hugues had manipulated the whole thing to free himself of inconvenient adversaries. The point was that, due to those indiscretions, Remigio's business underwent a collapse from which it never recovered, until he decided to return to his homeland and open a bank in Bologna.

Nowadays his clients were above all scholars at the *Studium*, but he had maintained contact with the Knights Templar and had continued to deal with them even after their order was put on trial. The Templars of Bologna who had avoided arrest came to him for loans and to negotiate in secret the sale of properties that the Church had not already confiscated. They recommended him to confrères from other cities too.

That evening, after supper, when the office had already been closed for some time, one of the two armed retainers, whom the banker employed for security purposes, had come to tell him that a traveller from Tortosa wished to see him urgently. Remigio had gone down to the hall imagining that he would find a Knight of the Temple but seeing that it was Hugues de Narbonne waiting for him in the corridor he suddenly felt faint and nearly collapsed.

The Frenchman was dressed with his habitual elegance. He wore a sky-blue tunic that went down to just below the knee, following the new mode which tended continually to shorten men's clothing, metal-grey stockings and black ankle boots. He had aged, and the curls poking out from under his floppy cap were more white than blond, but his presence was still intimidating. He was tall and robust, with a square head and cruel mouth. His forearms and hands, protruding from the sleeves of his tunic and covered in a thick fuzz of blond, recalled lion's paws. Remigio quickly decided that it would be better to receive him and talk in private, rather than to try to send him away by force. But he told the two retainers to wait behind the door and come in quickly if he called them.

As soon as they were alone in his office, not bothering with pleasantries, Remigio said harshly, 'Whatever the motive that has brought you this far, Messer, I will do nothing for you. Absolutely nothing.'

This time he was sure that he had the upper hand, but when the Frenchman got up, putting his fists on the table and leaning towards him, Remigio Sensi felt his breath fail him.

'I do not need to remind you of what happened last time you denied me a favour,' said Hugues de Narbonne, pinning him to his seat with hard grey eyes.

'Times have changed,' retorted Remigio, forcing himself not to show his fear. 'Your order is on trial, your Grand Master de Molay is in prison and risks being sent to the stake, the Inquisition is looking for you. I'd only have to shout and you'd have every guard in the city on to you.'

'So why don't you shout?' challenged the Frenchman.

Remigio simply looked at him, without replying.

'I'll tell you why you don't,' continued Hugues de Narbonne. 'Even if the Order of the Knights Templar is on trial, the Templars remain your best clients, and if it got around that you had betrayed the Commander of the Vault of Acre and had him arrested, you would lose them all. Furthermore, if you sold me to the Dominicans, I could reveal that you act as inter-

20

mediary in various business affairs conducted by Templars who are avoiding arrest, that you know many of their hiding places and that your house is a point of reference for members of the order who are passing through the city. How do you think they would react?'

'You would never do such a thing to your own confrères,' answered Remigio, in a voice now deprived of any strength whatever.

This time it was the Frenchman who looked at him without speaking and that look was more eloquent than an entire discourse. It was clear that Hugues de Narbonne was ready to sacrifice anybody in order to achieve his aims.

At that moment there was a knock at the door. Remigio said, 'Come in' and Fiamma entered. She had heard that he had a client with him and, despite the late hour, had come to take dictation from him, as always.

She was dressed in the inconspicuous manner that befitted a girl of her age. She wore house slippers and a simple gown of light wool that disguised her curves. But she must have already undone her hair for the night and not had time to comb it again, as her blonde locks, held only by a hair band, floated free around her shoulders. She held her head partially turned away from them, in such a way that the visitor could only see the healthy side, and Remigio did not miss the look that Hugues de Narbonne gave her.

'I do not need your help, my child,' he said, hurriedly. 'And anyway, we have nearly finished.'

Fiamma seemed surprised. Her dark eyes, made all the deeper by the contrast with her blonde hair, turned to the visitor with a mixture of curiosity and suspicion. Remigio almost physically perceived the excitement that such a direct glance provoked in Hugues de Narbonne, and his disgust for the Frenchman, buried by the years of separation, returned to break open like an egg brooded over for a long time.

'I said, you may leave us,' reiterated the banker, abruptly turning to Fiamma.

'As you please,' she answered, in a compliant tone that both her demeanour and her look fully contradicted. She made a slight curtsey in the direction of the guest, showing her full face for a second, and then left, closing the door silently.

'When we last met you were a widower,' said Hugues, thoughtfully, as soon as they were alone again. 'Even if you had married again straight away, the girl would be six or seven at the most if she were your daughter. And hers doesn't seem to me to be the body of a little girl.'

'Fiamma is nineteen years old and is my adopted daughter. I took her into service when I still lived in Tortosa, after you had done your best to ruin me. Then I became fond of her and adopted her. But I don't see why it should interest you.'

Hugues de Narbonne went back to sit down in one of the three high-backed chairs covered in purple silk cushions and stretched his hands over his thighs. He wore the calculating look that made the banker's heart race. However good the sources of information that the Frenchman might have at his disposal, he could not know about Fiamma. Nobody knew about her, not even Remigio's father confessor. It was the best-kept secret of his life.

'Shame about the scar that disfigures her face,' continued Hugues. 'Nevertheless, I don't believe that she'll have difficulty finding a husband. I imagine that plenty of young Bolognese bucks would aspire to becoming kin to an established banker.'

Remigio did not know what the man was playing at. His every word seemed to hide a threat. But what could he do about it? In the current situation Hugues was in no place to harm him and yet he was afraid of the Knight. It was an irrational feeling, perhaps based exclusively on the man's extraordinary physical appearance; he was still tall and strong even though he must be over fifty. Despite himself, Remigio had to acknowledge that Hugues de Narbonne was a born leader. He only had to speak and his interlocutor immediately felt the need to please him, to see the light of approval in his pale eyes. Not even the limited and scholastic Latin that he spoke to communicate with whoever did not speak his language diminished the impression of authority. It was not difficult to imagine an army of Templars on the battlefield ready to follow him to the death.

Everything considered, perhaps it would be better to find out what he wanted.

'Tell me what brings you here, Messer Hugues,' said Remigio, in a tone that was not steady enough to reinforce his self-confidence. 'Then I'll decide what to do.'

Mondino opened the door and found himself facing a Dominican friar. The man was surrounded by three guards from the *Podestà* who each held a lamp, creating an island of light in the dark street. When he recognised the Dominican to be Uberto da Rimini, his concern turned to something approaching dread. The Inquisitor was known for the intransigence with which he pursued anyone who crossed his path. From the moment he had arrived in Bologna to take up the trial of the Templars, the denunciations and sentences for heresy had multiplied. Until now, Mondino had not met him in person, but he had often seen him participating in religious ceremonies. Uberto was a delicate man, smaller than Mondino by a head, thin and completely bald, with a dry, heightened complexion. Particularly striking was the smouldering nervous energy that emanated from his whole body, draped as it was in the black and white of the Dominican's habit. His eyes, dark and close together, shone out in his hairless head.

'Peace be with you, Father,' said Mondino. 'Why abroad at such a late hour?'

'It's a question that I might ask of you too,' answered the Dominican. He was standing several steps away, a trick often used by small men to look taller people in the eye without having to lean back and look upwards. 'When a man stays up at night instead of going to bed, one fears it is for illicit purposes, and not to do the will of God.'

Mondino knew perfectly well that it was better not to react to the taunt. He knew that he should justify himself in some way and answer his questions, hoping that the guards would stay calm and the Inquisitor go away as soon as possible. But his impulsive nature betrayed him once again.

'In this city it is above all the ecclesiastics who devote the nocturnal hours to the will of God,' he said.

He could tell from the friar's face that he knew the students' euphemism. Since the Lord's command was to go forth and multiply, it was common among students to refer to the sexual act as *the will of God*. If Uberto had agreed with him, it would have been as though he were admitting that by night priests spent their time with prostitutes. But neither could he deny that they dedicated their nights to serving the Lord.

Uberto da Rimini barked two short words at the guards: 'Arrest him.' Before he had time to make a move, he found a man on either side of him and one behind.

'What do you intend to do, Inquisitor?' he asked, impassively. 'I am not a heretic and I have committed no crime. I am Mondino de Liuzzi, physician of the *Studium*.'

The grimace of disdain on the friar's face was accentuated. 'I know exactly who you are. You are the physician who corrupted the art of medicine by introducing the practice of dissecting human bodies, in open violation of a Papal bull. It does not surprise me that you are so insolent to those who spread the word of Christ.'

'The *De Sepulturis* bull prohibits the dismembering and boiling of corpses, not dissection for scientific purposes,'

24

responded Mondino. 'It was proclaimed mainly to avoid commerce in false reliquaries and the bones of saints.'

Uberto did not reply. 'We are looking for a murderer. He set fire to the house he lodged in and made his escape over the rooftops. Possibly carrying with him the corpse of the man he had killed.'

'And you've decided to look for him in the School of Medicine?'

'The neighbours who put out the fire told us that he is one of your students. Your school is only a street away, it would be logical that he would think of taking refuge with you.'

'What is not logical,' said Mondino, through clenched teeth, 'is to conclude that I would provide refuge to a murderer. There is no one here.'

There, he'd said it. He had lied. On opening the door to them, he was still not entirely sure that he wanted to run that risk, despite the promise he had made Gerardo and the interest he had in the corpse with the heart of iron. But the Inquisitor's arrogance and the instinctive antipathy that he inspired did the rest, and now Mondino could not go back, even if he wanted to: he would never be pardoned for that lie. Now, saving Gerardo was the same thing as saving himself.

'May we have a look?'

'No. My word must suffice.'

Uberto da Rimini made a sign to the guards and Mondino was seized by the arms. He tried to free himself with a tug, but the man behind held him by the waist. Mondino heard the noise of broken earthenware. One of them must have dropped a lamp.

'Let me go, immediately!'

'We only want to have a quick look round. If you're not hiding anything then you've nothing to be afraid of.'

'Many of my students live around here,' said Mondino, with a fury that he could hardly contain. 'I saw quite a lot of

25

them helping to put out the fire just now. Would you really like me to call for help?'

The guards loosened their grip imperceptibly. They knew well that the students welcomed any opportunity to create disorder, especially when one of them or their masters were under threat. Obviously Uberto da Rimini knew this too. He stared at Mondino with such an intimidating look that the physician required all his self control not to lower his eyes, then said quietly, 'Let him go.'

The armed guards took a step backwards, making the daggers that they wore at their sides clink together. Their faces were emotionless, and Mondino had the impression that they would have obeyed any order from the Inquisitor without blinking an eye, although they were in the employ of the city *comune* and not the Church. Besides, he imagined that refusing to obey an order from Uberto da Rimini could have unpleasant consequences.

'We will arrest this man soon and make him confess everything,' said the Dominican in a shrill voice, fixing him with a penetrating look. 'I hope for your sake that you are not lying.'

Uberto turned suddenly, making his black cloak undulate and the twisted linen cord encircling his white habit swing round, and he set off towards the Church of Sant'Antonino, followed in silence by the guards.

Although his throat burned with the desire to shout a stinging rejoinder after them, Mondino bowed his head and simply said, 'Peace go with you, Father.'

As soon as he heard the door close again, Gerardo got out of the chest in which the physician had made him hide, on top of the dead body of his friend.

'I couldn't breathe any more,' he said, taking great gulps of air.

'Neither could I,' replied Mondino. 'And I was out of doors.'

Silence fell. During his escape over the rooftops, Gerardo had not had time to think of anything else, and inside the chest his ears had been strained and his heart in tumult, as he waited, ready to carry out any desperate action if the Inquisitor had come in to search the house or if Mondino had betrayed him. Now that the danger had passed, his body, more than his mind, remembered the sensation of Angelo's cold corpse, of the close, intimate contact with death. Gerardo was shaken by a long tremor and had to sit down on the floor. Finally tears streamed down his cheeks.

Without taking the slightest notice, Mondino returned to the matter in hand.

'The gravediggers who I am waiting for cannot be far now,' he said. 'They have probably been hiding so as not to be seen by the firefighters and the Inquisitor, but as soon as the road is clear, they'll knock at the door.'

'You're waiting for gravediggers?' asked Gerardo, drying his eyes with the back of his hand. 'At this hour?'

'What did you think I was doing here in the middle of the night? Waiting for you? Help me lift up your friend, we must be quick.'

Minutes before, the physician had risked arrest and a heavy sentence if the guards had found what they were looking for, and yet he seemed perfectly calm. Gerardo looked at him closely, and perhaps because now their relationship was no longer that of teacher and student, it was as though he were seeing him for the first time. A man in his forties, but who appeared younger than his years. He was tall and thin, with intense green eyes beneath a large forehead. Judging by his rugged physique, wrapped in the black robe that went down to his ankles, Gerardo thought that he had been right not to try and disarm Mondino. Despite his training and the difference in age, a scuffle with the physician might have held surprises.

While they pulled Angelo's body out of the chest and laid it back on the marble slab, Mondino explained that he was waiting for the delivery of the corpse of a woman who had been put to death that day, and on which he wanted to carry out a dissection.

'I made an application to the magistrate and it is all legal,' he said, opening the dead man's breast once again and studying the iron heart as though it were a wonder and not the monstrosity that it represented. 'But I must do it secretly because the Church is opposed to scientific progress and loses no chance to interfere.' He turned to look at Gerardo as though the Templar were directly responsible for the Church's behaviour towards him. 'As long as the priests continue to meddle in everything instead of looking after the salvation of souls, we will never make progress.'

It was no mystery that Mondino was politically on the side of the Ghibellines, in favour of the Emperor's rule as against that of the Pope. His convictions had even earned him exile, and he had only been able to return to Bologna by paying a very high fine. Gerardo, being a monk, was naturally of the opposite persuasion and supported the Guelphs, but it was not the moment to object.

Silently, Mondino took the knife and started to cut the places where the metal gave way to flesh. Watching him work, Gerardo could not help feeling admiration. He was concentrated and precise. His actions never seemed hasty, and yet in a few seconds he extracted that horror of flesh and iron from Angelo's chest, passing it to Gerardo so that he could hide it in the wooden coffer. When he found himself holding what had been his friend's heart in his hands, Gerardo nearly cried out, but he restrained himself and carried out the order without arguing.

28

'Tell me what you intend to do now,' said Mondino, without looking at him.

He had closed Angelo's breast again and seemed more relaxed.

'In what way, Master?'

'We want to find out who killed your friend, don't we?' demanded Mondino, impatiently. 'So we have to draw up a plan of action.'

'You're saying that you'll help me in that too?'

Gerardo couldn't hide the annoyance in his voice. He was happy that the physician was prepared to help him get rid of the body, but he didn't want anyone hampering him and slowing him down in the search for the culprit.

Mondino was looking the other way, standing in front of the cupboard where he kept his surgical instruments. He turned with a reel of silk thread in one hand and a large needle in the other.

'Listen carefully,' he said, staring Gerardo hard in the eye. 'I have lied to the Inquisitor, I have broken the law and I am now in as much danger as you are. I do not intend to loiter around while a callow youth makes a mess of things and gets himself arrested, condemning us both. You wanted my help and it is too late to go back now. I will decide what we do from now on. Is that clear?'

'Not at all,' answered Gerardo, dryly. 'I respect you as a physician and I thank you for not reporting me, but I have no intention of being told what to do by you.'

He had not liked being referred to as a callow youth, and he certainly didn't believe that a layman, who was anti-religion and lacking any military training, could really help him find a murderer and defend the interests of the Knights Templar at the same time.

Mondino went up to the corpse and, without saying a word, started to suture the chest, piercing the flesh and pulling

29

the thread through with the expert and nimble fingers of a seamstress. When he had finished he asked Gerardo to help him put the tunic back on, then finally spoke.

'My involvement is not negotiable,' he said, louring at the monk with resolute green eyes. 'You want to find the assassin; I want to discover the alchemical secret. We must unite and it is not in your interest to refuse.'

'Why? Because otherwise you'd denounce me?' countered Gerardo.

'No, because pursuing two parallel lines of action can get us both what we want more quickly. The more time we waste, the greater the risk of being caught.'

'You speak as though you already had something in mind.'

'I do. But before I go on you must accept my involvement without reserve.'

Gerardo reflected. Although he had no military training, Mondino seemed strong and decided, a man who should not be underestimated in a fight. He had shown himself able to react forcefully to the unexpected. Besides, the idea of following two trails was not at all stupid. But there was still the fact that he didn't know whether he could trust Mondino once the corpse was hidden.

'You won't betray me?' he asked.

'It's too late for me to do that now, and I'm already beginning to regret the fact. Now make up your mind, we haven't got all night.'

'Very well, but we make the decisions together.'

Mondino thought a moment and then he nodded. 'First I will explain my idea, then you tell me yours and we will come to an agreement.'

It was obvious that the influence of his job as a teacher was taking the upper hand. Although he had just accepted collaboration as equals, Mondino continued to behave as he did when speaking from the podium. As soon as they had begun to discuss their plan, a hurried knocking at the door interrupted them. It was the gravediggers, just as Mondino had said it would be. They had been hiding in a courtyard with the woman's body on a barrow and only dared to come out when the street was deserted once again. As Mondino bade them come in, Gerardo quickly withdrew to hide in another room. From behind the door, he listened to their apologies: they had been frightened when the Inquisitor with the three guards had passed close by them and they'd thrown the cadaver into a sewer. Then they had retrieved it. Mondino was indignant and said that it was impossible to practise anatomy on a body covered in slime and filth. The two men asked for compensation to take the woman away again. The physician negotiated a fee and in the end doubled it, asking them to take away the corpse stretched out on the dissecting table at the same time. He explained that it was a body on which he had already finished experimenting, and should be buried in a mass grave. The two gravediggers lifted Angelo's body on to the wooden barrow, laying it on top of the woman, pocketed the agreed sum and went off satisfied.

A minute later Gerardo went back into the lecture room and only then could they finally talk in peace.

'As I said, there are two routes to follow,' resumed the physician, leaning against a desk. 'The first is to find out whom Angelo was meeting that evening and whom he had met since arriving in the city. The second is the trail of alchemy.'

'I understand your interest in the secret of how to turn human blood into iron,' replied Gerardo. He was exhausted and would happily have sat down, but he stayed on his feet out of respect. 'However, I don't see how it can help us to find the murderer.'

'I studied alchemy a little bit as part of my medical training, and yet I have never heard of such a thing,' explained

Mondino. He had an unfocused look on his face, as if he were rapidly trying to go back over all the books he had read. 'Very few people can know a secret such as this.'

Gerardo was surprised by the physician's mental clarity. They had not had a moment of peace since he had turned up at the man's door, and yet Mondino had already had the time to elaborate a plan that lacked nothing, except the finer details. Acting on impulse, he decided to share with Mondino what he knew. He put a hand into the little leather bag that hung from his belt and pulled out a piece of crumpled paper.

'This slid out of Angelo's tunic when I dressed him. It may have no importance, but it's the only clue I've got.'

Mondino examined the paper. It seemed to have been hurriedly ripped off a larger piece and it contained just a few words, engraved into the paper with a stylus, or perhaps with the pressure of a fingernail.

'Philomena, watering place, market,' read Mondino out loud. 'It's a woman's address. A prostitute?'

'I think so, Master. It is possible that Angelo did not fully respect his vow of chastity.'

Mondino's lips assumed a sarcastic smile and Gerardo prepared himself to rebut a comment on pleasure-loving priests, but the physician said nothing and turned back to the piece of paper.

'There are many places where they water and wash the animals and various markets in the city,' he said. 'But I would bet that it's the one near the Campo del Mercato.'

'How can you be so sure?'

'Your friend wasn't from these parts. If he only wrote down these words, without being more specific, it seems likely that he was referring to the biggest livestock market there is.'

He was probably right, but Gerardo was tired of praising him. 'So I'll begin my search there,' he said simply. 'For tonight—'

'Tonight you can stay here,' interrupted the physician,

pushing himself away from the desk. 'There is no bed, but you can spread the blankets in the chest on the table and sleep there.'

'I will spend the night in prayer for Angelo's soul,' replied Gerardo. The mere idea of lying down on the marble slab where so many cadavers had been eviscerated gave him the shivers.

'As you prefer. Tomorrow I've got a lesson after breakfast, but the steward comes around daybreak to prepare the lecture hall. Make sure that he doesn't find you here.'

'I'll be gone before dawn, don't worry,' said Gerardo. 'What will you do while I'm looking for the woman?'

'I'll go and talk to some alchemists that I know. In the afternoon, just before vespers, we'll meet in the Church of San Vitale and Agricola, near my house. You'll find me sitting in my family pew.'

'I'll be there, you can be sure of that.'

'Good,' said Mondino, opening the door.

'Until tomorrow, Magister,' said Gerardo. 'And thank you for everything.'

The physician turned slowly, looking at him closely. 'I have always been impulsive in my decisions,' he said. 'Helping you was not an exception. I hope you will make sure that I don't regret it.'

Then he went out into the dark street, without even a lantern to light his way, and turned his steps confidently towards home.

Gerardo stood motionless on the threshold listening to the peaceful sounds of the night. If the neighbours had already returned to their beds, it meant that the fire had not caused serious damage. Nonetheless, a description of him would have been given to the authorities and beginning the next morning it wouldn't just be the Inquisition that was after him, but the city guards too. He would have to find somewhere else to live, assume another name and be doubly cautious from now on.

33

He closed the door and secured it with the metal bar. Then he drew his hands through his shoulder-length hair, more to calm himself than to tidy it, and went to kneel at the linen chest. In the absence of a body, he would watch over Angelo da Piczano's metallic heart buried in the wooden chest beneath two blankets.

He was certain that Angelo's soul, wherever it was now, would have great need of comfort.

II

Beneath a leaden sky, Uberto da Rimini was crouching down on the narrow pathway of San Domenico's cemetery, pulling out the weeds around the tombs. He had woken early, still irritated that he hadn't found the dead body mentioned in the anonymous informer's letter. His annoyance had increased when he remembered the arrogant reception he received from the physician who had refused to let him enter by threatening to cause a student uprising. Uberto took it out on a friar who had knocked over a jug of water on the floor, ordering him to do a day's hard labour in the cemetery.

In theory, only the prior had the power to deal out punishments, but he was a weak man, who from the day that Uberto had arrived at the monastery had done his best to make himself invisible. So that when his authority was bypassed, he could always say that he had not been present, that he had not seen anything and that he knew nothing.

Consequently, it was really Uberto who was in command, and although it seemed proper, given that he was more than capable, he had to be careful not to fall into the sin of pride.

This was why he had later decided to join the monk in his punishment of weeding the cemetery. He took satisfaction in being as inflexible with himself as he was with anyone else. Besides, physical effort was the only thing that might help him give vent to his anger that morning.

They worked on in silence, each alone with his thoughts. Uberto bent down to pull out a dandelion growing from the crack between two bricks, but its long conical root broke just below the surface and he was left with a handful of leaves. This meant that the plant would reappear in a few days' time.

He straightened his back, observing the lines of tombstones before him. The requests of prelates and notables who wanted to be buried near St Dominic's tomb rose year on year, and the monastery had difficulty fitting them all in. The cemetery was full of tombs, and although the friars did their best to keep it in order, the weeds simply carried on reappearing.

Heresy carried on reappearing too, thought Uberto, after every effort to extirpate it. But it wasn't heresy's fault. It was the Inquisitors who, in order not to lay themselves open to criticism from the civil authorities, contented themselves with niggling trials and mild sentences. How could you frighten a heretic if, in the worst case, he was condemned to carry out a pilgrimage to St Peter's in Rome?

The only way to stamp out heresy completely was to extract it at the root, whatever the cost. There would be mistakes, certainly. The odd innocent man might finish at the stake, but his soul would be saved because he had died for the good of the Church. It had been the fate of the Cathars of the Languedoc, and, more recently, of Fra Dolcino and his acolytes too. Both Cathars and Dolcinians had disappeared altogether. And the same would have to happen to the Templars. The Holy Inquisition's job in this case was not to find certain proof of guilt or innocence, as the Archbishop of Ravenna, Rinaldo da Concorezzo, wanted. The accusations against the Templars were too serious and their power too great for the Church to run the risk of absolving them. The order must be destroyed, and its leaders burned at the stake. The job of every good Inquisitor was to help the Church reach that objective, even if it meant making difficult decisions.

Uberto da Rimini sat down at the foot of a tomb to think, while the friar went on working without stopping or raising his head.

The evildoers did not concern themselves with obeying the law when they committed their crimes. Why should those who fought against them have to be hampered by a series of useless regulations? If he wanted to find the corpse of a Templar showing signs of the Devil's work, as indicated in the informer's letter, Uberto could not follow legal channels. He had sent for a trusted man, a former priest who lived at the edge of the law. However, what he meant to ask of him would not receive the Archbishop's approval, so he had to be very careful.

The youth who had escaped arrest the night before was one of Mondino de Liuzzi's students. And the fact that the physician had denied Uberto entry to the School of Medicine still seemed highly suspicious to him. He would have to investigate, but in secret. Then, once he had found proof, Uberto would be able to work out how to do things according to the law. There was no doubt that this case could reveal itself as crucial in speeding up the fall of the Templars. If he were successful, many high-placed prelates, and perhaps the Pope himself, would approve of what he had done.

On the other hand, if he failed he would cover it all up. In that way he would risk nothing.

A friar came walking swiftly towards him and told him that a certain Guido Arlotti wished to speak to him on an important matter.

Guido Arlotti was the former priest whom Uberto had been

waiting for. He was anxious to see Arlotti but didn't want to be seen dirty and sweaty as he carried out his penance like a peasant.

He cut short the friar's explanations with an abrupt wave of his hand and told him that he would receive the visitor in his study. Then he set off towards a gate that led to the orchards, rapidly refreshed himself at the well, cleaning his hands of the stains of the weeds, and entered the monastery by a back door, while thunder sounded in the distance.

Guido stood waiting for him in the study. He was thickset with short reddish-brown hair. His knee-length sleeveless tunic showed off his muscular arms and thick calves clad in woollen stockings. On his feet he wore flat laced sandals, not elegant but made of good leather. Looking at him, no one would have said that he had once been a priest. Now he earned his living by exercising the questionable art of procurer of women, but he was still a Christian in his way. He had a genuine fear of hell and helped the Church in its job of singling out people suspected of heresy in return for money and indulgences for his sins.

Uberto greeted him and offered him a glass of water from the jug on the table, which Arlotti refused. Thus they immediately came to the point of the visit, both remaining on their feet. This was a way of underlining that Guido should not really be there and that the meeting would be as short as possible. Uberto was pleased to see that the discomfort was not only his own. The de-frocked priest also felt out of place in the house of God, and this made it easier to lend the right tone to their relationship.

'I came as soon as I received your message, Father,' said Guido. 'How can I be of service?'

Uberto took a step away from him. Guido didn't exactly smell bad, but his body and clothes still bore the cloyingly sweet odours of the perfumes burned in brothels.

'I must entrust you with a most delicate task,' he said.

'I'm listening.'

'I have reason to believe that a physician of the *Studium* has given refuge to a fugitive from justice, probably a Knight Templar disguised as a student. And that he has helped him to get rid of a cadaver. How could he have done this?'

Guido remained silent for a time, his face dark. He stretched a hand out towards the jug of water, and then thought better of it. 'There are plenty of ways,' he said, finally. 'What is the physician's name?'

'Mondino de Liuzzi.'

Guido nodded. 'I know who he is. Mondino is in contact with all the gravediggers in Bologna. He buys corpses from them for his dissections. He might have asked one of them for help.'

'And would you be able to find out?'

'It won't be easy,' answered Guido. 'As you know there are lots of small cemeteries in the city and a large number of gravediggers. If one of them has helped Mondino get rid of a body, he'll obviously keep quiet about it. But with the promise of safety, and perhaps a little money ...'

'Do as you think best,' said Uberto, cutting him short. 'The important thing is to find proof that Mondino is involved, and naturally find the hidden cadaver.'

Guido darkened again. 'That might not be possible. If I were a gravedigger charged with such a task, I'd throw the body into a mass grave with the lepers. Then it would soon be covered with quicklime, becoming unrecognisable.'

'Let's hope that not everyone has your intelligence,' said Uberto. 'If you get me what I ask, your pay will be twice the usual.'

'I'd also like a certificate of plenary indulgence, signed by the Archbishop.'

'Forget it. Rinaldo da Concorezzo must not even be aware

of your existence, at least until the trial of the Templars is concluded.'

Guido looked annoyed. 'I understand. But you know that I can't speak of many of my sins in confession. And more than a year has gone by since the last indulgence I received.'

He was referring to the crimes against the law, including murder, committed on his own account or by order of a man of the Church. Uberto knew that he was not the only one to take advantage of Guido's services. He needed to keep him sweet.

'I'll see what I can do,' he said. 'You concentrate on getting results.'

Guido Arlotti's wide face broke into a smile at last. 'Results are my speciality,' he said. Then he made a slight bow and left.

When Uberto returned to the basilica's cemetery, the cover of dark clouds had got thicker, but there was still time for a bit of work before it began to rain. He looked over at the friar with whom he had been sharing the penance. He had been working hard without rest since the early morning, bent down among the tombs. He was sorry for him, but they would have to start again from the beginning.

He went up to him and good-naturedly explained how the work should be done, gouged out weed by weed.

'But like that it will take weeks to rid the whole place of them,' the monk protested, raising his sweating face to look at him.

The good nature vanished from the Inquisitor's face with the rapidity of a dream, and the friar hurriedly excused himself for his impertinence. Then he knelt down on the ground and started to delve painstakingly into the cracks between the stones with the point of the sickle.

It was a good idea. In an élan of modesty, Uberto decided to do the same. He picked up a pointed shard of earthenware and dug around the dandelion root until he managed to extract the whole plant, avoiding breaking it even at its delicate end. Then he threw it on the pile of other weeds and filled the hole up with earth, without leaving even the smallest trace of the plant that had once grown there.

Gerardo walked in the rain, with the hood of his cloak falling over his eyes. He was tired from his vigil and the events of the night, which now seemed to him somewhat unreal. Other than praying for Angelo's soul, he had asked God's pardon for the manner in which he had been forced to dispose of the body. The idea that his friend was lying in a mass grave, without even a cross to recall his name, seemed to him almost more horrible than his death itself.

According to his agreement with Mondino, he had to start looking for the people with whom Angelo da Piczano had been in contact during the few days he had spent in Bologna. But first of all Gerardo needed money, given that he had left all his possessions in the burning house and all that he had now were the few coins in his pouch.

He had left the School of Medicine at dawn and immediately begun to look for new lodgings. Naturally he had changed neighbourhood, choosing the area near the Porta Stiera, and more precisely Borgo del Rondone, not far from the Church of San Naborre and San Felice. It did not seem to him that the dialect spoken in San Felice was so different from that of Strada Maggiore, as heard by Dante, the famous Florentine poet who had passed through Bologna, but it was also true that he didn't have much of an ear for languages. He had found it difficult enough to learn Latin. In any case, dialect apart, it had not been easy to find a room, because he wanted somewhere from which he could guarantee his escape if need be. Fortunately it seemed that there was hardly a family in the city that didn't rent out rooms to students. He

41

had found one near a bakery, with a separate entry at the rear so that he could come and go without attracting attention. He had presented himself to the owners using his real name. Since the identity of Francesco Salimbene was now compromised, he might as well revert to his own. Three years had passed since the order for the arrest of the Templars and no one would be bothering to look for a neophyte like him any more.

And that was the irony of it: Gerardo had dreamed of becoming a Templar since he was a boy, and just when, after years of spiritual and military training, he had finally taken his vows and was awaiting his first posting, Philip the Fair's offensive against the order had begun. To escape arrest, Gerardo had left Ravenna and come to Bologna, changing his name and breaking off all contact with his family. He had altered his physical appearance, growing his hair and relinquishing his beard and the robe worn by the order. He had enrolled in Mondino's lessons, but studied the absolute minimum necessary to keep up the fiction and was waiting out the end of the trial before deciding what to do with his life.

And now he was in trouble again, wanted for arson, not just for being a Knight of the Temple.

He had considered leaving the city, then decided against it, not only because if he left he wouldn't be able to find Angelo's murderer, but also because he was convinced that it would be easier to continue to hide among Bologna's forty thousand inhabitants, as he had until now, than in some little town in the countryside, where his presence would be noticed.

But now he had to venture back into the centre of the city, where many people knew him, not least his ex-landlord. It was the most dangerous part of town for him but it was also where the bankers had their offices and he needed to ask for a loan. Gerardo hoped that his hood would suffice to avoid discovery, but he couldn't relax and continually struggled against the temptation to look over his shoulder.

An insistent rain was falling and everyone was looking for shelter under the arches. The streets were left to the horses and carts and the people carrying things that were too bulky to allow them to thread their way through the columns. Gerardo stopped to wait for a small flock of goats to cross the paved piazza in front of the Church of San Francesco. The route was shorter by Trebbo dei Banchi but passed Mondino's *Studium* and it obviously wasn't the moment to show his face in that area. All of a sudden a kid goat nipped through the open door of a tavern, and by the time the goatherd followed, it had mysteriously disappeared. A loud altercation followed in which the shepherd dog also took part, barking furiously to keep the flock together while his master argued.

Gerardo walked on, thinking that the kid would already have had its throat cut by the taverner's wife to stop it bleating, and that the shepherd would never see it again.

He wound his way between the stalls of the Mercato di Mezzo, splashing his shoes in the mud, took the bridge over the Aposa and reached the chapel that housed the stone cross dedicated to the Holy Apostles. There he saw that two countrymen, sheltering from the rain beneath the canopy, were roasting a piece of pork on the church steps, perhaps ignorant of the fine they risked receiving from the city guards. Pretending to want to warn them, he took the opportunity as he spoke to have a good look round him.

The countrymen told him to mind his own business but Gerardo was already long gone. He turned right at the Asinelli Tower and found himself in the Trebbo dei Banchi neighbourhood. Once more he was seized by an irresistible need to look over his shoulder, but he knew that he would only attract attention, raising the likelihood of being recognised. He tried to remain calm; he put his head down and walked on.

He arrived at the office belonging to Remigio Sensi, trusted banker to the Templars. The wooden hatch, which when open and resting on two supports served as a counter on which to count out money and sign bonds, was beneath a portico that was too high to provide efficient protection against bad weather, and perhaps for that reason it was closed.

So Gerardo went up to the door of the banker's house, which he found open. Just over the threshold, in a badly lit hall, lounged two massive attendants in grey indoor tunics, daggers at their belts. He told them that he wanted to see Remigio. The two moved aside to let him pass. Gerardo walked down the windowless corridor that was lit by lamps even in the middle of the day, took off his wet cloak, laid it on a bench and entered the studio through a double wing oak door.

He was surprised to find a girl in the room. Her head was lowered and her blonde hair was covered in a silk veil of the same tone of green as her embroidered robe. She was writing on a piece of parchment with a quill, making a scratching sound. It was the first time in his life that he had seen a woman writing. Even his mother, who was perfectly able to read, had to dictate her letters to a scribe.

'Come in, Messer,' said a man's voice, and only then did Gerardo notice the banker sitting at the centre of the long table that divided the room in two. He was no longer a young man, had very little hair, a flattened nose and wore an avid expression. He had a prominent stomach that his well-cut long black tunic did little to hide. Behind him, against the wall, there was a very solid-looking coffer with two locks, and to either side of it, two bookshelves overflowing with documents held together by hard leather covers.

Gerardo went up to the banker and introduced himself, mentioning the name of the confrère who had sent him but without saying that he was a Knight of the Temple. He didn't know if he could trust the girl.

As though reading his mind, Remigio asked her to go and

find out what the kitchen girls were up to. She laid down the quill, blew on the words she had just written and turned to give the banker an annoyed look that was certainly not that of a servant. 'I checked on them a moment ago,' she countered. 'May I finish writing this letter first?'

She seemed to be avoiding looking in Gerardo's direction, with her profile turned towards the banker, and an elbow on the table.

Remigio Sensi sighed. It was clearly not the first time that his orders had been questioned. 'Do as I told you,' he said quietly.

The girl glared at him, she was on the point of answering back, then thought better of it. She nodded and rose. In order to get out from behind the table, she had to face Gerardo straight on, showing a terrible scar that disfigured the left side of her face. The young man was shocked, but even more so by her eyes, that were so dark and deep, shaded by an immense sadness.

It was only for a second, then she dropped her gaze, as befitted the modesty of a young woman, and walked swiftly out in her yellow felt slippers that matched her hair.

'I've never seen a female scribe before,' Gerardo felt the need to comment, sitting down on a silk cushion on the high-backed chair.

Remigio laughed. 'Fiamma is my adopted daughter. When I took her in, she already knew how to read and write.'

'Strange for a woman. Was she the daughter of a noble family?' Gerardo did not really want to know about Fiamma's family, but something inside him refused to let the matter drop.

'Her father was a Venetian merchant who ran his business in the Kingdom of Aragon, too close to the Saracen lands,' explained Remigio. 'One day the city was sacked and Fiamma's family killed. But a Knight of the Temple certainly did not come here in order to talk about that.'

45

'No, of course not.' Gerardo took a breath and added, 'To be brief, Messer Remigio, due to an unfortunate incident I have lost all my money and I need a loan. I have land near Ravenna that I wish to sell, and I will use a part of the proceeds to restore your money to you.'

'An incident? Of what type?'

'Does it matter?'

Remigio Sensi laid his palms on the dark table and looked him in the eye. 'You are a Knight of the Temple. If the incident of which you speak has anything to do with the Inquisition, the probability that you will soon be caught is high. And I must know the risks to which I am exposing myself.'

Gerardo nodded slowly. He could not tell him everything and decided to tell a half-truth instead. 'The Inquisition doesn't come into it,' he lied. 'The house where I had a room took fire and I had to escape. I have no way of paying my landlord back.'

'A fire?' said Remigio, with an alert look. 'You mean the house behind the Church of Sant'Antonino that burned down last night? I know the owner, he lives near here.'

Gerardo felt himself exposed. He wanted to make up an excuse, any sort of lie, but he paused a moment too long and the banker made a sign as if to say that it didn't matter to him.

'Your secrets are safe with me, don't worry,' he said. 'I certainly won't denounce you. But now let's get back to business.' He raised his eyes to look at a large painting of St Matthew, protector of the moneylenders, as if to ask for inspiration. Then he set out the conditions of the loan.

'As you know, the *comune* permits moneylending, on condition that the interest does not exceed four *denari* per lira a month. Naturally, in the case of a wanted man, this absolutely does not cover the risks.'

'So what do you propose?' asked Gerardo, knowing that the preamble was prelude to a hammering.

'It depends on how much money you need, in any case I would say that I cannot accept less than fifteen *denari* per lira a month, with full restitution of the debt a year from the agreement.'

Gerardo had been expecting an even more exorbitant request and he took heart. But his relief did not last long.

'Furthermore,' continued the banker, 'there would have to be a fine for default in case of failure to pay on the due date.' He sighed as though it displeased him to have to say such a thing, and added, 'Fifty per cent of the entire sum.'

Gerardo leaped to his feet in outrage. 'What? But this is usury! It is a very serious crime, condemned by—'

'Calm down, Messer. Do not insult me,' interrupted Remigio, without losing his composure. 'Are you or are you not aware of the risks that I run, lending money to a wanted man, a member of the order accused of heresy and filthy practices and currently under trial? And just so that you know, that is not all.'

'You don't need to go on,' said Gerardo, holding up his hand and walking towards the door. 'I will look for better conditions elsewhere.'

'You won't find them. Just as you won't find anyone you can trust absolutely, who understands your situation and who will not betray you. Think about it. Anyway, the other thing I wanted to mention besides the conditions that I have already put forward is not more interest but just two guarantors who will stand surety for you.'

Gerardo opened his arms slightly to let some air circulate between his shirt and tunic, to disperse the wave of heat that had overcome him. He too turned towards St Matthew on the wall and silently asked God's forgiveness for accepting conditions that benefited the sin of usury. Then, through gritted teeth, he said, 'You well know that I can't refuse. But I don't know where to find the two guarantors that you ask of me.'

'You are fortunate,' said the banker, in a conciliatory tone. 'In fact you need only find one. I can recommend the other myself.'

'Who would that be?' inquired Gerardo, warily.

'A Templar like yourself. He is French, he is rich and he has just arrived in the city. I've known him for some time. I will mention your situation to him and I am sure that he will agree to help a confrère in difficulty.' Remigio rose to his feet and added, 'I cannot abandon my work right now, but I would be honoured if you accepted to share my table. I will have someone accompany you to the kitchen, where Fiamma will serve you a bowl of *minestra*. After all it is nearly time to eat.'

It was clear that the offer of friendship was self-interested. Remigio certainly didn't want to make an enemy of the Knights of the Temple. After all, now that they were under trial, they brought him even better business than before. Hearing the name of the girl mentioned, Gerardo replied impulsively, 'I will accept to please you, Messer Remigio, but don't go to too much trouble. A bowl of warm milk and a slice of bread would do very well. However, first of all, I have a question to ask of you.'

'Go on.'

Perhaps the banker knew something of Angelo da Piczano. It was possible that the Templar had called on him during his brief stay in Bologna.

'I heard that my friend Angelo da Piczano, who is also a Templar, has been in the city for a few days,' he said. 'Has he by chance been to see you? I would be grateful if you could tell me where I can find him.'

The banker had started shaking his head even before Gerardo had finished speaking. 'I have never heard that name,' he said. 'And in any case, even if I did know the person you are looking for, I would not tell you.' He raised a hand to ward off the young man's protests. 'My profession is based on discretion,' he explained. 'If someone were to come here and ask for you, I certainly wouldn't tell him where to find you.'

'However, I happen to know that many Templars passing through the city have met thanks to you,' Gerardo answered back, annoyed.

'Certainly. But only after I've made sure that both of them were disposed to meet.'

He explained that the system was simple. A client said that he wanted to meet a person. Remigio answered that he did not know the man, then went to him and gave him the message. If the fellow agreed, he set up a meeting. If not, he did nothing.

'So if your friend should approach me in the next few days,' he concluded, 'I will not fail to pass on your request. And should his reply be positive, I will advise you. Otherwise it is futile to ask. I'm sure you understand.'

Gerardo nodded wearily. Angelo would not be returning from the afterlife to speak to Remigio Sensi, or indeed anyone else. To find out whom he had met during his sojourn in Bologna, he would have to look elsewhere.

The banker went over to open the door. He gave instructions to one of the servants to prepare bread and milk for their guest, and then he returned slowly to sit down at the table.

'Good, now tell me how much you need.'

Gerardo took a deep breath and said, 'At least forty Bolognese lira.'

'Find the guarantors and the affair is done,' replied Remigio, with a smile that was meant to be benevolent but only managed to convey avarice. 'Then we will occupy ourselves with selling that property of which you were speaking. A propos, where are you lodging?'

'I would prefer not to say for the moment,' answered Gerardo.

'As you wish.'

The smile on the face of the banker vanished, indicating that he didn't understand such a lack of trust after his speech about discretion. They bid one another goodbye and Gerardo left, following the servant to the kitchen.

It was a large room, lit more by the fire flaring in the hearth than by what little light came from the single window, which was fortified with thick bars. Fiamma was scolding a barefoot girl of about nine years of age with a runny nose who had a contrite air about her. A second, older girl wearing a grey bonnet sat at a shelf made of terracotta tiles near the fireplace, plucking a chicken.

'Forgive me,' said the mistress of the house immediately, making the delicate green veil that covered her head flutter as she turned to face him. 'This numbskull didn't find milk in the first place she tried, so instead of looking elsewhere she came back empty-handed. I'll send her straight out again, but I'm afraid you'll have to wait a little.'

'Please do not put yourself to any inconvenience, Mistress,' replied Gerardo. He went to sit down at the table in the centre of the kitchen and added, 'Bread and cheese will do very well, if you have any.'

Fiamma immediately sent the girl to fetch some cheese from the larder, and then she herself poured him a tankard of wine from the pitcher on the table.

The little girl walked off sniffling and soon came back with a piece of fresh cheese on a thick slice of bread. Gerardo took the food, thanked them and began to eat in silence. He was ravenous, but tried not to tuck in too voraciously because he was in the presence of a lady.

Fortunately the wine had been diluted with water, but even as it was, perhaps because of his exhaustion after the night's vigil, it went straight to his head, spreading a pleasant warmth through his body and a sensation of well-being that was most inappropriate in the circumstances. In the meantime the older girl had finished plucking the chicken, had scorched it by passing it over the flames and was now concentrated on gutting it, putting the heart, liver and throat to one side and throwing the rest of the entrails into a wooden pail.

'Is the fare to your liking, Messer?' asked Fiamma.

Gerardo was lost in thought, and contrary to both good manners and the Code of the Templars to which he had sworn obedience, he raised his head and found himself looking her in the eye. The young woman did not avert her gaze, and they remained looking at one another until Gerardo, painfully aware of the impure manner in which he was staring at the woman, managed to utter in a dreamy tone, 'It is all delicious, Mistress.'

He heard a muffled giggle and turned quickly round. The little servant next to the fireplace was facing the other way as she worked, but Gerardo was certain that she had seen everything. He rose to his feet as if the chair were scalding him.

'I must go now,' he said. 'Thank you for everything. I haven't felt like this for a long time.'

And after that strange comment, and a loud sneeze of adieu from the barefoot child, he went out of the kitchen, leaving the three females wondering what on earth he meant. They would have found it difficult to guess, for he didn't even know himself.

He recovered his cloak from the entrance hall, went out into the street and set off for the seven churches that made up the Benedictine Basilica of Santo Stefano, the fulcrum of the architectonic arrangement commissioned centuries before by Bishop Petronio and known throughout Christendom as Jerusalem Bononiensis.

Following an impulse he went through the spacious doorway of the first church, which went by the name of the Holy Crucifix. He felt ill at ease, and a brief visit to the house of the Lord could not but do him good. He walked quickly up the aisle and turned left to enter the church where the Holy

Sepulchre of Jerusalem had been reproduced. Around the small octagonal sanctuary that held the mortal remains of St Petronio, the main patron saint of Bologna, there were six monks kneeling in prayer. Gerardo stood contemplating the small but important work of architecture. It was said that it perfectly respected the proportions of the original and that under the floor there was a sacred wellspring whose waters were able to heal all illnesses. There was even a rumour of an underground temple predating the church, dedicated in remote times to the cult of the pagan goddess Isis.

And yet, Gerardo derived no relief from his visit to that consecrated place. Afterwards, he felt more worried than ever. Moving quietly so as not to disturb the monks in prayer, he walked out of the right-hand door, crossed the deserted cloisters and went into the Church of the Holy Trinity. He was on the point of leaving, when he saw a priest kneeling in a corner. The man had heard his steps and turned to look at him, without saying anything. Gerardo stopped, feeling uncomfortable. While he searched for something to say that would justify his presence there, the words came out spontaneously, as though they were the only appropriate ones for that place and time.

'Father, I would like to confess.'

The priest nodded, rose and beckoned him over. Gerardo went to kneel before him, waited for the priest to pronounce the customary words and then began to confess all the sins that he could remember, mentally asking God's pardon because he could not reveal the things that tormented him the most. In theory the lips of the priest were sealed, but he knew well that the superiors usually absolved a priest guilty of violating the sacrament of confession, if such a violation was committed for the greater good of the Church. At that moment the Church seemed to consider the elimination of the Order of the Templars as the greater good, and Gerardo could not take the risk.

While he searched his soul for hidden sins, still in the state of slight inebriation induced by the wine and his nocturnal vigil, at a certain point he heard himself say that he had thought with joy of being able to form a family, with a wife and children, and of dedicating himself to the glory of the Lord.

The priest interrupted him, curious. 'And why do think of that as a sin, my son?'

Gerardo realised his error. The thought was a sin in that it was contrary to his monastic vows, but he couldn't very well say that.

'The woman who inspires these thoughts in me is married, Father,' he lied. 'I am in a state of mortal sin.'

The priest nodded with a serious air, as though expecting that explanation. He asked if Gerardo had anything else to confess, and at his negative reply he imposed a heavy penance on him, then gave him absolution and moved away. Gerardo got up and left. When he found himself outside, he felt all the tiredness of his sleepless night descend heavily on him, as if the confession had emptied him.

The rain had got more intense. He pulled his hood up again, and crossing the piazza with unsteady steps, he took two decisions. First, he would go home and sleep for a bit before going to find the Philomena in Angelo's message. And second, he would make sure that he didn't find himself alone with the banker's daughter again.

The grey light of afternoon entered through an open window of the Liuzzi family home, in a side street to Via San Vitale, and a smell of wet earth rose from the courtyard. Summer was not far off, but the rain gave everything a wintry tinge. For the third time, Mondino took the quill from the table, dipped it into the inkpot, and for the third time he put it back down again. In front of him were a white sheet of paper, a new candle and an entire ream of cotton paper waiting to be filled with anatomical notes. But there was nothing he could do about it. He simply could not concentrate.

That day he had cancelled his lesson at the *Studium* and spent the entire morning speaking to three alchemists. They lived in the Porta Procola area, near the Circla. The Circla was the familiar name for the paling that for the moment constituted Bologna's third city wall. The work on the actual wall had yet to begin.

Unfortunately he had gathered nothing of use from any of the three, in part because he had not dared to be too specific in his questions. He did not believe that he was at great risk, because alchemists generally tended to keep their affairs to themselves and to keep away from judges and magistrates, but you could never be too careful. He had been told of another alchemist, who had settled in Bologna not long before, after years of travelling, and he intended to go and question the man soon.

However, he wasn't nurturing much hope, because the person who had suggested he try the alchemist had also said that he was given to the use of aqua vitae for more than alchemical and medicinal purposes.

With an effort of will, Mondino compelled himself to finish a drawing of the articulation of the muscle between the arm and the shoulder. Its form recalled the Greek letter Delta upside down and some medical men had thus begun to call it the deltoid muscle. To the side of the drawing, he noted down advice about how to detach the muscle from the bone and then he moved on to the pectoral muscles. But his thoughts automatically ran on to what the human body kept under those muscles and the thoracic cavity that they covered: the heart. From there to the mystery that he had stumbled on the night before was only a short step, and Mondino found himself once again with his quill poised in mid air, lost in a fascinating and dangerous dream.

Exasperated, he rose to go and fetch the bundle of pages he had already written. Passing the window he stopped to contemplate the rain. But the monotonous and almost soporific sloshing of the water on the leaves of the apple tree in the garden and on the roofs of the neighbouring houses couldn't relax him either. Looking towards the Caccianemici Piccoli Towers and the bell tower of the Church of San Vitale and Agricola in Arena that rose above the houses round about, he imagined Gerardo fleeing over the rooftops, dragging his friend's body behind him until he had managed to get down to the ground by traversing a series of terraces that dropped down to a fenced-in orchard. Mondino knew the owner of that house, a Ghibelline like himself who, by the irony of fate, had once saved himself from the reprisals of a Guelph family by taking the opposite route to that of Gerardo. He had clambered up from one terrace to another and then scrambled between the rooftops until he was within shouting distance of some friends' houses behind Piazza Maggiore. At that point he shouted for help until someone came. The retaliation ended up with three dead and numerous wounded on both sides and Mondino and his Uncle Liuzzo had given aid to everyone without distinguishing between factions.

Thinking back to that episode, Mondino shook his head. Bologna would never return to the splendour of the previous century if the Bolognese continued to tear themselves to pieces from rivalry between the Guelphs and the Ghibellines. But at the same time he was not disposed to surrender without a fight to the dominion the Church wanted to impose on the *comune*. The ideal would have been to hold on to freedom, without being accountable either to the Pope or the Emperor. But since this was not possible it was better to be in league with Enrico VII, crowned King of Italy in Milan a few months previously. A few days before, Enrico had set off in the direction of Lodi and Cremona. If he managed to subdue them, his reign would acquire solidity. Mondino thought of what he would do if the sovereign turned up at the gates of Bologna, as Barbarossa had done so long ago. His Ghibelline faith encouraged him to negotiate an honourable peace, but if the city decided to take up arms and fight, he would fight. In such an uncertain world, the freedom of the *comune* came before every other consideration.

A clap of thunder shook him out of his daydream, and he remembered the reason that he had got up from his writing table. He went to fetch the bundle of notes for his book from a shelf. There were hundreds of leaves, thick with notes and drawings, where the structure of the human body was described point by point and organ by organ. Mondino loved to imagine his treatise finished and bound in leather as a great book, with its simple title stamped in gold: *Anothomia*. A book that physicians in years to come would study with a respect equal to that which the jurists reserved for the work of the great Irnerius. And that, like the work of Irnerius, would be integrated and improved with the advance of human knowledge, while nonetheless remaining the discipline's essential foundation.

For the moment, however, the treatise consisted more than anything else of an accumulation of notes that Mondino continually revised, and that he did not yet dare to write down in fair copy. He needed to discover more and explore further before offering his findings to the world like a map to be followed without risk of getting lost.

Thus, to unearth the secret that enabled blood to be changed into iron could represent a step forward of enormous importance. It was risky, certainly, but the gift of never running risks belonged to Liuzzo, not to him. His uncle was an excellent physician, but he lacked the desire to go forward. He restricted himself to applying rules decided on by others, and perhaps precisely because of that he had managed to make his way rapidly in the *Studium*.

Liuzzo prized results, but was not prepared to expose himself in any way to obtain them. Mondino had decided not to say anything at all to him about current events. His uncle would take fright and try to stop him, making his life impossible.

As though conjured up by his thoughts, Liuzzo appeared on the threshold.

'Good evening, Uncle. I didn't know you were here.'

'You too could go down and visit your father, from time to time,' said Liuzzo, in a reproachful tone. 'He told me that he hasn't seen you yet today.'

'That's not fair. I went down not long ago. He was asleep and I didn't want to wake him.'

His father was ill. Mondino was sure that he had a carcinoma, or a sarcoma, as Galen defined it, in his left lung. Sure enough, if he turned on to his right side he couldn't breathe, because his good lung was compressed by the weight of his body and the left, overcome by the tumour, didn't inflate properly. It was incurable and there was nothing they could do but make the old man as comfortable as possible in the last months of his life. Mondino and his three sons, Gabardino, Ludovico and Leone, took turns sitting with the old man whenever they had a bit of free time.

Liuzzo came into the study and went over to the writing table, which was strewn with papers. 'All your time is taken up with making these notes,' he said, sighing. 'When you're not giving a lesson, you write. And at night, instead of going to sleep like any other good Christian, you dissect corpses. It's not only your father who never sees you any more. Even your children know that they can't rely on you nowadays. When Leone needs advice, he turns to Pietro and Lorenza.'

Pietro and Lorenza were a couple of family retainers whom Mondino had taken into service when his wife died. They were young and full of energy, and their little girl brought life to the house with her merry shouting.

'Have you nothing to say?' insisted Liuzzo.

'What do you want me to say?' burst out Mondino, irritated. 'That you're right? Well, you are right. Happy now?'

Liuzzo stiffened. 'I only came by to remind you that your presence is expected at the Sunday banquet,' he said, in a formal tone. 'I'll be waiting for you to pick me up at my house, as is the duty of a younger member of the *Studium*.'

Having said that, he turned round and left the room without a word of goodbye. Mondino stood listening to his steps on the wooden stairs that went down to the ground floor. Then he turned to the bookshelf and put the bundle of rough copies back in their place. It was clear that he wouldn't be getting any work done that afternoon.

It had stopped raining by the time Gerardo arrived at the Campo del Mercato. The working day had ended and the piazza was now full of people chatting and playing dice; taking their ease. There was no end in sight of the previous year's famine that had caused the price of grain to rise, but people just wanted to forget about it. Three young lads played at making pebbles ricochet off the low wall surrounding the watering trough, while opposite them a peasant was washing his donkey, throwing water over its back with a wooden pail held together with strips of tin. When Gerardo asked the boys if they could show him where a certain Philomena lived, they replied in a chorus, 'The hairy woman?' and bolted like jackrabbits. Gerardo didn't want to draw too much attention to himself by asking adults, so he decided to sacrifice some money. He showed the coin to the boys, who had stopped not far off. The one who seemed to be their leader, a blond, lank child, with knees covered in scabs beneath a short sleeveless tunic, came towards him, stopping at a safe distance. With a gesture he made Gerardo understand that he wanted the money first, and the Templar threw it at his feet. The boy pointed to an alley not far from the watering trough and shouted, 'The second last house on the right!'

Then he ran off with his companions, proudly showing them the coin he had earned without much effort.

Gerardo followed his directions, surprised, but not very, by the lads' strange behaviour. If the woman he was looking for was a prostitute, it was likely that their parents must have told them to keep away from her house and her clients.

The lane was foul-smelling, as were all the narrow alleys of the city. They tended to be overrun by filth and excrement despite the vigilance of the borough administrators, whose job it was to denounce anyone caught in the act of throwing rubbish away. The system worked in the main streets, but in the alleyways other customs were in force that were hard to eradicate. Gerardo walked up to the penultimate dwelling, stepping over a dead dog on which fortunately someone had thrown some quicklime, and knocked at the door.

It was opened by the ugliest woman he had ever seen. She was old, over fifty, with grey hair under a dirty bonnet and a slovenly gown. She had a dull look about her and it was quickly obvious why the boys had saddled her with such an offensive nickname. The backs of her hands were covered in dark bristly hairs like those of a man. She didn't exactly have a beard but her cheeks showed signs of the razor and her eyebrows were as thick as silkworms. With a shudder, Gerardo thought what her legs might be like. Fortunately her long grey tunic covered them down to her feet.

'Are you Mistress Philomena?' he asked, incredulous. Angelo da Piczano could not possibly have broken his vow of chastity for a woman of this sort.

'And who are you?'

'My name doesn't matter, I've been sent by a friend.'

The old crone asked who the friend was and Gerardo told her, but she didn't recognise the name. Angelo had obviously introduced himself to her under an alias. So Gerardo described him to her, saying that his friend had come to visit some days before and had been very happy with the outcome. Finally the woman's face lit up.

'Come in,' she said, in a croaky voice. 'Payment in advance.'

Gerardo tried to explain, but the woman did not want to hear another word before seeing his money. So he gave her a few coins, promising the rest later. He had absolutely no intention of sinning with her, but hoped that the avidity provoked by the money would induce her to answer some questions.

The woman led him into a kitchen with smoke-blackened walls. She closed the street door and immediately went to open another leading into a little corridor. Gerardo went in, thinking that she would follow him, but the old hag shut the door behind him, leaving him alone.

Or rather, worse than alone.

Now everything became clear. There was a boy of about six or seven, half-dressed, waiting on a reasonably clean straw mattress. The room had no windows and was lit only by a stub of candle, probably stolen from church. The child got up without a word, walked over to Gerardo, pushed his hands up under the monk's tunic and began to fumble with his breeches.

Only then did Gerardo react, pushing him away with more violence than was necessary. The little chap fell back on to the bed, but he got up again immediately to return to his task. While his expression had initially been empty and almost absent, now he looked terrified.

Gerardo brushed him away again, more gently this time, but the child came back and set to work again. Now he was on the verge of tears. In a flash of intuition, Gerardo asked, in the gentlest voice possible, 'Are you afraid that if you don't do your duty, they'll beat you?'

The child suddenly froze, stared at him for a while, and then nodded twice.

'Don't worry, it won't happen this time. But now please be still. I am not one of those wicked men who come to you. What's your name?'

Again, the little fellow looked at him with mistrust as though trying to work out whether he was telling the truth or if it were a trick. At the end he pointed at his mouth with a finger and opened his hands in a gesture of powerlessness.

'Are you dumb?'

He nodded his head. *Yes.*

'Did they kidnap you?'

Another soundless *yes.*

Gerardo had heard talk of such repugnant practices, but it was the first time that he had seen them in person. Initially he had reacted impetuously, concerned only to avoid sinning, and he had frightened the child. Now he tried to reassure him and inspire his trust. One thing was clear: although he was here for another purpose entirely, he would never leave the little boy in the hands of that woman.

'Don't worry,' he said softly, sitting down on the bed next to him. 'I'll take you away from here.'

To see the apprehension in the child's expression transform itself into hope was more than he could bear. He got up from the mattress, making the candle's flame waver, and went to open the door. It was bolted from the outside. He started beating it and shouting and the hag came quickly.

'Why did you lock me in?' asked Gerardo, his face now a deep magenta.

'I always do,' explained Philomena, her breath smelling of wine. In the half-light her hirsute hands and bushy eyebrows seemed to belong to a hellish being. 'To stop the boy running away. I paid dearly for him and I'm not going to take any risks. If he runs off, who'll chase after him? I'm too old.'

She gave a throaty cackle, showing her yellow teeth. Gerardo walked out and she bolted the door again with a wooden bar and followed him into the kitchen, looking a bit perplexed. A half-full jug of red wine stood in the centre of the table.

'What is it? Does Masino not please you? I must say you are the first. Your friend—'

'My friend what?' he snapped, forcing himself to control the rage that had taken hold of him. For the moment, finding out about Angelo was the most important thing.

'He enjoyed him greatly. He even said he'd be back soon.'

Gerardo had seized her by the throat. 'You're lying!' he said. 'Angelo would never do such a thing.'

The shrew didn't reply. In her eyes, Gerardo read obstinacy and cunning. She had realised that letting him enter was a mistake and had decided to say nothing further. There was no time to think. Someone might come along and there was the risk that she might cry out for help. All his instincts held him back from hitting a woman, but he overcame them and gave her two hard slaps, continuing to throttle her with his free hand to stop her from shouting. She growled an oath, trying to strike him with her fist. Gerardo caught her wrist and squeezed it harder than her throat, finding that her rough skin, her hair and her masculine appearance made it easier for him not to yield to compassion.

Philomena began to entreat him. 'What do you want from me?' she wheezed. 'I beg of you.'

'You must tell me everything that you know about Angelo,' replied Gerardo, harshly. 'Then I'll let you go. If you attempt to shout or I find out that you are lying, I'll kill you.'

She nodded, and this time there was genuine fear in her eyes. 'He's not really your friend, is he?' she said. 'You want to harm him, accuse him of sodomy.'

Without removing his hand from about her neck, Gerardo

reflected rapidly. If he replied in the affirmative, the woman would not collaborate, because in a trial for sodomy of her client she would be condemned to death too. But he preferred not to tell her that Angelo was dead.

'I only want to make him understand that he must get out of my way,' he lied. 'Now that I know his secret, he'll be more careful. Talk.'

He loosened his hold and the crone started to speak. She said that his friend had turned up and mentioned the name of a man whom she knew well, so she had let him in.

'What was the man's name?'

She shook her head, with a defiant expression. Gerardo squeezed again, harder this time, and after a second's hesitation he shook a fist in her face. Before he had to hit her again, Philomena relented.

'His name is Francesco,' she stuttered. 'He's a priest, an Augustinian.'

At those words, Gerardo started. Another monk who betrayed his vows in the most abject manner.

'And what did Angelo do with the child?' he asked. He felt a fierce anger mixed with disgust and shame, but he had to know.

'What they all do,' answered the old woman, shrugging her shoulders.

Gerardo thought once again that he could not leave the poor little lad here, even if it meant killing his keeper.

He asked her to repeat to him all that Angelo had said that evening, but she shrugged her shoulders again. 'He didn't say anything. People don't come here to talk to me.'

Gerardo clutched her throat again, with force. Philomena's eyes goggled and she went purple. She made a sign to say that she wanted to talk and as soon as he freed her, she coughed violently.

When her fit of coughing had passed, she leaned on the

table with one hand, as though she needed to support herself, and said, 'I remember one thing.'

'What?'

'That evening my legs were aching terribly, as they do every time the fog descends on the city, so when he left I didn't get up to open the door. I said it was an ailment of old age and told him to enjoy his youth while he still had time.'

'And then?' pressed Gerardo, impatient.

'He looked at me in a strange way, and he said—'

'What did he say?' Gerardo couldn't contain himself.

'He said, "I will never grow old. When your house falls beneath the weight of the centuries, I will still be here." I remember it not just for the words, but for the look he had. He seemed almost mad.'

Gerardo let go of her. He was puzzled. Did Angelo know that he would be dead within a couple of days and was that why he had said that he would never grow old? But what did the second sentence mean?

Taking advantage of his brief inattention, the woman wriggled out of his grasp, knocking over the jug of wine. She managed to grab a knife from the tiled shelf next to the chimney, and before Gerardo could get hold of her again she was already on the other side of the table and shouting like one obsessed. 'Help! Geremia! Bernardo! Come quickly!'

Gerardo realised that she must have accomplices, whose job it was to settle any problems she had with clients. He could hardly shout for someone nearby to call the city guards; that was the last thing he wanted. He had to get away. With a leap he got to the door, threw it open and started running up the alleyway. At that moment two brawny silhouettes came out of the house opposite. He did not stop to find out if they were following him or were running to the old woman. He bolted with all the speed that his feet could muster, and when he looked over his shoulder there was no one following him.

Only then did he become aware of an irksome sensation of wetness on his breeches. Looking down, he saw that they were drenched with wine.

It was already almost evening, but he couldn't go to his meeting with Mondino dressed like that, so he decided to go home first to change. He walked along, exhausted by lack of sleep and prey to a nervous trembling at the horror of what he had discovered about the Templar who had been his friend. Only once he had got to his room did he manage to calm himself down, swearing to himself that he would free the poor Masino, even if it cost him his life.

III

The sight was hardly worth the long journey, thought Wilhelm von Trier, looking around the crowded piazza in front of the Basilica of Santo Stefano. True, the idea of creating a copy of the holy shrines of Jerusalem was interesting, and the name of Jerusalem Bononiensis had become famous throughout Christendom. Yet he, who had seen the real Jerusalem with his own eyes, found it pathetic and almost blasphemous that holy names like 'Valley of Jehoshaphat', 'Golgotha' and 'Mount of Olives' were attributed to piazzas and urban slopes, infested with merchants, inns and bawdy houses, although to some extent ennobled by the presence of the churches.

Nonetheless he decided to go and have a look at Santo Sepolcro. But first he would find lodgings, sleep for a bit and restore himself, hoping that in the meantime the afternoon would become less damp. Age brought its handicaps.

Wilhelm von Trier was an old man and he would certainly not have travelled all the way from the island of Cyprus, where he had found secure refuge from the wave of accusations and trials that had assailed his order, just to see the replica of something that he had already admired in its genuine form when fighting in the Holy Land. There was another reason, a much more important one, that had induced him to undertake the journey, despite the discomfort and the necessity of travelling incognito. In a reflex he put his hand under his tunic and checked the pocket sewn into his breeches where he had stored the map. He had almost left it in Cyprus, and then at the last minute had decided to bring it. It had been extorted from a man by torture, but had turned out to be entirely useless. And yet it had been sketched out with too much care for it not to mean anything at all. All these years Wilhelm had asked himself whether it hid a secret that they had been incapable of deciphering, and perhaps now that question would finally be answered.

He walked slowly towards an alley to the left of the piazza, thinking that it was the ideal place to find an inn where there wouldn't be too many questions asked. On his journey, he had passed himself off as a pilgrim heading for Santiago di Compostela. His shabby look and poor clothes had protected him from robbers and bandits, but had also meant that he had had to lodge in hovels. He couldn't wait to get back to Cyprus, once this business had been dealt with.

He still had to find out what the mystery 'friend' who had written him the letter wanted in return for the promised secret. And after that he had to find a way of obtaining the secret and silencing the friend. But it would all have to wait until that evening. If the letter were genuine, he would discover everything after vespers.

Finding an inn that suited him, he entered and was struck by the fact that the owner spoke fairly good Latin. During his journey through the lands of Italy, Wilhelm had found it difficult to communicate: in his pilgrim's disguise he frequented mostly humble environments, and the poor spoke only the local dialect.

The innkeeper explained that in Bologna they were used to accommodating people from all over the world, among them clerics, scholars and pilgrims, and a bit of Latin was necessary for business. 'When I was a lad my father made me study with a Benedictine monk from the basilica nearby,' he said. 'And now I know how right he was.'

Wilhelm asked for a room to himself, saying that he suffered from insomnia and couldn't sleep in a shared room. The publican had a little room with a double bed and Wilhelm agreed to pay double to occupy it alone. He went up the narrow wooden stairway to the first floor. Once inside the room, he dropped the two saddlebags that served as luggage, took off his shoes and lay down on the cloth bag full of straw with a sigh of relief.

In Cyprus he had been used to sleeping on a wool mattress and the discomfort of the beds over the journey had taken him back to the years of his youth. Now too, savouring the pleasurable relaxation of the limbs that preceded sleep, Wilhelm von Trier began to think of that time, long ago, when his search had begun.

He had entered the Order of the Knights of the Temple when he was still very young, more due to his spirit of adventure than as a religious vocation, and he had immediately left for the Holy Land. He was assigned to the Templar House in Tyre and it was there that a comrade-in-arms had spoken to him of the secret. From that moment on, its discovery became his chief reason to live.

Al-iksir, was what he had called it. A secret possessed by the Arabic alchemists even before the birth of Christ, perhaps originating in the far Indies. It was what the European sages referred to as the 'elixir of long life', a powder that was able to prolong life indefinitely and to cure any wound or illness of the body.

The monk who told him about it maintained that in the city

of Alessandretta, now for some time in the hands of the Saracens, there lived an alchemist who knew the secret. The confrère had been trying for a long time to organise a trip to Alessandretta incognito, but had not managed. And now he had heard that the man he was looking for had moved to the Moorish lands in Spain.

'And that's why I mention it, brother,' he had explained to Wilhelm. 'I need your help. In return I will offer you the possibility of taking part in the search. I have been able to observe you over these months and I know that you are the right person: valorous, intelligent and decisive.'

Wilhelm had ignored the compliment and asked exactly what he wanted of him. It didn't take long. Wilhelm had the grade of sergeant and also carried out the duties of company officer. All the transfer orders of the Templar House passed through him. The confrère wanted to be transferred to Spain so that he could continue his research.

Thus, a few months before the fall of St John of Acre confirmed the definitive loss of the Holy Land by the Christian forces, the two of them turned up at the Tortosa Templar House in Spain, where another Knight of the Temple joined the group. The three had made a pact to take possession of the elixir. Then Wilhelm's friend died of fever and they were two once more. In the meantime the Turkish alchemist whom they were looking for was killed, and his corpse found at the gates of Granada, or Gharnata as the Arabs called it, with his heart missing. This had caused a fresh outbreak of hostilities between Granada, in the hands of the Saracens, and Tortosa, the stronghold of the Kingdom of Aragon. Now that the alchemist was dead, Wilhelm and his companion despaired of ever bringing their search to a conclusion. But suddenly a new ally appeared, he too a Templar, who had pointed out a different trail to them, right there in Tortosa ...

Wilhelm von Trier's musings went no further. His conscious

thoughts were confused with strange images that blossomed in his mind without any constructive logic, and in the blinking of an eye the old Templar was asleep.

Mondino crept on tiptoe into his father's room on the ground floor and watched him quietly. Rainerio lay facing the window, looking at the little bright-green fruits just forming on the apple tree in the garden after the flowers had fallen. He was thin and pallid, with strangely shiny skin and an expression that grew daily more distant. Mondino repressed the pain it gave him and sat on a stool by the side of the bed.

'Good evening, Father.'

He didn't ask how Rainerio was. Everyone who visited the old man invariably did just that. He never did. What was the point of asking how a dying person was feeling? It only served to make the man lie, to answer in bland replies made with a forced smile. Because if he had told the truth, people would feel ill at ease and would have submerged him with gentle reproaches, showing a hypocrite's optimism. Mondino wasn't sincere with him either because when he entered he lowered a mask over his face so as to hide his true emotions from his father. But that wasn't hypocrisy. It was compassion. Towards both of them.

Rainerio turned and smiled. 'Mondino. We don't see much of you nowadays.'

The physician nodded, once more distracted by the thought that had tormented him since the evening before. Gerardo had not turned up at the meeting place. And however much he tried to force himself to think of all the possible innocuous explanations for the Templar's absence, his mind turned in circles around a single fear: Gerardo had got himself arrested, and soon the city guards would be knocking on Mondino's door too.

'That was exactly what I wanted to talk to you about,

70

Father,' he said, expelling his ill-omened thoughts. 'It's possible that for a while I may be away from home more often than usual.' He looked away, searching for the right words. 'Please believe me when I say that it is not a question of indifference with regard to yourself.'

Despite the strength of will he felt, his voice had abandoned him for a second. He hoped that his father hadn't noticed.

'You've found another mystery on your path?'

'How do you know?' asked Mondino, struck with surprise and not managing to hold back.

Rainerio didn't smile, but a playful spark appeared in his eyes. 'Do I have to remind you of the story of the apples? I was just thinking about it.'

Mondino remembered the episode only too well, not least because it had earned him a decent dose of lashes. One day, when he was a boy, he had stolen all the apples off the tree. He'd taken them to the loft and hidden them in a wooden case lined with waxed paper, on which he had then nailed down the lid. He had heard his Uncle Liuzzo speak of the spontaneous generation of maggots and had decided to experiment. If, after two or three weeks, he opened the case and found maggots in the apples, he would believe that they were born spontaneously.

'No, there's no need,' he answered with a smile. 'But I still wonder how you found me out.'

'Because I know you,' answered Rainerio. 'You are attracted by what you can't explain and you have no peace until you find an answer that satisfies you. Not even the divine Aristotle escaped your investigation. And now you must have found something that has stimulated your imagination. That's why we never see you around the house any more.'

Mondino and his father had never communicated very much. They both had the thorny character typical of choleric temperaments, dominated by the humour of the yellow bile. Between them there had always been precious few hugs and a great number of arguments. Mondino was convinced that his father wasn't interested in him. And now Rainerio showed that he knew him much more thoroughly than he thought.

It was true that Mondino loved to uncover secrets. That was why he'd become a physician. Even greater than the idea of alleviating his neighbour's suffering, it had been the impulse to discover the workings of the human body that drove him to take up his profession. And this was why he had developed a passion for anatomy too. But it would be better if his father didn't even suspect the nature of the mystery that preoccupied him now.

'Well, Father,' he began, dropping his eyes, 'I am studying a new technique for—'

'Let it be,' said Rainerio, interrupting him dryly. 'If you don't want to talk about it, never mind. You don't have to lie.'

Mondino felt himself blush. For a second he thought about denying it, and then he told himself that it was ignoble to spend the little time he had left with his father telling untruths. 'Forgive me,' he murmured. Then, in almost as quiet a voice, he added, 'It is something dangerous. The less you know, the better. I would ask you not to speak of it to Liuzzo.'

'Does the danger regard the Inquisition?' asked Rainerio.

'Yes,' answered Mondino, omitting to say that the concealing of corpses and the help given to an arsonist were also of interest to the civil authorities. He had accumulated an impressive collection of crimes, in just one night. 'But there is the possibility of obtaining something that is very important, for the good of humanity.'

His father turned towards the apple tree. 'Be careful, I beg of you,' he said, in a prophetic tone that sent a long shiver down his son's spine. 'I have a bad feeling about it.'

When he left the room, Mondino felt indescribably sad. And not only for his father's fate.

*

Passing beneath the huge sign affixed to the wall of the Garisenda Tower, which proclaimed the law against carrying arms in the city, Gerardo remembered that he was not armed. For what he intended to do, he couldn't decide whether this was a good or a bad thing.

When Gerardo had announced his decision to enter the order, his father began to summon a Templar Master of Arms to their castle three times a week. According to his teachings, the sword is like the cross for a Knight of the Temple. A weapon against evil, but a sacred weapon, to be used sparingly. *It is only used in battle*, the bearded old monk said. *We are not vulgar mercenaries. We are the soldiers of Christ, and we are only permitted to fight against the enemies of the faith.* An axiom that he often repeated was that the only way to be sure not to kill someone for the wrong motives, in a street fight or a tavern brawl, was to avoid carrying arms when not at war. *If I have not got my sword with me, I can be certain that I will not use it*, he used to say.

As he walked along under the arches and distractedly watched the artisans, bread-sellers and cheese-slicers who were putting away their wares and taking down their stalls, Gerardo was overcome by an excess of anger for the life that he had dreamed of and which had been denied him. He had put on the chain mail and the white robe with the cross on his chest only once, the day when he had been ordained a monk. He could remember the weight of his helmet, his shield and his sword perfectly. And the pride of feeling himself a powerful instrument in the hands of the Lord, a member of one of the most important and legendary orders in the history of the Church. Not long before, he had left the home where he had been born and brought up and moved to the Templar House of Ravenna. He had been waiting for his first posting, when like a flash of lightning in a clear sky the warrant for the arrest of all the members of the order had arrived, signed by Pope Clement V himself.

Many of Christ's soldiers had thought that it was a mistake and stayed serenely awaiting the Inquisitors, convinced that they had nothing to fear. Gerardo had followed the advice of his Master of Arms, who had immediately left for the island of Cyprus. *Retreating is not fleeing*, he had told him. *Find a place of hiding, watch what happens from safety, and then only if it's appropriate, make yourself known.*

Gerardo had never regretted following that counsel. He had escaped to Bologna and changed his name. He had broken off all contact with his family, more for their good than for his, and in three years had only once sent them a message, in which he said that he was well and as soon as the storm had died down would come home. He had been hoping that his situation would take a decisive turn for the better with the conclusion of the trial, expected within the next few weeks.

Despite all this, he would have felt more comfortable with a knife at his belt. He had no intention of killing the old woman, even if she deserved it a thousand times over for what she had done to Masino and almost certainly to other children too. But perhaps if he had a weapon, it would be easier to make her obey him and he would be able to defend himself should the two accomplices he had seen last time make a reappearance.

He didn't have a real plan. He thought he would knock at the door, disguise his voice so that she would open up and then push the woman inside, putting her out of harm's way, while he freed the child and took him away. His exhaustion the evening before had prevented him from thinking clearly. He hadn't even gone along to his meeting with Mondino, because as soon as he got to his room he'd collapsed on the mattress and slept the whole night through, the next morning and part of the afternoon, waking up when the sun was already descending in the west. Now he felt restored and had no doubt that he would succeed in what he had decided to do.

He avoided the market place as he had done the previous evening and he kept close to the walls, turning down a couple of streets before, and approaching Philomena's doorway from the opposite alleyway.

This was his chance. He knocked and waited, preparing to disguise his voice.

No one came to the door. He knocked again, louder, and called out her name.

Still no answer.

He climbed up to the window, a few feet above him, and tried to look through a crack between the closed shutters, but everything was dark inside. Not even a lamp was lit. It was quite possible that Philomena had gone out, leaving the boy at home, but somehow Gerardo knew that this was not the case. With a heavy heart, he kept his balance with one hand and forced the shutter open with the other, shouting to Masino to make a noise or to throw something on the ground if he was in his room.

Nothing happened. Behind the wooden shutter, the kitchen looked deserted. The fire was out, and on the table and shelves there wasn't even a frying pan, a wooden spoon or a knife. Under the table he thought he could see the pieces of the jug that had been broken the night before.

The old hag, perhaps afraid that he would come back with some guards in tow, had hastily moved out, taking her little prisoner with her. It was too risky to ask her neighbours where she'd gone and, anyway, he doubted that they would know. He was about to get down when he felt someone grab his ankles. He managed to kick out with one foot, hitting his assailant in the face, who swore and let go of him. Gerardo jumped down and found himself facing a man who was as thin as a nail, with an unkempt beard, missing incisors, long hair and a tunic that was too short and from which appeared a pair of patched breeches. But the thing that attracted his attention the most was the long knife that the man quickly took out from under his tunic.

'By God. Quick, Bernardo!'

Hearing that name, Gerardo was reminded of Philomena shouting the night before. They were her accomplices, left behind to watch over the house, perhaps awaiting her return. He heard a sound behind him, four or five paces away, and without turning round to look he attacked the man in front of him, catching him by surprise. With one hand Gerardo grabbed his weapon arm, twisting his wrist to make him drop the knife, while with the other he swiped him in the throat making him flop to the ground wheezing.

Gerardo bent down to pick up the weapon and immediately rolled to the side to avoid the attack of the second man who had launched himself at him. The man found himself grabbing thin air and Gerardo gave him a kick to the head, sending him flailing on top of his ally. Then, while his aggressors were trying to get to their feet, Gerardo turned and ran towards the piazza at breakneck speed. He emerged from the alleyway near the trough where the same three boys from the day before were playing with a ball of rags. Before they recognised him, Gerardo hid the knife beneath his arm and turned sharp left, walking twenty or so yards at a normal pace until he arrived at the first arcade. There he hid behind a column and waited for the two men, who didn't take long to appear at the end of the alley. They looked around them for a second, trying to work out which way he'd gone, then decided to turn right and ran on.

Gerardo finally relaxed and suddenly all the fear that he had repressed during the fight overwhelmed him, causing his hands and legs to shudder. It was the first time that he had encountered an enemy in the flesh, outside his lessons with the Master of Arms. He had indeed risked his life and this knowledge did not cease to frighten him. His fear was only tempered by one fact: his training had saved him. All those hours spent learning to fight without letting himself be hampered by emotions had turned out to be useful. He went over each different phase in the brief altercation in the alleyway and couldn't help smiling. Those two cut-throats were not what his Master of Arms would have defined 'enemies of the faith', but when it was a question of saving one's skin, academic definitions lost their importance.

With care he inspected the knife he had wrested from his aggressor. The handle was made of wood and the blade of steel; low quality but sturdy and well sharpened. Gerardo hid it under his tunic, wedging it beneath the cloth belt that held up his breeches, and then he set off for his hired lodgings.

The fact that he hadn't managed to save the boy caused him a pain in the centre of his chest like a closed fist. But at least he was no longer weaponless.

Leaning against the wall of a house from where he had a full view of the Church of San Giovanni in Monte, Wilhelm von Trier looked around him continually. In the Bolognese reconstruction, the church symbolised the Mount of Olives, the place at the foot of which Christ had retired before the Passion, in the garden of Gethsemane. Wilhelm wondered to himself why the anonymous 'friend' in the letter had chosen that particular place for their meeting. The friend had shown himself to be too precise for it to have been by chance. Vespers had rung a while before and several people had passed by but no one had come near Wilhelm. He asked himself how he would recognise the man, but knew that it was pointless to concern himself with such a thing. The friend probably knew what he looked like. He'd made it clear that he knew rather too much.

After sunset, the to-ing and fro-ing in the piazza had lessened to the point of almost stopping completely and the only other person besides Wilhelm who was stationary was a beggar who sat beneath an arch about twenty yards away. He was reaching out for offerings from passers-by with the stump that was his right hand and the palm of his left. Wilhelm watched him closely. Instead of the habitual makeshift sackcloth tunic with which all the poor clothed themselves, the man was wearing a very greasy black cassock that must originally have been made of good cloth, probably a charitable donation.

Suddenly the church bell rang compline. As though waiting for precisely that signal, the beggar got up and came rapidly towards him.

Wilhelm watched, trying to work out whether he was a real beggar or the friend in disguise. But when the man got to him every doubt vanished: the smell and filth that he had about him couldn't possibly be part of a disguise. Wilhelm got ready to refuse a request for alms, but the man said a phrase in laboured Latin in which the Templar recognised the word *amicus*.

Suddenly wary, he asked the beggar to repeat himself and after various attempts managed to make out the message: the friend with whom he had a meeting could not come. He asked Wilhelm to return to his lodgings and wait for him there.

The beggar held out his good hand and Wilhelm grudgingly let drop a coin. How did the friend know where he was staying? After eating and resting, the only place he'd been to that afternoon was the office of a trusted banker to the Templars, where he had changed some silver florins into Bolognese lira. But he had certainly not told the banker that he was staying in a low order of tavern.

Beginning to feel concerned, he turned back to the inn. When he got there he was surprised not to find the innkeeper sitting at the entrance to check on the comings and goings of his clients. However, loud shouts and the cackle of hens could be heard coming from the garden. He went to have a look and saw the innkeeper struggling with a stray dog that had got into the hen coup and killed two hens already. Wilhelm shook his head and went upstairs, going into his room.

He immediately felt a terrible pain at the nape of his neck and everything went black.

When he came to his senses, Wilhelm von Trier found that he was paralysed and couldn't speak. He had a bitter taste in his mouth. Someone must have made him swallow some poison while he was unconscious. He knew that he'd been caught in a trap. The hunter, had become prey.

He heard a slight movement in the room and a clinking of metal, as though someone were preparing metallic instruments. He pretended to be unconscious, trying to discern what was happening from the noises and whether it would be possible to free himself. But he couldn't figure it out. In the end, terrified, he slowly opened his eyes.

By an association of thoughts, what he saw took him back to the name of that evening's rendezvous, to the word 'passion' from the Latin *patior*, to suffer. It was about to begin.

At the end of his bed was death, looking him squarely in the face and smiling.

IV

Mondino walked into the banqueting hall with a heavy heart. When a new physician hosted the customary entertainment to celebrate getting his *licentia docendi,* even the older and more respected masters abandoned their usual gravitas to laugh and enjoy the pleasures of the feast. Mondino, who was closer in age to his students than to the other teachers, given that many of the students were nudging forty, made the most of these merry occasions and thoroughly enjoyed the music and singing. As a rule, he never had to be asked twice to dance a stampita or a farandole, even if he had absolutely no sense of rhythm and was always hopelessly out of step.

He was firmly of the opinion that humanity gained something with the arrival of a new graduate in the world of medicine, jurisprudence or the liberal arts. So it was right to rejoice. And this particular banquet was being given by a student from Syracuse with ample means who certainly hadn't stinted. All the teachers from the faculty of medicine had been talking about it for weeks.

And yet, as he glanced around the great hall with its cross-vaulted ceiling and Florentine tiled floor, filled with three long tables placed in a horseshoe and covered with snow-white tablecloths, Mondino felt listless. And as he watched the servants busying themselves arranging bowls, cutting boards and spoons, he didn't even feel the slightest pleasure at the thought of eating. He'd not yet received any news from Gerardo and the joy of the banquet was ruined by the thought that if the young man had been arrested, it would be his last supper.

'Magister, what a pleasure to see you at my humble table,' said the graduate, coming over to welcome him. He was a tall, bulky man of about thirty-five, with drooping cheeks. Mondino was convinced that he would make a good physician, once he had returned to his distant Syracuse.

'I wouldn't have missed the graduation banquet of one of my best students for the world,' Mondino answered, in an affable tone. 'Not to mention that many of my colleagues only got through the rigours of Lent by thinking of this event.'

The student laughed, replied that Mondino was too kind and that he hoped he would not disappoint his guests' expectations, then he accompanied Mondino to his place and went back to supervising the last preparations.

Mondino noted with satisfaction that he had been put at the centre table where the roasts would be carved. It was a sign of great respect. Seated there were the rectors of the two universities, ultramontane and cismontane, and the two head bursars, whom Mondino went to greet before going to take his place next to Liuzzo. The black or brown robes of the notables from the *Studium* contrasted with the red robes of the physicians. The other guests had been anything but sober in their choice of dress and the room was a riot of colour. There was not a bare head in the place and even in headwear there was noticeable variety, although everyone had chosen light materials because the warm season was approaching and with the wine and dance they were likely to sweat.

81

'I came by to collect you, Uncle, as we had agreed, but you had already left,' said Mondino, as soon as he sat down.

'I had to go out on rather a strange errand,' Liuzzo replied. He seemed to have recovered his temper since the day before. 'A murder in an inn near the Basilica of Santo Stefano.'

'But haven't you seen plenty of murders before?'

His uncle looked at him, as if uncertain whether to go on or not. Liuzzo sighed. 'The fact is that the man who was killed, a German who had arrived in the city not long ago, had something particularly horrible about him. The woman who found the body ran out of the inn screaming. Some passers-by heard her and went to have a look. Then someone went to inform the authorities. They said the thorax was opened in the manner of a dissector and the heart transformed into a block of iron, so the judge thought that it would be better to take a physician along with him, and he sent for me before going to the house. But is there something wrong?'

Mondino called on all his strength to put on a strained smile. 'Nothing, Uncle. It's just that these stories are not made to increase the appetite. But what you are saying is interesting. Please go on.'

'I don't know if I should, Mondino. You've gone very pale. Are you sure you are feeling quite well?'

'Yes, yes, I'm fine. You were saying that the heart had been turned into a block of iron? That seems incredible.'

'I thought so too,' agreed Liuzzo. 'In any case we didn't have the chance to see anything for ourselves. The innkeeper had informed the priests and when we arrived, the Inquisition barred the door. I was already late for the banquet, so I made my apologies to the judge and left. It seems that the dead man was a Knight Templar in disguise, and the Dominicans want to use this death to demonstrate that the Templars are involved in devilish practices. Just imagine, they didn't even want the cadaver to be removed. They asked for nothing to be touched until it has been seen by Uberto da Rimini, who is returning from his visit to the archbishop in Argenta this evening.'

'You mean to say that the dead man is still there?' asked Mondino. 'And for how long?'

'I don't know. The fact is that no one dares make any decisions in the absence of the Inquisitor. It seems that they're all petrified at the idea of making a mistake.'

Mondino nodded. During their brief encounter, the Inquisitor had not appeared to him to be a man inclined towards clemency. He was about to ask more questions, when their host requested silence for the commencement of the banquet. By now the guests were all seated and the steaming soup tureens containing the ravioli in broth for the first course were already towering over the tables.

The speech of thanks given by the graduate was suitably brief. Then the rector of the cismontane university, to which the new doctor belonged, spoke of his appreciation. After this there was a prayer and then they began to eat. Fortunately there was a bowl for every two guests and everyone had their own spoon. This was not always the case and sometimes resulted in detestably ill-mannered scenes. At some of the poorer banquets where Mondino had been present, the less important guests, who were often left without bowl or cutlery, forgot all sense of decorum and launched themselves on the tureen itself, slurping the soup with cupped hands and dirtying their sleeves up to the elbows.

The servants refilled the bowls with broth teeming with pieces of ravioli about the size of half a chestnut, and the assembly of serious professors dedicated all due attention to eating. However, Mondino left most of their shared bowl to his uncle, hardly even tasting the broth. He didn't know how to get more information out of Liuzzo without arousing suspicion, and he certainly couldn't reveal to his uncle what he had done with Gerardo: Liuzzo would be absolutely furious.

And yet he had to do something. If another corpse had appeared in the city, similar to that of Angelo da Piczano, then he must see it. Perhaps he would find some clues that would help him catch the murderer before the man was taken by the Inquisition. If the priests got their hands on him first, under torture the man would surely confess to the killing of another Templar in the same way, and that would soon lead to Gerardo's arrest. For the moment, at least so he hoped, the *comune* would have better things to think about than pursuing a student suspected of causing a fire that had not done much damage. But two murders such as those of Angelo da Piczano and the German in Santo Stefano would set off a manhunt from which Gerardo would not be able to escape. And the arrest after that would be his own.

General conversation took up again while the servants removed the now empty tureens and brought great platters full of civet of hare à la française. Liuzzo did not even make as if to serve himself, simply waiting for his nephew to serve them both. Out of the platter, Mondino picked three fine pieces of meat covered in abundant dark sauce, laying them out on a thick slice of bread, which he placed on the tablecloth between the two of them.

'Mondino, there is something tormenting you,' said Liuzzo.

He said nothing more, but it was clear that he was waiting for an explanation.

'Well yes, Uncle,' replied Mondino, taking up a piece of hare between his fingers and starting to eat it more for appearance's sake than because he had an appetite. 'If you want to know, the idea that the priests are taking it upon themselves to administer justice in our homes does not please me one bit. That death of which you were telling me was a Templar? Fine, let the *comune* judges be consulted and no one will deny the Inquisition permission to treat the murder as their own. But it's this deceit, this presumption, that I dislike.'

He had begun his speech more than anything to divert his uncle's attention, but then he'd become genuinely heated, as he did every time that he spoke of the interference of the papacy in the life of the city. He was suddenly silent, while an idea that had come from those words, took form in his mind.

Liuzzo finished his mouthful and carefully licked his fingers before speaking. 'I know that you don't like it, Mondino,' he said, slowly, as though weighing his words. 'And I also know where your antipathy for the papacy has led you. I'm not asking you to renounce your principles. I would not ask that of anyone: what is left of a man, if you take away what he believes in?'

'What is left is an empty sack, which inflates and deflates according to the wind around it,' replied Mondino, in an acidic tone, without managing to restrain himself. Liuzzo's was a rhetorical question, obviously not needing a reply. But he had not liked the reference to exile. That was where his hate of the papacy had led him, more than ten years before.

Liuzzo scooped up a bit of sauce with two fingers, licked them and said, 'I know that you would do it again. That is what I admire in you. The ability always to see a thing to its conclusion. But,' he went on, cutting short his nephew's protests with a wave of a hand, 'now you are a Magister of the *Studium* of Bologna, the first and the best university of Europe. You are a father, you no longer have a wife at your side and you are not as young as you were ten years ago.'

'So? I am still myself.' Mondino's tone was more abrupt than he had intended. 'I know how much I cost you,' he added. 'You and my father. And I've often asked to pay off that debt.'

This time it was Liuzzo who lost his self-control. He lowered his voice even more, so as not to be heard by the fellow diners seated opposite them, but his words came out as dry as the sound of a blade being sharpened on stone. 'The thousand lira that your father and I had to pay for your return was a sacrifice because we are not rich, but we have never considered it a debt. If you are too small-minded not to be able to accept the disinterested help of your own family, that is your problem. What I want to say to you is that you have a responsibility towards your children. If you get into trouble, they will be the ones to pay for your pride this time. And to publicly accuse the Church of prevarication and arrogance means trouble.'

As soon as they got to the pause between courses, with musicians starting to play cheerful and slightly irreverent songs, the guests took the opportunity to get up, stretch their legs and go through to the garden to satisfy their bodily needs. It was the moment that Mondino had been waiting for.

'Uncle, may I speak to you please?' he asked.

Liuzzo turned and seeing him already on his feet, he got up too. 'Only if you intend to apologise,' he answered, curtly.

They moved a few paces away from the table, over which the servants were leaning to remove what was left of the roast, which was not much, and make room for the cheeses and pudding.

'Please forgive me,' said Mondino. 'I was stupid and churlish to speak to you like that.' He raised his eyes to look Liuzzo in the face. 'Now I need to leave this banquet. I must ask you to help me do so in the least discourteous manner possible.'

'Leave the banquet?' asked Liuzzo, appalled at such a violation of good manners. 'But you can't. You'll offend our host, who has gone to so much trouble to do it as it should be done.'

Mondino made a sign to him to lower his voice. Mondino said nothing while two other guests passed them going towards the garden, then he said: 'I want to go to the Captain of the People to ask for a pass to see that corpse.

And I have to go right now, before they take him away. I have no intention of letting the Pope get away with running the place.'

Liuzzo stood staring at him, in a silence that was more eloquent than words. Mondino did not add anything further, and through gritted teeth, his uncle finally said, 'I will say that you have been called to the bedside of a patient and I'll make your excuses to our host. But let it be clear that I am doing it for the good of our family and not for you. Now you may as well go, if you absolutely must. But when we see each other next, I want to talk about the new terms of our association. I have spent more than fifteen years setting up my School of Medicine and I will not permit you to throw it all away for your confounded principles.'

This said, he turned and walked back to the table. He was seething, and yet he smiled to left and right and exchanged pleasantries about the music and the acrobats who were entertaining them in the pause between courses. Mondino envied him his talent for being at his ease in society; one that Mondino himself possessed in such paltry measure. Not by chance, when in 1299, eight well-informed Guelphs had compiled the list of the two hundred Ghibellines to be sent into exile, they had chosen him and not his uncle and his father, who were Ghibellines nonetheless.

Thanks to his principles, Mondino had been banished to Faenza for three years, leaving his father and uncle to take care of his family. And then they'd used up everything they had to pay the fine so that he could come home, and it still wasn't enough. Of course, being a good physician, Mondino had been able to rebuild the family patrimony since then, but now Gerardo had turned up and dragged him back into trouble again.

No, he thought, not even that was true. Gerardo had only come to ask for help, but he could have refused him. If Liuzzo

87

had been in his place, he would have called the guards and let justice follow its course.

And Liuzzo certainly wouldn't have let himself be tempted by the dream of uncovering the mystery that transformed blood into metal.

Before the pause ended and someone noticed his absence, Mondino walked quickly out of the hall. He didn't want to say goodbye to anyone or give any sort of explanation. It was better this way. His uncle would make his excuses for him.

As soon as he was in the street he stepped in some horse droppings because he was absorbed in thought and not looking where he put his feet. He had to stop to clean his leather shoe with a stick. He couldn't stop thinking about what Liuzzo had said.

There being no way he could tell the man the truth, he had had to lie to him. The danger in which Mondino had put himself and his family by helping Gerardo had got much greater with the appearance of a second corpse. He knew that Liuzzo would criticise him severely if he knew everything. He would call him an impulsive and irresponsible idiot, as he had done in the past. And this time Mondino would not be able to stand it.

Above all, because he was beginning to think that it might be true.

The meeting was not going well. Uberto da Rimini had undertaken the journey all the way to Argenta, through hazardous and marshy country, because he intended to present an important request to the Archbishop of Ravenna, Rinaldo da Concorezzo, and was certain that he possessed the arguments necessary to convince the man. However, the prelate had immediately started by criticising his efforts with regard to the fire on the previous Thursday because it had not resulted in the discovery of a corpse.

'Monsignor, forgive my boldness,' said Uberto, resolutely, while doing his best to appear submissive. 'But the person who gave us the information has always shown himself reliable in the past.'

'I do not doubt that,' answered the Archbishop. 'The fact remains that you have found no proof of anything at all.'

It was this quibbling mentality that had carried Rinaldo upwards through a brilliant career at the Curia. But Uberto did not understand how a man with such a bland spirit could have been charged by the Pope to direct the trial against the Templars of northern Italy. It was a job that required someone made of altogether different stuff. Someone who, faced with an exceptional situation, would be prepared to take exceptional action and bend the rules of normal behaviour. Someone like himself, for instance.

'We didn't find any proof because there was someone else in the house. Instead of opening the door, he set the place on fire and escaped over the roofs, taking the corpse with him.'

'You do at least have proof of that?' asked Rinaldo, stolidly.

They were in the great hall where the Archbishop received important visits, and this sign of respect had pleased Uberto. But Rinaldo da Concorezzo had not sat down, so he too had to remain on his feet, shivering in the middle of that enormous draughty room. He had the suspicion that the Archbishop was doing it on purpose, and felt the colour rise to his cheeks.

'No, Monsignor, we are not absolutely certain that there was someone in the house, still ...'

'So why are you talking of murder, of commerce with the Devil, of people escaping over rooftops with corpses on their backs? These are serious allegations, and I am not disposed to accept them in the absence of concrete facts to support them.'

Uberto made a visible effort to control himself and said that perhaps it would all be simpler if the Archbishop gave him permission to start again from the beginning.

Rinaldo da Concorezzo walked over to the open window and turned around so that the hot early afternoon sun warmed his back.

'Please do, Father,' he said.

Uberto began with the anonymous letter delivered three nights before at the San Domenico Basilica. The bearer had slipped it under the door of the monastery, knocked hard and then disappeared. It was not the first time that they had received information in that manner, always from the same person as shown by the handwriting in the letter, and always revealing itself to be useful. Various Templars who escaped the first wave of arrests had been caught thanks to this mysterious informer.

'And have you ever tried to find out his identity?' asked Rinaldo da Concorezzo.

'If someone gives us factual help but prefers to remain anonymous, Monsignor, I don't see a reason to waste time and resources trying to find out who he is.'

Uberto immediately regretted those words. If one of the friars had addressed him in that tone, he would have found a way to send him off to spread the Lord's word in the most remote corner of Christendom. Uberto scrutinised the Archbishop's face, anxious to know what price he would have to pay for his insolence, and he realised that from where the prelate stood, with the light behind him, it was impossible to make out the man's expression. Once again Uberto asked himself if the Archbishop were not doing it on purpose.

'However, I do see a reason not to accept anonymous information or accusations, Father Uberto,' replied Rinaldo, coldly. 'And so that you can see it too, I order you to reflect upon it while weeding the tombs in the cemetery of your abbey for a whole day from sunrise to sunset, without stopping to eat, drink or rest. Now go on with your tale and do not dare to show me such disrespect again.'

Uberto swallowed his humiliation, happy to have got away with so little. And at the same time he absorbed an important piece of information. The punishment given to him by Rinaldo could not have been chosen by chance. Someone must have informed the Archbishop of his initiative to weed the cemetery. Uberto made a mental note: the prelate had spies in the monastery. From now on, he must tread very carefully.

In the meantime, in language as respectful as possible, he explained that having received the letter he had gone to the *Podestà* to request some guards be assigned to him. He had then gone with them to the house where, according to the letter, he would find a horrendous crime. A Templar from Bavaria had been killed in the course of a ritual to propitiate Baphomet, the pagan idol adored by the Knights Templar. Only, as the guards knocked on the door, flames were seen issuing from the top floor. They had tried to break the door down, but a neighbour who lived on the ground floor arrived just at that moment and opened it for them. By now the fire had spread, making it impossible to go upstairs. And once the flames had been overcome, there was nothing to be found in the debris.

'Who does the house belong to?' asked Rinaldo.

'A wool merchant, Monsignor, who is above suspicion,' replied Uberto. 'But he had rented an apartment on the top floor to a medical student, a certain Francesco Salimbene from Imola. We suspect him to be a Knight Templar.'

'You suspect him? Is his name not in the registers that you sequestered?'

'He is obviously using a false name, Monsignor,' said Uberto. 'Besides, he might also be a foreigner, so there would be no mention of him in the registers of the Templar house of Bologna in any case.' He took a deep breath and added, 'But perhaps one of the Templars who are already under arrest might know him. That was actually the reason for my visit.'

'Really? Would you be a little more clear, Father.'

Uberto was certain that he could perceive a nuance of irony in the prelate's voice, but, once again, when he looked the man in the face he was unable to make out his eyes as they were against the light. Was it possible that an Archbishop of the Church of Christ would make a fool of an Inquisitor friar?

'I have come to make a humble request that I made to you once in the past, and for which you refused your consent. But perhaps now—'

'You are not going to tell me that you have come all this way to ask me to authorise torture!' exploded Rinaldo. 'What makes you think that I would say yes if I have already expressed my absolute opposition to the practice?'

The Archbishop had abandoned his good humour and now his tone was imbued with all the authority of the position that he held. And yet Uberto da Rimini was certain that he could make him change his mind.

'Monsignor, there is little more than a month before the conclusion of the trial and no proof to condemn the Templars has emerged. I am certain that our pope, Clement V—'

'Do not dare to interpret the wishes of Christ's Vicar on earth with your feeble mind!' thundered Rinaldo, striding over from the window and bringing himself up to his full height in front of Uberto. 'As long as I am responsible for this trial, I will never authorise the extortion of confessions by torture. You have made a fruitless journey, Father Uberto. Now go, and do not forget your penance. I will ask the prior to let me know when you have completed it.'

Having said this, he turned his back and went to sit down on one of the great hall's comfortable seats.

'As you wish, Monsignor,' said Uberto, through clenched teeth. Then he made a bow and left, closing the door behind him.

He hurried down the stairs, waylaid a passing novice and

sent him to call the two guards who made up his escort. They were no doubt lazing around in the kitchen. When the two men arrived, they found him already in the saddle and waiting. They thought better of asking questions and quickly mounted their own horses.

Not long afterwards the little group left through the castle gate, heading in the direction of Bologna at a lively trot. The sun had disappeared behind a grey scud that fitted Uberto's mood perfectly. The meeting had been a total failure.

However, the one thing that bucked up his morale was the possibility that Guido Arlotti, the lowlife whom he had ordered to investigate Mondino, might have made an interesting discovery when interrogating the gravediggers. If he had found concrete proof to lay at the door of the physician, he would have him arrested and, using any method whatever, Mondino would be made to confess the whereabouts of the Templar who pretended to be his student. Then he would present the archbishop with a *fait accompli*.

Uberto was not stupid, even if Rinaldo persisted in treating him as such. He knew very well that to accuse someone of something you needed proof. But proof, he thought to himself, while brutally pulling up his horse to stop it nibbling the grass at the roadside, is only to be had by those who know how to find it.

Gerardo da Castelbretone was lying on his bed staring at the ceiling when the knowledge that he had been a complete idiot hit him with a thump. Old Philomena had let drop a significant fact and he had completely ignored it.

He leaped up, hurriedly pulling on his breeches and coat and not forgetting the baggy cap with the pleat that fell down over his forehead to help cover his face. He left his room and went down to the street door, treading as quietly as possible so as not to draw the attention of his landlady, who since receiving payment in advance for a month's rent had shown herself particularly kind and protective towards him.

The matron did, however, manage to intercept him in the corridor and kept him talking about Emperor Enrico VII's taking control of Lodi and Cremona and the siege of Brescia, begun recently.

'Do you think he will reach us here?' asked the woman. 'I tremble at the idea that our experience with Barbarossa will happen all over again.'

'It won't happen again. I don't believe that Enrico, if he should succeed in forcing Brescia to surrender to him, would come as far south as Bologna. But should he do so, we will be here waiting for him.'

Gerardo was not interested in the subject, but he had spoken with feeling. The idea of letting Bologna fall into the hands of the Emperor made him shudder.

The baker's wife was distracted by the sudden cry of one of her small children in the room next door and Gerardo took his chance to nip out of the door with a wave and a smile, hurriedly making his way towards the Church of San Filippo and San Giacomo of Savena. The Augustinians were living there, while awaiting the completion of the new basilica that was being built not far away, in a piazza next to Via San Donato.

Making his way along the nearly deserted streets lit by the soft afternoon sun, Gerardo felt a strange sadness that he recognised only too well. He would never have admitted that he did not like Sundays, the Lord's day, but it was true. Since he was a child, Sunday had always been an empty day for him, with nothing of interest to do and too many adults getting in the way. Whereas on weekdays he felt much freer and happier. And that feeling had stayed with him even now that he was a grown man.

Passing Asinelli's the fishmonger at Porta Ravegnana, he

pinched his nose against the smell of rotten fish that polluted the air even when the shop was closed. When he arrived at the door of the monastery, he knocked and said to the novice who came to open the shuttered window that he wanted to speak to Father Francesco. The boy asked him to wait and closed the shutter.

Standing in front of the closed door, Gerardo became aware that he didn't have a plan. He had hurried to the monastery as soon as he realised his oversight, intending to force the priest to tell him everything that he knew about Angelo da Piczano. If Angelo had introduced himself to the old harridan in the priest's name, it was clear that they must have known one another. Perhaps Father Francesco could reveal something that would help him to find the murderer. But he certainly wouldn't tell the Augustinian anything voluntarily, given that the man, like Angelo, engaged in a vice that was punishable by death. The only way, thought Gerardo, was to try to lure him to an isolated part of the monastery and frighten him, using the knife and the knowledge of his secret.

As the wait continued, his concern grew greater. Supposing the old woman had warned him? Perhaps the priest had left immediately to go on a pilgrimage to another monastery, to avoid trouble. But no, that couldn't be. Gerardo couldn't imagine the woman, as ugly as sin and hairy with it, turning up and telling one of her trusted clients that she had betrayed him. What would she get out of it? It was much more likely that she had disappeared without telling anyone where she was going. Now she was heaven knows where, spending the money earned through her repugnant trade, and perhaps, God forbid, setting herself up somewhere else.

The little shutter opened and the novice's beardless face appeared in the window again. 'Unfortunately Father Francesco is ill,' he said. 'He's asleep and I've been told not to wake him.'

'What's wrong with him?'

'Nothing serious,' answered the boy. 'His hernia has been giving him a lot of pain recently and last night they took him to the infirmary, where our apothecary has administered a calming potion.' He gave an apologetic smile. 'That's why I kept you waiting so long. I couldn't find him anywhere.'

'I see,' said Gerardo. 'I'll come back another day.'

'Would you like me to tell him that you came to see him when he wakes up?'

Gerardo forced himself to give a reassuring tone to his words. 'No, thank you. Better that he rests peacefully, if he can.'

The inn was right behind the Basilica of Santo Stefano, in a short, dark, muddy alley. Mondino high-handedly showed his pass to the soldier sitting on the doorstep.

'I've come to see the German's corpse,' he said. 'By order of the Captain of the People.'

It had all been much easier than he had thought. He had gone to the *Podestà's* offices, where he ran into a judge who was an old friend of his and who immediately took him to meet Pantaleone Buzacarini, the Captain of the People. Mondino had explained that it would be very useful for his anatomical research if he were able to have a look at the strange cadaver, and the captain, a Ghibelline like himself – called to office as part of the Guelph city government's recent policy of openness – had given his permission on the spot. 'We can't get into trouble with the Inquisition,' he said. 'So we're not beginning investigations ex officio on this case, unless they ask us to. Nonetheless, a physician is not a judge, and I can find nothing to take exception to in scientific curiosity.'

What he was really saying was clear: his hands were tied, but it suited him that a lay citizen went along to have a quick look. So he had written the pass, signed it and given it his

96

personal seal next to the people's stamp that bore the bust of St Peter.

The soldier didn't even pretend to read the pass, although he examined each of the stamps with attention. Satisfied, he said, 'As far as I'm concerned, you can go in. But you'll have to convince the monks who are guarding the room.'

'Do you know the dead man's name?' asked Mondino.

'Wilhelm von Trier, or so I'm told.'

'How did they discover that he was a Templar?'

The man shrugged. 'I think he had a letter on him. The innkeeper knows Latin and when he found it among the man's possessions he went straight to the priests.'

Mondino nodded and went up the wooden staircase that led to the first floor. He could tell immediately which room it was because standing in front of the door were two very young Dominicans with a frightened air about them. They told him that their orders were not to let anyone past, but Mondino ignored them completely, as if they hadn't even spoken. He just pushed open the door and went in. The two young monks stood undecided for a fraction of a second too long, so Mondino simply closed the door and bolted it from the inside. Then he took out the half-orange full of dried flowers and lavender that he used to combat the stench of illness and death and pressed it to his nose, turning a deaf ear to the shouts of the two boys who were ordering him to come out.

Liuzzo's description of the body did not prepare Mondino for what lay before him. He had been expecting something resembling what he had seen the last time, and naturally there were similarities. But it was all much cruder. The corpse was sitting on the bed with his back against the wall. He was an old man, tall and thin, with a prominent chin. He had no shirt on and his open chest revealed the obscene transformation of the heart. But this time the mysterious assassin had not confined himself to that. He had also disfigured his victim's face.

A deep incision in the shape of a cross went from the forehead to the chin and from one cheek to the other, passing over the nose. The effect was chilling.

There was blood everywhere: on the dead man's arms and face, in his hair, in his white beard, on his fustian breeches, on the walls and naturally on the mattress, which was drenched with it.

One thing he noticed immediately was that no one had touched the body. This was remarkable because the confusion of footprints in the bloody dust on the floor indicated that a good number of people had been in the room. There had been the cleaning woman who had found him, the passers-by who had come to her aid when she ran down into the street and the priests who had come to appraise the situation, but no one had dared to disturb the macabre *mise en scène*; perhaps out of fear of the Devil, perhaps perceiving that it had some particular significance.

Indeed it was clear, as in Angelo da Piczano's case, that there was a symbolic aspect to the crime. The heart of iron must mean something, and also Angelo's truncated arms and the cross cut into Wilhelm von Trier's face.

Working out the significance of the mutilations might help Mondino and Gerardo to discover the author of the atrocities.

Thinking of Gerardo brought on a rush of anger. Where was that hopeless individual now that he needed him?

However, Mondino did not let himself be distracted by such unproductive thoughts. He listened. Outside the door, all was quiet. If the monks had run for help, he did not have much time.

Rapidly, he examined the room, looking at everything quickly but with minute attention. He didn't bother to search the dead man's saddlebags. The innkeeper had already done that and anything important that he had found, besides the letter, would already be in his pocket or in the hands of the Dominicans.

Struck by a sudden inspiration, Mondino decided to check the body. If there was anything left to find that might set him on the path of the murderer and his alchemical secret, it could only be on the dead man himself, because no one had yet had the courage to touch him.

Feeling no repugnance – due to his long familiarity with death – Mondino patted the German's body with care. Almost immediately he felt a bulge at the height of his belt. He slipped his hand between skin and clothes, and in a pocket sewn inside the breeches he found a piece of valuable parchment, soft and carefully rolled, and a hard object. When he pulled out the latter, he saw that it was the index finger of a human, stripped of flesh, with the veins transformed into metal, like the heart in the man's chest. But it was not the man's finger. A quick look at the dead man's hands confirmed that he still had all ten of them.

Mondino thought that perhaps it was Angelo da Piczano's finger, because his hands had been missing. But there was no time to be lost in suppositions. Someone might arrive from one moment to the next.

He unrolled the parchment and saw that it was a map, with sketches showing woods and mountains, a series of symbols that he had never seen before, and a mark in red ink surrounded by some Arabic characters. Knowing perfectly well that he was committing another crime, he put it into his bag along with the metal finger. Then he quickly opened the door, frightening the two monks who had remained motionless in the corridor, put the pomander back in his bag and went downstairs.

Perhaps he had found something important, he couldn't tell yet. More than anything he wanted to know the secret that turned blood into metal, but now the most urgent thing was to find the perpetrator before the Church did. The murderer – still supposing that there was only one of them – represented

99

a serious danger, and there was only one sure way of avoiding having him talk.

However, Mondino found the idea of killing in cold blood insufferable, even if it was someone who had already killed two people in a manner that to describe as horrible would be an understatement.

He saluted the guard with a nod of the head, walked quickly out of the street door and immediately bumped into a fruit seller under the arches, almost knocking the man over. Nonetheless it was the fruit seller who excused himself, intimidated by the red robe and the fur-trimmed cloak that Mondino had put on for the banquet.

Rapidly distancing himself in the crowd that filled the piazza to overflowing, Mondino forced himself not to think of what would happen once they had found the author of the crimes. First they needed to find him. Then he and Gerardo would decide what to do.

He had never, in his whole life, had so many things about which it was easier not to think.

V

Mondino went out early. He had a lesson that day, but first he wanted to speak to another alchemist. Paying no attention to the pedlars of every description that swarmed through the streets, he walked the length of the San Donato arcade and finally arrived at the solitary house next to the Circla paling. He found the man he was looking for in a courtyard throwing handfuls of broad bean skins to the hens. He was an imposing man, with thick dark hair and big brown eyes. Mondino had been told that he was likely to find him prey to drunkenness, and to avoid this problem he had decided to go to his house early in the morning. But he was obviously not early enough. The alchemist had a nebulous look about him and at first it was not easy for Mondino to make himself understood. Together they went into the man's laboratory, where, despite the open window, the dense vapours of distilling alcohol impregnated the air. They seemed to be having an effect on the hens, which scratched about unsteadily in the chaos of pliers, hammers and other tools. A bean soup was boiling in a pan over the fire, hanging from a hook fixed to the wall above. On a stone platform a little coal fire had been lit, over which sat a strangely shaped alembic, the like of which Mondino had never seen before. Its various components, boiler in riveted copper, swan-neck still head and cooling flask, were positioned one above the other instead of side by side. The object seemed more primitive than the normal serpentine alembics, but it looked very functional.

'It's called an *alquitara*,' said the alchemist, noticing his interest. 'As the refrigeration vase is directly above the swan neck, the vapour can condense immediately and drip into the recipient.'

'From the name, it would appear to be Arabic,' said Mondino. 'I've seen other alembics from those parts, but nothing like this one.'

'Nor had I, but I can assure you that it works even better than the normal ones. I got it from a sorceress, a converted Arab who earns a living preparing potions and love philtres. She gave it to me in exchange for a book. But tell me, why are you here?'

The alchemist's large eyes gazed at Mondino with a confused expression and he belched. It was now clear, if there had been room for doubt, that the *aqua vitae* distilling in the alembic was not for alchemical purposes. It occurred to Mondino that the death of the German Templar at least meant that he could be more precise in his questions without arousing suspicion.

'I imagine you've heard of the strange death of that man in Santo Stefano?' he said.

'Who hasn't heard? The news has done the rounds of the city. But to me it's an absurdity.'

'Why?'

'Because I'm an alchemist, Messer, and as such I know perfectly well that the heart of a human being cannot be turned into a piece of metal.'

'Are you absolutely certain?'

The man straightened his shoulders and managed to assume a relatively lucid expression before answering: 'Absolutely. But you still haven't told me the reason for your visit.'

He knew nothing. It was therefore pointless for Mondino to expose himself. He looked around to find a pretext and once again his eyes fell upon the *alquitara*. 'I'd like to buy an alembic like this one,' he said. 'Where can I get one from?'

'Perhaps the person I got mine from. But I warn you, she is a strange woman.'

'The sorceress?' Mondino had never met one before, but he had no trouble imagining that they were strange women.

'Yes. But is that really why you came?'

Mondino merely nodded, without going into particulars. He had just had an idea. 'The woman speaks Arabic, doesn't she?' he asked.

'With me she spoke in the Italian vernacular,' said the man, shrugging his shoulders. He went up to the fireplace and gave the soup a stir with a long wooden spoon.

'But she speaks Arabic too.'

'I imagine so,' replied the alchemist, irritated. 'She is Arabic.'

'And she knows how to read, since you gave her a book,' said Mondino, almost to himself. Then, in a louder voice, 'Do you know where she lives?'

The man was having difficulty concentrating and kept looking from the pan to the alembic. 'She lives in Bova,' he said. 'I don't know exactly where, but they should know her thereabouts. She's called Adia Bintaba. Now, if you would excuse me.'

Mondino left and walked to the School of Medicine with a smile on his lips. He would ask the woman to translate the phrases in Arabic on his map. He was sure that they held precious information.

*

Gerardo arrived towards the end of the lesson. He came up to a window from the outside, moved aside the curtain that let the air circulate, yet prevented the students from being distracted by what was going on in the street, and made a sign to Mondino. None of the students noticed him, hunched as they were over their folios of Avicenna's *Canon*.

Mondino stared at him for a moment, with what looked like a mixture of surprise, anger and relief, and then went on talking. He must have finished the lecture and was now dealing with questions. Gerardo let the curtain fall and began to wait. He had never been a real student and yet he missed the world of the university already. It was years since his first lesson, but he remembered perfectly how Mondino, with the slightly monotonous voice of someone who has repeated the same thing many times, explained how to ask questions according to the four Aristotelian causes. It was a system that Mondino's own teacher, Taddeo Alderotti, had used before him: 'You must think of the material cause, or rather what it is made from, then the formal cause, that is its form or essence, then the efficient cause, in other words the author of the work, and lastly the final cause, or rather the end and purpose of the chosen argument. At this point you formulate a series of *dubia*, which will be followed by the *disputatio* and, finally, the *solutio*.'

Thinking back to those days, which though not particularly happy had been considerably less complicated than the present, helped Gerardo to while away the time, and suddenly he found that the lesson had ended.

Mondino came out last, quite a long time after the students, when the steward had already begun to restore order in the lecture hall, and he set off towards Piazza Maggiore without looking behind him. Aware of the necessity for prudence, Gerardo let him go on a dozen yards before coming up beside him. He was about to greet Mondino when the physician suddenly turned.

104

'You took your time,' he snapped, angrily. 'I thought the worst had happened.'

'Forgive me, Master. Let's go somewhere quiet, please, and I can explain everything. I need to speak to you urgently.'

'And I want to speak to you too,' answered Mondino, as if nothing could be more irritating to him. 'But I've got to go to the cutler to collect a surgical fork that I need urgently. Come with me, we can talk on the way.'

'As you wish, Magister,' replied Gerardo.

'And you can stop calling me Magister in that deferential way, at least when we are alone. I never really was your master, given that you didn't come to my lessons to learn, but to hide.'

'Magister,' said Gerardo, calmly, 'I owe you an enormous debt for the help you have given me, and for that alone you deserve all the deference that I can show you. Besides, to carry on pretending to be master and student is the best way not to attract too much attention, even if I am no longer attending your lessons.'

The physician was silent for a while and then he nodded, almost against his will. Gerardo followed him across the road, careful where he put his feet in the mud. Soon afterwards they surfaced beneath the arcade opposite, professor in front and student walking respectfully half a pace behind.

Mondino asked him what he had been doing over those days, and Gerardo told him about the lodgings he had taken in Borgo del Rondone and about his visit to the banker, but it was not the moment to ask him the favour he wanted, so instead he told him about Philomena and Masino, of his visit to the old woman's house and of the horrible discovery he had made.

'I have almost begun to think that Angelo da Piczano deserved that ghastly death,' he concluded. 'But what concerns me most now is that I don't know what to do to save the child. Philomena has taken fright and vanished, gone who knows where.'

'That friar of whom you spoke,' said Mondino, without turning to face him, and continuing to walk on. 'I think I know who he is. If I'm not mistaken his cousin is the master builder in charge of the works at the new basilica of San Giacomo Maggiore, in Via San Donato.'

'Father Francesco.' Gerardo said his name with contempt. 'I tried calling on him yesterday, but he had been taken to the monastery infirmary and they wouldn't let me see him.'

They were crossing Piazza Maggiore, passing the *Podestà*'s offices. On their right were some houses that for some time there had been talk of demolishing to build a huge basilica dedicated to San Petronio.

'What's wrong with him?' asked Mondino.

'He suffers from a scrotal hernia, as far as I could understand. It's rather too bland a punishment for his particular sins. I wanted to talk to you about that too.'

'About his hernia?' Mondino stopped and looked at him with an expression that was anything but benevolent.

Gerardo gathered up his courage. 'Well,' he answered in a low voice, so as not to be heard by the passers-by and the pedlars who thronged the piazza. 'I was thinking that a visit by a great physician such as you might be a good way of getting to him and making him talk. He might know something important about Angelo da Piczano. And maybe even about Philomena too.'

'You were thinking!' the physician burst out. 'And who are you to tell me what to do?'

Gerardo looked around him and saw that a few people had turned to look at them.

'We're attracting attention,' he said, with a conciliatory smile for the benefit of the curious. 'All right, if you don't want to help me, I'll find another way of speaking to that degenerate priest.'

Mondino moved on, Gerardo followed him and after a few yards no one took any more notice of them. They got to the other side of the piazza and turned into the fishmonger's street, first passing the silk market and Cornacchina Tower on their right. Only then did the physician turn to look at him briefly.

'The idea of the visit is a good one,' he said. He no longer seemed annoyed.

'So you'll go?' asked Gerardo. The smell of rotten fish coming from the corner behind the rows of stalls was so strong that he felt he could almost see it.

'Yes. But first there are more important things to talk about. Have you heard about the other Templar who's been killed?'

Gerardo jumped. 'Another? No, I hadn't.'

Outside one of the city's most famous fish-shops, the physician paused to pay his respects to the wife of one of the Lambertazzis with a courteous bow. She was an eccentric lady who went to the market herself to check up on the servants while they were doing the shopping. Then he told Gerardo all about Wilhelm von Trier's death and the fact that he had managed to examine the cadaver before the Inquisitors, purloining a map full of alchemical symbols.

'A map? Of what?'

'I don't know yet. We can talk about that later, when I show it to you. I've been carrying it on me since yesterday, expecting to see you. The main thing is that our assassin has produced another victim. The German's body has been seen by quite a few people, and the fact that it had a piece of iron where the heart should have been is on everyone's lips.'

'Had his hands been amputated too?'

'No. But he had a bloody cross carved into his face. Does that mean anything to you?'

'Nothing, apart from the fact that these murders seem to want to communicate something specific. The hands, the cross, the heart of iron . . . they're all symbols. But of what?'

'When we know that,' replied Mondino, darkly, 'perhaps we shall also know who the murderer is.'

A woodcutter, bent beneath the weight of a stack that was too big for his shoulders, came between them. Gerardo walked round him and joined Mondino in front of a bakery, from which the smell of bread and spices wafted. He was convinced that their disjointed conversation, held in the commotion of the crowded street, was the result of pique on the part of the physician because he had not turned up to their meeting.

'Master,' he began, 'it's not wise to discuss these things in public.'

'On the contrary,' replied Mondino, who continued walking a step ahead of him. 'We would attract more attention if we went to confabulate in a tavern.'

Gerardo did not agree, but he preferred not to insist. Mondino was highly strung and it was better not to provoke him, above all because Gerardo wanted to ask him a favour.

They turned into a quieter side street, and not much further on entered a large well-kept courtyard, where there was only the metallic sound of a file to be heard.

Gerardo took advantage of the relative peace to take up their conversation again. 'So you think he was attacked by surprise?' he asked.

Mondino nodded. 'When I examined him, I saw that like your friend Angelo he had a bruise on the back of his head. This is the second murder committed in this way, and tells us something about the perpetrator.'

'You mean to say that it must be someone who is physically strong?'

'Exactly,' replied the physician. His aggravation at having been anticipated was obvious, and Gerardo had to stop himself from smiling. 'Quite strong, but certainly astute enough to convince his victims to trust him to the point of letting him enter their lodgings.'

The sound of the file came from a cutler's workshop, where a boy in a leather apron was sitting on the entrance steps sharpening a knife. As soon as he saw them he ran in and a moment later a man who seemed to be his father came out. He was holding a fork with a thin handle and two points ending in hooks, like the ones that surgeons use to lift the edges of skin and muscle during an operation. 'It has been ready since yesterday, Master,' was all he said. Mondino examined it with a satisfied expression, paid without bargaining and turned back towards the street. They walked out of the courtyard, passing two women carrying baskets full of dirty clothes on their heads, and Mondino made as if to go home, but Gerardo took his arm to hold him back.

'Master, I have a favour to ask of you.'

'Another? Haven't I done you enough favours?'

Gerardo was silent for a moment, his head bowed, while the physician asked him what he wanted.

'As I told you, I went to a banker to ask for a loan, but he wants two guarantors. He's got one already, the other ...'

'Will have to be me,' concluded Mondino.

'I know that it's an inconvenient thing to ask of you, but I don't know who else to turn to,' admitted Gerardo. 'I promise you will be taking no risk at all, I have the means to honour my obligation.'

'Where does this banker live?' asked Mondino, brusquely.

'Not far from here,' Gerardo replied, immediately. 'If it were possible, it would be best to go now, before his offices close.'

A servant knocked and put his head around the door, announcing that Gerardo da Castelbretone had arrived with a guarantor for the loan. Remigio Sensi nodded and told him to go straight to the gentleman he had spoken of, requesting him to come as quickly as possible. Then he dismissed the servant with a wave of the hand and went back to speaking to the client sitting in front of him.

'Everything is ready, Messer. My daughter has the documents here ready to sign.'

The client, a corpulent landed proprietor from Casalecchio, read the documents attentively, following every line with his finger. Then he took the quill that the banker was holding out to him, dipped it in the ink and signed the bottom of each page.

'Very good,' said Remigio, happy that the affair had been concluded. He handed over the money. The man made a brief bow to him and to Fiamma and went down to join the escort that awaited him in the street. Immediately afterwards Remigio ordered the two servants to close the window hatch that opened on to the arcade and to invite Gerardo and his surety to come inside.

When Gerardo introduced Mondino, Remigio paid him the compliment of saying that the great Mondino de Liuzzi had no need of introduction. Fiamma got to her feet and addressed a curtsey first to Mondino, then to Gerardo, placing one foot behind the other and slightly bending her knee. But while she had demurely dropped her head in front of the physician, with Gerardo she exchanged a glance that Remigio did not like at all.

'There will be a short wait,' said the banker to his guests. He struck a piece of steel on to the flintstone and lit three lamps, because with the shutter closed the office became dark even in broad daylight. 'As for you, my girl, you may leave. I can manage these gentlemen alone.'

'With your permission, I must finish the letter that you asked me to write this morning,' responded Fiamma, firmly. 'If I put it off any longer, it will mean that we will not have it ready to deliver this evening.'

That said she went quickly to sit down at the table, as though to close the discussion. She took a piece of parchment, dipped the pen in ink and began to transcribe the words of a rough copy on to parchment.

Remigio pursed his lips and addressed Mondino. 'You must be a little bit patient, Magister,' he said. 'I have sent for the second backer, but he will take a moment to get here.'

Gerardo burst out, suspiciously. 'You have not betrayed me, have you, Messer Remigio?'

He slipped his hand quickly under his tunic and then looked at Fiamma. The banker had the feeling that it was only the presence of the girl that stopped Gerardo from pulling out a knife.

Remigio lifted both hands. 'Calm down, calm down. I don't know if I can speak ...'

'The Magister is abreast of everything that concerns my situation,' replied Gerardo, still looking about him as though he feared the arrival of the Inquisition from one moment to the next. 'You can talk freely in front of him.'

'Just as well,' approved Remigio. 'Otherwise I would have had to ask you to advise him. I cannot accept a surety who is not aware of all the risks that he is taking on.'

'Does the other man of whom you speak know all the risks?' asked Gerardo.

'Naturally. I have already told you that he is a Knight of the Temple like yourself.'

Remigio indicated the seats covered with silk cushions and the three of them sat down. One of the lamps was on the table just next to Fiamma, to allow her to write with ease, and it lit up her face in full. Mondino scrutinised her with a professional eye.

'A red-hot cautery,' he said almost to himself, shaking his head. 'Five or six years ago, to judge from the thickening of the tissue.' Then, turning to Remigio, 'Was the cataract really bad enough to justify the use of the cautery on the child?'

The banker was about to reply, but Fiamma looked up from her writing and spoke first. 'The cataract gave me terrible pain throughout the left side of my face,' she explained, with a sombre look in which all the suffering she had gone through seemed to be concentrated. 'The doctors said that cauterising it was the only cure that would guarantee recovery.'

Mondino shrugged. 'As far as I'm concerned the cautery is a barbarous instrument that will soon be abandoned by science.'

'And what do you use instead, Magister?' asked Remigio. He did not really want to know but he always tried to make his clients talk of their own work a bit. It was a thing that put them at their ease and made them feel secure, so that they relaxed and were more malleable. Mondino briefly explained that cauterisation was a difficult method requiring great skill. It was painful for the patient and unfortunately in many cases did not obtain the hoped-for result. Physicians still used it a great deal, but for the cataract he preferred to use a cure based principally on a warm dry diet, taken with compresses made of resin, cloves, cubeb and galangal.

'Please excuse me,' said Fiamma rising to her feet, as soon as the physician had finished. 'I must go and check on the girls in the kitchen.'

She hurried out, making the wicks of the lamps oscillate, and Remigio was pleased that Mondino's interest in her scar had achieved the purpose of making her leave the room. He felt he had to explain that the scar was a subject of great sensitivity for her. The two agreed without further comment.

'Tell me at least the name of the man whom we are waiting for,' Gerardo insisted, returning to the reason for their presence in the office.

'His name is Hugues de Narbonne,' replied Remigio. 'He was Commander of the Vault of Acre, perhaps you have heard of him.'

Gerardo opened wide his eyes and mouth, without saying anything. He was the picture of surprise. Remigio almost felt sorry for him, and turned to close the lid of the safe so as not to look him in the face. The youth almost certainly believed that a man so high up in the Templar hierarchy must be some kind of saint. He would discover to his cost how wrong he was. Hugues' interest in him was certainly not dictated by generosity.

After Gerardo's first visit, Remigio had informed Hugues de Narbonne straight away. That was the demand that the Frenchman had put before Remigio: to immediately make known to him every incognito visit by a Knight Templar, above all those who had arrived in the city recently. When the banker had told Hugues that a Templar had come to see him needing a loan because all his possessions had been destroyed in a fire, Hugues showed himself to be most interested. And he had instantly accepted to stand surety for the loan.

A servant appeared at the door and announced the arrival of the Frenchman. Remigio told him to show the man in and as soon as Hugues de Narbonne entered the office, he made the introductions in Latin, to respect formalities and because Hugues did not speak the vernacular. The matter of the loan was settled speedily, but in the absence of Fiamma it took longer to prepare the documents. While Remigio wrote, Hugues chatted animatedly with the other two. They spoke of castles and garrisons, of sea voyages and Arabic medicine, which Hugues maintained was more advanced than European medicine. To which Mondino responded, 'Not for long.'

However, everyone paid due attention to reading and discussing the clauses of the contract, and at the end Remigio was less satisfied with the affair than he had foreseen. His dissatisfaction reached its peak when Gerardo asked if he might lend them a room so that they could talk privately for a short while. Mondino's irritated expression at hearing those words did not escape Remigio. It was clear that this was something they had not discussed beforehand. In any case, he had no intention of complying with the request.

'My house is not a public meeting place,' he replied, curtly. 'If you have to talk, go to a tavern.'

Gerardo and Mondino nodded and got to their feet, but Hugues de Narbonne stayed seated. 'As you will appreciate, Messer Remigio,' he said, with a cold smile, 'we must be very careful with regard to what we say and to whom we say it. This young man has had a good idea. Your house is the only place in which we can be sure that we will not be betrayed.' He laid a hand on the leather bag that he wore on his belt and took out some coins, which he threw nonchalantly on the table. 'We will pay you for the inconvenience.'

Despite the retainers outside the door, Remigio did not dare throw him out, as he wanted to do. Hugues had already shown how dangerous it was to oppose him. Besides, granting the request could turn out to be useful. Remigio might be able to find out something that he could use against the Frenchman. And then perhaps he could rid himself of that scourge once and for all.

'My office is at your service,' he said, getting up without touching or even looking at the coins. 'I will have wine and nuts brought for you, but don't take too long. I have other business to conclude today.'

As soon as they were alone, Hugues de Narbonne excused himself for his bad manners, adding that unfortunately it was necessary. 'I've known Messer Remigio for some time,' he explained. 'I know how to deal with him.' Then the Frenchman addressed Gerardo. 'What did you want to talk to me about?'

Mondino looked at de Narbonne closely. The sky-blue tunic, embroidered shirt and light wool stockings that he wore did not hide his animal nature. Whereas his clear eyes were most definitely not the obtuse eyes of an animal. On the contrary, they showed a menacing intelligence, always ready to take advantage of every situation.

Gerardo, on the other hand, did not seem to see anything of the sort. He was happy as a lark because of the attention shown him by such an influential personage, who in less difficult times for the Templars wouldn't even have deigned to speak to him. And without being asked, he said that he was worried about the impact that the recent strange murders in the city might have on the trial in progress.

'Why are you speaking in the plural?' asked Hugues, quickly. 'As far as I'm aware, there has only been one murder.'

Mondino tried to warn Gerardo, but the young man went on regardless. He explained that there had been two murders: the first he had managed to hide because it had happened in his own house, but he hadn't been able to do anything about the second. He wanted to find the assassin before the Inquisition and he wished to share the information he had with Hugues. Surely the Commander of the Vault of Acre would know things that a mere knight did not.

Of the whole rambling speech, Mondino was struck by only one thing: Gerardo had left him out entirely, not even mentioning the part he'd played in getting rid of Angelo da Piczano's body. But he was very worried by the trust that the young man showed the Frenchman with the gelid eyes.

For Mondino, unlike Gerardo, did not trust him at all. Their meeting at Remigio Sensi's house seemed to him to be prearranged, and he was certain that Hugues de Narbonne's interest in Gerardo hid something more than the simple desire to help a confrère in a spot of trouble.

To prevent Gerardo mentioning the map, the only thing that came to mind was to anticipate him. Mondino said that he was the physician who had been to examine Wilhelm von Trier's corpse on behalf of the *comune*, before the arrival of the Inquisitor.

They were interrupted by the arrival of Remigio's two servants who were carrying a pitcher of wine, tin cups and an olive-wood bowl filled with walnuts, plus two slabs of curved marble with which to break the shells. Their behaviour expressed amazement at, and mistrust of, the clients who had convinced their master to leave his own office. Perhaps it had never happened before.

When they had gone, Hugues went to check that the door was properly closed and then he asked Mondino a large number of questions about Wilhelm von Trier, in a brusque and practical tone. Mondino found himself replying to the questions without quite understanding how the Frenchman had assumed command. It was something that obviously came naturally to him. Hugues wanted to know exactly what wounds the body had sustained, in what state the room was, if there were the remains of a fire, if there was a smell of sulphur and above all, if the material into which the heart had been transformed were really iron or something else.

As a whole, his questions revealed that Hugues was something of an expert on the subject of murder. He admitted to having gained experience in such things during his sojourn at the Templar House in the Kingdom of Aragon, but it did not extend to alchemy. His ideas on alchemical processes were outlandish and confused, and Mondino, who had in fact studied the texts of Arnaldo da Villanova, Raimondo Lullo and above all, those of Albertus Magnus and Roger Bacon, explained to him that the alchemical transformation carried out in that sordid inn behind Santo Stefano had nothing canonical about it at all. There had simply not been enough time to go through the four operations and three phases of transmutation, which could take weeks or even months.

'The alchemist is not a magician, as the common man would believe,' he went on, taking a walnut and placing it on one of the little concave slabs of marble. 'To obtain a result of this kind, you don't just need to light a fire, recite some magic words and click your fingers.'

'So how do you explain what you saw?' asked Hugues de Narbonne.

Mondino cracked the nut with the second piece of marble, crushing the shell. 'I don't know how to explain it. I only know what cannot have happened.'

'I too have thought long and hard about it,' intervened Gerardo. 'Could it be that the murderer made his victims drink a substance, something that set off the transformation from the inside, and only after that, opened the thorax and displayed his work of art to the world?'

The Frenchman's eyes lit up at the question, revealing an interest that according to Mondino went well beyond the desire to obtain justice for his order and for the poor victims. 'I have never heard mention of a poison of that sort,' replied Mondino. 'But perhaps it's not a poison ...'

They both looked at him, waiting for him to continue. He took his time, separating the flesh of the nut from the pieces of shell and eating, before he replied. 'If you believe that it's a question of some other alchemical preparation,' he said, finally, addressing the Frenchman, 'I cannot prove you are wrong. But I've never heard of any preparation capable of such a thing. Besides there are other knotty points.'

'What are they?'

Mondino drank a gulp of wine and the others did the same. 'How is it possible that a man drinks a poison and that the poison, instead of passing down the throat to end up in the stomach, goes straight to the heart? How did it get there? How is it possible that it left no trace of its passage through the rest of the body? And most of all, if the victim was first stunned and then stabbed with an awl, as the bruising on the nape and the hole in the chest of both bodies would suggest, how did the liquid make its way around the body? When the

117

vital processes cease, the whole pumping system that is triggered by the heart stops functioning.'

'And what are the answers to those questions?' asked Gerardo.

Mondino saw an expectant light in his eye and was sorry to have to disappoint him. 'I have no answers,' he admitted, morosely. 'Only questions.'

'You have spoken of both corpses,' said Hugues de Narbonne, fixing him with penetrating grey eyes. 'Why didn't you tell me before that you had seen the other one too?'

Mondino realised that he had said too much, distracted by his scientific interest in the subject. But the threatening undercurrent of Hugues' words induced him to defend himself by attacking.

'Messer, I do not know you and I am under no obligation to tell you anything,' he said. 'Perhaps Gerardo owes you obedience, I do not.'

The Frenchman let fall any pretence of friendliness. He rose in a flash and took hold of Mondino round the neck, lifting him and pushing him against the wall.

'Messer, perhaps resolving these cases of murder only represents an intellectual curiosity for you,' Hugues said through clenched teeth. 'For me it is very different.'

Mondino grabbed his wrists to free himself, but it was Gerardo's intervention that brought the situation back to normal.

'Commander, please,' he said, in a decisive tone. 'Let him go, or I will have to defend him.'

Hugues de Narbonne turned to stare at Gerardo, stunned by such insubordination. Then he changed tack. 'Very well,' he said, in his low and throaty voice, relaxing his grip around the physician's neck. 'Excuse my vehemence, Messer Mondino. The fact is that if the King of France succeeds in his intention of suppressing my order, a large part of the Templars will be condemned to mere *purgationes*, or at the most a few years in prison. But those occupying positions of greater responsibility, like myself, will end up at the stake. Or if they do manage to escape, will spend the rest of their lives in hiding, living in poverty, without ever drawing attention to themselves. Surely you must understand why I will do everything in my power to avoid that happening.'

'What I understand, Messer,' replied Mondino, overheated and breathing heavily, 'is that I do not like you and that I disapprove of Gerardo's decision to reveal what he knew about those deaths.'

'Please control yourselves,' Gerardo intervened, standing between them and opening wide his arms to separate them. Then, addressing Hugues, he said, 'It's my fault that the Magister finds himself involved in all this. Please don't ask more of us than we can give you, Commander, but know that we will not hide anything important from you.'

Hugues de Narbonne nodded and took a step back, as though nothing whatever had happened. Mondino felt his heart thumping hard, but did his best to appear impassive. He said that he would have to leave them, as it was time for him to go back to his family for dinner. In the end the Frenchman had given him the perfect pretext to extricate himself from the discussion.

Gerardo looked at him with a maddened expression. 'I have just said that we will not hide anything important from the Commander,' he said. 'Please would you show him the map you were talking about, Master.'

Mondino gave him a harsh piercing look, but the damage had been done. Gerardo had obviously decided to share everything he knew with Hugues de Narbonne, and at that point to pull out the map would add nothing to the problems they already had. Perhaps the Frenchman could even tell them something useful about it.

Letting out a sigh of resignation, Mondino slipped his hand beneath his tunic. 'I found a map in a secret pocket sewn into Wilhelm von Trier's breeches,' he explained, extracting the roll of parchment. 'I do not know what it represents nor if it bears any connection to his death, although I am inclined to think so, given that this was in the same pocket.'

With a rapid gesture he opened his palm and showed them the fleshless finger that he had found with the map. The two Templars looked at him in amazement and Mondino quickly put it away before Hugues could manage to take it from him.

'You saw it quite well,' he said. 'The veins of the finger have been turned into iron, just like the hearts of the two dead men. The finger does not belong to Wilhelm von Trier, and I don't know where it comes from.'

'Master, but this means ...' said Gerardo, without finishing his sentence.

'What?' asked Mondino. 'That our man was drawn into a trap? Maybe. That was exactly what I wanted to talk to you about.'

'Let's look at the map,' interrupted Hugues.

Mondino moved the pitcher of wine and the bowl of walnuts away and brought the light closer before he rolled out the parchment on the table. It was a small sheet of the best-quality vellum, soft and devoid of stains, made from the inside of the animal's skin. The drawings had been executed with great care, first with leadpoint and then shaded with pigments of three colours: white for the roads, red for the mountains and black for the fields and woods. In the two top corners were the sun and moon. In the bottom corners were a green and a red lion looking upwards. Between the two lions there was a red circle beneath which were the Arabic characters ءامرحلا written in copper salts ink that had taken on a greenish tone as it had faded. In the same ink other groups of words

120

were written in smaller letters, filling up almost all the blank spaces on the map. At the top in the centre, between the pictures of the sun and moon, there was another little red circle, with no clarification. The route indicated by the map united the two points, crossing through the woods and over the mountains. Mondino had studied it in every particular, but not knowing what it referred to and not understanding Arabic, he had made no sense of it at all.

'Does it mean anything to you?' he asked Hugues.

The Frenchman examined the map attentively. Then he said, 'Nothing. Other than that it describes a place in Spain.'

'How do you know?' asked Gerardo, surprised.

'Under the circle at the bottom there's the word *al-hamrã*, or Alhambra, as the Spanish say. It means "the red one", and indicates the fortress in the city of Gharnata, in the south of Spain. It's a Moorish stronghold. It must be the starting point of the journey.'

'Since you understand Arabic,' said Mondino, 'can you tell us what the other words mean?'

'They seem to be verses written for a marriage,' replied Hugues de Narbonne, without looking at the map. 'They praise the spouses, but they don't make much sense and it looks as though there are some stanzas missing. Perhaps they were only written to fill the empty spaces.'

Mondino knew about the habit of the Bolognese notaries of copying down verses in the margins of acts and documents, to prevent unauthorised persons adding false riders. Perhaps the Arabs did the same thing.

'It's possible,' he said, crisply, as he rolled up the parchment. 'In any case, if the dead Templar had taken such trouble to hide it and kept it with the finger that I showed you, knowing more about the map could prove useful to us.'

Hugues took a swig from his tin cup and dashed it on to the table with an abrupt gesture, making the lamp's flame waver.

'We're wasting time,' he said, his hand still on the cup. 'We have got to get to the murderer before the Inquisition does. And we don't need a map crammed with abstruse symbols to do that. We need to know whom the two men met when they arrived in Bologna. We must split up and discreetly interrogate anyone who saw them, beginning with the places where they lodged and working outwards from there. Obviously, first, Gerardo, you must tell us everything that Angelo da Piczano said and did while he was in your company.'

Hugues had again assumed the role of commander and was independently deciding their plan of action. With his coarse voice, grey eyes and imposing physique, he had a natural charisma that checked any desire to challenge him.

However, Mondino drew himself up and confronted de Narbonne.

'I don't agree, Messer. As I've already make quite clear, I do not owe obedience to you and I will follow my own trail, while you and Gerardo look into the meetings and movements of your two dead confrères.'

Hugues turned puce in the face, as though he had been slapped. He obviously wasn't used to hearing his decisions disputed. He looked at Mondino in silence, holding the empty cup firmly in his large hand covered with blond hair.

The physician met his gaze and, in the end, the Frenchman asked through gritted teeth, 'What would your idea be?'

'The secret of how to turn human blood into iron cannot be known to many. I myself, even though I studied alchemy during my medical training, have never heard of it. I am making inquiries among the city's alchemists, asking them for information about who might know a secret of that sort. Finding that person would almost certainly mean finding the murderer.'

Hugues gratified him with a contemptuous smile. 'Making inquiries among the alchemists is the first thing that the

Inquisition would think of doing. To follow in their footsteps is a mistake. This is a race in which we cannot afford to arrive second.'

Gerardo, while not losing his adoring attitude towards the Frenchman, intervened in defence of Mondino. 'Forgive me, Commander, but it's likely that the alchemists said as little as possible to the Inquisitor friar. While it is possible that they would speak freely to a lay physician, who after all knows the subject as well as or better than they do.'

Hugues reflected a second before speaking and then he nodded his great curly head. 'Very well, we'll split up. We'll talk to ordinary people, you to the alchemists. And we will keep each other informed of the results.'

Put in that way, Mondino's role seemed once again to have been Narbonne's decision. But the physician decided to let it drop. After all, it was true that rooting out the murderer of the Templars was in the interests of all three of them, and given that Hugues was now part of the group, to collaborate was the wisest thing he could do.

'Very well. Now we'd better leave. I don't want that poor banker to have an outflow of bile.'

All three of them rose. Hugues de Narbonne left the coins he had thrown on the table lying there and walked out of the office. Remigio did not turn up to say goodbye and they left without anyone seeing them out.

As soon as they were in the street, Mondino said, 'Now I must leave you. I will expect news through Gerardo.'

Having made it clear that he would prefer not to see Hugues de Narbonne again unless it was absolutely necessary, he turned and walked briskly away beneath the arches.

VI

Remigio Sensi stepped back from the two small holes in the painting of St Matthew that had allowed him to see and hear what had gone on in his office, and wiped the sweat from his forehead with the sleeve of his tunic.

He often made use of the hideaway to watch the behaviour of clients whom he did not trust. He would find an excuse to leave them alone for a moment and retire to the little hidden cubbyhole, cut into wall behind the painting. If his clients nosed around among his papers, appeared too happy or too afraid, went up to the safe or even (as sometimes happened when there were more than one of them) spoke in low voices of their fraudulent intentions, when Remigio returned to the studio he found an amiable but firm pretext not to conclude their business. In that way he avoided putting anyone's honesty in doubt.

Now, however, it was not a question of a loan or a deed of sale, but of something much more serious. What he had overheard required immediate measures to be taken.

He left the hideaway, beckoned to one of the servants at the door and sent him to deliver a message. Not long afterwards, a gaudily dressed young man entered Remigio's office. He wore a yellow surcoat and red breeches bordered in orange; his shoulder-length dark-brown hair was partially hidden beneath a brown cap embroidered in gold.

'I was about to sit down to eat when I received your message,' he said, by way of a greeting, taking a chair opposite Remigio without waiting to be asked. 'I hope you called with such urgency because you have good news for me.'

'Indeed I have,' replied Remigio, looking him straight in the eye. 'I want to propose the total cancellation of your debt. You will owe me nothing and your father will never know what trouble you have got yourself into through playing dice.'

The young man regarded the banker for a long time without showing any enthusiasm. Then he asked, 'What do you want in return?'

Remigio explained. His guest listened intently and at the end he said, 'Are you absolutely sure that it's as simple as that?'

'The place and time have to be chosen carefully, that's all,' replied Remigio. 'I shall decide when the time's right and send you word.'

'And afterwards I won't owe you anything.'

'We'll tear up the promissory note together, you have my word.'

'It's a done deal, then,' said the young man, rising with an agile movement that revealed his familiarity with physical training. 'I'll await your instructions.'

He left the room with a jaunty step and when the servant had closed the door, Remigio smiled to himself. Soon he would have eliminated a potential problem in his life and at the same time he would finally have his revenge.

*

Mondino had taken a gig to Porta Lame and then got out and continued on foot as far as Bova, where the Moline and Cavadizzo canals converged with that of Navile. There he asked directions from some farm workers and left the main road heading towards the right, across two fields where the wheat was still short and green. The city was beginning to spread beyond its gates, but there were still only a few houses around there, separated by vines and cultivated land.

The little grain plants had a feeble air to them because the recent rains had drenched the earth so. Another long period of bad weather would seriously damage the crops. Mondino was tired and had sore feet. He had decided to leave the gig and continue on foot so as not to stand out too much, but he was beginning to regret it.

At last he saw a modest house, one storey high with a thatched roof. For the moment, the laws to prevent fires were only valid within the city walls; but soon, with the advance of the houses and the retreat of the fields, even the sorceress would have to put on a tiled roof.

'Here we are,' he said to himself, recognising the place from the description that some of the labourers had given him.

The house had solid walls, albeit a bit lopsided, and outside there was a yard paved with irregular stones, a saddled donkey tied to a post and a cane chicken run, certainly not safe from foxes. A wisp of smoke was rising from the chimney pot, which the wind almost bent into a right angle. The garden was full of plants but invaded by weeds. As a whole, the dwelling produced a strange impression, as if someone knew the proper way to do things, but did not have time to do them. Which was absurd, given that if there were one thing there seemed to be no lack of, in that place miles from the uproar of the city, it was time.

'Hail!' shouted Mondino, at the top of his voice. 'Anyone home?'

He waited, but no one appeared. Only the donkey turned to look at him with mild curiosity, making its wooden saddle shake.

'I've come to speak to Mistress Adia!' he shouted again.

He started to go up to the door, but had only taken three or four steps, when from behind the house there appeared two enormous dogs. They had iron-grey coats falling in thick pleats around their eyes and snouts, and they stood watching him in silence with an expression that seemed almost sad. He had seen dogs like them before, during his exile in Faenza, and the owner had explained their origin. They were an ancient breed, descendants of the great Molossers described by Columella in *De Re Rustica*, and they had spread throughout Europe with the Roman legions, at whose sides they fought. As a result, Mondino did not make the mistake of taking their mild behaviour for tameness, and stayed right where he was. He was sure someone was at home. Apart from the smoke coming out of the chimney, the windows were open and the door ajar. And it was impossible that his shouting had not been heard.

While he reflected on what to do next, he heard a sharp whistle, a few words in an unknown language, and the dogs turned and trotted off, disappearing behind the house again.

'Come in, there's no danger,' said a woman's voice, in perfect vernacular.

Mondino went forward, warily. Then out of the house came a woman carrying two empty baskets. She proceeded to hang them from the donkey's saddle, one on either side, and she turned towards him smiling.

'I was just going out. What can I do for you?'

Mondino had imagined her old and wrinkled, but she was the opposite. Young, with amber-coloured skin and a lithe body. She wore a white silk veil on her head which, rather than covering it, set off her shiny black hair particularly well. Her shapeliness was clearly outlined by the long indigo gown she wore, and her eyes were two dark wells.

'An alchemist gave me your name, Mistress Adia,' he said, trying to hide his surprise. 'He told me that you are Arabic and know how to read.'

'So?'

A certain hardness had insinuated itself into her voice. Mondino hurriedly smiled, to placate her. 'I'd like to show you a map with some sentences written in your tongue,' he explained. 'And ask you to translate them.'

'Are you sure that you don't want a potion to melt the resistance of a loved one or to increase the power of your loins? Almost all the men who visit my house do.'

'No,' replied Mondino. 'I came for …'

'For the map. There's no need to repeat yourself, I'm not deaf.'

'Really?' said Mondino, who was starting to get irritated. 'Judging from the way that you didn't reply to my greeting when I got here, I thought that you might be a little hard of hearing.'

The woman burst into a throaty and melodious laugh. 'I didn't answer immediately because I was busy reading a difficult passage,' she said. 'And I wanted to finish it before leaving.'

Mondino was annoyed that she didn't even seem to consider the idea of putting off her departure in order to help him. 'Naturally I shall pay you for the disturbance, mistress,' he said. 'I certainly wouldn't presume to ask you to do it gratis and for the love of God.'

'I understand,' answered Adia. 'But I have an important meeting in Corticella, and I'm already late. Couldn't you come back tomorrow?'

Mondino had never met a sorceress before, but he knew for certain that they were highly sensitive to the power of money. Perhaps she was only trying to raise the price.

'Are you in too much of a hurry to close the door of your house behind you?' he asked, ironically. He reached to the purse hanging from his belt. 'Listen, I'll give you two soldi, no more,' he said. 'Now, would you please have a look at this map?'

Adia Bintaba stiffened. Then she put a foot into the stirrup, leaped agilely into the saddle and looked down at him from where she sat on the donkey. 'There's not much to steal in my house, and anyway I don't advise trying to enter in my absence,' she said. 'My dogs make good guards. As for your request, come back when you have learned some manners.'

She gave a light kick to the donkey's side with the heel of her leather slipper and rode away without looking back.

Incredulous, Mondino watched her go. Sitting upright astride the donkey, she was even more beautiful, but he certainly hadn't come all that way to contemplate a fine-looking woman. More time wasted, another blind alley. Perhaps Hugues de Narbonne was right, the trail of alchemy led nowhere. Now, however, it was the only one he had left.

Gerardo looked at Hugues de Narbonne without knowing what to do. The most logical thing would have been to say goodbye and walk away, but he didn't want to do that. He had never known anyone who had lived and fought in the Holy Land apart from a knight from the Templar House of Ravenna, where he had taken his vows. His mind was full of stories and legends, and now he had before him the Commander of the Vault of Acre, no less. But what could he do? He could hardly invite the man back to his lodgings and ask to be regaled with tales of bravery and battles. Hugues de Narbonne would simply laugh at him, and with good reason.

It was the Frenchman who saved him from his embarrassment. As though he'd been reading his mind, Hugues said,

'Why don't we have supper at my house? Then we could have a chat.' He put his hand on Gerardo's shoulder. 'I imagine you've got plenty of things to ask me.'

During the meeting with the banker, Hugues had addressed Gerardo in the formal manner but now he used the more familiar second person singular. His rank in the order fully gave him the right, but Gerardo liked to think that it was a sign of intimacy and not superiority. He accepted the invitation with enthusiasm and they set off for the paper-maker's borough, for a brief stretch walking along the canal that carried the waters of the Savena into the city. Along the way, Hugues showed himself to be an amusing conversationalist, and when they got to his house he laughed with pleasure at Gerardo's amazement when the young Templar saw the disorder that reigned in the kitchen.

'When I rented the house I decided I didn't want servants around,' Hugues said. 'For reasons of solitude. I tried to cook for myself a couple of times and then I stopped bothering. I eat at the tavern or I get them to bring meals over for me.'

He took a coin out of his bag, went to the door and whistled to two small children playing at jumping puddles at the edge of the street. The larger of the two ran over straight away and pocketed the coin with a wide grin.

'Tell your mother to bring us something good to eat,' said Hugues, in a stuttering vernacular, which made the small boy and Gerardo laugh.

The child ran away, while his little brother peed into the puddle he had just jumped over. Hugues closed the door. 'His mother is the wife of the taverner on the corner,' he said, leading Gerardo into a small room sparsely decorated with a table, chairs and a long black chest, on which two candelabra sat. 'Nice-looking woman, very bountiful.'

Gerardo preferred to say nothing and sat down where Hugues indicated, but the Frenchman, after making himself comfortable, went on: 'You're thinking, How could this man betray his vows in such a shameless manner? Am I right?'

'Commander, I wouldn't dream of—'

'Forget it, I can read your face like a book. The important question is a different one: what is a vow? Answer me.'

'Well, it's a solemn commitment that we take on before Christ ...'

'Before Holy Mary.'

Gerardo felt his breath fail him. He thought he had understood perfectly, but wanted confirmation. 'What did you say?'

'I said, "It is a solemn commitment that we take on before Holy Mary."'

Hell's teeth, thought Gerardo. Among the dozens of imputations against his order, he well remembered that in which the Templars put the mother of Christ on a level with her son. For his own part, while honouring Mary with due veneration, he had never done that. And he had thought that the accusation, like all the others, was fruit of the warped fantasy of Philip the Fair, who had every reason to suppress the Knights of the Temple, so as not to have to pay the enormous debts he had contracted with them.

Hugues de Narbonne seemed amused at his bewilderment. 'Now you're thinking that the accusations against us, which you had thought false, are in fact true.'

Gerardo shook his head, confused. 'What am I supposed to think, Commander? To consider the Virgin Mary to be equal to Christ is heresy.'

'I was not referring to the Virgin Mary. And I do not consider her equal to Christ, but above him,' the Frenchman said, without losing his composure.

By now Gerardo had only one wish: to walk out of that house and leave the man to his heresies. The position of responsibility the Commander held, or rather, had held, given that Acre had been in the hands of the Saracens for more than twenty years now, forbid Gerard from openly criticising him, but he wanted nothing more to do with him.

Hugues de Narbonne burst into a cheerful laugh. 'Forgive me for pulling your leg,' he said. 'Right now your face is priceless.'

Gerardo breathed a sigh of relief. 'I knew that you couldn't be serious, but for a second I believed you.'

'But I've never been more serious. I wasn't apologising for what I said, but the manner in which I said it. I could have introduced the subject a little at a time, sounding you out, preparing you … Instead I wanted to do what my master did to me, a long time ago. Now I understand why he laughed so much.'

Gerardo couldn't make sense of his own reactions. He knew that he should get up and leave, and yet he just sat there, paralysed by the mass of questions that filled his mind. If not for the Mother of Christ, for whom did the Commander reserve the title of Holy Mary? Why did he speak of a master, as if those heresies were a recognised practice within the order? During his training and the preparation of his vows, Gerardo had never heard of such things. Was this secret knowledge? And if so, why had Hugues de Narbonne decided to communicate it to him, without even knowing him properly? But one issue tormented him above all the rest: did listening to this without opposing him constitute a mortal sin?

'Listening isn't a sin,' said Hugues, showing once again that he could read the young man like an open book. 'If what I'm telling you seems a heresy, incompatible with the truths of the Christian faith, you can leave and not come back. I shall still stand surety for you, and I consider you released from the obligation of obedience that you owe me in so far as I am your superior. Which do you choose?'

Gerardo had already chosen and Hugues' words only acted

as the spur that he needed to give voice to his burning desire to understand.

'Go on,' he finally managed to say.

'I imagine you will have heard of Baphomet, the demoniacal idol that we are accused of worshipping,' began the Frenchman.

'You don't mean to tell me that is true too?' murmured Gerardo in a reed-like voice. All his convictions were shaken to their foundations.

Hugues made a slight movement with his hand, as if calming a nervous filly. 'It is true that some of us, the better part, I would presume to say, venerate something that we call Baphomet. But it is false to call him an idol, much less demoniacal. Everything lies in the meaning of the words.'

He got to his feet, went into the kitchen and returned with a pitcher of white wine, without tankards. He took a long draught and then offered it to Gerardo. 'Drink, you look as though you need it.'

The young man obeyed mechanically and then he put the pitcher down on the table between them, without saying anything.

'Do you know the language of the Jews?' Hugues asked him.

'Certainly not!' responded Gerardo, indignantly. The mere idea of having anything in common with Christ's murderers horrified him.

'Neither do I. But I know its alphabet. The Jews, like the Saracens, reject Christ's message and for this reason they are damned for eternity. But that doesn't mean that they are stupid or ignorant. The knowledge of the infidels can be profound.'

'And what has this got to do with the Hebrew alphabet?'

Hugues smiled at his impatience. 'I'm getting there.' He stretched out an arm to open the piece of furniture behind him, and took a piece of notepaper and something to write

133

with. After which he started drawing two rows of mysterious signs on the page, one above the other, while Gerardo watched him in silence.

When he had finished, he turned the page towards Gerardo, showing him the two sequences of letters:

אבגדההוזחטיכלמנסעפצקרשת
תשרקצפעסנמלכיטחזוההדגבא

'They are the opposite of each other,' said Gerardo, having examined them.

'Exactly. It's a Hebrew code, called the Atbash, from the name of the first and last two letters of their alphabet. The letters are written from right to left, then from left to right. Then you take a word and substitute each letter with the corresponding letter in the row beneath.'

'The result is a completely different word,' interjected Gerardo. 'Comprehensible only to those who know the code.'

'What intellectual promptitude,' said Hugues, smiling with approval. 'As you say, it's easy to decipher but you have to know the original language. And this is a secret that none of us will ever reveal to the Inquisitors, even under the worst torture.'

'Why?'

'Let's take the word Baphomet,' said Hugues, indicating some symbols on the top row. 'In Hebrew it is made up of five letters: Tav, Mem, Vav, Pei and Beit.' He pointed to the letters and copied them below.

תמופב

'Reading from right to left, as the Jews do, we have BA.PH.O.ME.T. Now, let's take these letters and substitute them with the corresponding letters on the row below. He joined the letters with little dashes of the pen, and then copied them down beneath the first five.

א י פ ו ש

He looked at them a moment with a strange respect and read, 'Alef, Yud, Pei, Vav and Shin. Or rather, from right to left, S.O.PH.I.A.'

'The goddess of wisdom!' exclaimed Gerardo, surprised.

'Exactly. Now tell me, in what way could honouring wisdom be a heresy?'

'But why didn't you say!' demanded Gerardo. He was angry and his face burned as though he had a fever. 'We should reveal the code to the Inquisitors and show them that there is nothing wrong in it.'

Hugues shook his head, with a sad look in his grey eyes. 'Our order is condemned, make no mistake about it. We have become too powerful for our own good. We cannot say or do anything to change our fate, but we can safeguard the knowledge that has been handed down to us.'

On an impulse Gerardo seized the pitcher and took a long draught of wine. Hugues did the same and then he started a complex discourse, punctuating it with intense looks and quick drinks. He spoke of the Greek goddess Sophia, derived from the World Soul of the Gnostics, the Great Mother who gave life to the world and who is higher than the Redeemer himself, because without her there would be no world to redeem, and therefore no Redeemer. And he concluded by saying that the female divine principle was incarnated in the Christian religion in the figure of Mary Magdalene, the wife of Christ.

'But Christ was celibate!' shouted Gerardo, thumping the table with his fist and leaping to his feet, quite beside himself. 'And Mary Magdalene was a—'

'Do not say that word!' In a sudden bound Hugues had jumped round the table and grabbed hold of him by the neck. 'Do not take her name in vain.'

Gerardo was struck dumb, not so much because of the strength or the speed of the Frenchman's reaction, as for the passion in his words, unexpected after the cynicism with which he had expressed himself until then.

At that moment someone knocked at the door. Hugues let go of Gerardo's throat and went to go and open it. Voices and laughing were heard coming from the kitchen, then the Commander returned to the room in the company of a woman in her thirties. She was dressed in a grey sleeveless surcoat on top of a décolleté linen tunic. Her auburn hair was gathered into a white cap. In one hand she carried an earthenware pot, with two thick slices of bread balanced on top, from which came a good smell of stew. She leaned over to put it on the table, showing her breasts and giving Gerardo a lascivious smile.

'Gianna doesn't have much time, or her husband will begin to suspect something and come looking for her,' said Hugues. 'I told her that I have a guest and she is disposed to satisfy both of us for a bit more, but together, not one at a time.'

Hugues was obviously quite able to make himself understood even by those who spoke no Latin, when he wanted to. Gerardo merely shook his head. They both laughed at his blushing face and went off to the bedroom. On the threshold the woman turned to look at him with an expression of nostalgia, and then blew him a kiss from the tips of her fingers.

'If you change your mind, come and find me later,' she said.

Hugues murmured something in her ear and she laughed in a coarse manner, then they closed the door.

Gerardo sat at the table, immobile, as though he had been touched by paralysis, asking himself why he didn't get up and leave. A part of him, that he tried to silence, told him that he was so obviously excited that he had already sinned, so he might as well join them in the room and have the woman.

In an effort to distract himself from those thoughts, he went back to looking at the Hebrew alphabet lying on the table. The avalanche of revelations that he had received in such a short time came back to occupy his mind. Christ was married. And to Mary Magdalene, a prostitute, although redeemed and sanctified. It couldn't be true. Perhaps the accusations of heresy formulated against his order, that he had always thought false and made up intentionally, had the basis of truth.

However much he tried to think clearly, he couldn't manage to do anything other than repeat mangled phrases devoid of a logical connection. First, he thought that he knew too little to judge. Then it occurred to him that it was a sin to hide behind the pretence of ignorance. But what was his duty? To come out of hiding and turn himself over to the Inquisition, proclaiming his own good faith? No, it was too dangerous. He risked being interrogated under torture, and even if he were believed and freed in the end, he would be crippled for the rest of his life. After examining his conscience, Gerardo decided that he did not possess the vocation of martyr.

Besides, there was always the possibility that Hugues had in fact been telling the truth. Perhaps the Templars, as the rumours would have it, had discovered secrets in the Holy Land that contradicted the Church's official story. He looked at the word Baphomet, and underneath its transformation into Sophia, goddess of wisdom. Who knew how many mysteries he might uncover, following Hugues de Narbonne.

He fought off that sacrilegious thought, but before he had managed to control his agitation enough to make a decision, be it only that of leaving, Gianna came out of the bedroom, hurriedly rearranging her bonnet.

'I'll come back another day,' she whispered as she passed him. 'And I'll make sure I have more time for you.'

The street door closed with a soft click and immediately afterwards Hugues de Narbonne came back into the room. He had a serious expression that Gerardo did not make the mistake of thinking might be due to the knowledge that he had committed a grave sin. The Commander evidently considered himself above the laws of the Church, so the reason for such seriousness had to be something else. Perhaps the revelations were not over yet. Gerardo ceased struggling with himself and prepared to listen, putting off every decision until he finally left the house.

'When I entered the order,' said the Frenchman, sitting down to the pot of stew, 'I took my vows, just like you, even though from the beginning I considered them unnecessary restrictions. Then someone decided I was ready to share a higher wisdom and my vows were overridden. What you saw is not a banal violation of the vote of chastity. In the sense that it is not a sin and does not need to be confessed to be forgiven.'

Gerardo understood the concept, even if it seemed blasphemous to him. In practice the Commander was saying that for those initiated in the secret knowledge of the Templars, the laws of common behaviour did not hold. And that only the non-initiated had to respect the Rule. The thing that he still could not understand was why Hugues had chosen to make him party to the secrets, given that, as he had just stated, they were things that he would not have revealed even under torture.

'Commander,' he said when he had managed to calm the jumble of thoughts that were dancing in his head. 'Why me?'

Hugues laughed and slammed a hand down on the tabletop. 'Finally the right question!' he said, nodding with his large white-blond head. 'Haven't you asked yourself why I agreed to stand surety for a person I didn't even know?'

'Remigio told me—'

'You can forget the banker, he knows nothing. The truth is that since the evening when I found out about your involvement with Angelo da Piczano, I have wanted to meet you.'

'You knew about that before I told you!' exclaimed Gerardo. 'But how is that possible?'

'It is simpler than you think. I knew Angelo and when he arrived in Bologna we met up.'

Hugues lifted the lid of the pot and peered inside with a critical eye. Then he put in a hand and pulled out a piece of meat, well covered with the greasy sauce, and put it on one of the two slices of bread.

'You were the person that Angelo was supposed to meet on the night that he was killed!' cried Gerardo.

Hugues shook his head and dipped his fingers into the sauce again, wiping them on the bread to soak it well. 'No. He led me to believe that the meeting was on the next day. If he hadn't done so he would still be alive now.' Hugues paused and his grey eyes darkened. 'However, as soon as I heard about the fire, I ran to the house. The Inquisition had turned up straight away but had found nothing. Asking around, I discovered that the student who had vanished and that everyone was talking about was probably a Knight of the Temple too. And his was a difficult and risky undertaking, to get away without abandoning Angelo's corpse to the Dominicans.'

'So you went to see Remigio and told him that if I turned up, he was to put me in contact with you,' said Gerardo. 'That's why he was so interested, when I told him I had been in an accident.'

'That's more or less it. Well done. Quickness of mind is an important quality for a future initiate.'

'You haven't answered me yet, Commander. Why do you want me to share this secret knowledge?'

With a gesture Hugues encouraged him to help himself to

the food, but Gerardo shook his head, without dropping his gaze. The Frenchman shrugged his shoulders and bit into a piece of meat, then put the other half on to the greasy bread.

'God talks to us by putting what we must confront in our path,' he said, with his mouth full. 'Sometimes they are tests and obstacles that are destined to form our character. Sometimes good fortune, great or small, of which we should not become too proud. On other occasions, he makes us meet the right people at the right time.' Hugues paused and swallowed his mouthful with a gulp of wine from the pitcher. 'Those of us who found true wisdom in the Holy Land are growing old,' he continued. 'Many of us are already dead. We need young blood so that the torch is kept alight. And I found you on my path. So, if you wish, when this affair is over, I will share what I know with you.' He picked up the piece of meat again and pointed to the pot. 'Now you must eat. You'll need all your energy for the mission I'm about to entrust you with.'

When he got to the construction site of the Basilica of San Giacomo Maggiore, being built on the San Donato road, Mondino stopped beside a row of stonecutters sitting on the ground working on the capitals of the columns. Without much difficulty, he picked out the master builder, a robust Augustinian with a long grey beard, who was standing upright on a block of stone watching the workmen.

Mondino called to him and the monk turned quickly and jumped down, winding his way between the square blocks of stone and the beams that cluttered up the little piazza in front of the church.

'*Pax vobiscum*, Magister,' he said, shaking the dust off his robe. 'Forgive my messy appearance.'

'*Et cum spiritu tuo*,' replied Mondino. 'I see that you are getting on well, Father Paolo. When does the roof go on?'

The monk turned to look at the site with a pride that was almost paternal. The four perimeter corners were already complete, connected by stretches of wall on which masons and labourers were at work.

'It will be nearly two years before we can start thinking of the roof,' he said in a dreamy tone, as though in his mind's eye he could already see the finished basilica. 'But tell me, what can I do for you?'

'Actually I wanted to do something for you. Or rather, for your cousin Francesco.'

The priest's mouth opened into an almost perfect 'o'. 'My cousin? But how?'

Mondino smiled benevolently. 'A student of mine knows him and told me about his complaint. As you know, the inguinal hernia can become strangulated at any moment, endangering the patient's life. Rather than run such a risk, it would be better to remove it without losing more time.'

The master builder's spry face was the picture of astonishment, but genuine happiness was spreading across it as well. 'You seriously mean that you would do it yourself? Francesco will be delighted. His hernia has given him great pain lately.' Then, all of a sudden, his expression darkened and he touched his beard, embarrassed. 'But, well, I don't think we can stretch to ...' He interrupted himself to shout to a couple of workmen to get out of the way. They were standing underneath a huge beam being lifted with a pulley. Hearing him, they lazily moved away a few steps.

'Three weeks ago a rope broke and one of their colleagues was killed, but they still don't learn,' he said, shaking his head. 'But going back to my cousin.'

'Don't worry about the money,' said Mondino, who had foreseen the question. 'As I want to carry out this operation for reasons of research, I would ask your cousin a third of my normal fee.'

141

The priest's face brightened behind his beard. 'Thank you, Magister. This is truly a gift from heaven.'

'Let's not exaggerate.'

'I'm serious. When someone advised him to have his hernia removed, Francesco immediately thought of you. However, knowing that he could not afford your prices, he thought he would ask Bertruccio or Ottone, who use your method too.'

Bertruccio Lombardo and Ottone da Lustrulano were the only ones among Mondino's students who were capable of carrying out that operation without risk of the patient dying of septicaemia or blood loss.

Mondino was surprised that the master builder was abreast of the innovation that he had introduced in the treatment of the inguinal hernia, but then it occurred to him that it wasn't so surprising really. The priests fought stubbornly against the progress of science, but they were quite prepared to take advantage of it when it suited them. The previous manner of operating on the inguinal hernia, practised by his master Taddeo Alderotti, meant first cauterising the scrotum then gradually scraping away the layers of burned flesh. In this way the castration of the patient was inevitable. Mondino fully understood why a dishonoured priest such as the master builder's cousin was keen to be operated on with his method, which almost always meant that the reproductive capacity was preserved intact.

'I too am glad that is his preference,' he replied, without managing to smile. 'It makes it much easier. Even though, to tell you the truth, I must say that either of the physicians you named would have been perfectly able to perform the operation.'

'I don't doubt that. Still, given the choice, always better the teacher than the pupil, don't you think?'

The master builder's pleasure for his cousin was moving,

and Mondino felt somewhat guilty for the way in which he was using him.

'Certainly, Father,' he said, avoiding eye contact. 'If it suits you, I will come by the monastery tomorrow afternoon.'

'Very good. We will be waiting, and thank you again.'

The priest turned and went back to work. In the noisy piazza, full of stones, carts, stonecutters and masons, the Church of San Giacomo raised its roofless walls like a ruin from the olden days.

VII

Walking along a foul-smelling alleyway between two rows of houses, Gerardo put a hand over his nose and mouth so as to shut out the stink. He only hoped that some housewife didn't choose precisely that moment to empty the slops out of her window. He glanced upwards and seeing all the shutters closed, he pressed on. He could have taken the main street to get to the inn where the German had died, but he had decided not to for two reasons.

The first was that he was afraid he might be recognised. Three days earlier, when Hugues de Narbonne had ordered him to piece together Wilhelm von Trier's movements from his arrival in the city to his death, Hugues had pointed out to Gerardo that the proprietor of the house that he had set on fire lived in the area. But the order remained unchanged and Gerardo did not dare to argue. Although he was still devastated by the Frenchman's revelations, he was nonetheless a Knight of the Temple and the Rule prescribed absolute obedience to one's superiors.

The second reason that he wasn't using the main road was

that the area around Santo Stefano bordered on that of Trebbo dei Banchi, so that several times a day he passed right in front of Remigio Sensi's bank. He didn't want the banker, sitting at his counter on the street, to ask the reason for all the to-ing and fro-ing, and above all he didn't want to see Fiamma, sitting at the long table behind her adoptive father, busy transcribing documents.

Remigio had shown himself to be most discreet, simply saluting Gerardo with a slight nod of the head, and not addressing a word to him. Whereas Fiamma seemed to sense his presence even before he arrived, and every time he walked past their premises, she glanced up from her papers and gave him a forceful look that he was at a loss to interpret.

Despite all his intentions, Gerardo couldn't drag his eyes away and he felt his heartbeat accelerate. During those days he did nothing but think of the things that Hugues de Narbonne had told him. Of the possibility of being privy to secrets known only to a small minority of Templars. Secrets that would change his life in unforeseeable ways, and were perhaps already changing it.

In his mind's eye, Gerardo often went back to what Hugues and that woman had got up to in the bedroom. Some years previously, when he was still living in the small family castle, a serving wench by the name of Assunta, married with two children, had introduced him to the pleasures of the flesh. They had met many times, during the quiet hours of the summer, in the cool of the stables or in the shade of the vine. It was those memories that had been the most difficult obstacle for him to overcome when he took his vows. It had taken months of prayer and spiritual exercises to forget what the blood insisted on remembering, but in the end he had done it.

And now he found out that it wasn't even true.

Just the idea that it was possible to violate the Rule without committing a sin, in the name of a superior wisdom forbidden to the majority, had been enough to haunt his mind. Over the last few days, Gerardo had repeatedly asked himself what he wanted from life. For the first time he found himself doubting that his destiny were really that of the soldier monk vowed to the defence of Christianity. But he still hadn't managed to come to a conclusion.

He had got to the point where he took longer routes; cutting through alleyways deep in mud, excrement and rubbish, just to avoid seeing Fiamma. At the same time however, he wanted nothing more, and at least once a day he gave in to the desire and walked down the main street that ran from Porta Ravegnana to the St Jerusalem quarter.

Coming out of the narrow lane, he finally removed his hand from his mouth and breathed freely. He avoided walking past the inn again, so as not to arouse suspicion. The first day he had gone in pretending to be curious like so many people, and he had asked some questions about Wilhelm von Trier's murder. The innkeeper was literally besieged by people who wanted to know about the dead Templar and the heart of iron, and he had not noticed the fact that Gerardo's inquiries were more precisely targeted than those of the others. He had told him, and five or six other people who had stopped to listen, about the German's arrival, his request to have a room to himself, the fact that he had gone out in the afternoon and no one had seen him come back in.

'A stray dog got into the hen coop,' the innkeeper said, happy to repeat his adventure yet again. 'I heard the hens cackling and went out to have a look. I'm certain that the murderer let the dog into the coop so that he could get into the German's room without being seen. Then my customer must have come back too, and gone up to the first floor.'

'Who found the body?' asked a pimply youth.

'The woman I paid to clean the house.'

'Would she tell us what she saw?' Gerardo had asked.

'She doesn't work here any longer. The experience frightened her off.'

'Where does she live?'

'In Via Galliera, beyond the market square.'

Gerardo got the innkeeper to tell him the name of the woman and went to see her that afternoon. Handing over a few coins, he persuaded her to tell him everything that she had already told the Captain of the People's men. He didn't find out much more, other than the fact that after vespers she had to go out on an errand. She had taken the stable boy from the inn, a strapping lad quite able to defend her if need be, and she'd noticed the German waiting by a wall opposite the church of San Giovanni in Monte. He was talking to the beggar with a missing hand who hung around thereabouts.

She remembered that the man, tall despite his advanced age, was leaning over the vagrant as if listening to him. Beggars could usually be got rid of in a few words, with a handout or a shove, and it had seemed strange to her that the German was taking such a lot of trouble to listen to the monk's woes. Immediately afterwards he walked away in the direction of the inn.

Then, the following morning, opening the door of his room to clean the floor, she had seen him lying on the mattress, with his chest wide open and his heart transformed into a block of iron.

Wilhelm von Trier's meeting with the beggar probably wasn't important at all, but you couldn't be sure. Gerardo asked the woman for a description of him and began to look along the route to St Jerusalem.

He went twice round the churches that represented the sacred places of Jerusalem, peering into every part of the piazza and the surrounding lanes near San Giovanni in Monte,

147

but he could find no trace of the maimed tramp described by the woman. And yet he should have been easily recognisable: he wore a filthy black tunic that must once have belonged to a man of the church, he had a long beard, long hair and used a pilgrim's walking stick made of ash.

Gerardo had decided to go and look for him not long before nones sounded, because the working day was at an end, the shops would soon be closed and a mass of people would be spilling into the streets on their way home. It was the best time of day for anyone living off charity.

Afraid that the description he had was mistaken, he stopped other beggars and got the same reply from all of them: the maimed beggar was from Ferrara; in fact they called him the Ferrarese as though it were a proper name. They hadn't seen him around the place for a while and supposed that he had returned to his city. Gerardo asked other questions and with a bit of effort managed to verify that the Ferrarese had disappeared on the day that the German's corpse had been found. He might easily have gone away by chance on that very day, tramps moved around a lot. But there were beginning to be too many coincidences in the whole affair.

If the man had taken the trouble to disappear after the murder, he might genuinely know something and not want to run any risks. At this point it was imperative to find him. But the idea of setting off for Ferrara in search of a mendicant with a missing hand seemed ludicrous.

A crippled boy who was begging for alms on a wheeled board, about fifty yards from Remigio Sensi's premises, was the only one to give him any new information. He said that perhaps the beggar with the missing hand had not gone away after all, but could be ill. In that case, he could easily be in the underworld.

'What underworld?' asked Gerardo.

'I'll show you for a lira,' answered the boy.

'A lira?' Gerardo laughed at such an absurd request. 'Don't you think that's a bit much?'

'Not at all. Another person I showed it to gave me that without quibbling.'

'Really?' smiled Gerardo. 'Tell me his name and I'll believe you.'

The boy's face grew sullen. 'No chance. The person gave me that amount so that I would never mention it to anyone.'

'Very convenient,' replied Gerardo, who began to find the conversation amusing. 'You can't tell me who it is and yet you are free to tell me how much money he gave you.'

'I'm not lying,' insisted the boy. 'Why do you think no one else has told you about the underworld yet?'

'They didn't think that the Ferrarese was ill.'

The boy shook his head, with a serious air. He can't have been older than eleven or twelve, but he was trying to behave like an adult. The top half of his body was normal, but his legs were two dry sticks folded on to the wheeled cart.

'They didn't tell you because it's the beggars' secret.'

Gerardo got down on his heels so that his face was level with the boy's. 'And you, so respectful of your word given to a stranger. Why are you prepared to betray the secret?'

The lad looked at him angrily. 'Because I've never promised anyone that I wouldn't tell!' He began to manoeuvre himself with his hands on the paving, turning the board and moving away. 'Anyway, if you are interested in finding out where the underworld is, the price is one lira.'

Gerardo got up and saw Remigio Sensi looking at him from a distance, standing erect behind his bench. When their eyes met, the banker saluted him with a nod of the head as usual. Gerardo replied in the same way, and then he ran to catch up with the boy and he stopped him by grabbing hold of his shoulder. 'I'm interested. But I can't pay you that much. I've just taken out a loan, because I had nothing left.'

'I don't believe you. Let me go.'

It really did seem as though he had decided to go on his way without bartering. Gerardo put his hand in his purse. As soon as the boy heard the rattle of coins he stopped, and in the end they agreed on ten soldi, a decent labourer's pay for two weeks' work.

'I'll give you five straight away,' said Gerardo, putting the coins in the boy's hand, which was so dirty and calloused that it almost couldn't close, 'and five after I have seen this famous underworld.'

'Done,' said the boy. 'Come with me.'

He slipped the money into the smaller of two bags that he wore across one shoulder, over his torn coat, and set off on his cart, pushing himself along with his hands.

Gerardo couldn't help liking him. He decided that even if the secret of the underworld turned out to be a hoax, he would still let the boy keep the five soldi that he had already given him.

'What's your name?' he asked.

'Bonagrazia, at your service,' he replied without turning round. 'But everyone calls me Bonaga.'

They left the piazza, walking past the inn where Wilhelm von Trier had been killed, and entered a maze of alleyways between Santo Stefano and the high street. Bonaga manoeuvred his cart with skill, but in some places piles of rubble and rubbish blocked his way. So as not to lose time, when the going was rough, Gerardo picked him up, trying to ignore the fact that he reeked, and carried him and his wheeled cart together.

At a certain point the boy stopped in front of the ruins of a house. 'Here we are,' he said. He went round a pile of square stones but then he suddenly stopped, making a sign to be silent. From his larger bag he pulled out a rolled up catapult, placed a stone in the piece of concave leather in the centre and a finger in the ring at the other end of the cord. Then, with a rapid movement, he whirled the sling twice above his head and let it fly. Gerardo ran quickly to his side, with a hand on the hilt of his knife, but as soon as he saw the boy's satisfied smile he relaxed. He followed the direction of his gaze, and on a bit of grass growing between the rubble, at about eight paces distance, he saw a blackbird with its head smashed.

'That's my supper,' said Bonaga. 'A right piece of luck.'

'Yes. It was a long way to have hit it at your first shot.'

The boy took on an offended air. 'I could have hit it had it been twice as far away. I meant that it was a piece of luck to find a blackbird. The innkeepers slaughter the things, to serve them warm to their customers, and there are almost none left in the city now.'

Gerardo went to pick up the dead bird by its tail and handed it to him. Bonaga immediately put it away in the big bag that seemed to be half full of pebbles from the river. Then he pushed off with his board to go into the house, crossed into the entrance hall that no longer had a front door, and went on into the darkness.

'Come. It's this way.'

For prudence's sake, Gerardo waited until his eyes had become accustomed to the dim light before following him. A strange silence reigned in the ruined house, perhaps due to the fact that the noise from the main streets did not reach such a secluded place. As soon as Gerardo reached him, Bonaga showed the Templar a large hole opening out beneath a wall.

'That is the underworld,' he said, holding out his hand for the rest of the money.

'One moment.' Gerardo held him back. 'You must tell me exactly what this place is and why the man I am looking for should be down there.'

The boy paused before speaking, then he said, in a low

voice, 'It is the beggars' secret refuge. I've heard that it's very old and stretches for miles under the city. Lots of beggars come to sleep here at night. Others are there in the day too, when they are too ill to go out.'

'How is it possible that no one knows anything about it?' asked Gerardo.

Bonaga explained that one day, before he was born, someone had wanted to add a new floor on to the house and it had collapsed, because the cellar beneath it could not hold its weight. That was how the underworld was discovered. The house was abandoned because, with the hole beneath, it wasn't worth rebuilding and the underworld was explored and colonised by the beggars. Then the citizens gradually began to forget about its existence.

'I've never been down there,' said Bonaga, gloomily. 'I can't get down on my own and no one has ever wanted to take me.'

His voice had become harder. Perhaps that was the reason that he had decided to betray the secret, more than for the money. He felt his brothers in misfortune had left him out.

'Haven't you got any friends?'

The boy shook his head, looking Gerardo in the eye. 'We poor are all enemies. I have to spend any alms that I receive immediately, otherwise they steal them off me because they know that I can't run away.' He sat there in silence for a moment, then added, 'But if I have time to get out my catapult and can get my back against a wall, they keep their distance.'

'Do you want to see what it's like down there?' asked Gerardo, on an impulse.

Bonaga shrugged his shoulders and dropped his eyes without saying anything. Gerardo bent down, lifted him off the cart and started to carry him down through the rubble. When they got to the tunnel, he set him down on a square-shaped stone and looked around. In the shadowy light that filtered down from above he saw a torch fixed to a wall and looking more closely he noticed that next to it was a piece of steel and a flintstone. He struck the steel and the torch soaked with cheap oil immediately took fire, letting off a dense black smoke.

The boy exclaimed in thrilled astonishment. They were in what must have been an ancient Roman sewer pipe, with a drainage canal in the centre, now dry, and a narrow passageway leading off on the left-hand side. There was a slight breeze in the tunnel. Obviously other ways down there existed and a circulation of air was created, but the smell carried by the wind was anything but pleasant. The bottom of the canal, dry for centuries, was studded with rubbish, through which rats scurried.

'Over there it goes underneath the Church of Santo Sepolcro,' said Bonaga, pointing to a stretch of tunnel to their right. 'No one goes there any more, they say that it has a curse on it.'

Gerardo peered into the darkness of the tunnel. It wasn't difficult to imagine that such a spooky place caused people to believe in the supernatural. 'A curse? What sort of curse?'

'I don't know. As I told you, no one speaks to me much. I only heard that some vagrants disappeared and were later found down there. Dead.'

'I see. And where does the other tunnel lead?'

'If you go down that tunnel, at a certain point you get to an enormous room,' replied Bonaga, who was staring at the squalid sight as though it were one of the Seven Wonders of the World. 'They told me that all the walls are painted, like in a church. I know that the Ferrarese sleeps there.'

'I'm going to find him,' said Gerardo. 'You wait for me here, I'll carry you back up when I get back.'

'No!' exclaimed the boy, terrified. 'We've got to leave immediately.'

In an agitated voice he explained that if Gerardo entered the underworld dressed like that, he wouldn't get out alive. And if he himself were left abandoned on that stone without being able to get away, he would soon meet the same end.

Gerardo hesitated. He wanted to get the thing over with and speak to the Ferrarese in order to find out if he knew anything useful about the death of the German Templar. But the urgency in Bonaga's voice and above all, his expression, made Gerardo take the threat seriously. He put out the torch, took the little mendicant into his arms again and went back up to the ruined house.

Without saying a word he deposited the boy on his cart, gave him the other five coins that he had promised him and they began to retrace their steps. As soon as they were back in Piazza di Santo Stefano, Gerardo said goodbye to the boy and set off towards Via San Vitale, where he had a meeting with Mondino. He looked skyward. The sun was hidden behind a thick cloak of clouds and the afternoon promised rain.

As he was in a hurry, he took the main street and found himself walking past Remigio's counter almost without realising it. The banker had already told his servants to raise the wooden hatch and was waiting for them to close and bolt it from the inside. In the few seconds in which he could still see in, Gerardo saw Fiamma raise her head and stare straight at him.

Incapable of going a step further, he stood looking back at her and, without thinking, waved a hand by way of greeting. The hatch closed with a dry crash and Gerardo had the impression that a second later Fiamma would have smiled at him.

Somewhat annoyed, Uberto da Rimini walked out of the street door and headed for Trebbo dei Banchi. The two young priests that he had decided to take along with him followed a few paces behind, with heads down, not daring to disturb him while he was thinking.

He had just been to see the owner of the house where the arsonist-cum-student had lived. However, the wool merchant hadn't seemed particularly pleased that the Inquisition was taking his interests to heart. On hearing that the officers of the *comune* had obtained no results as yet, he became reluctant to collaborate. Uberto couldn't work out whether this was because he was a stupid Ghibelline or because he had something to hide. Perhaps both.

However, at least he had been respectful, not so much towards him, but towards his office. This was one of the reasons why Uberto took pleasure in the job of Inquisitor. He would not have liked to belong to an order lacking in notoriety and celebrity like the Augustinians or the hermitical monks of San Girolamo, for example. He enjoyed the fear that the Dominicans' black and white habit inspired in people. The populace was wicked by nature, and the one thing capable of keeping the people in line was a healthy fear of God. Something that the Inquisition, through its work, continued to nurture. Uberto was convinced that sooner or later the privilege of investigating heresy and behaviour that was contrary to the faith would be entrusted entirely to his order, removing power from the Franciscans who often showed themselves to be too weak.

In any case, he had managed to get a physical description of the young man from the merchant, since his research on the basis of his name had led nowhere. By this time he was certain that Francesco Salimbene was a false identity. This, more than anything else, indicated that he was guilty. It wasn't quite legal proof, thought Uberto with a rush of irritation as he was reminded of his recent meeting with the Archbishop, but it was more than enough to convince him that he was on the right path.

If they could find the young man who had vanished and who was almost certainly a Knight Templar in disguise, he was convinced that a great deal would become clear and the Archbishop would no longer be able to get out of taking the decisions that his cowardice had stopped him confronting until now.

Another lead he wanted to follow was that of Mondino de Liuzzi. Uberto had been livid with rage when he had found out that the physician had been the first person to examine the corpse of the German Templar in Santo Stefano. But then he realised that that too was an important pointer. Mondino's presence at the scene of the crime was suspicious. Since the evening of the fire at Sant'Antonino, it became increasingly clear that Mondino had something to hide.

Uberto keenly hoped that Guido Arlotti had managed to discover something useful too. The former priest had not yet reported back, but time was tight and he didn't intend to sit around waiting for him to do things at his leisure. He had decided to go and speak to Arlotti in the tavern that he used as a base for his nefarious trade. Guido had promised results and the time had come to make him understand that he should never make vain promises.

Walking with rapid steps, Uberto soon arrived at Porta Ravegnana, followed the road to the Mercato di Mezzo as far as the bridge over the Aposa, then turned right into the black-smiths' neighbourhood, still followed by the two friars, who were now chatting among themselves. The noise of hammering on anvils and the acrid smell of steel tempered in water surrounded him like a cloak. He picked his way along the road, walking on the dry mud in the centre of the street, passing the array of swords, metal cauldrons, knives and other wares displayed outside the workshops.

The members of the populace whom they happened to notice turned away with a hostile air. Uberto knew why: a rumour was spreading through the streets that the rise in the price of bread was the fault of the Church.

A boy with thick blond straw-like hair, busy polishing a breastplate with a cloth, spat on the ground as they passed. Uberto stopped, turned and looked at him in silence until the boy got down on his knees, offering a stream of excuses in an almost incomprehensible dialect. The spit had not been a gesture of disrespect towards them, it had been by chance, and he had not seen them, no one would dare to spit in the path of the Dominican Inquisitor ...

Uberto, mollified by the terror of a rat in a trap that he had seen in the boy's eyes, and content to have been recognised even by an ignorant peasant such as he, told him to be more careful in future and went on his way. His companions had witnessed the scene with expressionless faces, and they carried on walking behind him without breathing a word. They were both bright boys whom Uberto had picked out to be his personal assistants in order to prepare for the job of Inquisitor. It was above all the smaller of the two, a friar by the name of Antonio, who knew the value of obedience.

So he had decided to take them to Guido Arlotti's den. They had to begin to learn that one could not always do everything according to the rules, and that to combat the Devil it was sometimes necessary to get one's hands dirty.

Once they had left the blacksmith's borough, with their ears ringing from the clamour of the hammering, it took him a moment to hear the normal noises of the street. He turned to check that the two novices were still behind him and led the way along a route made circuitous by the necessity to avoid dangerous roads and at the same time not be seen by too many people. They finally reached Torresotto di Galliera. Not far ahead, in a street without a name, they stopped in front of the door of a tavern.

Uberto ordered Friar Antonio to go in, find Guido and

bring him out. If possible, the Inquisitor preferred to save himself the sight of what he imagined would be inside. Scantily dressed women, depraved men, dirt and the stink of sweat. The young man nodded and went in without hesitating, a determined expression in his eyes and his jaw set. But he came straight out again, visibly shocked. He said that Guido Arlotti was not in a condition to come outside and perhaps not even to speak. The publican had told him that he was in bed in the room upstairs, still drunk from the night before.

Uberto reflected on what to do. Given that he had come this far, he wasn't about to leave without getting any answers. He told the two of them to follow him and marched into the tavern.

Inside, the filth and stench were exactly as he had imagined them. However, the prostitutes and drunks must have taken advantage of those brief seconds to get out of the place. There was almost no one in there, only three men with evasive expressions who were sitting in silence at a square table. Uberto stepped with sandalled feet on to the damp straw strewn across the floor and went over to the publican, a man with broad shoulders and thighs like tree trunks. He asked the way to Guido's room and then went up the stairs, followed by the two friars.

He left them to wait outside the door and went in alone, saying that he wanted to save them from the sight of a man reduced to living like a brute beast. In realty, although he trusted them both, he did not want witnesses to his conversation with Guido.

He immediately threw open the small window, letting the air and light in, and when the stocky man lying on the large bed covered with a sendal drape protested, swearing with his eyes shut, Uberto went up to him and simply said, 'Guido, it's me.'

The result was astonishing. Guido Arlotti immediately sat

bolt upright, his eyes popped out of his head and in a hoarse voice he stuttered, 'You? But how …?'

'I cannot wait any longer, Guido,' said Uberto, cutting him short. 'Don't disappoint me. Have you found out anything useful?'

'My head aches,' Arlotti moaned. He rubbed his face with his hands in an effort to regain the lucidity that the wine had removed. When he looked at the Inquisitor again, he was smiling. But the smile, perhaps because of his headache, seemed more of a contorted grimace.

'I found the gravediggers,' he said. 'They had buried the body in a mass grave. I paid them to dig him up and I discovered something interesting.'

'What?'

'The dead man had a suture on his chest. I opened it and inside it was empty. His heart was missing.'

Uberto had to force himself to appear impassive. After the German Templar being found with his heart transformed into a piece of iron, a detail of the sort was almost an indictment. Mondino would have a lot of explaining to do. One way or another, his fate was sealed.

'Do you know what will happen to you if someone recognises you?' asked Mondino, for the tenth time.

Gerardo just shrugged his shoulders, without replying. Where they were going that possibility was almost nonexistent, and the physician knew it. They walked along as they usually did, the master in front and the student a step or two behind. Mondino had been the first to say that it was a pretence, and so it was. Gerardo respected him, but didn't accept orders from him. When Mondino had tried to convince the younger man to go back home, promising that he would tell him everything the next day, Gerardo had replied that he wouldn't dream of it, and had walked on at his side.

159

'Well, at least promise me that you will not let your anger get the better of you,' continued Mondino.

'I can't promise anything.'

Suddenly Mondino stopped in his tracks and turned to look at Gerardo in the uncertain evening light. He let past four women who were proceeding in a tight group with their heads down and in silence to avoid any kind of approach from unknown men. When the women were out of earshot, he said, 'Then you can forget it. I am prepared to run risks, but only on condition that they are not rash ones.'

Gerardo sighed, exasperated. And yet he saw that the physician had a point. It wasn't worth increasing the risks involved in an already very dangerous situation just because he wanted to take the man by the neck and make him rue the day he was born.

'I promise,' he said. 'I will only do what you tell me to do and I will not get carried away. Now can we go on?'

At Borgo San Giacomo they turned and not long afterwards arrived at the entrance to the monastery. Mondino knocked, said his name and explained that Father Francesco was expecting him. The friar closed the hatch and soon afterwards opened the door, bidding them come in. Father Paolo, the master builder at San Giacomo Maggiore, was waiting for them in the corridor, beaming behind his grey beard. He told them that unfortunately the friars were at supper just then and the prior couldn't come in person to greet the great physician Mondino.

'If you'd like to join us, we would be very happy,' he added.

Gerardo smiled to himself. Mondino had told him that that was exactly what would happen. The physician knew perfectly well that the Augustinian prior did not like him, and for once the Church's antipathy was to his advantage. This was the reason he had chosen the supper hour to turn up at the monastery. The priests would have an excuse not to see him and Mondino was quite happy to be seen as little as possible.

'Unfortunately I need to go and see another ailing patient immediately afterwards,' replied Mondino. 'But don't worry about supper. I work better on an empty stomach. Please, take us to your cousin.'

Father Paolo, visibly relieved, led them down a long, deserted and almost pitch black corridor, where no one had yet lit torches or candles. When they went past the deserted dormitory, he didn't stop, explaining that they had moved Father Francesco to a private cell, which even had a door.

'His wailing kept everyone awake at night and come the daytime the monks kept dozing off,' Paolo explained, smiling. 'So the prior decided to accord him the distinction of the room kept for important guests.' They went on until they reached a bare but comfortable cell. The friar languished on a straw palliasse on a rough-hewn wooden bed, covered in a sheet and his habit.

Father Paolo made the introductions and asked if they needed a brazier, to which Mondino replied with great gentleness, that he had all he needed with him.

'How will you close the wound?' asked the master builder.

'I will not cauterise it, if that's what you want to know. I will use silk thread.'

'I see,' said the priest, with the air of someone who didn't understand at all.

'The only thing that I shall need is a basin of water, but I see that there is already one here,' said Mondino, pointing to the bowl and the jug on the table beneath the window. 'As for the rest, my assistant will see to everything. Go back to supper, Father. We will still be here when you have finished eating.'

The priest bowed his head, thanked him again and left, closing the door. Mondino asked Gerardo to prepare the patient, accompanying his words with an admonishing look, and then he started to take his instruments out of his bag, laying them out in a row on the table.

Gerardo was too surprised to think of being angry. He had been expecting a man who looked brutish, black-hearted or at least deceitful, whereas Father Francesco was the picture of sweetness. Blue eyes, very short hair, a shaven face and an open smile, despite the pain his hernia caused him. He was the type of religious man to whom one would naturally turn, for advice or a comforting word.

Without saying anything, he lifted the sheet and helped the priest to sit up on the bed. Then he made him lie down again, but across the bed, with his back on the mattress and his feet on the floor. He explained that he would have to immobilise him to avoid involuntary movements during the operation, and Father Francesco consented with good grace.

'Do what you must,' he said, opening wide his arms and smiling.

Gerardo tied his hands to the frame of the bed and then took another two pieces of stout cord from the bag. While he lifted up the man's knees and opened his legs, he told himself that there was nothing to be surprised about. Angelo da Piczano had appeared to be an exemplary Knight Templar, dedicated to the Rule and the defence of the faith. And yet he did those unspeakable things to innocent children, the very children whom Christ loved above all else. *Suffer the little children to come unto me*. The way in which people like Angelo and Father Francesco perverted those words set the anger inside him aflame and he pulled too hard on the cord, prompting a cry of pain from the patient.

'Be careful!' snapped Mondino immediately.

'It doesn't matter, Magister,' said Francesco, with an angelic smile. 'The fault is my own, I am too sensitive.'

Gerardo tied the rope in a double knot, and then he lifted up the priest's shirt, laying bare his genitals. Turning away so as not to see the spectacle of a grown man with his legs wide open like a whore, he said: 'The patient is ready, Master.'

Mondino nodded, he asked him to put the basin filled with water on the floor beside the bed, then he sat on a stool in front of Francesco's open legs and with expert movements began to shave his thick pubic hair, moving his member this way and that with his free hand to facilitate the passage of the blade, and rinsing the razor in the basin every so often.

Watching the scene, Gerardo thought that he had been right not to study in those years when he had pretended to be a student: he could never have made a surgeon.

When his genitals were completely free of hair, Gerardo put a rag into the monk's mouth so that he could bite it against the pain. They had decided not to use sedatives, because if Father Francesco had gone to sleep it would be impossible to interrogate him. While Mondino lay down the razor, took up the knife and began to cut, Gerardo looked away again. The sight of blood had no effect on him, however while a cut with a knife or sword was one thing, it was quite another to watch the surgeon's knife invented by Guglielmo da Saliceto cutting and poking around in a man's private parts.

The operation was quicker than he thought it would be. Francesco was groaning with pain while the mattress became covered in blood and then something that was not quite recognisable ended up in the basin with the blood, water and hairs. Mondino cleaned the wound several times with vinegar, applied a healing poultice and waited for the blood loss to lessen. Then he asked for the needle and silk thread and sewed up the incision.

'All done' he said afterwards, raising his head and looking the patient in the eye. 'The operation has been successful.'

Francesco spat out the cloth and tried to smile, repressing a grimace of pain. 'I don't know how to thank you, Magister,' he said, weakly.

'Oh, I do,' replied Mondino, without smiling back. 'You knew a Knight Templar by the name of Angelo da Piczano. I need some information about him.'

'What?' answered Francesco, his clear eyes wide and sincere, still dazed by the pain. 'No, I don't know anyone of that name. Why do you ask?'

'Because Angelo da Piczano is dead,' replied Mondino, in the same tone. 'And we are trying to find out who killed him. We know that you were one of the last people to have seen him alive, so don't bother to lie. Just tell us everything you know about him, to help us track down his murderer.' The priest opened his mouth, but Mondino went on, taking a firm hold of the monk's member with his left hand and raising the knife with his right. 'Needless to say, if you lie, the outcome of this fine operation could be compromised. It is a regrettable fact but it is sometimes necessary to remove the genitals too. Nobody would blame me.'

His tone was calm, but his expression was unambiguous. Father Francesco realised he was caught in a trap. 'This is what you really came here for,' he whispered, furiously. 'You tricked my cousin into trusting you with the story of the operation, just to ask me about this Angelo da Piczano. Well, sorry to disappoint you, but I don't know him. I have never even heard of him. And you would not dare to hurt me. If you try I will shout for help, and in seconds my colleagues will be here.'

The look of pain in his blue eyes was momentarily cancelled out by a challenging expression. He no longer seemed to be the personification of goodness. Gerardo took a step forwards to take hold of him round the neck, but Mondino stopped him.

'No,' he said, without taking his eyes off the priest.

Then, slowly, he moved the razor nearer to the man's member, so that he could see quite well through his open legs.

164

'You wouldn't do it,' said the priest.

'You don't know me,' replied Mondino. He lowered the blade, ready for the incision.

Father Francesco shouted with as much breath as he had in him, but he had to stop because the effort increased the pain in his groin.

Alarmed, Gerardo turned to the door, but Mondino remained quite calm.

'Your colleagues are at supper in the refectory,' he explained, in a mild tone. 'Besides, everyone knows that removing a hernia is a painful operation, and they would expect to hear some yelling. No one will come.'

Gerardo saw a flash of doubt pass through the priest's eyes, then his stubborn pride returned.

'If you do not let me go immediately, I will call for help,' he threatened. 'I will shout murder. You can be sure that someone will come.'

'In that case,' said Mondino, 'I will inform your confrères about what you do to little boys in that old crone's cavern. Perhaps they'll tear you apart themselves or maybe the prior will manage to stop them in time and you will be saved for the executioner, for a humiliating trial that will end up at the stake.'

Gerardo was literally on tenterhooks with anxiety. If Francesco called for help and the monks really did turn up, someone would call the guards, he would be recognised and arrested, and the same fate would await Mondino, since he was his accomplice. Knowing that Father Francesco had been condemned to death would be meagre consolation. Mondino's hold on him was based entirely on the fact that the priest could not know that Gerardo was a wanted man, but the risk was still enormous. The young man could not understand how the physician managed to keep his sang-froid.

A gleam of real terror could now be seen in Father

165

Francesco's martyr's eyes. He stared fixedly at Mondino and what he saw convinced him not to cry out.

'Which old crone?' he attempted to say.

'Her name is Philomena,' replied Mondino. 'Don't waste time lying; it was she herself who betrayed you. We know everything but that's not the reason that we are here.'

Francesco shook the ropes that were binding his arms, and again the effort caused him to groan with pain.

'If you don't stop twisting and shouting,' said Mondino, without losing his calm, 'the only result will be that the wound will reopen. In such an eventuality I might not be able to close it in time and the excessive loss of blood could be fatal.'

This time the man was left in no doubt that the threat was genuine. He nodded and said, 'If I admitted knowing Angelo da Piczano, what would you do?'

His situation was desperate and yet he still tried to negotiate. Gerardo thought that it was just as well that he hadn't been able to speak to the man three days earlier. He wouldn't have got anything out of him and would only have succeeded in putting him on his guard.

'We shall ask you some questions,' said Mondino, 'and then we'll go away. We are not interested in denouncing you; otherwise we would already have done it. It's a threat that we will only carry out in extreme circumstances. And by the way, it will not be worth your while talking about what has been said between these walls.'

Francesco seemed to reflect on the offer. His self-control was frightening.

'First undo my legs,' he said, after a pause.

'No, first you speak,' intervened Gerardo, incapable of containing himself any longer.

'You heard what my assistant said,' affirmed Mondino. 'Tell us what we want to know and everyone will be better off.'

The priest capitulated with a sigh. 'Very well. But I warn you: I know very little.'

His confession was disappointing. He had met Angelo da Piczano some days before his disappearance, at the public baths near Porta Govese. Angelo had noticed the looks that he was giving the young men and had approached him. After a brief conversation, Francesco gave him Philomena's address and received some money in return.

'I haven't seen him since then, and I didn't know that he was dead,' he concluded, his voice cracking from the pain the wound gave him. 'If you don't believe me, I'm not sure what I can do about it.'

Gerardo was convinced that he was telling the truth. By now he had admitted enough to condemn himself to death and he had no reason to hide anything to cover up a dead man. The knight was just thinking that they had run a heavy risk for nothing, when Mondino got up from the stool.

'One last thing,' the physician said. 'The address of the house that Philomena has moved to, and we'll go. I know you know it.'

Francesco nodded. He no longer had the strength to resist.

'Borgo del Pratello,' he murmured. 'A house with a green door, in the first lane on the right after the Wild Boar Tavern.'

Then he closed his eyes and began to groan quietly, overcome by the pain and weakness due to the loss of blood. Mondino put his instruments back into his bag while Gerardo untied the patient and laid him properly on the bed. As soon as they left the room, they found Father Paolo waiting for them in the corridor.

'Supper has just finished,' said the master builder, embarrassed. 'Unfortunately the prior—'

'It doesn't matter,' said Mondino, interrupting him. 'As I told you, we must go. As far as my fee is concerned, I shall send a servant along in a few days.'

'Certainly, as you wish,' replied the priest. 'Did it go well?'

Mondino took on a contrite air that amazed Gerardo. 'Yes and no, Father, yes and no.'

'Please, don't keep me in suspense.'

The physician explained that the operation had been successful and Francesco was doing well. They would only have to change the sheet and palliasse and let him rest. They should also ask the father apothecary to give him a calming decoction twice a day.

'Within a week at the most Father Francesco will be on his feet again,' he concluded.

'So what is the problem?'

Mondino sighed. 'The hernia was in a difficult position,' he replied. 'I had to remove anything in the way of the surgical knife so as not to risk puncturing the peritoneum.'

'Could you be clearer please?'

'Well, Father, I could not avoid castration. I advise you to wait until your cousin is quite well again, before telling him.'

At those words the master builder's tense expression relaxed. 'Oh don't worry about that, Magister,' he said, with a slight smile. 'The important thing is that Francesco is well. As for the rest ... For a priest, the fact of not being able to succumb to temptations of the flesh is more of a help than a hindrance.'

By now it was dark outside. While they walked down the middle of the road to avoid any nasty surprises that might be hidden behind the columns of the arcade, Mondino reflected on what he had just done. He had taken it upon himself to judge and condemn another human being.

'You didn't have to castrate him, did you?' asked Gerardo, in a low voice, as though reading his thoughts.

Mondino didn't reply at once, but when he did any doubts

had vanished. 'Yes, I did. We can't denounce him, but at least this way he won't be able to do any more wrong.'

'No, I meant—'

Mondino stopped and turned to look at him. 'Did you really think that the explanation I gave the master builder was the truth?' he said, offended by the idea that the youth could question his expertise. In a crisp tone, he added, 'I am perfectly capable of operating on a hernia without jeopardising the male functions.'

Gerardo nodded silently and they set off again in the direction of Pratello. They walked along side by side without bothering to stand on ceremony. The moon had not yet risen and in the dim light of the few lanterns hanging above the entrances to the houses, it was almost impossible to recognise anyone unless they were very close.

'Master,' Gerardo took up again, after a short while. 'How did you know that Philomena had stayed on in the city and that he'd know her new address? I had told you that she took fright and fled.'

Mondino shrugged. He didn't feel like talking, but replied just the same. 'Women like that one don't frighten easily,' he said. 'She just realised that her house was no longer safe and moved elsewhere, probably to a place that she had ready just in case.'

'I see, but how did Francesco know where she'd gone?'

'Because she would have told him. Once she had moved to the new house, she would have sent someone to inform all her regular clients. Otherwise who is she going to sell him to, the poor child?'

Those words ended their conversation. They walked on through the almost deserted streets, passing groups of students going in or out of taverns, shady-looking men on their own and prostitutes winking at them from windows. They reached the Wild Boar Tavern, turned into the lane, which was empty,

169

muddy and dark, and after a few yards found themselves in front of the house with the green door. Compline had not yet rung.

'Let me go in first,' said Mondino, in a low voice. 'Even if you disguise your voice, she'll recognise you.'

'Master, this is my business. I promised Masino that I would rescue him and I intend to keep my word, but I don't want you running any unnecessary risks.'

There were a couple of reasons why Mondino had decided to help him. First, the idea of leaving the boy in the hands of the old woman was abhorrent to him. Second, he wanted to protect Gerardo, not so much and not only because his help was indispensible in solving the mystery, but also through a strange sense of loyalty that Mondino didn't feel like elaborating on. In any case, now was not the moment for long and embarrassing explanations.

He grabbed Gerardo by the collar of his tunic and pushed him against a wall. 'If you think that I am going to hang around out here in the dark waiting to find out what's going on inside, you are quite wrong,' he said, thrusting his jaw at him. 'We shall go in together, whether you like it or not.'

He let him go, and before the youth had the chance to recover from the surprise, Mondino had knocked on the door.

What happened next occurred with the speed and twisted logic of a dream. The woman opened the door; Mondino grabbed her by the throat to stop her shouting and went in, followed by Gerardo, who immediately shut the door. This time Philomena was not alone. Sitting at the table was one of her two accomplices, who quickly got up and threw himself at them, brandishing an iron bar. Gerardo thumped him in the chest, just below the solar plexus, and while he dropped to the floor ran towards the other rooms in search of Masino. Mondino pushed Philomena down on to a bench, pulled the surgical knife out of his bag and pointed it at her to keep her at bay. It probably wasn't necessary, but he felt more comfortable holding a weapon when faced with the bristly-headed woman with hair on her hands.

A minute later, Gerardo came back carrying the little boy in his arms. He was dressed in tunic and cap but had no shoes or breeches on. Masino had his face buried in Gerardo's neck and was clutching a small wooden crucifix in his hands, presumably the only thing he wanted to take away with him.

While Mondino was looking at the child, the old woman took her chance and threw herself on him with a loud screech. She had pulled out a long stiletto from her gown and gave such a forceful thrust that had it met its target it would have speared him like a thrush on a skewer.

Mondino didn't manage to get completely out of the way and the stiletto ripped his tunic, nicking the skin on his left side. Reacting instinctively, he plunged his knife into the woman's neck and was hit in the face by a spray of warm blood.

Gerardo shouted something that he didn't hear, but Mondino saw him open the door and went out after him, wiping his bloody face with the sleeve of his tunic. They were glad of the pitch darkness outside. Mondino followed the Templar and the little boy through the empty streets. They went past the Church of Sant'Antonino and the house that Gerardo had set on fire, but they didn't stop to look at the blackened beams on the top floor and the wooden scaffolding where repairs would be starting the following week. Mondino passed it every day, going to and from the School of Medicine. They carried on towards the hospital of San Procolo, where they had decided to leave Masino. Taking in abandoned children was the monks' main activity. At the door of the hospital, Gerardo gave the boy some money and spoke to him softly for some time. Then, leaving him on the doorstep, they knocked on the door and quickly moved away into the shadows, each finding his own way home.

As he returned home, in a ripped and bloody tunic, Mondino was busy contriving something to say to his family to justify his appearance, as though with that preoccupation he could avoid thinking about the fact that he had just killed a human being. All of a sudden he understood why murderers loved the night.

The dark provided shelter and allowed them to hide from themselves as well.

VIII

On his way to the monastery of San Domenico, Mondino kept repeating to himself that he had nothing to be afraid of, but however much he said it, he knew that it wasn't true. The knowledge of all that he had done since that moment eight days earlier, which now seemed a lifetime away, when he had decided to help Gerardo, never left him. And now an urgent summons from the Inquisitor had increased his anxiety to an almost insufferable level.

As he walked, he could feel the bandage rubbing beneath his clean clothes. At home he had had to lie, saying that by a miracle he had escaped the violent onslaught of some wretch, who contented himself with grabbing his bag and disappearing into the night. Naturally, before going home, Mondino had taken the precaution of cutting his belt and throwing the bag into a canal.

Everyone had accepted his explanation without question, but as far as he was concerned, the fact that he was such a convincing liar was nothing to be proud of at all.

It was the last day of April and although already late afternoon, the air was warm. Everyone was more lightly dressed than a week before and there was the feeling that summer had finally arrived. Mondino too had stopped wearing his fur-trimmed cloak over his red robe, which made him sweat when he walked fast, but he had put it on for the meeting that awaited him. He preferred to be bolstered by the signs of his profession at the meeting with the Inquisitor.

Making himself slow down, he began to walk at a more measured pace. He envied Gerardo, who at that hour would be sleeping blissfully to prepare himself for some exploit that night, which he had decided to tackle with Hugues de Narbonne. Mondino didn't approve of the Frenchman's involvement in their investigation, but he couldn't do anything to avoid it, and anyhow he was grateful that someone else was running risks with Gerardo.

The physician had lain awake most of the night, troubled by nightmares in which the dominant theme was the sensation of the knife sinking into Philomena's neck. It continued to torment him, camouflaged in different ways but always recognisable. And when he had risen, his servant Lorenza told him that a Dominican monk had come to summon him to an urgent meeting with the Inquisitor that evening.

At that hour the streets were less frenetic. The working day had ended and people seemed more relaxed. Only a few carders, working from home, who had opened mattresses in their courtyards, were still hard at it, hurriedly separating the wool fibres.

Mondino usually enjoyed the sight of the daily life of his city, but just then he hardly took it in at all. He had already prepared his defence should the Inquisitor question his interference in the case of the dead German, and as he walked along he tried to identify its weak points. That must be the reason that he had been called to see the man. If it were the other thing, the concealment of Angelo da Piczano's body, they would have come to get him with city guards in tow.

Or perhaps not, so as to avoid stirring up protests by the students. Perhaps the Inquisitor had cunningly thought of inviting him to a friendly meeting and would have him arrested the minute he set foot in the monastery. Then there might be protests anyway, but without a public arrest they would be more moderate.

And anyway, if they had managed to find proof of what he had done, Mondino knew that he had no hope. His students certainly wouldn't be able to defend him in a trial of that sort.

So as far as the German's murder was concerned, he couldn't do anything but continue to play the part of the *comune's* envoy. The Church must have been annoyed because he had demanded to examine the cadaver before the Inquisitor. But then why hadn't they protested through the official channels, complaining to the *Podestà* or the Captain of the People? Mondino had entered the inn with a pass that was entirely in order.

It was pointless torturing himself over it all. He had now arrived and would soon discover the reason for the summons. He walked diagonally across the piazza, passing the memorial tombs of Egidio Foscarari and Rolandino de Passeggeri, the great commentator who had resisted Emperor Federico II, refusing in the name of the Bolognese to give the Emperor back his son Enzo, a prisoner in the city. Mondino would have liked to have a tomb like that one day, for his scientific discoveries. But perhaps that meant he should restrict himself to writing his treatise instead of dreaming of the secret that transformed the veins into iron so as to reveal the blood's circuit in the human body. In any case, it was a bit late now to back out.

He knocked at the door of the monastery, gave his name to the friar on guard and said that the Inquisitor was expecting him. The friar immediately let him in and ordered a novice to accompany him to Uberto da Rimini's study.

Mondino walked through halls and along corridors,

following the faint sound of the young friar's bare feet flapping on the floor. At last the boy knocked on a door, listened for an answer that Mondino couldn't hear, entered and almost immediately came out again. With a respectful smile he stood aside, let Mondino past and closed the door behind him. Mondino imagined his bare feet padding away down the corridor and felt an irresistible desire to follow him. The physician could already feel himself suffocating in that monastery.

He walked into a large room decorated with taste but without excessive opulence. At the other end, seated at a walnut table in the light of an open window, the Inquisitor Uberto da Rimini raised his eyes from an illuminated manuscript and looked at him with an expression that was almost benevolent.

'Mondino de Liuzzi,' he said, dryly. 'Thank you for coming.'

'It's my pleasure, Father,' replied Mondino. 'I imagined that you would want to see me, and only this morning I was thinking of asking to see you. Your summons just beat me to it.'

The Inquisitor's small, thin body appeared even smaller behind the large table at which he was sitting and the great bound volume on it that he was reading. 'That's just as well,' he said, almost to himself. 'Just as well.' After which he paused for some time without saying anything, his dark eyes fixed on those of de Liuzzi.

'Why did you send for me?' asked Mondino, finally.

'Ah,' replied the friar, with a flourish of his child-sized hand from the sleeve of his black and white habit. 'About the murder of that German Templar, Wilhelm von Trier. They told me that you examined the body.'

'I see,' said Mondino. Then, since the prelate still didn't ask him to sit down, he went over to the table and sat on a seat, from where he could see the sky out of the window. 'Please ask anything you'd like.'

The discussion had become a delicate fencing match, where they had to dance round the crux of the matter rather than deal with it head on. Mondino confirmed what the prelate already knew, after which there were another couple of general questions and answers and then Uberto asked him if he had determined how many mortal wounds there were.

'One, Father.'

'Only one?'

Uberto seemed disappointed, and Mondino could guess why. The maximum number of people that you could condemn to death for murder could not be more than the number of mortal wounds found on the corpse. The Inquisitor must have been hoping to rid himself of a number of enemies in one go.

'Actually it doesn't surprise me,' said Uberto.

'Why not?' asked Mondino.

'In Devil worship there is often only one fatal wound, inflicted after the victim has been subjected to prolonged suffering.'

Now they were getting to the point. Mondino considered what he could say without compromising himself, but he could find nothing better than repeating the priest's words in an interrogative tone.

'Devil worship?'

'You don't deny that's what it is about, I hope.' The Inquisitor's tone had suddenly hardened. 'The Templar was offered up in sacrifice to their idol, Baphomet. And I believe I know why.'

'Why?'

Mondino knew that he couldn't go on for ever just repeating the priest's words like an echo. But he was determined not to say anything of importance until he had found out exactly what it was that the Inquisitor wanted from him.

Uberto da Rimini abandoned the mask of cordiality that he

had been wearing up to that point. His face became taut, all corners and straight lines. 'Because there is a trial in process against the Templars,' he said. 'And with abominable acts like this one, they hope to ensure the protection of the demonic forces. Ah, when I think that this nest of vipers came to life and prospered in the bosom of the Church …' Uberto shook his head slowly and said nothing more.

This time it would have been confrontational to repeat the Inquisitor's words, so Mondino chose to remain silent. He sat motionless, quietly waiting for da Rimini to go on.

'In short,' said Uberto, tracing a vein in the wood of the table with his finger, 'you can confirm having seen definite signs of adoration of the Devil and moral degradation in the manner in which the murder was carried out?'

'I cannot confirm that,' Mondino replied. 'I didn't see that.'

Now he had openly opposed the Inquisitor's will. The boundaries were marked out. The battleground had been identified. The moment for wielding the sword had arrived.

Uberto da Rimini seemed to reflect on what he was going to say, as though wondering whether he might not in fact be mistaken in judging the German's death to be Devil worship.

'And yet,' he said, as if to conclude his interior reasoning, 'the man's heart was changed into a piece of iron.'

Mondino also chose his words with care, before speaking. 'I saw that, I cannot deny it …'

'And so?'

'It is an unusual phenomenon. I have never heard or read of such a thing before. But it is not enough to be certain of the Devil's participation. An alchemist might have been able …'

'An alchemist!'

'Father,' said Mondino, raising his palms to invite quiet. 'It may seem strange, but you know better than I do that the principle of metallic content of matter, as Geber explains in his *Book of the Composition of Alchemy* …'

Seeing a fierce smile appear on the lips of the Inquisitor, Mondino didn't go on. He knew immediately that he had made a mistake, but it was too late now to put it right. He automatically hunched his shoulders, as if preparing himself for the blow.

'I don't possess your scientific knowledge, Magister,' said Uberto, in a honeyed voice. 'And I do not know much about the metallic principle and of that which is inflammable contained in matter. But I do know that this Geber of whom you speak is an infidel, a Saracen, part of that same stock which we fought in the crusades and we still fight on our coasts. You are not by chance telling me that, to support the lack of Devil worship in the murder about which we are speaking, you are going on the words of an unbeliever?'

'The Arabic religion is in error, without any doubt,' Mondino hurriedly clarified. 'But their knowledge is great. Avicenna's *Canon*, as you know, is one of the most studied medical texts in Christianity, and even in the *Studium* we value ...'

'The *Studium*!' Uberto burst out, managing to make the word sound as though he were spitting. 'A rabble of folk who invade the city, propositioning honest women and fornicating with strumpets, spending their time in taverns drinking and playing dice, and other depravities that I won't mention. People who, as Maurizio da San Vittore said, "seek wisdom not for wisdom's sake, but to prostitute it, either out of vanity or for money". And I should be surprised that the texts on which they base their studies come from the land of the heathens?'

It was as close to a direct insult to Mondino that he could expect. Speaking of his students with contempt, the prelate obviously intended to spite him: in Uberto's opinion, the teachers of that 'rabble' were certainly no better than their disciples. The discussion was taking a dangerous turn. Mondino knew that he would do better to ignore the cutting remark and agree with the priest. But it was more the insult to knowledge than to himself that drove him to respond in like spirit.

'And yet even renowned Christian scholars have taken up alchemy,' he insisted. 'Albertus Magnus himself, Doctor Universalis, who apart from anything else was a Dominican like yourself, and taught at the university of Paris.'

'That's enough!' shouted Uberto, slamming his hand down on the table and leaping to his feet. 'I will not permit you to compare a celebrated Christian, who was also archbishop of the Church, to that mob I was talking about before. Albertus was given the title of Doctor Universalis, or Doctor Expertus, precisely because he soared to heights that were unattainable by that scum. And I should remind you that although he certainly taught in Paris, he taught theology! He understood the need of many young people, in danger of losing their souls in the pursuit of worldly pleasures and profane knowledge, and he went among them. And the young prized him. They deserted the halls of law and medicine to follow his lessons, and so many of them came that Albertus had to start teaching in the public square, because there was no hall big enough to contain all his students.'

Mondino had also got to his feet, to respect etiquette but in part too because he didn't want to let himself be dominated. Now the Inquisitor came towards him. Thin as Uberto was, and shorter by almost a head, he still managed to be frightening.

A silence fell that neither of them bothered to bring to an end. The light coming from the window was failing, a sign that the sun was about to go down. A lamp needed to be lit in the room, but Uberto da Rimini did not seem to notice. He was clearly satisfied at having finally reduced his adversary to silence. He allowed himself a smile, in which a flicker of anger still resonated.

'Alchemy,' he said, in a calm voice, 'will soon be rejected

by Christian science. It will be likened to sorcery and oppressed, as indeed it should be. And when that time comes, scientists, physicians and philosophers would do well to have purged their learning of the influence of the infidels. However,' he added, and again his smile took on a wild look, 'I did not only want to talk to you about the German Templar's death.'

Mondino felt his heart sink in his chest. He did his best to assume an impassive attitude and asked, 'Perhaps you have need of my medical services? Your complexion seems to me somewhat heightened; you probably suffer from an excess of yellow bile. In that I could certainly be of help.'

Uberto circled around him, forcing him to turn round. The Inquisitor moved with an almost feminine grace, but there was nothing attractive in his expression. Spontaneously, the banal comparison came to Mondino of a cat preparing to finish off a mouse. 'If your medical services consist, as I have heard,' said the priest, 'of tearing the heart out of dead people and making bodies disappear, then no thank you, I have no need of them.' He looked at Mondino with a malicious joy in his eyes, and gently added, 'Magister, you have been found out.'

Gerardo felt extremely ill at ease dressed as he was. His shirt was sweaty, encrusted with dirt and ripped in more than one place. He wore no stockings or breeches, and he was covered in a grimy sackcloth that could in no sense be described as a tunic. Perhaps that was the reason for his bad mood and his inclination to address the Commander without due respect.

'Mondino maintains that you had already seen the map before he showed it to us in the banker's study,' he said, suddenly. 'Is that true?'

Hugues de Narbonne astonished him by making a sincere reply. 'It's true.'

'So why didn't you say so?'

The Frenchman stopped in the middle of the street. Even dressed in rags like a beggar, he had the authoritative appearance of a leader. 'I'm the one who chooses what I say or don't say, Gerardo,' he answered, in a tone that did not admit a reply. 'Mondino is not one of us and I don't know how much we can trust him. All you need to know is that the map is useless. Some people believed that it could lead them to a place where the secret of immortality was kept, but after years of trying they had to conclude that it was false.'

'The secret of immortality,' repeated Gerardo, incredulous.

As usual they were speaking in Latin, but in very low voices, to avoid giving themselves away. Latin certainly wasn't the language of beggars.

'Imagine what people of superior intelligence could do if they were not subject to death,' said Hugues. 'They could defend the faith better and explore human knowledge more deeply than it has been until now. In the right hands, it would be an inestimable gift.'

'But the map is false, you said so yourself.'

'Exactly. Or it is hiding its secret too well. But perhaps there's another way to get the same result.'

'What other way?'

'That's enough now, Gerardo. If I think it appropriate, I will tell you about it on our way back.' He pointed in front of him. 'There's the ruined house. Am I right?'

'Yes.'

They started walking through the debris and Gerardo made his way towards the entrance of the underworld, listening carefully. A dim light was coming from below. Reassured by the silence among the ruins, he turned towards Hugues de Narbonne and simply said, 'All clear.'

Hugues made a sign that he should start to go down. Barefoot and dressed as a vagrant, the Frenchman was unrecognisable. Gerardo hoped that his own disguise was equally effective. The smell coming from their clothes was unbearable, but now at least he was starting to get used to it.

He began to pick his way among the rocks and bricks, thanking heaven that he still had shoes on. That had been Hugues' idea. He had said that the only hope of getting the information they needed and escaping the underworld alive was to pass themselves off as vagrants. To achieve a realistic effect, that morning they had hit two genuine vagrants over the head, taking their beggar's bags and their clothes, which were stiff as suits of armour with dirt. They had left their own clothes at the Frenchman's house and just before sundown they had set off.

Hugues had no problem doing without shoes and he moved naturally in bare feet. Gerardo had tried, but continued to hop and trip, and in the end they both decided that he would attract less attention if he kept his shoes on. A beggar with nearly new shoes was an impossibility, but Gerardo had dirtied them with grease and dust and trusted that in the dark he would get by without arousing suspicion.

Once they had entered the tunnel, they stopped again to look around them. The torch that Gerardo had used the previous day was no longer there. It was probable that the first beggar returning in the evening had used it to light the others along the way.

'Is everything clear?' asked Hugues. 'Remember that you are the only one to speak, I am mute.'

'I remember everything perfectly,' answered Gerardo, tetchily. He was annoyed because it was the third time that the Frenchman had asked him if everything was clear. 'Now please try to use your Latin as little as possible. Someone might hear us.'

Hugues can't have been used to letting the initiative fall into someone else's hands, but in this case it was inevitable. He only spoke French and Latin so he had decided to pretend to be dumb. Whereas Gerardo could talk in the dialect of Ravenna, which he knew well having learned it from the family servants during his childhood. They already had a story ready to justify their presence and why they were looking for the Ferrarese. Gerardo only hoped that the beggar really would be able to tell them something useful about Wilhelm von Trier's death. He didn't quite know how he was going to raise the subject without arousing suspicion, but he'd tackle that problem when he came to it. Now he needed to find the room with the frescoes that the boy had told him about.

They made their way down the narrow raised passage, Gerardo in front, Hugues behind, each with their beggar's bag across one shoulder. A fetid smell rose from the dry canal, coming from the putrefied rubbish that had accumulated there over the years. There were torches sticking out of the walls, placed every twenty or thirty yards and these gave enough light to prevent them tripping over. As he went, Gerardo began to think that perhaps it was not a sewage system after all, but an ancient secret passage. The tunnel was neither narrow nor wide. Stretching his arms he could touch both walls. The lancet vault, just above their heads, and the whole passage itself were made out of bricks and stone and seemed very solid, despite being centuries old.

Only at one point, where the tunnel widened slightly and turned to the left, did a stretch of wall seem in danger of collapsing in on itself, but it was held firm by a horizontal beam wedged between the walls. The two Templars had to bend down to pass beneath the prop, and soon after they came out into a great circular hall, lit by small fires dotted around the place. Gerardo counted about fifteen people, but other beggars could be heard coming along the tunnel. In the city above them, compline must have already rung.

'We're here,' he whispered.

Hugues nodded without saying a word.

The smoke from the fires and the torches had covered the

walls in a blackish patina under which the remains of the frescoes that had once decorated them could still just be made out. The ground in the hall was not flat but descended towards the tunnel in a series of low steps. Gerardo was more and more convinced that it was an old Roman house, or perhaps a spa, buried by later buildings.

But they were not there to admire the work of the ancients; they had a job to do. Going up to one of the fires, he began to ask about the Ferrarese.

The first beggar that Gerardo spoke to was a gaunt youth covered in a sack with bloody bandages around his head and hands. Without even looking up, he said that he didn't know the maimed man they were looking for. He was in the process of unwrapping the bandages around his wrists, revealing dirty but perfectly healthy hands, and then he began to rummage among his belongings, taking out a dead cat that his two companions welcomed with smiles and shouts of approval.

As Gerardo was approaching the next fire, Hugues touched his shoulder.

'Don't turn round too suddenly, but look to your right,' he whispered in his guttural Latin.

Gerardo's first reaction was irritation. Then he said to himself that if Hugues was prepared to risk exposing his illiterate mute's disguise, then he must have a pretty good reason for it. Smiling as though he wanted to greet someone, he turned in that direction and his blood froze: a few steps away from them stood a strapping great man, wearing only a rag wrapped around his hips. He still had an obvious swelling and a scab of blood on the top of his shaved head, where he had been hit by a club. Gerardo recognised with horror the first beggar whom they had hit over the head in order to steal his clothes. If he recognised them, they were doomed.

At that moment the man looked up and caught his eye.

*

The Inquisitor spoke in a soft, unthreatening voice that somehow made his accusation all the more powerful and definitive. His tone affirmed a fact, without leaving room for doubt.

Mondino realised that his career as a physician, and probably even his life, had come to an end. Absurdly, he didn't think of his dear ones or the trouble that awaited them. He had just one thought, one regret that filled his whole being: the treatise on anatomy would never be finished.

'I don't know what you are talking about, Father,' he said, without much conviction. 'It is true that I dissect corpses for study, but ...'

'But not long ago one came along whose appearance quite markedly resembled that of the German found in Santo Stefano. The chest was open and the ribs broken and bent outwards. What's more, even the dead men's profession when they were alive was the same: they were both Knights Templar. Is that not strange?'

It was clear that the Inquisitor knew everything. So it was therefore pointless to continue denying it. However, to admit anything voluntarily was suicide. If Uberto wanted his head, thought Mondino, he would have to come and get it. He would not be offering it up of his own accord.

'What are you getting at?' he asked.

'It's simple. The only difference between the two corpses was that one of their hearts had been transformed into a block of iron, while the other's had been removed. It is reasonable to suppose that the second had received the same treatment. You could be accused of committing both crimes, but that is probably not true, and the Church is only interested in the truth.'

Mondino made an effort to control his breathing. He desperately wanted to sit down again. The Inquisitor's game was clear up to a point. He was saying that the Church had nothing to gain by accusing him of the murder of the two

Templars. This was good news, however Mondino had a nasty suspicion that worse was yet to come.

'Indeed it is not true, Father. I didn't know the people you are talking about and I wouldn't have a motive for killing them. What's more I don't possess the necessary knowledge to do what was done to them.'

'You mean you are not a sorcerer.'

'Father, I don't know if this is the work of one—'

'Certainly it is, Magister! This is definitely the work of a sorcerer. And one who obtained his macabre power through a pact with the Devil. There is no room for discussion.'

Mondino said nothing. Uberto da Rimini could believe what he wanted. The main thing was that his accusation of Devil worship fell on someone else's head.

'Do you agree with me that to transform the heart of a man into a block of metal is a work of sorcery?' asked the priest.

He had been very precise in his question. Quite obviously he had an objective, but however much Mondino racked his brain he couldn't work out what it was. He had the uncomfortable feeling that he was walking along the edge of a precipice in the pitch dark.

'It could be.'

An authentic, almost friendly smile appeared on Uberto's face. Mondino felt that he would do anything to keep that smile intact, and he hated himself for his cowardice. Outside the window came the screech of a pulley. Despite it being nearly dark, someone was drawing water from the garden well.

'Good, I see we are beginning to understand one another,' said Uberto. 'I shall put you out of your misery, Magister. It was the gravediggers who betrayed you.'

Mondino was perspiring. He had the feeling that his body was both hot and cold at the same time. All those words were designed to frighten him; he was being softened like wax in the hands of the clergyman. However, he couldn't give up yet. His pride would not allow it.

'I don't deny that I used that corpse for my anatomical studies,' he said. 'But—'

'Be quiet!' interrupted Uberto violently. His kindly smile had vanished. 'Don't you realise that you have no way out? In the German's saddlebag there was a letter that identified him as a Templar. It accused him of the brutal murder of a Christian, committed with some of his confrères, and invited him to come to Bologna, to find out an obscure secret. These Knights of the Temple whom you seem to want to defend, do you understand who they really are?'

'I am not defending anyone, Father. And I know little or nothing about the Templars.'

'That's just as well, although your actions seem to contradict you. Now, in the light of what you have done, do you not agree that it would be easy for us to put you on trial, identifying you as the assassin of the first Templar and hence also the second, by similarity of *modus operandi*? Thus obtaining your death sentence, as well as the confiscation of your family's possessions. Answer me: do you agree or not?'

The Inquisitor's voice had been increasing in volume until he was shouting. Beads of spit formed at the corners of his mouth. He wiped them away with the back of his hand without taking his eyes off the physician. Mondino looked down at the terracotta tiles at his feet and realised that he didn't want to look up again. But he made himself raise his eyes and look straight into Uberto's, before admitting defeat.

'I agree, Father.'

'And you are right to. That way you can save yourself and not throw your life away. As I said, despite the proof against you, the Church is inclined to believe in your innocence, at least for the moment, and you will not be accused of anything.'

'I am grateful to you.'

A murmur of voices could be heard in the garden. The Inquisitor went over to the window and peered into the night. Suddenly the voices stopped and Uberto turned back to face him.

'Let's say that you shall show your gratitude in more than just words, Magister,' he said. 'If the Inquisitor's tribunal required you to give evidence, in your capacity of doctor and professor at the *Studium*, that the heart of that German monk was transformed into metal thanks to a work of sorcery, would you do it? Just answer yes or no.'

His intentions were finally clear. The Church had spotted an opportunity to exploit that mysterious killing as grounds for proof in the trial against the Templars. To condemn Mondino was not ideal because it would shift the attention from those whom the Inquisition wanted to be the guilty parties, despite the two dead Templars being victims and not murderers. This was why they were offering impunity in exchange for his witness statement. Mondino was in a trap; he had no choice. His whole being wanted to reply yes. Instead the word that came out of his mouth was the exact opposite.

'No.'

Uberto reacted by hitting the table with one of his little fists, making the inkstand wobble, fall over and spill ink over the polished surface. He distractedly took a piece of high-quality parchment and pressed it on the growing stain, without taking his dark eyes off Mondino.

'Do not try to leave this room, you will be stopped the minute you go through that door,' he said, stretching his free hand towards a little silver bell. 'In a moment the guards will come and take you away.'

'One moment,' said Mondino, lifting up both his hands in a gesture of surrender that cost him a terrible struggle with himself. 'Can we talk about it?'

'There's nothing more to say,' said Uberto, rolling up the parchment and throwing it on the tiled floor. 'Is it to be yes or no?'

'What you are asking of me is not easy,' said Mondino. 'I might be able to do it, but I need a few days to think about it.'

He said this in order to secure a bit more time and put off the arrival of the guards, but as he said it he realised that he was telling the truth. In just a few seconds his life had threatened to change direction. He found himself at a crossroads and he didn't like either of the options open to him, for different reasons. He felt confused and needed to be alone to think it over properly.

Uberto da Rimini opened his lips in a taut smile. 'Not so arrogant now, are we Magister?' he said. 'The prospect of ending up in prison tends to have that effect. All right, I'll give you two days. If you have not decided to testify by sunset on Sunday, you will be arrested. I trust you not to run away. If you do, I will make the accusation against you public. You will be hounded wherever you go, and you could no longer teach at your beloved university.'

Mondino nodded, saying nothing. The Inquisitor rang the silver bell and two friars, as vast as bulls, appeared at the door.

'See this man out,' said Uberto. 'He is free for the time being.'

Mondino made a slight bow and went over to the door. As he was leaving, the Inquisitor called him back.

'There's one more thing. Other than giving evidence at the trial, you must say where the person who brought you the corpse is hiding.'

Mondino turned towards him and was on the point of saying something, but Uberto stopped him with a wave of his hand. 'Think well before you lie. I know that he is one of your students and I imagine that he is a Templar in disguise. I am certain that it was he who killed these men in such an ignoble manner.'

'I am certain of the opposite,' replied Mondino, in a decided voice. 'He is a young man who has found himself involved in something much bigger than him.'

'If it wasn't him, then it has to be you,' said the Inquisitor with a cherubic expression. 'We need a culprit. You choose who it is to be.'

As soon as Mondino had left, Uberto sent for Guido Arlotti. The defrocked priest was waiting in a room next door and came straight in.

'From now on, you must never leave Mondino's side,' ordered the Inquisitor. 'I want to know where he goes, what he does and whom he meets. And above all I want to know where that phoney student who used to live in the house that was set on fire is hiding. He passed himself off as Francesco Salimbene, but it's a false name and by now he will have changed it. Mondino will definitely go and advise him to escape.'

'It will be done, Father,' replied Guido. 'Don't you think that Mondino will run too?'

'No, his life is here, he won't bolt. He is useful to us free and he knows it.'

Guido Arlotti nodded. 'I will get straight to work.'

Then he turned on his heel and left the room.

Gerardo turned away from the beggar whose clothes he had stolen and slowly began to move to the other side of the subterranean hall, followed by Hugues de Narbonne. The man couldn't have recognised them, because they had attacked him from behind, but there was still a high risk of being discovered. If they didn't find the Ferrarese in that part of the hall, they should leave, without going back to the place where, in a loud voice, the semi-naked beggar had begun telling the story of his

191

misadventure, obviously not mentioning the silver coin that Gerardo had left in his hand in return for his bag and clothes.

They took small steps, careful not to stand on the odds and ends scattered all over the floor. Meanwhile the room was gradually filling up as more and more men and women were arriving in dribs and drabs. Fortunately, many seemed not to know each other, so the presence of the two Templars in disguise went unobserved. Gerardo asked them in turn if they knew where to find the Ferrarese, but without much success. Some didn't know him, others said that over the last few days he hadn't left the hall, but they couldn't say where he was just then. The two moved towards the top of the steps, going to a fire over which two men and a woman were cooking green apples in a small earthenware saucepan. Gerardo asked them about the cripple and the woman looked at him suspiciously. She was about twenty and would have been beautiful if it were not for her excessive thinness and for the fact that she was missing three front teeth.

'Why are you looking for him?' she asked.

Gerardo told her the story that they had made up beforehand. They had been driven out of Ravenna and on the road another vagabond had told them to look for a beggar missing a hand called the Ferrarese once they got to Bologna. He was a good man and would help them to find their way around the city.

'A good man, the Ferrarese?' laughed the older of the two men, a squat fellow with grey curly hair. 'Whoever told you that must have been blind and deaf!'

The other two laughed scornfully and the woman changed position in an unseemly manner, uncovering her legs to some way above the knee. Gerardo looked away.

'There are no good people here,' said the older man. 'Only bastards who will do anything to live another day.'

'It's like that in Ravenna too,' said Gerardo, imitating the common vernacular of the servants at home and sitting down next to them. 'Anyway, even if he is a bastard, I want to meet the Ferrarese.'

All three of the vagrants suddenly went silent. The eldest was stirring the apples in the earthenware pan with a piece of wood. The younger man, who had fair hair, a long beard and who hadn't yet spoken, whispered menacingly, 'No one asked you to sit down. You don't scrounge a meal with your story about the cripple, get it?'

The woman, looking at Gerardo in a way that made him blush, said, 'We only have these apples, and they are for us.'

'Sour apples,' mumbled the beggar with the grey hair. 'You have to cook them until they become mush, otherwise they give you stomach ache.'

'But if you've got something too,' continued the woman, 'you can stay. The Ferrarese will be here soon.'

'Harlot!' exclaimed the young bearded man. 'I know why you're asking him to stay.'

'Go to hell,' she answered, aggressively. In a flash, a shard of broken crockery appeared in her hand. 'Or I'll cut off what isn't any use to you any more.'

The old man chortled. Gerardo and Hugues joined in the laughter, hoping to play down the situation. The blond man looked at Hugues sceptically.

'Didn't you say your friend was deaf and dumb?'

'So?'

'Then why did he laugh, if he can't hear?'

Gerardo sighed, pretending to be exasperated. 'Because he's not blind.'

'What the hell's that got to do with it?'

'He saw everyone laughing and so he laughed too.' Gerardo got up. The conversation was starting to get dangerous. 'We're leaving.'

'Didn't you want to meet the Ferrarese?' asked the woman.

The fair man glared at her and then he looked at Gerardo with open hostility and started to get to his feet. Hugues took on a combat position, slightly bending his knees. The young beggar looked at them both and fell back down next to his miserable fire.

'If you know where we could find him, mistress,' said Gerardo, 'please tell us now.'

'Mistress my arse!' The fair man laughed bitterly, taking hold of the woman by the arm. 'She's a sow, that's what she is.'

'Leave me alone!' shouted the woman, abruptly getting up and hiding behind the two Templars. 'If you touch me, they'll protect me.' Then, turning to Gerardo, 'So have you got anything to eat or not?'

The situation left no alternative. Gerardo only wanted to get away from the three of them, but that would have aroused their suspicion. 'Sure,' he said, feeling the bag and congratulating himself for having looked inside before coming down into the underworld. 'Five sparrows and a piece of bread. Much better than your apples.'

At these words the men's expressions became docile. The older one with the grey hair said, 'Sparrows in apple sauce; exquisite. You certainly can sit down with us.'

'First, I want to know about the Ferrarese,' insisted Gerardo.

'Oh, that pain in the arse,' said the woman, smiling. 'The Ferrarese has been acting strange lately. He spent a whole week down here. Didn't say why. Perhaps someone caught him stealing and he wanted to lie low for a bit. He went out yesterday and when he came back he wouldn't shut up, he said he was going to be rich, that he had a benefactor and he didn't care if it was the Holy Virgin or the Devil in person. He went out early today but he hasn't come back yet. He usually sleeps over there,' she said, pointing at the wall a few yards from them. Then she sighed. 'That's all I can tell you.

194

Now let's sit down and eat. I can't wait to have meat in my mouth again.'

The double entendre didn't escape Gerardo because the woman squeezed his thigh at the same time. He was now desperate to extricate himself from the situation, but Hugues, in his role as deaf and dumb man, was in no position to help him.

'Five sparrows and a piece of bread, did you say?'

The voice resonated behind him, gruff and ominous. Gerardo turned and found the beggar with the rag round his hips standing there.

'What's it to you?' he challenged the vagrant, stupefied by his own quick-wittedness. 'There's not enough for you. There are five of us, if you don't go away immediately we'll slay you.'

The others moved, confirming his words. They were prepared to kill, to protect their supper.

'Five sparrows and a piece of bread,' repeated the man, too furious to be intimidated, 'was what there was in my bag. The one you stole off me,' he said, pointing at it. 'And you're even wearing my clothes.' He turned towards his friends. 'He's the one who robbed me!' he yelled. 'Help me get my stuff back!'

IX

By the time Mondino left the Church of San Domenico it was almost dark. Vespers had just rung. Mechanically, he turned homewards but when he found himself passing a tavern he decided to go in and have a jugful of wine. He had to think clearly and preferred to be alone in a crowd of strangers rather than to go home and have to deal with all the problems that were waiting for him there.

He sat down on a bench at a wooden table that was so massive not even two strong men would be able to turn it over. As he took sips of the white wine from the hills, he watched the furtive coming and going of the occasional rat in the straw covering the floor.

The tavern was full of legal and medical students from various countries who filled the air with their Latin, punctuated with jokes and swearwords in other languages. Mondino recognised the guttural sounds of German and Danish, the French words with the stress on the last syllable, the singsong of Spanish. Thanks to the university, Bologna was one of the liveliest cities in the world. As he sat there contemplating the students, the thought of spending the years to come in the shadow of a secret made every voice and look seem more intense than usual. Mondino stared closely at the smallest detail and perhaps for that reason noticed a man in the throng who, like him, was not joining in with the general merry-making. He was dumpy and muscular, with thick arms and legs protruding from a short grey wool tunic. His large face showed boredom and annoyance at the chaos around him, and yet he didn't seem in a hurry to finish his wine or the bowl of olives in front of him. A couple of times, Mondino saw the man briefly looking over in his direction. Perhaps he was wondering what a physician was doing among that rabble. Mondino took another gulp of wine straight from the jug, because the tavern didn't provide glasses, and went back to his thoughts.

He had two worries: reporting Gerardo and testifying against the Templars. To betray a person who trusted him and who he was beginning to trust was unthinkable, but he could not sacrifice himself and his family to save Gerardo. As far as he was concerned, the Templars could burn at the stake, at least it would mean one less ecclesiastic order.

But the problem hadn't changed. If he declared under oath something that was contrary to science, it meant swearing a falsehood. He could always ask absolution in church for the sin of perjury and do penance. The more serious consequence for him was that he would lose the respect of his colleagues, Italian and above all French. At the School of Medicine in Montpellier they would have a good laugh at his expense. Not to mention the fact that if he were to testify, a dangerous murderer would go free and be at liberty to kill again.

Thinking of the pros and cons, in the false mental clarity produced by the wine, Mondino saw the scales tip clearly to one side. And in the end he made his decision.

He would spend the next two days trying to find the

murderer. He was convinced that he was getting close and if he could discover without a shadow of a doubt who had killed the Templars, Uberto's accusations and threats would fall to the ground.

On the other hand, if he didn't manage to find out, he would give Gerardo time to get out of Bologna, and then he would denounce him as he had been asked to do. He didn't want to, but his altruism didn't stretch to martyrhood.

However, it wouldn't necessarily get to that point. Without wanting to, Uberto da Rimini had given him an important piece of information when he revealed the contents of the letter he had found among Wilhelm von Trier's personal effects. Mondino's suspicion that the two dead Templars had been drawn into a trap was confirmed. Now he just had to find out who had set the bait.

He would have to go back to the sorceress. It was possible that the murderer were a Saracen, given that the map in his possession was written in Arabic. And there couldn't be many Arabs in Bologna. They probably all knew each other. If he were clever, he could get the woman to translate the map and possibly even give him information about the local Arabs at the same time.

At that moment two German students came up to his table. Neither of the two studied with him but they recognised his face and told him how much they admired his work and the courage with which he defied the Church's opposition to anatomical experiments.

Mondino was not in the best frame of mind to receive praise on his courage, but he forced himself to smile. 'I'm only trying to find out about the things in the human body that will one day allow us to understand it,' he said.

Then, so as not to appear pedantic, he offered them his jug of wine. They drank from it with long draughts and then thanked him by singing an irreverent song about a physician who was a charlatan. At the end of every verse they repeated Avicenna's famous words: 'An ignorant physician is the aide-de-camp of death.'

Soon afterwards Mondino paid for the wine and set off home. With the coming of night, the air had got cooler and his fur-trimmed cloak now seemed almost too light. The streets were deserted and his steps produced a slight squelch in the mud of the road. Suddenly he lifted the hood of his cloak and turned round. He thought he could hear steps behind him. But he must be mistaken; there was no one there.

He stopped to listen for a moment, his heart thumping despite himself, and then he walked on in the middle of the road, keeping an eye on the shadows under the arcades to either side of him.

Fear and darkness took him back to what he had done the night before. The awareness of having killed Philomena had never left him, but during and after his meeting with the Inquisitor he had been too busy to think about it.

In his mind's eye he could see himself sinking the surgeon's knife into the old woman's neck and could feel the sensation of the blade cutting through the flesh; flesh that was much more resistant and elastic than that of his corpses.

The woman had been evil and hadn't deserved to live, but he would never have wanted to be her executioner. Of course, if he hadn't reacted, he would have been the one to die, and Philomena would have had no scruples about cutting him up and giving him to the dogs to eat, to get rid of the evidence.

Mondino sighed and, in a low voice, he started to recite a *requiescat in pace* for Philomena's soul, although he doubted if the prayer would do her much good where she was now.

When he turned off Via San Vitale into the street where he lived, he noticed that all the windows were lit up and thought at first that he must be mistaken. At that hour the lamps would normally be out and his father and sons in bed. He went up to the street door and saw that it was ajar. Now worried and on the point of shouting for Pietro and Lorenza, whose job it was to turn out the lights and lock the door before they went to bed, he rushed across the little courtyard that led to the kitchen. The fire was still lit but there was no one there.

Mondino went into the main hall and saw his two servants bending over the big brazier under the window, but before he could say anything, Liuzzo came striding in from the other side of the hall and laid into him: 'Where are you when you're needed? We've been looking everywhere for you. Your father's much worse and the children didn't know what to do, Gabardino came to get me and of course I came immediately.'

Mondino felt himself go white. 'My God, is it serious? I must see him.'

He went to his father's room, followed by his uncle. The curtains of the four-poster bed were open and his three sons were standing in silence around their grandfather. Mondino nodded hello to them, receiving hostile stares in return. Old Rainerio was asleep, and he didn't want to wake him. But from the yellowish colour of his skin and the veil of perspiration that covered his face, it was clear that he was indeed much worse. His breathing was laboured and his body under the cover seemed even thinner than before. Mondino knelt down next to the bed, laid his head on the mattress and began to cry silently, with his eyes closed. No one said a word and for a while all that could be heard in the room was the hoarse breath of the old man.

When he had calmed down, Mondino said a prayer, then opened his eyes and stood up. With a nod of his head towards the door he signalled to Liuzzo that he wanted to speak to him and left the room. Mondino's two smaller sons followed them while Gabardino stayed to watch over his grandfather. In

200

the corridor, Mondino briefly paused next to the vertical loom, covered in a drape since the death of his wife Giovanna. In that house, death was about to claim its second victim. He shook his head silently and went on.

They went back into the hall. Mondino sent the two boys to bed, telling Ludovico to get up and take over from Gabardino at his grandfather's bedside in a few hours. He told Leone to take Ludovico's place at lauds.

Refusing Lorenza's offer to make him something to eat, he sent her and her husband to bed too. Fortunately their daughter had not been woken by all the turmoil in the house.

When they were alone, Mondino asked Liuzzo what he had given his father.

The old physician shrugged his shoulders. 'The usual mixture of hyssop and henbane to help expectoration and relieve the pain. Only this time I doubled the dose of henbane, to allow him a bit of sleep.'

'Have you stopped the hot brick compresses?'

'Only while he's asleep. Then I've told them to carry on. I know they don't do any good, but Rainerio seemed to take some relief from them, and it helps your sons feel they are being useful.'

Mondino nodded. The hot compresses sometimes dried the excess of black bile that caused the tumour, rebalancing the four humours and allowing the patient to get better. But this could only happen in the initial phases of the illness. Now only God could help Rainerio.

'Do you think it's time to call the priest?'

'No. If anything happens suddenly, the Church of Sant'Antonino is right next door. It won't take a second to send for one. But you can't carry on disappearing like this without telling anyone where you are going.' Liuzzo's expression was severe and as he spoke he came up to the great dining table in the centre of the room, without motioning to

Mondino to sit down. He leaned his fists on the wooden table-top and said, 'Now tell me where you've been all day.'

The moment that Mondino was dreading had arrived. Liuzzo would not be satisfied with vague explanations and he certainly couldn't involve him in the problem.

'I can't tell you,' Mondino said, with a sigh. He had neither the strength nor the desire to make up a lie.

Liuzzo took two quick paces to the brazier under the window with the barred shutters and leaned over it as if he wanted to pick it up and throw it at Mondino. But naturally that wasn't his intention. He checked that the brick that had been put there to heat up was well covered by the embers, then he straightened his back and said, 'At my School of Medicine, I do not intend to keep an associate who hides things from me.' He raised a hand to stop his nephew's protests. 'Don't deny it,' he said, in an irritated tone. 'First, you walk out of a graduation banquet making vague excuses. Then you disappear for hours every day without telling anyone where to find you. Now you've begun to come home in the middle of the night. Do you think I am stupid?'

'No, Uncle, of course I don't. You are right in thinking that I am hiding something from you, but I really can't talk about it.'

Liuzzo sighed and returned to the table, his expression a mixture of worry and exasperation. 'While they were out looking for you this evening,' he began, 'a man said he had seen someone wearing a physician's cloak come out of the Priory of San Domenico. Tall, thin and looking nervous. Was it you?'

'Yes.'

'What on earth were you doing at the Dominicans? Please don't tell me that you went to visit a patient.'

'No, Uncle, I did not go to visit a patient.'

'Did you go there to speak to the Inquisitor?'

'Yes.'

'Why?'

'I was the first person to examine the body of that German Templar who was killed in Santo Stefano last Saturday. Uberto da Rimini asked me to stand witness at the trial against the Templars. I must declare under oath that it was an act of sorcery.'

'You answered yes, I hope.'

Once again their difference in character prevailed. In his place Liuzzo would have no hesitation.

'I answered no. Uncle, you know perfectly well that sorcery—'

Losing his patience, Liuzzo thumped the table. 'Forget what I know or don't know!' he said, reddening with anger. 'Don't you realise that both because we are physicians and because we are Ghibellines, we must keep up good relations with the Church? Have you thought what it means if the Inquisition owes us a favour? And what does it matter if you believe that it was an act of sorcery or not? The Church wants to dissolve the Order of the Templars and it needs to amass valid pretexts. Since when have you cared about what happens to the priests?'

Mondino, standing on the other side of the table, didn't reply. His uncle had understood the situation perfectly. Liuzzo's political abilities had always enabled him to root out the hidden motives behind people's words and to act accordingly. It was an ability that Mondino, on the other hand, entirely lacked. His stubbornness in always trying to draw out the truth only caused problems.

But he preferred not to tell Liuzzo that, if he did give evidence, it would be he who owed the Church a favour, not the other way round. And if he didn't, he would be arrested and sentenced, with serious consequences for his family and the School of Medicine too.

Disheartened, he thought that he would never be able to

extricate himself from the whole mess in the two short days he had. He stood there in an obstinate silence. When Liuzzo realised that he wasn't going to get a reply, he said, 'I've had the bed made up in the room next to your father's. I shall stay here tonight to look after him because I don't want him left on his own if you suddenly decide to go out on more mysterious business.'

Then he turned on his heel and walked out of the room.

The only man who got to his feet in response to the semi-naked beggar's cry was a small ruffian who had a nasty look about him. Gerardo reviewed the situation. Hardly anyone seemed to want to help his accuser. He was repelled by the idea of fighting a beggar, particularly the one he had hit over the head to steal the man's miserable belongings, but at that point it was the only way to make him shut up.

However, Hugues de Narbonne was a second ahead him. He stepped forward and punched the beggar full in the face, making him topple backwards. He was about to hit the vagrant again when, seeing something out of the corner of his eye, he turned to Gerardo.

'*Heus! Post tergum!*' he shouted.

Gerardo turned round just in time to dodge the bearded man about to knock him on the head with a rock grabbed from beside the fire. Gerardo managed to push him backwards, but then he began to shout: 'Did you hear that? The mute speaks Latin! It's either a miracle or he's not really one of us.'

'Let's get out of here,' said Hugues, in a low voice. And without waiting for a reply he began to run towards the mouth of the tunnel, jumping nimbly in his bare feet over the fires and bodies lying on the floor. Gerardo followed him without hesitating. In the meantime the subterranean hall was transforming itself into a representation of hell. Between the smoke and the fires, the beggars got to their feet, yelling and trying to steal off each other in the commotion. Scuffles broke out all over the place. But a compact group led by the fair, bearded man and the beggar they had robbed began to chase after them.

Hugues ran down the centre of the drainage canal, between the filth and the rats. He was twice Gerardo's age and in bare feet and yet Gerardo had difficulty keeping up with him. They could hear the echoing shouts of the incensed beggars at their backs.

He finally caught up with Hugues at the turn in the tunnel. The Frenchman was puffing, but he hadn't stopped because he was out of breath; he was pushing the beam that held up the walls with all his might.

'Help me!' he yelled.

'But they'll die,' said Gerardo. The idea of saving his own skin at that price appalled him.

Hugues de Narbonne gave him a quick, piercing look. 'They certainly won't die and I can assure you that I'd rather they did,' he snarled, and went on gasping and pushing. 'Now stop behaving like a child and help me. Otherwise that lot will kill us and throw us in the pot for supper.'

What he said had the worrying sound of truth. Rumours about the vagrants' tendency to eat absolutely anything, including human flesh, did not seem exaggerated just at that moment. Gerardo stood beside the Frenchman and began to push the beam with all his strength.

All of a sudden, he saw the bearded man's face appear about four or five yards away. At first the beggar's expression was one of malicious joy but it soon changed to one of terror when he realised what they were doing. He sped up in order to throw himself on them, but in that second the beam finally gave way. Having now lost its support, the precarious wall collapsed, taking a part of the roof with it and completely blocking off the tunnel.

205

'Run,' said Hugues. 'I don't know how long they'll take to clear it.'

They ran on, at a less breakneck speed, until they got to the cascade of rubble that served as the entrance to the tunnel. Outside it was already dark, but the almost-full moon lit their way.

Hugues leaped up the rocks with ease and this time Gerardo kept up with him. As they came out of the gap in the ruined house, they both stopped to get their breath back, only then realising how unhealthy the smoky and fetid air had been below ground. Then something, perhaps instinct sharpened by years of warfare, made the Frenchman turn round suddenly.

'Get down!' he shouted, jumping back down the hole.

Without stopping to think, Gerardo automatically followed him. He fell raggedly down between the rocks while three crossbow darts whistled over their heads. From above, they heard the muffled sound of someone swearing.

'It's an ambush,' murmured Gerardo, sitting up with difficulty and massaging his bruised shoulder.

Hugues de Narbonne agreed, still out of breath. 'They were waiting for us.'

'I owe you my life, Commander.'

Hugues shook his head. 'You owe it to your own quick reflexes.'

'Who do you think they are?' asked Gerardo, nodding towards the gap above them.

'I've no idea. First let's try to get out of here, then we'll worry about that.'

It was clear that the men had been waiting for them and that they were used to killing in silence. Apart from the whistle of the arrows and the muffled blasphemy, not even the slightest noise had betrayed their presence. Now Gerardo could hear them having a confab in low voices, hidden behind the pillars of the ruined house.

'Give yourselves up and come out with your hands raised,' said a gruff voice. 'We won't harm you.'

Hugues replied in French. It was a phrase that Gerardo couldn't understand, but which sounded deeply vulgar, above all coming from a monk, albeit a soldier monk. Something like, 'Go and bugger the Devil.'

There was silence from above them, probably because Hugues had spoken in a foreign language; but they could now hear the beggars' angry voices in the tunnel. Their pursuers must have already cleared a way through the fallen debris and it wouldn't take them long to widen it in order to get through.

On one side were the beggars, on the other, the archers. There was no way out. Gerardo turned to look at Hugues de Narbonne and only then saw, in the light of the moon, the blood staining his hair.

'You're hurt,' Gerardo said.

'It's nothing,' replied the Frenchman. 'I just hit my head on a rock.'

Then his knees buckled and he fainted.

Gerardo caught him just in time to stop him from falling face down on the ground, and leaned him against a boulder. The voices coming from the tunnel were becoming more distinct. Soon the beggars would be upon them.

Gerardo was sweating. He was alone and he had to decide whether to die at the hand of the beggars or to try his luck with the arrows in a desperate attempt at escape. Quietly, he clambered up to the top of the rubble, but as soon as his head emerged into the half-light an arrow whirred past his ear. He crouched down instantly.

At that moment he heard a cry of pain. One of the archers had been hit. But by whom? He raised his head slowly and saw two shadows emerge from behind the safety of a column and go up to something on the ground behind them. It was his moment and there wouldn't be another. Shaking with courage and fear, Gerardo pulled out his dagger and leaped forward.

Mondino sat at the table in the hall for a long time. Suddenly he heard a noise coming from his father's room and thinking that the old man must have woken up, he went in on the tips of his toes. When he saw what was happening he couldn't control his anger.

'Lorenza!' he hissed.

The woman was talking quietly to Gabardino and in her hands she had a wooden cup full of milk. Hearing his tone of reprimand, she turned round guiltily, her face scarlet under the white cap that covered her hair. Mondino signalled to her to join him in the kitchen and there he told her off harshly for disobeying his orders. Still holding the cup in her hands, Lorenza burst into tears and Mondino's fury immediately vanished, a deep sadness taking its place.

'I told you not to give milk to my father,' he said, 'because milk encourages the production of damp humours which he already has in excess.' Perhaps by trying to explain the reason for his orders in simple terms, it would be easier for the woman to respect them. 'In short, giving him hot milk could hasten his death.'

'This milk is different,' she murmured, head bowed, but in a stubborn tone nonetheless. 'And he likes it so much.'

Mondino's voice immediately lost its understanding tone. 'Do not question my orders. If I find you giving milk to my father again, you will be driven from this house. Do you understand?'

Lorenza nodded twice without raising her eyes, then asked meekly if he'd like something to eat. Mondino dismissed her with a brusque wave and she left the kitchen. To tell the truth, his stomach did feel rather empty but he knew quite well that it was not hunger. It was a nervous impulse brought on by anxiety. Instead of eating or trying to get some rest, he decided to watch over his father's slumber and let his elder son go to bed.

Sitting on an uncomfortable chair that he had brought in from the hall, Mondino was amazed that he didn't feel like sleeping after the accumulated tiredness of the past days. However, he was tormented by a sense of guilt. His father was dying and he couldn't be near him. His children needed a guide at that delicate moment, an authoritative presence that would help them to accept the mystery and reality of death, and he was always away. And the worst thing was that he couldn't explain the reason for his absence.

Perhaps to escape the pain or perhaps because the scientific part of his brain was destined always to take the upper hand, he began to think about Rainerio's illness. He had seen plenty of tumours in the dead bodies he studied. Lumps of organic material that genuinely resembled crabs clinging to the organs and bones, justifying the term 'carcinoma' coined by Hippocrates from the Greek *karkinos*, crab. Sometimes they were compact and well defined; sometimes they spread, sending out fistulas or metastatic branches to the organs nearby. Then the cancer looked more like a malign octopus. In those cases there was nothing to be done besides praying for a miracle. However, when there was no metastasis, Mondino believed that there was a possibility of surgical intervention. He had carried out the operation on cadavers and had often been successful, managing to isolate and remove the carcinoma without damaging the vital organs.

The problem was in the fact that you couldn't open the body of a live man as you could a dead one because the operation would kill the patient. Mondino was convinced that one day internal surgery would be possible but much depended on the better understanding of the mechanisms of the body.

Take the blood, for example. Galen taught that there were

two types of sanguinary circulation, that of the veins and that of the arteries. The idea was confirmed by the observation that the venous blood and the arterial blood were different shades of red. But as for the idea that the left cavities of the heart received blood from the right, in his dissections Mondino had never found evidence of the tiny holes in the interventricular septum or of the 'wonderful network' described by Galen.

But what if the arteries and the veins were in some way linked by other veins that were as thin as hairs, so small that they escaped observation altogether? And what if such a link could allow the closure of one or more veins without cutting off the circulation of the blood?

Perhaps that was the mystery that represented the key to attempting internal surgical operations in the future. It had been the deciding factor that drove Mondino to help Gerardo without thinking of the consequences. But now those consequences had come back to haunt him and there was no getting away from them.

Mondino put a hand in the inside pocket of his tunic, where he had kept the map from the day that he had removed it from the German's body. Unlike Hugues de Narbonne, he was convinced that it had something to do with the secret of the heart of iron. He pulled out the little rectangle of parchment, unfolded it and looked at it long and hard. The three colours of ink – black, white and red – alluded to the three phases of the alchemical process: dissolution, coagulation and union. The green and red lions in the bottom corners represented the beginning and end of the process. The sun and moon at the top stood for gold and silver, the incorruptible metals, but also mercury and sublimated sulphur.

These meanings had been clear to him from the first time he had set eyes on the map. But however much he tried, he couldn't understand the message. He was convinced that the key to reading it was hidden in the Arabic script and he didn't trust Hugues de Narbonne's interpretation of them. Mondino knew various priests who would be capable of translating from the Arabic, but at that moment the last thing that he wanted to do was to put the map in the hands of a cleric who could testify against him later. The only other person whom he could ask for a translation was Adia Bintaba, the sorceress. He hadn't liked the imperious manner in which she treated him, but if he wanted to understand the message, he would have to swallow his pride. He would pay her another visit and he hoped not to find her on the point of going out again.

Exhausted, Mondino put the map back in his pocket and closed his eyes. He didn't want to sleep, but his thoughts began to become entangled, interweaving with images that had nothing to do with the map or the Inquisitor's bribe. One of the last things that he saw before dozing off where he sat, while old Rainerio continued his restless sleep in the bed, were the dark eyes of the sorceress, looking at him with an ironic expression.

The light of the moon coming in from the entrance hall and through the cracks in the ruined house allowed Gerardo to pick his way over the uneven ground and creep right up to his aggressors.

There were three of them. One was lying on the ground, the other two standing. They were wearing short swords at their sides and carried crossbows, and they had their backs to him.

By pure instinct, Gerardo went up to the one who was closest to him and grabbed his collar with one hand, as he had done many times in training. But this time, instead of just miming the action of slitting the man's throat, he plunged in the knife and pulled hard to the side.

The man collapsed with a horrible gurgle and his accomplice quickly turned round. He had just let fly an arrow towards a shape crouching in the dark about ten yards away and knew that he would not have time to reload the crossbow. Instead he threw it at Gerardo and unsheathed the weapon at his side.

Gerardo jumped sideways and the crossbow glanced off his shoulder. He looked at his enemy and knew that he was going to die. The man in front of him was taller, had a larger frame and carried a sword against his dagger.

But if he were already dead, then he had nothing left to lose. There was no need to be afraid. He studied the man, ignoring an indistinct sound that he couldn't quite identify at that moment.

Suddenly his adversary stepped on a loose stone and lost his balance. He didn't fall over, just moved his sword arm to the side a bit, and only for a second.

Before he even saw his chance, but anticipating the man's movement, Gerardo darted forwards, planted the knife under the man's ribs and grabbed the wrist of his sword arm with his free hand. The man fell to his knees. Before Gerardo could ask himself if he should finish him off or leave him alive, a sword fell on to the archer's forehead, splitting it in two.

Gerardo turned quickly. There was Hugues de Narbonne, with his curly hair full of blood and a staring expression. In his hand was the sword of the man whose throat Gerardo had cut.

'Well done, lad,' he said. 'Excellent work.'

His voice didn't seem to belong to him either. It was as though it came from a long way off.

'Do you feel all right, Commander?' asked Gerardo, while Hugues dropped the sword and knelt down to pick up the dead man's crossbow and arrows.

'No, I'm not feeling at all well,' replied Hugues. 'Go and see who that is over there,' he said, pointing at the dark shape groaning in the shadows. 'And finish him off. Meanwhile I'll welcome our friends.'

Only then did Gerardo realise that the noise behind him was the sound of the beggars about to burst out of the tunnel. Hugues loaded the crossbow, with an effort that made him grit his teeth, let the arrow go and the first of the beggars who had emerged from the gap in the ground fell back with a stunned cry.

Silence returned to the ruined house.

Gerardo hurried over to the shape lying in the dark just outside the entrance of the house. He recognised the wheeled board and stick legs of Bonaga, the little cripple. He had a dart stuck into his shoulder and another in his stomach. Although still alive, he had little chance of making it. He was crying and moaning softly, with his catapult gripped tight in his hand. When he saw Gerardo, he tried to speak, but the Templar put a finger to his lips.

'Thank you for your help,' Gerardo said. 'Don't worry, we'll get you out of here.'

He moved the little cart out of the shadows, trying to work out if he could carry the boy to Mondino's house and still avoid being caught by the beggars.

'I betrayed you,' Bonaga managed to stutter in a small, shaky voice. He smiled weakly. 'Then I regretted it. But I didn't know they wanted to kill you.'

He was about to say something else when his smile changed into an expression of absolute terror. Gerardo quickly turned round but he was not in time to stop the blade that hit the boy's forehead, splitting his head in two just like the archer's.

'Commander, no!' shouted Gerardo, almost crying. 'He saved our lives!'

'And what were you going to do, leave him for the rabble that are about to turn up?' replied Hugues, still sounding distant. 'Or did you think you could make your escape dragging him along behind you?'

Gerardo was horrified. He looked at the body of the poor

boy that had shown him the beggar's hideaway for ten soldi
and he felt his heart tighten. Blood was pouring out of the
crack that divided the mop of hair in two. Bonaga had died
instantly. If he had stayed put in his corner and kept quiet, no
one would have seen him. But he had wanted to help them,
and had lost his life at the hand of one of the two people he
had saved.

Gerardo shook his head, trying to hold back the tears, but
without success. To kill your enemy was one thing. To kill a
friend was betrayal. And no secret knowledge could justify an
act of that sort. For the first time it occurred to him that he
had made a terrible mistake in trusting Hugues de Narbonne.

'He was about to tell us something important,' he said,
aghast. 'He said that he had betrayed me, then that he had
repented.'

The Frenchman didn't seem to give the matter any importance. 'Well, it's too late to ask him now,' he said, cynically.
Then, seeing the expression on Gerardo's face, he added, 'He
was done for, don't you see? I only shortened his suffering.'
Hugues winced and let the sword fall, putting a hand to his
head. Then he stumbled, but this time Gerardo didn't hold him
up. Hugues started groping around as if he couldn't see very
well and eventually found Gerardo's shoulder. 'Take me home,'
he said, in a whisper. 'I can't stand up any longer, and that lot,'
pointing towards the gap in the rubble, 'will be on us as soon
as they realise that there's no one threatening them with a
crossbow.'

X

Mondino woke with a jolt and couldn't immediately understand where the noise was coming from. Then he realised that someone was knocking at the street door and he got up hurriedly to go and see what was going on. He came out of the kitchen and walked briskly across the courtyard. Before opening the heavy door, he asked who it was, but he knew already.

'Magister, it's me, Gerardo. Please open the door.'

Mondino opened up. The street was immersed in silence. The bells for lauds hadn't rung yet, but the dark of the night was already beginning to pale. His ex-student seemed tired in the uncertain light. His hair was scruffy, his eyes bloodshot and there was a nasty smell on him as though he had been rolling in dung.

'What is it?' asked Mondino, darkly. 'Do you know what time it is?'

'Master, you must come with me. The Commander has been hurt and is delirious.'

'Hurt? By whom?'

'He hit his head.'

Mondino asked what had happened, but Gerardo simply said that Hugues had fallen into a deep sleep and he couldn't wake him up.

'My father is dying,' answered the physician. 'I can't leave his side to come and treat that Frenchman.'

Gerardo sighed. 'I understand, Magister. But in his delirium the Commander spoke of blood and iron. And of a dead man …'

Still befuddled by sleep, Mondino leaned on the doorjamb while the meaning of the words sank in. 'You mean,' he said slowly, 'that the murderer we are looking for is Hugues de Narbonne?'

Gerardo moved his head in a manner that was neither negation nor affirmation. 'That's what I want to find out. But he's got to be woken up first.'

Mondino left the young Templar there in the street, waiting in front of the open door. He went back into the house, up to his room, put some instruments that he might need into a bag, took an ointment and some pieces of silk and linen, and then changed his clothes. For what he had to do it was better not to be too recognisable. He took off his robe and put on a pair of grey breeches and leather boots, and over his shirt a brown knee-length tunic leaving much more freedom of movement than the almost floor-length ones that he usually wore.

He put on a light cloth cap that matched the grey of his breeches, quickly glanced at himself in the silver mirror hanging on the wall and then went back down to the kitchen.

While he was getting ready to go out into the courtyard, he sensed that there was someone behind him. He turned round quickly and saw Liuzzo at the hall door, in nightshirt, cap and felt slippers. He was watching Mondino fixedly without saying a word.

'Uncle, I've got to go. There is a wounded man who needs my help.'

'Then I'll go. You stay with your father. Today might be his last.'

Mondino felt the full weight of that sentence. Liuzzo was right and yet he had to go. The stakes were too high: it was a question of his freedom and that of his family. In that moment he felt himself hate his uncle for cornering him like this.

'No, I must go,' he said, between gritted teeth. 'I can't explain, but ...'

'I am tired of you telling me that you can't explain!' replied Liuzzo, without moving from the doorway. 'Tell me what is more important than watching over your father in the last hours of his life, for God's sake!'

The blasphemy was so utterly out of place coming from Liuzzo that Mondino was momentarily speechless. He shook his head slowly, then said, 'I will not be able to take my lesson today. Please would you take my place, Uncle.'

'Certainly I can take your place, don't worry about that. But not only for today. From now on! If you go out of that door without telling me where you are going and why, you can consider our collaboration at an end.'

Mondino bowed his shoulders, he turned towards Gerardo who was waiting outside in the street, and went out in silence, closing the door behind him.

A phase of his life had ended. Everything was beginning to fall down around him.

Guido Arlotti congratulated himself on not giving in to the desire to go home to bed. If he had done so, he would have missed a piece of good luck. A physician of Mondino's fame did not wander around seeing patients at dawn, unless it was a case of extreme gravity.

Or illegal business.

He followed them at about twenty yards, being very cautious. The physician had highly acute senses, and the night before he had almost caught him. Mondino seemed to think he was being followed now too because as he crossed the city he looked over his shoulder a couple of times. But now Guido knew what he was up against so there was no danger of being spotted. He walked under the arcade that was still in darkness, moving warily from one column to another.

A noise made him suddenly turn round, automatically clenching his hands into fists. At night it was always better to walk down the middle of the street, like Mondino and his companion. You had to watch out for muddy puddles, horse dung and the uneven surface of the road, but at least you avoided nasty surprises leaping out of darkened doorways or from behind the columns of an arcade. In the space between two columns, Guido heard a sound: the rustle of cloth followed by a hurried panting. He unsheathed the dagger that he carried hidden under his tunic and leaned round the pillar to have a look. He could make out an indistinct shape in the dark that on closer investigation revealed itself to be two bodies clutching one another. A man and a woman with ripped clothes; two vagrants with no home to go to at night had nonetheless found the time and inclination to dedicate themselves to the pleasures of the flesh.

Guido relaxed and went on, taking up his furtive pursuit again. In the hotchpotch of the streets in the centre of town, the two men always chose those that were wider and better lit. They talked with their heads close together and Guido would have given a golden florin to hear what they were saying, certain that the Inquisitor would give him twice as much in turn. But unfortunately he couldn't get close enough and had to resign himself to sneaking among the few remaining shadows while the walls took on the pink tinge of dawn. Mondino and his companion crossed the silk weaver's arcade, turned into the fishmongers' and then the key-makers' road, appropriately named Keyholers. The first artisans were beginning to open up their shops, calmly bringing out their wares. The poor who had slept under the arches got up in a hurry before someone arrived to move them on. Guido gave a sharp kick to a boy who took hold of him by the hem of his tunic, asking for charity, and then he shot behind a column. Mondino certainly wouldn't have heard the beggar boy's shout, or if he had would have assumed it was a quarrel between the dispossessed.

He emerged from his shelter when the two had already turned the corner and hurried after them. First they went south towards San Niccolò of the Vines, where the Basilica of San Domenico was slowly taking shape. Then they turned east. They crossed the bridge over the Savena and went into the neighbourhood of the paper-makers, who were pulling out large bundles of cotton paper to sell to students and notaries for their notes, and piles of parchment leaves divided according to quality and whiteness, held down by pebbles from the river to stop the wind carrying them off.

It was the worst time of day to be shadowing someone, thought Guido furiously. He didn't have the cover of darkness and there weren't enough people out on the streets so he could get lost in the crowd. On the contrary, the few people around might notice a man dashing furtively from one column to another and try to stop him. He decided to change tactic and adopt a relaxed pace, pausing every so often in front of a stall, exchanging the odd word with an artisan or shopkeeper, and turning away from Mondino and his friend whenever he could.

In the end the two men stopped at a relatively modest house, perhaps the home of a small tradesman or a successful artisan. The younger man opened the door with a large key that he took out of the pocket of his tunic and they went in.

Guido quickly noted that all the shutters were closed so he wouldn't be able to peer through to see what they were up to.

He found a spot from where he could keep an eye on the front door and settled down to wait. If they opened a window, he would go closer to hear what they were saying, otherwise it was pointless running any more risks.

The house was immersed in darkness and, before going inside, Mondino waited while Gerardo lit a candle in an earthenware candlestick. Stepping over the threshold, he saw in the flickering light of the wick that the kitchen had been left in complete disorder. Every single object – plates, jugs, pans, crockery, chairs and cloths – was somewhere other than its proper place. It seemed as though someone had been having fun emptying the cupboards but without actually using anything.

Gerardo placed the candle on the chimneypiece and confirmed the fact.

'It was me,' he said. 'After putting the Commander to bed I was looking for something to eat, but I couldn't even find a bit of stale bread. Oh, by the way, there are no servants here, we don't have to whisper.'

Mondino nodded. 'Take me to him. Is he in the bedroom?'

'Yes. But first we must finish our conversation.'

'What conversation?'

In fact Mondino knew very well to what he was referring. Along the way, the physician had told him about the meeting with the Inquisitor and what it implied.

'Magister,' said Gerardo, in a serious tone. 'You can't do that to me.'

Mondino felt a dull rage rise in him. 'What can't I do? Who was it that knocked on the door of my *Studium* with a corpse in tow? If I am in this situation, it is entirely due to you. Besides I'm not saying that I will send you to your death. If I am forced to denounce you, I will let you know beforehand so that you've got time to get away. After all, it doesn't change much for you. You are already a fugitive from justice.'

Gerardo was standing next to an oak table, on which stood a huge copper basin surrounded by a set of plates and other tableware. At those words he picked up a wooden spoon and started brandishing it like a weapon. For a second Mondino was afraid that he was going to set upon him, but the young man only used the spoon to beat it against the palm of his hand while he was speaking.

'I am wanted as a Templar monk and as a probable arsonist,' he said. 'The fire is difficult to prove and in less than a month, if the trial came to an end with the acquittal of the order, I might even be able to go back to living as a free citizen. Whereas, after your testimony I shall be a murderer on the run. I will no longer have home or friends, I will have to emigrate to a distant land, change my name and rebuild my life from scratch.'

'You should have thought of that before dragging me into this affair.'

'You can't say that!' said Gerardo, beating the ladle against a tin plate with a dry clang. 'If you didn't want to help me, you should have said so that night. If you denounce me now, it will be a betrayal, just like that of Hugues.'

Mondino jumped forward, knocking the castle of tableware with the bag that was slung across one shoulder and making the two wooden bowls precariously balanced on top fall off. 'Don't you dare liken me to a murdering bastard who happily killed a poor cripple whose only mistake was to want to help you,' he said, grabbing Gerardo by the folds of his tunic. 'It is true that I decided to help you that night, that I killed that old hag and that I decided to come with you now, leaving my father on his deathbed. I know very well that I didn't have to do it, and I take full responsibility.'

He stared at Gerardo who simply nodded, without trying to free himself. Mondino got his breath back and added, 'The Inquisitor was very clear: he needs a culprit quickly to use as leverage in the trial against your order. If I don't accuse you, then he will accuse me of the murders. It was me who paid the gravediggers to get rid of your confrère's body. They only saw me, not you. It was me again who first examined the German's body. It will be easy to deduce that I did it to hide the proof of my guilt. If you believe that I would be prepared to be put to death in order to save you from having to leave the country and being forced to work for a living, you are making a big mistake. Now take me to him.'

Gerardo gently put the spoon back in the copper basin, took the candle from the shelf and walked out without speaking. As soon as he was outside the kitchen he said, 'At least promise that you will only denounce me if we don't find the real murderer.'

Mondino had no difficulty replying. 'I promise you. If Hugues de Narbonne is the murderer, as you suspect, your order will suffer anyway, but we'll both be safe.'

Gerardo nodded gravely. 'I understand, Magister,' he said. 'When one can do no more for others, it would be stupid not to think of saving one's own skin.'

'Let's get on with it. Remember that we've only got until sunset tomorrow.'

In the light of the flickering candle, they walked past a small room with a table and chairs. The entire house was in chaos, not only the kitchen.

They went into the bedroom in which there was a tatty four-poster bed that had lost its curtains. Gerardo put the candle on a poplar chest of drawers and went to open the shutters and pull down the linen blind. The room filled with a milky light.

Hugues was lying on the bed awake, looking at them.

It was strange that he didn't say anything when he saw them come in, or even acknowledge the fact in his face. Mondino noticed the vitreous expression. He went up to the bed and passed his hand in front of Hugues' eyes. The Templar blinked, but apart from that he didn't move a muscle. Mondino spoke to him, touched him and even shook him, without managing to wrench him from his vegetative state. The physician tried to prick him on the arm with the point of a surgical knife and Hugues quickly drew his arm way, but without changing his expression. He reacted to stimuli, but was not really present.

'Did you say he hit his head?' asked Mondino, examining him.

'Yes. Initially there was a lot of blood and then it stopped. First he fainted and then he came round. He managed to walk all the way here, but he was raving. It was then that he said the things I told you about.'

'And then what happened?' asked Mondino, signing to him to help sit Hugues up with his back against the bed head.

'I told you. At one point he fainted and didn't come round again. I tried slapping him and throwing water on his face … Nothing had any effect. He was breathing, but other than that it was as if he were dead.'

'Whereas now he's awake, but he isn't reasoning,' said Mondino, almost to himself. 'Let's look at the wound.'

He moved back the hair, which was clotted with dried blood, to reveal a three-inch cut where the skin was swollen and broken. With a razor, he shaved the hair around the wound, then began to press gently with his fingers as Rogerius advised in his book on surgery. Mondino established that the bone had a fissure. The pus would certainly have entered the brain cavity too.

'We need to perform a trepanation,' he said. 'Help me tie him down.'

Gerardo went to get the cords. He tied Hugues's hands and feet to the posts of the four-poster, leaving him in a sitting position. Unfortunately Mondino had not brought a somniferous sponge soaked in an analgesic solution to relieve pain and cause a state of stupefaction. So they had to gag the Frenchman to stop him from crying out. He didn't put up any resistance and probably didn't even know what was going on. Mondino took a small crown saw out of his bag and asked Gerardo to hold the patient's head still.

Despite his almost unconscious state, as soon as he saw the trepan, Hugues began to move and pull at the ropes, trying to shout through the gag.

Mondino avoided catching his eye, took a deep breath and made a brief prayer to God, asking him to steady his hand. He had already carried out operations of the sort before and knew that the possibility of it resulting in the death or irreversible paralysis of the patient was very high. It would take only the slightest inattention, once the point of the trepan had gone through the last layer of bone, for it to sink into the cranium itself. Or if he opened the sides of the fracture too far, they might not close properly afterwards. In that case the patient survived, but only bedridden and needing constant care to avoid the miasma in the air getting into the brain. Sooner or later he would contract a high fever and pass away in extreme pain.

Hugues de Narbonne might well be a murderer, but Mondino intended to operate on him with the same precision he would have used if he had to trepan the cranium of Enrico VII himself. Not only because Hugues would have to survive if he was going to tell them everything that he had been keeping to himself until now, but also and above all out of respect for Mondino himself and his profession. These days, the Hippocratic oath seemed to have fallen into disuse, reduced to a mere formality in this degenerate age, but for him it represented the foundation of medicine.

Finally he turned to face the Frenchman. In the unlikely

event that Hugues could actually hear or understand him, Mondino forced himself to sound calm and authoritative as he said, 'We must trepan the cranium in order to purge it of pus. It will be painful, but afterwards you will get better.'

Hugues gave no sign of having heard. His eyes had gone glassy again and he let Gerardo hold his head still without resistance. When the saw began to bite into the bone he struggled and groaned in pain, then he lost consciousness and his head dropped on to his chest, unintentionally helping the operation.

Mondino made four small holes, inserted a spatula between the edges of the opening and widened it so as to place a strip of silk inside to soak up the pus. He repeated the process several times, each time with a clean strip, until there was no pus left. The blood had begun to flow again from the scalp but by now the operation was finished. Mondino cleaned the wound well with a piece of linen and treated it with an unguent made of myrrh and herbs.

'I've done what I can,' he said, finally. 'But the damage is serious, I don't know whether he'll come round.'

'You mean he might die?' asked Gerardo.

'It depends. If he gets a high fever, he won't survive. Otherwise he might, but it's too early to say if he will ever be able to speak or reason in a coherent way again.'

'When will we know?'

Mondino shrugged. 'An hour, a day, a week ... When there is damage to the brain there is no precise timing and you should know that, considering that I gave a lesson on the subject a couple of months ago.'

The young man glanced at him with a guilty look and Mondino gave a bitter smile. Only nine days had passed since he had discovered Gerardo's true identity and he had thrown himself into finding out the secret of the heart of iron. However, the time when Mondino had given his lessons with

225

no other thought than that of expressing himself clearly now seemed distant as a dream that faded a bit more every time he woke up.

'So what shall we do?' asked Gerardo.

The tired sound of his voice caused Mondino to turn round. He looked at the Templar closely. In the light of day that now made the candle on the chest of drawers redundant, he could see that the youth was exhausted. Gerardo had come close to being killed that night, had killed someone himself and had watched over a wounded man. He had not closed his eyes once. Much like the physician, as it happened.

Mondino could not imagine anything more wonderful than lying down on the dirty palliasse that he had spotted in the room next door and slipping into a restorative sleep, forgetting all the problems that were raining down on him for a few hours at least.

But there was no time to rest.

'I'm going to speak to that Arab sorceress,' he said. 'She lives in the country not far from Bova. I want to ask her to translate the verses on the map.' He pointed to Hugues, who was still tied to the bed and unconscious. 'I don't believe what your commander told us.'

'Ex-commander,' said Gerardo. 'Killing that poor boy was an act that was entirely contrary to our vows.'

Mondino nodded. 'You should carry on looking for the maimed beggar,' he said. 'If he told his friends that he was about to become rich, it's possible that he really does know something. But first I wanted to ask you to go back to Remigio Sensi and get him to give you the names of all the Templars who have arrived in the city recently.'

'Why?'

Mondino was surprised by the question. Gerardo was usually so quick. Tiredness must have dulled his intuitive capacities.

'If it's true that the Templars who were killed had been lured into a trap, it might also be the case that the trap was not laid just for two people.'

'One of the new arrivals in the city might be the next victim,' concluded Gerardo.

'Exactly. We must find out how many and who they are and warn them. We should try to work out who the most likely target is and shadow him discreetly. I can help you with that when I get back, while you look for the beggar.'

'Good idea,' said Gerardo. 'I'll go right now.'

'Don't you want to get a bit of sleep first? It's still early, you could rest until breakfast time.'

'I'd better not. If I have time, I'll sleep in the afternoon.' He turned to Hugues de Narbonne, who might have been asleep or unconscious. Or pretending to be. 'What should we do with him?'

All the admiration and respect that Gerardo had shown the Commander in recent days had left his voice.

'I'll give him a calming potion to make him sleep,' replied Mondino. 'Come back later and check on him, but wait for me before you interrogate him. All right?'

'All right.'

Administering a sleeping draught to a man suffering a cerebral trauma was certainly not an ideal therapy, but it was the only way to make sure that Hugues would rest for the whole morning and that even if Gerardo wanted to contravene his orders and interrogate the Frenchman alone, he wouldn't be able to. Mondino was afraid that the young man lacked the ruthlessness necessary to force his commander to tell the whole truth, or indeed the shrewdness to understand if the man were lying.

They went into the kitchen. Gerardo lit the fire with the embers from the night before and Mondino prepared the decoction in a pottery saucepan, mixing lavender, passionflower and valerian. When it was ready he gave it to Hugues, who in the meantime had opened his eyes, although he still seemed absent. Then they agreed to meet each other there that afternoon, between noon and early evening, and went out leaving him tied to the bed with his head bent forward and his arms apart like a sitting crucifix.

Mondino immediately set off in the direction of Piazza Maggiore while Gerardo paused to lock the door. He hid the key in a gap in the wood below the window and left for Trebbo dei Banchi.

Guido Arlotti saw the young man hide the key and hesitated for a moment. The Inquisitor had given him orders to follow Mondino like a shadow, but also to find out where the student arsonist was hiding. Now, it seemed, the student and the young man who Mondino was addressing as Gerardo were almost certainly the same person. So which of the two should he follow?

What's more, he would have liked to go into the house and have a look around. Judging from what he had heard as he eavesdropped from outside the window, something very strange had been going on in there.

He regretted not bringing any men with him. He had done it so as not to have to split the lucre with anyone. But if his friends had been there to share the work, he would have been able to ask double the money from Uberto da Rimini. And that didn't include the plenary indulgence for his sins that he had been accumulating for a year now, since the last time he'd earned one for a crime of a certain gravity.

Guido had been a monk and he believed in hell and eternal damnation, but some time before he had accepted that he was too weak to resist his passions. So whenever he found himself doing a job for some powerful ecclesiastic, he took the opportunity to ask for forgiveness and the remission of his sins in exchange for light penances. Once he had only had to spend the night on a bed of nettles to be pardoned for murder, a sin that he had committed at the order of the very prelate who had granted him absolution. So it was that Guido remained convinced that he could carry on leading the life he wanted while not paying the penalty. The only thing that terrorised him was the idea of dying in a state of mortal sin. That is, without obtaining forgiveness and being able to repent. But for the moment the possibility of death seemed remote.

In the end he decided to keep to the original plan and follow Mondino. In any case the two of them were to meet again in the afternoon. In the meantime he would try to find a way to get hold of a pair of trusted men who could stick to the Templar and the physician like shadows. In that way he would have time to go and have a look in the house. Then once he had gathered all the information, he would be able to go and report to the Inquisitor.

As the young man walked away in the direction of Santo Stefano, Guido came out from behind the column of the arcade where he had been hiding and set off after Mondino. He had lost sight of the physician, but had heard where he was going so he would have no trouble finding him.

XI

Gerardo left the paper-maker's borough and then passed the Basilica of Santo Stefano and headed for Trebbo dei Banchi. He walked along in a dreamlike state rather than fully awake and he was finding it difficult to think coherently. Particulars of the night before kept coming back to him: the underworld, the beggars and their narrow escape ... At times he saw Bonaga's pained smile transforming itself into a mask of horror seconds before Hugues de Narbonne split his head open like a mature melon.

All of a sudden, he felt a violent shock and heard a shout and a string of curses. Only then did he realise that he had been walking with his eyes closed like a sleepwalker and had bumped into the wheel of a vegetable cart, knocking over the costermonger pulling it along. He apologised and quickly moved on before the man's shouts began to attract attention. He was ready to drop from exhaustion but he had to make it through the afternoon. There were still too many loose ends to tie up, time was short, and the enigmas were growing in number rather than diminishing. It was now clear that Hugues de Narbonne might be a murderer and a traitor to his order. Gerardo still had to find the beggar with a missing hand and he hoped that the great effort of tracking the man down would be worth it. He had to identify the Templars who had arrived in the city and find out which of them might be the next victim.

And then, as if all that weren't enough, there was a worrying problem about which he and Mondino had hardly spoken because they didn't have enough information to form even a vague hypothesis. But the problem remained: who were the archers who had been waiting for him and Hugues de Narbonne outside the underworld? Why did they want to kill them? Who had sent them?

Gerardo had no idea. He imagined that it was Bonaga who had told them they were in the underworld, and this was why he had confessed to betraying them. Shame that he hadn't had time to say more.

There was the strong possibility that once they heard about the abortive assassination attempt, whoever had sent those three men would dispatch others to finish the job off. And all he could do was ask himself when and where the next attack would happen, without being able to do a thing to stop it.

Walking into Piazza di Santo Stefano, Gerardo stopped short when he saw a group of guards emerging from one of the foul-smelling lanes that led to the beggar's tunnel. Behind the guards were two gravediggers pulling a cart on which lay a pile of corpses. Although he knew that the wisest thing he could do would be to walk away fast, Gerardo was rooted to the spot. He stayed to watch while the little cortège passed not far from him.

The archers had been well dressed, with short, light wool tunics over their shirts, wool breeches, good quality shoes and light cloaks that were obviously being used to hide the weapons they'd carried. One of the three, a young man with long dark-brown hair, had been dressed more elegantly than the other two, with a mail and tooled leather jerkin under his cloak. It hadn't however saved him from Bonaga's stone, which had broken his nose, or from Hugues' cracking blow that had almost taken his head off. The passers-by were exchanging shocked expressions, as though they knew them, but Gerardo didn't dare ask who they were.

Catching sight of Bonaga's slight body and bony legs sticking out from under the other corpses, he looked away, deeply shaken. One of the onlookers next to him misinterpreted his gesture and said, 'This city is no longer safe. It's all the fault of the foreign students who come here and behave as if they owned the place.'

'Ah,' said Gerardo dryly, without looking at him.

'You're not one of them, are you?' said the man, as though he regretted his comment. 'I didn't mean to offend, it's only that ...'

Gerardo reassured him with a wave of his hand and moved hurriedly on. Despite all the confusion in his mind, he asked himself if he hadn't quickened his pace simply to bring the job to an end and finally get some sleep. However, he had to admit that, above all, what made him hurry was the hope of seeing Fiamma again while he spoke to the banker.

He arrived at Remigio Sensi's house and immediately saw that something was wrong. The hatch that opened onto the street was closed but that was normal given the hour. Less normal was the fact that the front door of the house was open, while the two armed retainers usually posted there were nowhere to be seen. Then he saw one of them come out of a narrow lane that ran adjacent to the internal courtyard of the house. The other immediately followed and they both appeared worried.

Gerardo stopped them and asked what was going on.

'There's a dead man back there,' said one.

'A vagabond,' added the other. 'The women are very shaken. But that's not the real problem.'

'What is it then?'

The man was about to reply, but his colleague nudged him, pointing to the entrance of the lane with his chin, and he suddenly went silent. Fiamma was coming out of the little lane dressed in her indoor clothes, with her blonde hair escaping from her linen cap on all sides. The white scar on her cheek showed up more than usual in her flushed face.

'Messer Gerardo, thank God you are here,' she said. 'I don't know what to do.'

'What's happened? I heard someone had died.'

In the heat of the moment, Gerardo put a hand on her shoulder to calm her. Fiamma blushed even redder and looked at him hard before stepping away.

'Come and see,' she said, and began to walk towards the lane.

Gerardo hurriedly followed her. The alley was unpaved and on top of the dried mud were layers of rubbish that someone had pushed up against the walls so as to be able to get past. On top of one of the piles lay the body of a human being.

Fiamma stood aside to let him past and Gerardo went forward to have a better look. He immediately recognised the pilgrim's ash wood walking stick and the black cleric's cassock, greasy and frayed. When he saw the left wrist ending in a stump, there was no more room for doubt. It was the Ferrarese. The man was holding his bloody hand tight against his stomach, where he had been stabbed by a knife or short sword. His eyes were open and his teeth bared in a grimace of pain.

'Who killed him?' asked Gerardo.

Fiamma looked at him as though deciding whether she could trust him. 'I have no idea,' she said, dropping her gaze.

'Have you called the guards yet?'

'For a dead vagrant? They wouldn't come. I've sent for the gravediggers. Why are you so concerned about this man?'

'Me? You seemed to be the ones who are concerned. There is great distress at your house.'

Fiamma put both hands to her face in a gesture of desperation as though she had just remembered something terrible. When she took them away, there was a resolute expression in her eyes. Gerardo thought that perhaps she had decided to trust him after all.

'The distress you noticed is not for the death of this man,' said the young woman, on the verge of tears.

'Why is it, then?'

'Remigio has disappeared.'

In order to get to Bova, Mondino had decided to take a barge up the Cavadizzo canal so as to make the journey quicker. He patted the pocket in which he kept the map, keenly hoping that his meeting with the sorceress would not turn out to be a waste of time. He tried not to give in to despair, but could not avoid thinking that his life was plunging towards a chasm. And he couldn't even count on the support of his family. On the contrary, he had to put up with their disapproval in silence, as well as hiding all the anxiety that came from knowing that he deserved it.

It must have been shortly before daybreak and the city was waking up. Mondino could hear the characteristic morning sounds of spitting and the clearing of throats that had always turned his stomach in the past. Now they only reminded him of his father's painful condition. Rainerio suffered from prolonged coughing fits and spat out enormous quantities of mucus that the handkerchiefs on his beside table weren't large enough to contain.

Mondino reached the iron gate in front of the chapel that housed the Apostle's Cross, one of the four placed there by St Ambrose to protect the city almost a thousand years before. Then, following an impulse, he turned sharply into the little chapel. As he went in, he saw someone dash behind a pillar about ten yards off. The person seemed strangely familiar but Mondino didn't take much notice and knelt down to pray. He addressed the Most Holy Apostles of Christ, to whom the cross was dedicated, asking them to help his father to pass away and to forgive his own guilty absence at the bedside. Then he asked St Ambrose to give him the strength necessary to come out of this battle victorious and to protect him from his enemies.

Mondino knew and loved the power of prayer, but he would have wanted a Church that was closer to Christ's teachings and not obsessed with temporal power. This too was probably a dream, like the idea of discovering the secret of the circulation of the blood. Perhaps it was normal for a scientist to be a dreamer; the point was to give the right direction to the dreams. He had let himself be dragged into a mistaken dream and now things were getting out of hand and threatening to overwhelm him completely. He absolutely had to find the murderer of the two Templars. Only then would he be able to avert, at least in part, the misfortunes that were raining down on him.

And he had very little time left.

To calm the distress that had taken hold of him, he quietly intoned the hymn *Te lucis ante terminum* that was normally sung at compline, after sunset. It was the only hymn composed by St Ambrose that he knew, and he found it appropriate to the situation. A dark night full of horrors was about to submerge him, even if it was early morning.

When he left the chapel he felt much better. The sun filled the street and the heaviness that had weighed on his soul just before seemed to have vanished. Mondino leaned on one of the stone griffins at the corner of the railings and breathed deeply, mentally thanking the apostles and St Ambrose. At that moment he noticed a man standing in front of a fruit seller. He had his back to Mondino and seemed to be negotiating the purchase of a punnet of cherries. From his stocky build, Mondino recognised the man that he had seen drinking alone in the tavern the night before. In a flash, he remembered the shape that he had noticed behind him when he came out of the hostelry, and that of the man who had disappeared behind a pillar just before he turned to go into the Chapel of the Cross. It was the same person every time.

He made himself pretend indifference and walked towards the Torresotto at Porta Govese. He was bewildered. The man was definitely following him and almost certainly by order of the Inquisitor. He might have seen him speaking to Gerardo after Mondino had told Uberto da Rimini that he didn't know him. On no account should he see him speaking to the sorceress as well.

What to do?

Without stopping, Mondino began to look around him, searching for a way to give the man the slip. When he got to the Moline canal, just beyond Porta Govese, he should have turned left towards the Cavadizzo, but there was no sense in taking a barge now. It would be too easy to follow him. On an impulse he turned right and followed the canal in the opposite direction, towards the windmills that gave the canal its name.

The closer he got to the market square, the more crowded it became. There were men, women, children and animals clogging up every road leading to the piazza. It was Saturday and the weekly livestock sale was in full flow. Many farmers and shepherds had arrived the night before and slept beside their animals to protect them from thieves. As far as they were concerned there was no reason not to begin buying and selling, so they went ahead without waiting for the official opening of the fair. In any case, the presence of notaries and bankers only served for the more important deals; for one or two beasts it was much easier to agree with a shake of the hand.

Mondino saw a jurist whom he knew walking past, followed by a train of assistants in clerks' clothing, and he stopped to exchange a word or two, taking the opportunity to check on his stalker. He didn't see the man this time, but knew he was there. Then Mondino said goodbye to the jurist and mixed in with the crowd. Now, as often happened with him, fear gave place to anger.

Then it occurred to him that running away was not the only solution. He had not had much time to observe the man following him but he was sure that he was smaller than him, although possibly broader. Perhaps he could get the better of the stalker after all.

Looking around for a suitable place for a fight, he left the busy road and went as close as possible to the edge of the canal, beneath the jerking and screeching of the blades that turned the grain milling machines. There was no one around. When he reached the fifth windmill, familiarly referred to as 'Fantulino, the Little Mill', he noticed a large recess behind a tiled wall. He took a step to the side and hid in the shadows. The only noise he could hear was the roar produced from the vertical wheel in the centre of the canal, held up by a wooden truss stretching between two identical cabins on either bank. With his heart in tumult, he waited for what seemed like an age, but was in reality not much longer than that needed to recite a Pater Noster. Then he heard a footstep close by and a second later his pursuer appeared. Mondino didn't give him time to think. He stuck out a foot and tripped him up. While the man was stumbling and trying to keep his balance, Mondino grabbed him by the shoulders and dragged him over to the shelter of the wall. Before he could interrogate him he had to immobilise the man somehow, but from the way the man was struggling he realised that he had underestimated him. He was short, but extremely strong.

Fortunately the man didn't seem to want to attract attention either. He didn't shout or call for help. Snorting like a bull, he pivoted on one of his stumpy legs and, freeing himself from Mondino's hold, he turned and charged at the physician with his head down. Mondino received a headbutt full in the chest and fell back against the wall. He managed to get out of the way before the man could seize hold round the waist and thumped him on the nape of his neck. They grappled in silence, putting as much force as possible into their punches, both aware that they needed to hurry before someone came along. Suddenly Mondino felt himself being bitten on the neck, then he gradually began to run out of steam. Somehow, in the midst of the struggle, without intending to, he planted a finger in the other man's eye. His aggressor let out a strangled cry and let go, covering his face with both hands. Mondino took a run up and bundled him like a sack to the edge of the canal.

The man stuck his feet in but didn't manage to put up enough resistance. He tried to catch hold of Mondino by the hair, but only got his cap. Stumbling against the low parapet wall, the stalker's knees buckled and a second later he fell into the water with a splash. He stood up almost immediately, dripping wet and furious, and began to wade towards the bank, his eyes alight with a ferocious determination.

Two men on the other side shouted and jumped into the water, not to help the man but to catch Mondino, who they had obviously taken for the villain. Another two people ran towards the bridge just ahead to cut him off. If they caught him, they might even kill him. It was not infrequent that thieves were lynched by citizens and came before the judge either dead or as good as. Mondino turned and began to run between the houses, vines and orchards, knowing that his lungs wouldn't hold out for ever.

When Guido Arlotti climbed out of the canal he was just in time to catch a glimpse of Mondino's spare form disappearing behind the wall of the house, already a good distance from his pursuers. If they managed to catch him, Guido hoped that they'd give him a good going-over before bringing him back to the windmill.

Boiling with rage inside, Arlotti told his rescuers that the man had tried to rob him, but fortunately hadn't succeeded. Perhaps they'd noticed how Mondino was dressed? He certainly didn't look like a common pilferer. Guido said that he, Mondino, was a penniless student who had resorted to crime to pay his debts. But the others didn't seem to think it mattered much. They asked if he was all right and Guido thanked them and accepted the offer to go into the windmill to get dry and wait for news. But first he gave a coin to a boy and told him to go and fetch two men from the tavern that he used as a base in Borgo di Galliera, which luckily was not far away. He promised the boy another coin if he brought them back in good time.

The windmill was small and full of people. There were clients bringing sacks of grain to mill, others who came to buy flour from the miller's wife and people who were just dropping by to talk about the weather and the price of goods, which gave no sign of dropping. The miller lent Guido a spare tunic and his wife, a plump blonde with a generous bosom, went to hang out his clothes in the sun to dry. Guido had to repeat his story an infinity of times: the attack, the fight, his fall in the canal and the crook's escape.

He smiled and thanked them for their help, but inside he was beside himself with fury. When the crowd finally tired of his tale, he retired to a corner to wait for his accomplices and to plot his revenge. Even if the people running after him didn't catch Mondino, he would find him and make him pay for what he'd done. In fact he rather hoped they didn't catch him. After all, he knew where to find him.

It had now become a personal issue.

*

Mondino was now sure that the men trying to catch him had abandoned the chase so he slowed down to a normal pace, then he stopped to get his breath back, leaning on the wall of a house. He was exhausted. That sort of exercise made the blood too hot and burned the lungs, but also produced a pleasant feeling of euphoria. Alternatively, he thought, perhaps it wasn't the exercise that produced it, but the satisfaction of having fought and come out on top. He was certain that the man would come after him again, after all, he must know exactly where he lived. But it didn't matter. On the following evening, the time the Inquisitor had conceded to him ran out and one way or another the question would be resolved. At that point even the spy would go back to his master. Right now the important thing was to have got away. Mondino wanted to ask for the translation of the map as quickly as possible and then get back to Hugues de Narbonne's house to see how he was. He had decided that if the Frenchman was conscious, he would interrogate him before Gerardo got there.

Mondino crossed the Circla paling near the postern of Borgo di San Pietro, passed a wool-fulling mill and cut left through the fields, still following the canal that ran parallel to the city walls towards Porta delle Lame.

There were more people around than last time, perhaps because it was a Saturday, and this made it easier to pass unobserved. From early in the morning, the traffic was almost all moving in the direction of the city. For the most part they were farmers and artisans heading for the market on foot or with hand-pulled carts. Every now and then someone walked or trotted by on a horse.

Since he now knew the way, it took him less time to get to the sorceress's house than he had thought. No one came out to greet him this time either, but as soon as he shouted her name the woman called for him to go in. Mondino went forward cautiously, however the dogs were nowhere to be seen. He reached the door, pushed it open and stood on the threshold, transfixed by surprise. The single room, made up of kitchen, study and bedroom, was much bigger than the outside walls suggested and it was well lit. The place was full of a seemingly immense quantity of objects and yet order reigned supreme. It was not a conventional order, thought Mondino, taking in the piles of books that made towers and columns across the floor, the clumps of medicinal herbs hung to dry head down in a corner, the shelves full of terracotta and glass jars, the Arabic alembic and numerous copper and wooden objects for which he couldn't imagine the use. But the general impression was that the owner, bent over the pages of a great volume that was open on the table in the centre of the room, would immediately be able to put her hand on anything she needed. Mondino had never been inside a sorceress's house before but he had imagined it quite different.

'Come in, do,' she said, looking up. 'You've returned. So I imagine you will be more polite this time.'

Mondino made a slight bow that could be understood as a greeting or an affirmative response. He went in and stopped in the middle of the room. The woman closed the book, smiled and seemed to remember her own good manners. She gestured regally towards the only bench in the house, at one of the long sides of the table, and added, 'Sit down, please. You haven't yet told me who you are.'

Mondino said that he was a scholar from the *Studium*, using the name of one of his students. The woman gave him a sharp look and then introduced herself too: 'Hadiya bint Abi Bakr, at your service. But you may call me Adia Bintaba like everyone else.' She sat down on the bench at an easy distance from him. Then she added, quite naturally, as though they had only left one another minutes before, 'You mentioned a map.'

Mondino hurriedly took out the parchment, without talking

of money this time. If the woman wanted payment for the translation, she would have to ask him for it.

Adia looked at it carefully. 'The Arabic sentences are verses alluding to a marriage,' she said, confirming Hugues de Narbonne's opinion. 'But they are incomplete, as though some words were missing. Written like this, they don't make sense. As for the map itself, the characters between the two lions indicate something red, which seems strange to me.'

'Why?'

'Because there's no point in writing "red" under the red circle. It must mean something else.'

'Could it be a place in Spain?'

Adia's face lit up. 'But of course. The red fortress in the city of Gharnata that you call Granada. It probably indicates the point of departure, while the red circle at the top that has no writing next to it represents the point of arrival.'

Hugues de Narbonne had been telling the truth. Mondino slumped forward, putting his elbows on his thighs and his head in his hands. To say that he was disappointed did not do justice to his state of mind at all. Only then did he realise that he had doubted the Frenchman's word on purpose, to cultivate the dream that an important message was hidden in the verses. But they really were meaningless words and if they were hiding anything, it was directions to reach a place in Spain.

'Are you absolutely sure? I mean, you know, this map has got something to do with alchemy—'

'Really?' she interrupted him, with the same indecipherable expression in her eyes. 'So perhaps you are about to suggest that the marriage to which the verses refer is that between mercury and sulphur, the metallic and inflammable principles of matter. Have I guessed right?'

'How do you know about such things?' was all that Mondino managed to say.

This woman produced one surprise after another. She didn't talk like a country sorceress. In fact she didn't even talk like a woman.

Adia leaned an elbow on the table and smiled, showing her white, regular teeth. 'I come from a family of alchemists. My father didn't have any sons and so he passed all his knowledge on to me. It's not common, but it happens.'

'But the man who gave me your name spoke of you as a sorceress,' said Mondino.

Adia leaned towards him slightly and Mondino saw that she wasn't actually all that young. She must have been about twenty-five, and yet there was no sign of the presence of a husband or children in the house. Could it be that such a beautiful woman had not found a man prepared to ask her to be his wife? Or perhaps it was she who didn't want to get married? It seemed absurd, but then she was a strange woman.

'People don't trust sorceresses,' said Adia, seriously. 'But they would trust a woman of science much less. I chose the lesser evil.' She smiled again, and it seemed to Mondino that there was the shadow of sadness in her eyes. 'Besides, the title of sorceress keeps the men at bay,' she added. 'The good ones and the bad ones.'

'I see,' said Mondino, in embarrassment, just to say something. 'So if you say that the verses have nothing to do with alchemy, I can believe you.'

Adia Bintaba straightened her back. 'I said nothing of the sort. The fact that there are verses referring to a marriage on a map full of alchemical symbols cannot be by chance. I only said that the verses are incomplete. If we knew the missing words, it would all be much clearer. Have you got anything else? I don't know, a letter, a book ... If you want me to help, you must tell me the truth.'

'This map is all I've got,' said Mondino, shrugging his shoulders.

'And how did you get it?'

'I can't tell you that.'

Adia's expression made quite clear what she thought of his lack of trust without the need for words. 'You can't tell me,' she repeated, in a reflective tone. 'Could you at least tell me what the secret is that you hope to discover by deciphering this map?'

Mondino had not anticipated that question and for a moment he was at a loss. He wanted to put her on the right path in the hope that she would see a link that had passed him by, but he certainly couldn't talk to her about what he had done. He decided to make something up.

'As I told you, I study medicine. Some friends and I are doing research on the circulation of the blood and it occurred to someone that if blood could be transformed into solid metal, we could get a very precise idea of the vascular system. Now, this map—'

'To whom, precisely, did this idea occur?'

Her interruption took him by surprise and Mondino replied, 'To my master, Mondino de Liuzzi.'

'Mondino,' repeated Adia. 'Taddeo's student?'

'That's right,' said the physician, unable to hide his amazement at finding she knew his name as well as that of Taddeo Alderotti. 'Do you know him?'

'Only by name. The man is ignorant.'

The smile vanished from Mondino's face. 'My master is considered one of the best physicians alive,' he replied, curtly.

Adia seemed to be trying not to laugh in his face. She lifted up both her hands to diffuse his protests and said, 'I am not doubting his merits. In fact I have great respect for Mondino's anatomical research and I am looking forward to reading the treatise that he is writing. But as far as I'm concerned whoever makes progress only externally and not internally will remain ignorant.'

'I don't follow you.'

Adia looked at him with an expression of condescension. Then she said, 'Science must develop man just as man develops science', as though it explained everything.

'What do you mean? Be a bit clearer.'

'I will explain in simple words so that you can understand,' she replied. It was obvious that she was having fun at his expense and Mondino felt ill at ease, as if he were the only one in a group of people who didn't get the joke. 'But first tell me something. Why did your master send you and not come in person?'

'He had no idea that you were an erudite alchemist,' Mondino answered, shifting his position on the bench. 'And he thought I could manage to talk to a sorceress on my own.'

When Adia Bintaba looked back at him she was no longer smiling. 'As it happens, I once attended one of Mondino de Liuzzi's anatomy lessons dressed as a man. Now tell me why you have come to my house using a false name, Magister, and what it is you want from me.'

XII

Eventually the boy came back with the two men he had sent for. Guido Arlotti put on his now dry clothes, gave the tunic back to the miller and thanked him. The boy held out a hand, asking for the coin he had been promised.

'I told you that I'd give you another coin if you brought my friends quickly,' said Guido, making short work of the lad. 'Off you go, before I give you a kick in the arse for keeping me waiting so long.'

The customers and hangers-on who were standing around the mill laughed at the boy's forlorn expression and an old man put a piece of bread in his hand as consolation. Guido was already on his way to Porta Galliera, almost at a run. He didn't know how much time the physician would spend with the sorceress and wanted to catch them there together.

'Where are we going?' asked one of his accomplices.

'Beyond the Circla,' replied Guido, without slowing his pace. 'We must find the wretch who pushed me into the canal.'

When he was eavesdropping at the window earlier, he had

heard Mondino talk about a converted Arab sorceress. What 'converted' meant, given that the woman exercised practices that were contrary to the Christian faith, remained to be seen. However, for now, the important thing was that he remembered perfectly where she lived: in the Bova area. There couldn't be many Arabs in those parts.

'Do we kill him?'

'No. The person who's paying me wants him alive. But he didn't specify *how* alive.'

The others laughed. Guido often used them when he needed a helping hand. They were trustworthy, didn't flinch at the toughest job and knew the value of discretion.

'Are you armed?'

The man next to him lifted up the side of his coarse hemp tunic, showing the dagger that he kept hidden under the shirt next to his skin. The other simply nodded.

'There will be a woman with him. A witch.'

He said it to see how they would react. He didn't want them to run off at the crucial moment, terrified at the threat of some witch's curse. The two were silent for a few seconds, then the first asked, 'What's she like?'

'I don't know.'

The other man, who had been quiet until then, smiled. 'Let's hope she's young and soft, and not some shrivelled old harlot. Does she have to stay alive too?'

Guido didn't think that the Inquisitor would object if they had a bit of fun with the witch.

'No,' he answered. 'She's of no use to anyone.'

Thinking about it, Mondino was a problem too, alive. He was an important man, a professor at the *Studium*, and he could report Guido and have him arrested. Arlotti knew well that if there were any trouble, the Inquisitor would not contradict the *comune* judges in order to defend him. It was up to him to save his own skin.

He thought about it for a while, but by the time they arrived at Porta Galliera, he had made his decision. He would kill Mondino too. Then he would tell the Inquisitor that he had been rumbled and had had to defend himself. Uberto da Rimini would be furious, but there wouldn't be much he could do about it and he would just have to accept the fact.

At last a smile appeared on Guido's face. The morning was turning out nice after all.

Adia Bintaba went to the chimney at the end of the room. She took a strangely shaped saucepan that was lying beside the embers and said, 'I was forgetting my duties as the lady of the house. Please, would you accept a drink from my country?'

She poured an amber liquid from the saucepan into two tin cups and returned to the table. 'It's called *atay*,' she said. 'I've heard that it came to Arabia from distant China, centuries past. It's very good for the health, clears the mind and fights the symptoms of poisoning.'

Mondino brought the cup to his lips and tried a sip. 'It's good too,' he said, surprised. 'Thank you. But where were we. I've no wish to seem rude, but the fact is that, for reasons that I can't go into, I have very little time.'

He had told her everything. Beneath her expectant stare, he had admitted who he really was, said why he was there and what he was looking for. He had even told her about Wilhelm von Trier, although without going into too much detail and without mentioning the long list of criminal acts that he had carried out in the past few days. He instinctively trusted the woman, but prudence held him back.

Adia took a sip of *atay*, then another, with obvious pleasure. 'Time is something we must use, not a thing to be used by,' she said. 'Otherwise it becomes a cage. Calm down and listen to me please.'

'I am.'

'You want to know who managed to turn that German Templar's heart into a block of iron,' said Adia. 'The only thing I can tell you is that it is a distorted application of the principles of alchemy. It can bring no good. You must drop it.'

Mondino felt himself blush with irritation. He didn't like her professorial tone one bit. 'I don't agree,' he said, leaning an elbow on the table and looking her straight in the face. 'The application is distorted because it has been used to commit murder, but the scientific knowledge necessary to obtain that transformation is in itself neither good nor bad.'

Adia sighed, as though he were a stubborn child. 'I'll give you an example. Let's pretend for a moment that the aim of your life was to climb to the summit of a mountain, all right?'

'Certainly. Go on.'

'You begin to climb. You suffer from the cold and from hunger. You have to escape from wild animals and brigands. On your way you come across huts belonging to shepherds and woodcutters who offer you hospitality and food. You pay them back by helping with their work and curing sickness since you are a physician, then you say goodbye and go on your way. Until the day when you finally discover that you are at the peak of the mountain. How do you feel?'

'Satisfied, I imagine. But I don't understand the meaning of the story, and as I told you I haven't got much—'

'I haven't finished yet. On the other face of the mountain, there's a man who has the very same objective as you. He begins to climb and to protect himself from the cold he steals some clothes and blankets from the first woodcutter he meets. In order to eat, he kills some sheep, and when he is caught he kills the shepherd too. To combat solitude he rapes the shepherd's widow and takes her with him for a few days, ignoring her pleas for mercy. Then he tires of her, abandons her in the middle of a wood and continues to climb. He meets other shepherds, other woodcutters, and takes something from each of them, often their lives, but without ever giving anything in return. One day he gets to the top of the mountain, at the very moment when you too arrive.' Adia paused, looking him straight in the eye. 'The result is the same, obtained at the same time. But now can you say that the way in which it was achieved is unimportant and that in both cases the aim is in itself neither good nor bad?'

Part of Mondino could not but admire the clarity with which Adia had illustrated her thoughts. But he couldn't stand the fact that she had done it at his expense. He, *magister medicinae* who was famous and respected throughout Italy and even in France, had been made to look stupid by a woman. Out of pure stubborn pride, he refused to reply.

'I am not here to discourse on philosophy, mistress,' he said. 'My original question was a different one. Do you know how it has been possible to make iron out of the blood and veins of a human being? And who might have done such a thing?'

Adia sighed again, almost ostentatiously. It seemed as though she simply wanted to make a fool of him.

'Abu Ali al-Husain Ibn Sina, who you know as Avicenna,' she replied, 'said that the knowledge of something could not be called complete until its causes are known. Do you agree with that?'

'Yes, but what's that got to do with it?'

'I can't tell you much about the processes necessary to obtain the transmutation of human blood into iron and successively into gold, but—'

'Into gold?' broke in Mondino, sceptically.

'Yes, into gold. Aren't you a physician? Then you must know the works of Jabir ibn Hayyan, the man you call Geber, of Michael Scot, Arnaldus de Villa Nova, Albertus Magnus ...'

'Of course I know them,' said Mondino, offended. 'But in the *Studium*, the more modern masters teach their students to take from alchemy only what is useful to medicine, discarding the rest. I personally tried Michael Scot's formula to transform lead into gold and got nothing useful out of it at all.'

'Really?' said Adia. 'And what did you do exactly?'

'I followed his instructions step by step. I took the lead, I blended it three times with lime, red arsenic, sublimated vitriol and sweet alum, and then I immersed it in essence of sea-purslane and wild cucumber. After which—'

'The lead did not turn into gold,' she interrupted. 'And you concluded that the formula was false.'

'Precisely.'

'Well, you are wrong.'

Mondino was beginning to get annoyed. Adia Bintaba might well be a scientist, but she showed the typical feminine tendency not to take facts into consideration, relying exclusively on her own ideas.

'Something cannot be true if experience demonstrates that it is false,' he replied, in a dry tone.

'You really don't understand, do you? You don't see that the result doesn't only depend on the formula, but on the person who is putting it into practice,' she answered, exasperated. 'And yet you are an intelligent man. In alchemy, scientific progress is the mirror of interior progress. An alchemist who has not perfected his personal qualities can follow formula and processes explained in books all he likes. He will never obtain a result.'

Mondino decided that the game had been going on long enough. 'Listen, mistress Adia, I would love to sit here discussing these things with you, but I have already told you that I haven't got time. Have you any idea how someone managed to kill the German Templar in that barbarous fashion, or not?'

Adia burst out laughing and Mondino felt himself flare up.

251

His journey had been fruitless: he had wasted almost an entire morning of the two days he had left and he couldn't sit there acting as laughing stock to that woman.

'I most certainly do have an idea, yes,' said Adia, when she had finished laughing. 'I have been trying to expound it to you, but you won't let me speak.'

'I won't let you speak? That's a bit much.'

The woman looked austere. 'That's enough. I haven't got all day. So either listen in silence or go.'

Mondino's opinion of women scientists was falling rapidly. He wanted to turn and walk out of the house. But he forced himself to relax. He was there now, he might as well listen right to the end.

'Go on,' he said.

Adia gave him an ironic glance. 'As I told you, this mystery will never become clear to you until you make yourself understand the causes. You must know that the way to the House of God, that is the perfection of the soul and the matter sought by alchemy, is not immovable. The point of arrival is always the same, but the paths to get there can be quite different, as in the example of the mountain that I gave you before. The most famous is the one that passes through the transmutation of base metals into gold.' Mondino made as if to say something, but she stopped him with a sign of her hand. 'To obtain such a result does not depend on reading a treatise and applying a formula, as you did. The transmutation of metals is like a scale. The higher the state of perfection the soul has reached, the closer the transmutation comes to success. Do you follow me?'

Mondino nodded and she went on: 'As I told you, it is not possible for an impure soul to obtain perfect transmutation. However, there are those who don't accept this, who want power for power's sake, and who want to create *al-iksir*, what you call "the elixir of long life", by forcing the progressive steps. They make pacts with obscure forces and even if they can't reach perfection, they sometimes manage to obtain some power. For a brief moment they taste the illusion of victory, then inevitably, the power itself turns against them and kills them. To control the forces of nature, you need a soul in harmony with the universe. If the soul is closed, then the forces, once awoken, will crush it like a nut. Not out of wickedness, but because such is their nature.'

'Come to the point, please,' said Mondino.

'I am convinced,' said Adia, 'that the man you are looking for has found a way of bringing human blood back to the First Matter and successively turning it into iron. Then, from alchemical iron, a material that is very different from common iron, he might have managed to obtain gold.'

'But didn't you say that transmutation was not possible for an impure soul?' asked Mondino, now interested despite himself.

'Exactly. As long as the person is not helped by dark powers, as I said before. I think that is the reason for which the Templar was killed. In such a perverse transmutation, death is probably an essential ingredient.'

Adia was talking about black magic tied to alchemy, using more precise arguments than those of Uberto da Rimini, but not dissimilar in substance. Mondino sat there in silence. His scientific mind was rebelling at the idea that such a thing could be possible, but the point wasn't whether he believed it or not. The point was that someone else might have believed it. If that was the case, the two dead Templars were nothing more than the efforts of a perverse alchemist to obtain the transmutation of metals and the idea of a trap or a vendetta fell apart. Gerardo was wasting his time looking for Templars who had arrived in Bologna recently.

More precious time thrown away. He had to get back to Bologna immediately.

Just as he was about to take his leave, the door was suddenly kicked open and in walked three men. Mondino immediately recognised the thickset individual whom he had thrown into the canal. The other two had the faces of jailbirds, which lit up with a deviant light the minute they saw Adia. All three of them were armed with daggers.

'Stay where you are,' said the stocky man, who seemed to be the leader. 'You and the witch are under arrest.'

Gerardo got up from the kitchen table and began to walk up and down under the worried gaze of Fiamma and the scullery maids. He had just drunk the mug of milk that the lady of the house had offered him while he listened to her story and now he didn't know what to think.

That morning, as usual, Fiamma went to wake her adoptive father. She had knocked several times and receiving no reply opened the door of the room. The bed was untouched and her father wasn't there. She looked all over the house without finding him. No one had seen him go out and anyway the front door was bolted from the inside. If Remigio had gone out, he could only have left by the kitchen door that gave on to the courtyard, where they kept the hens and the pig. Fiamma and the two servants had gone to look and as soon as they had opened the door from the courtyard into the alley-way, they had seen the mendicant's body. They were still trying to work out what had happened when Gerardo arrived.

'Do you think that it was your father who killed him?' asked the young man.

Fiamma looked at him warily. 'If he had, it would have been in self-defence. Perhaps the beggar tried to rob him when he saw him come out. Or perhaps my father's disappearance and the death of the beggar have nothing to do with one another.'

The very moment that Remigio Sensi had disappeared

without any explanation, a body had turned up behind his house. Quite by chance it was the body of the man missing a hand that Gerardo had been looking for. The possibility that the events had nothing to do with each other, that it was a mere trick of fate, was practically inexistent.

Gerardo carried on pacing back and forth between the table and the chimney. In a brusque tone, Fiamma gave orders to the girls to start preparing dinner. Perhaps she wanted to keep them occupied or perhaps she was trying to convince herself that everything would soon get back to normal. Gerardo didn't know what to think.

The maimed beggar had told his friends from the underworld that he was about to become rich. He obviously knew something about the German Templar's death and had tried to get himself paid for his silence, but it had all gone wrong. If it was Remigio who had killed him, as everything seemed to indicate, it meant that the banker was involved in the mystery of the heart of iron. Perhaps he was the murderer of the Templars and not Hugues de Narbonne after all. But why had he vanished like a thief from his own house, leaving by the back door?

It was essential to find him as quickly as possible, and not only in order to relieve Fiamma's anxiety. And then what if Remigio and Hugues de Narbonne were in league with each other? Perhaps the banker had gone to Hugues' house after killing the vagrant. It just might be, thought Gerardo. After all, it was Remigio who introduced him to Hugues, and the two had known each other from before. If the Templar had regained consciousness and the banker undid the ropes that held him to the bed, Gerardo and Mondino risked losing every possibility of clearing their names.

All of a sudden, Gerardo stopped pacing and brought his fist down on the table. The three women turned as one, evidently alarmed.

'Forgive me,' he said. 'There's something I must go and find out. Mistress Fiamma, I will do my utmost to help you find your father. Now I must go, but I will be back as soon as possible.'

Fiamma didn't say anything; she simply accompanied him to the street door. The two servants had gone outside and were hanging around not knowing what to do. Gerardo was about to say goodbye when the young woman took his hands in an impulsive gesture. 'Remigio Sensi is not my father,' she said, her face set in a serious expression.

'I know that, mistress, I only said it for brevity's sake.'

Fiamma shook her head and a few more blonde strands of hair escaped from underneath her cap. 'It's not that. I just wanted to say that you mustn't be afraid of hurting or shocking me when you find out what's happened. Do you really think he killed that beggar?'

In the time it would take to say Amen, several different answers flashed through Gerardo's mind, but in the end he decided to be truthful.

'Everything would point to that, mistress. Still, we must try not to jump to conclusions. First, we must find him.'

At that moment they both realised that they were still holding hands. Embarrassed, they pulled apart and without another word Gerardo walked away, his heart in tumult.

He could feel Fiamma's eyes on his back, but he didn't give in to the temptation to look back. He thought confusedly of his vows. Perhaps he could give up the monk's habit and marry. But even if he did, he could never ask that beautiful young woman with the scarred face to be his wife after unmasking her father as a murderer. Lost in such troubled thoughts, he bumped into someone walking down the street in the opposite direction. The man, a noble to judge by his clothes, aimed a string of insults at Gerardo and seemed on the point of ordering the two retainers accompanying him to teach the Templar a lesson, when from further down the street there came a shout.

'It's him!' cried Gerardo's ex-landlord, pointing an accusatory finger at the knight. 'The one who set fire to my house! Grab him!'

Gerardo sidestepped the noble's vassal, who tried to grab hold of him, and started sprinting. Out of the corner of his eye, he saw Fiamma running down the street, trying to get in the way of his pursuers, but there was nothing she could do. Suddenly he felt himself clutched around the shoulders and he was rolling on the ground with one of the noble's servants on top of him. The other caught up a second later and kicked him hard in the side. Then again, and again.

Between flashes of pain, Gerardo could hear Fiamma shouting and thought that it was all over. He wouldn't be able to choose between earthly or godly love. He would finish at the gallows.

'Under arrest? In the name of whom, for goodness sake?' asked Mondino, contemptuously, moving in front of Adia. 'I hadn't heard that the Captain of the People was employing cut-throats to administer justice.'

The man puffed up his chest and straightened his back. 'I am Guido Arlotti, special agent in the service of Father Uberto da Rimini, Inquisitor of Bologna. Your wrists will now be bound. If you come quietly you will not be hurt.'

One of his two henchmen took the piece of stout cord that he wore round his waist in the guise of a belt, and stood waiting for orders. Mondino looked around for an escape route. That Guido Arlotti was in the Inquisitor's service was certainly true. That his was an official duty was highly unlikely. The Church didn't stick its neck out in these things and would never have sent an agent to arrest them, openly bypassing the responsibilities of the *comune*. Guido Arlotti must have dreamed up the story so that they didn't put up any resistance. Then he would make Mondino pay for his swim in the canal, and no doubt he'd also harm Adia. His two sidekicks couldn't keep their eyes off her.

At that moment she took a step forward, not the slightest bit afraid. 'Go now and no harm will be done to you,' she said in a tranquil tone.

The two ruffians guffawed, but looked at their boss uncomfortably.

'Are you really trying to frighten us with your witchcraft?' said Guido Arlotti, in a sneering tone. Then he began to walk straight towards Mondino.

Adia whistled loudly and shouted something in Arabic. The three men looked at each other, perplexed, but their confusion didn't last long. The grey Molossers burst on the scene, lolloping side by side through the open door, and without showing the slightest hesitation, without a bark or a snarl, sank their teeth into the men's backs.

In a second the room was full of shouting and noise. Guido Arlotti, who was standing in front of his accomplices, turned to see what was happening, and Mondino took the opportunity to jump on him and block the arm in which he held his dagger. Guido threw a punch, but Mondino managed to knee him sharply in the groin, at which point he dropped the dagger and the two of them fell to the floor, rolling in a wild embrace.

Mondino didn't know what was happening around him. He couldn't see where Adia was or who was getting the better of it out of the dogs and the men. All he could see were Guido's huge hands trying to hit him, claw out an eye or grab his throat, and all his attention was focused on stopping them. His elbow reached its target beneath a cheekbone, resulting in a grunt of pain. However, the triumph didn't last long, because Guido gave him a headbutt that almost knocked

Mondino out, although absurdly it was Guido who cried out in pain. While the agent was gasping on the floor trying to get up, Mondino suddenly felt the blade of the dagger under his hand. He took the knife and sat up, slightly stunned, but ready to defend himself.

He looked around, with the dagger in his hand and his jaw set. Guido Arlotti's henchmen were lying on the ground, bloody and bruised, with their clothes ripped and having lost their knives, which were on the table behind Adia. The two mastiffs stood over them in silence, with their red eyes and sad faces, ready to spring as soon as either of the thugs attempted to move. Guido was sitting on the floor, massaging the nape of his neck, livid with rage. Adia Bintaba had hit him over the head with a walking stick and was now watching him with a challenging look.

Despite the situation, Mondino could not but find her beautiful, in her warrior's pose. He struggled to get up, brushed the dust from his tunic and went over to the man. 'Now tell us who sent you and why,' he said in a threatening voice.

The man spat at his feet. 'Go to hell, and the whore too.'

Mondino leaned down to grab hold of Arlotti by the collar, but Adia stopped him, touching his chest with the walking stick.

'That's enough,' she said. 'You've already brought enough disturbance to my house.'

Mondino had no intention of taking orders from her, in the circumstances. 'Forgive me,' he said, controlling himself with difficulty. 'I need to know why this man has been following me since last night. It is a question of vital importance.'

'I decide what is important in my house,' replied Adia. 'You three, out of here. Otherwise I'll tell my mastiffs to attack.'

She made a sign of command with the stick and the two men on the other side of the room got cautiously to their feet, obviously in pain. One had his arm half crushed, the other's thigh was bleeding. Guido Arlotti was the only one not seriously wounded, but his face and arms were covered in bruises nonetheless. Mondino imagined that he didn't look much better himself.

'Mistress,' he said, in a gentler tone. 'This man possesses information that is very important to me. It could even be a question of life and death.'

Adia said two words in Arabic and the dogs went to lie at her feet. 'Go,' she said then, addressing their aggressors. 'Now. Before I change my mind.'

The three staggered hurriedly towards the door and a moment later were outside, under the vigilant guard of Adia and the dogs. When they were far enough away to consider themselves safe, Guido Arlotti shouted, 'We'll meet again, witch. You'll burn on the pyre, with your dogs from the Devil.'

Then he turned and caught up with the others, who were in too wretched a state to shout threats of revenge.

'It was a mistake to let them go,' said Mondino, watching them walk towards the main road. 'Now you are in danger too.'

'And what should I have done, in your opinion?' replied Adia, putting down the stick and leaning over to examine the two mastiffs. 'Kill them?'

'No, but ...'

'But what? In what other way could I have stopped them telling the Inquisitor about me? The correct practice of alchemy does not involve murder, Magister. I thought I had made that clear.'

'So what will you do now?'

Adia straightened and looked around. She seemed to embrace the room with a glance. Various books had fallen on the floor and the bench was on its side, but the strange order that Mondino had noticed on his arrival had not been disturbed too much.

'I've been happy here,' she said, with a tinge of nostalgia in her voice. 'But the moment has come to move on.'

'You're leaving?' asked Mondino, surprised. 'For ever?'

'Yes. I have been accused of being a witch by a man who, as far as I understand, is in the pay of the Inquisition. It's not something to be taken lightly, wouldn't you agree?'

She was right, even if the danger was not as immediate as she seemed to believe. Uberto da Rimini was only interested in the Templar's trial and time would pass before he would think of bothering about a country sorceress.

'And you're just going to leave everything like this? All this ... knowledge?' He couldn't find a more appropriate word to describe what he saw.

Adia smiled. 'I'll take everything I can with me. The rest I'll leave to the landlord, as compensation for what I still owe him. I haven't got time to call on him and settle up.'

'And where will you go?'

'To the port of Corticella. A trusted friend there will have me to stay until I find a place on a boat bound for Venice. And you?'

'Me what?'

'The way back to Bologna is not safe. Those men seemed in too much of a bad way to attempt anything, but they might wait for you in an isolated place, and you wouldn't have much hope on your own against the three of them, even if they are unarmed now.'

Mondino had been struck by a strange feeling of melancholy when Adia said she was leaving. But what she said now made him cross.

'If I run that risk, I owe it to you because you let them go,' he said, dryly.

'That is exactly what I meant,' Adia said, without losing her composure. 'I feel in some way responsible for your safety, so I'm offering you company. If there are two of us and the dogs, we'll be safe.'

'But I'm going in the opposite direction.'

261

She sighed impatiently. 'Are you really that slow or do you do it on purpose to irritate me? It's true that you'd have to go slightly out of your way, but at least you won't be risking your life. At Corticella you can take a boat up the Navile to return to Bologna. It won't take you more than an hour longer. Are you in a great hurry?'

'No, it was only that your decision surprised me. If I think of my house, my books ... Are you really going to just leave it all like this?' he asked. 'Without regret, without thinking about it any more?'

Adia wore a distant look. 'It's certainly not the first time. Even though I have converted to the Christian faith, wherever I go I'm barely tolerated, and I've already had to run away. Besides,' she continued, forcing a smile, 'this way I see new places, get to know the world, and meet lots of people who, like me, are looking for the truth.'

Mondino would have liked to ask which truth she was referring to, but it wasn't the time or place.

'I'll accept with pleasure, mistress,' he said, warmly. 'I'll help you pack, if you'll allow me.'

Adia's lips opened in a smile. 'That's the first nice thing you've said to me since you got here.'

XIII

Gerardo woke to the sound of a key turning in the latch of a door in the distance and opened his eyes, pointlessly as it happened, because it was pitch dark. The kicks and thumps he had been given had swollen his face and every movement he made hurt him.

He didn't know how much time had passed. There was the acrid smell of excrement that he had noticed when he was first brought into the cell. It came from a pile of dirty straw not far from him. Gerardo had lain down on the bare stone, as far as possible from the pile of dung, and, after a bit, not even horror of his situation had kept him from falling asleep.

He tried to get up, but hit his head. He had forgotten that the ceiling was less than five feet high, which meant that he couldn't stand up. Air entered through a small window to one side of the door, through which the food was also passed to the prisoner inside. Or so Gerardo supposed, given that since he had arrived, he hadn't been given anything to eat or drink.

Initially they had shut him in a shared cell with another four or five prisoners. Then, without any explanation, two burly guards had come and moved him to this little room that must once have been a larder, then turned into an isolation cell when the municipal jail had been moved to the *comune*.

From that moment Gerardo had been left in the dark, waiting to be interrogated. All of a sudden, the door opened and two guards appeared on the threshold. They were so tall and broad that they couldn't get into the room at the same time. One of them grabbed him by the wrists and dragged him out. The sudden light caused him acute pain in his eyes and he shut them quickly. Then the guards picked him up by his armpits and carried him off with his feet hardly touching the ground. They passed some shared cells, from which there came a very strong stench of sweat and excrement, and one that had the smell of a dead body. The youth didn't ask where they were going. He knew that instead of an answer he'd probably get a thump across the head. They went down a wooden staircase and another made of stone and Gerardo, noticing a decrease in the light, tried opening his eyes again: they were in an underground room, obviously used for torture.

He was very surprised to find that he had been brought in front of the *Podestà* in person, standing next to the Captain of the People. Although he was no expert in matters of prosecution, it was clear to him that something strange was going on. The arrest of a student and arsonist was not important enough to require the *Podestà's* intervention.

However, Gerardo was determined not to let himself be intimidated. Despite the dazed feeling he'd got from the blows to his head, in the cell he had worked out his defensive strategy, very simple but difficult to refute: he would deny everything.

The fire had happened; there was no getting away from it. But there was no evidence that he had started it. No one had seen him go into the house and no one had seen him escaping over the rooftops. The only proof they could lay at his door was the fact that after the fire he had disappeared. He hadn't gone to see his landlord to ask for an explanation, or to the judge to ask for compensation, given that all his belongings had been burned in the fire. They would ask him why he had behaved in that way if he were innocent?

Gerardo would maintain that he hadn't gone home that evening, and once he found out about the fire he had decided to hide for fear of being unjustly accused.

It wasn't a very solid defence, but neither was it very easy to prove the contrary. And anyway he had to do everything he could to avoid a sentence. Arson was considered a crime against the city and the punishment was severe. Only a few months earlier, an arsonist had had his eyes put out after boiling lead was poured down his back.

However, Gerardo's strategy depended entirely on the fact that he would be interrogated without torture, while the place where he found himself now seemed to deny that basic premise.

He stood in silence and stared at the floor in front of him as behoves a prisoner, observing the *Podestà* out of the corner of his eye. Enrico Bernadazzi from Lucca was *Podestà* in charge for that quarter. He was a bearded man with a large face, who just then was looking at a spot somewhere above Gerardo's head, as though deep in thought. Over his yellow, fine wool tunic, which reached his feet, he was wearing a sky blue, sleeveless surcoat and a cloth cap of the same colour that vaguely recalled a helmet. His elegant appearance was decidedly out of place in that damp, dirty room full of machines and gruesome devices.

There was a heavy silence, but Gerardo waited patiently, head down, until the *Podestà* asked him, in his soft Tuscan accent: 'Are you Francesco Salimbene from Imola, medical student?'

Gerardo tried not to show his relief. They hadn't found out his real name.

'Yes, your Excellency.'

'Do you know why you have been arrested?'

'Yes, your Excellency. For a fire that they say I started, but I'm innocent.'

The Captain of the People, Pantaleone Buzacarini, exchanged looks with the *Podestà*, and then he took over.

'You are not innocent. A witness saw you go into the house on the night of the fire, but no one saw you come out again.' He sighed, as though tired of having to continually convince stubborn criminals of their wrong-headedness. 'Your fate is decided, Messer. We can easily find other witnesses to testify against you, and furthermore I am certain that, under torture, you would confess.' He was a man with an angular face and athletic body, of about Gerardo's height. With a circular gesture of his arm, he indicated all the instruments of torture dotted around the room. The action was accompanied by the rustle of the dark surcoat that he wore over his short military-style tunic and striped red and black breeches. There was the pendulum, the torture most regularly used because it was among the blandest, in that it only caused the dislocation of the limbs. There was also a breaking wheel and a furnace to heat irons and pincers, which, fortunately, was not lit just then. Gerardo shivered involuntarily, which did not escape the captain's attention.

'But this is a civil trial!' he protested. 'The use of torture is not allowed.'

'The fire in that house in the parish of Sant'Antonino is the last of your problems, believe me,' intervened the *Podestà*, touching his beard. 'When the Inquisitor, Uberto da Rimini, was informed of your arrest, he asked that you be transferred to the Dominican prison, near the Basilica of San Domenico. But he was somewhat mysterious about the motives for his request. Before deciding whether to consent to it or not, I would like to know from you what you are accused of by the Inquisition. You can tell us of your own free will, or under torture. The decision is yours.'

Gerardo stood in silence. His mind was racing, but despite all his efforts he couldn't work out what he should say. Mondino had explained that the Inquisitor's accusation towards him would be the murders of Wilhelm von Trier and Angelo da Piczano using black magic and a pact with the Devil. But it wasn't in his interest to tell them that, even if he were innocent, because it was a much more serious crime than arson. Besides, any admission he made on the subject would implicate Mondino and that was a thing he should avoid at all costs. Apart from the moral considerations, just then the physician represented his only hope of salvation. Gerardo would only be exonerated if Mondino could find the real murderer. The chances of him convincing the *Podestà* or the Inquisitor of his innocence were precisely none, unless a culprit were found.

He had to play for time by continuing to deny everything.

'I have nothing to say,' he said, first looking the *Podestà* in the eyes, then the Captain of the People. 'Other than that I declare myself innocent of the crime of which you accuse me.'

The two exchanged looks. With a finger, Pantaleone Buzacarini scratched at a white mark on one of the black stripes of his breeches.

'As you will have noticed, Messer,' he said, raising his eyes to stare Gerardo hard in the face, 'we have had you brought here without the presence of a judge or an executioner. We were hoping to resolve the matter in a friendly manner. You tell us what we want to know, and we will offer you the guarantee of a just trial and a sentence that is not too excessive. I am asking you for the last time: why is the Inquisitor so keen to see you?'

Gerardo finally began to understand. The *comune* of Bologna, although it was part Guelph and therefore favourable to the papacy, disliked the Inquisition's tendency to meddle in the administration of justice. The killing of the German Templar was first and foremost a penal crime, and hence fell into the jurisdiction of the *Podestà*. The Captain of the People had allowed Mondino to go and examine the German's corpse because he was irritated by the fact that the Inquisition had claimed the right to investigate the murder.

They had had him brought down there to frighten him with the sight of the instruments of torture and now they were soothing him with the promise of a mild punishment. They could sense that something was afoot that was much bigger than mere arson, and they wanted to know what it was in order to be able to take the necessary countermeasures and to protect themselves from an eventual usurpation of their powers.

And yet, he couldn't trust a verbal promise. The two notables would be able to go back on it without a second thought as soon as they found out what they wanted to know. And the stakes were too high. It wasn't just a question of his personal safety, but of the survival of one of the most glorious ecclesiastical orders. If he agreed to the Captain of the People's proposal, everything he had done up to that moment would lose its justification. The fire, the hiding of Angelo da Piczano's body, the death of that poor crippled boy, the lies, his escape ... There would no longer be a superior motive. Gerardo would become, in his own eyes more than in those of secular justice, a common criminal.

'I have nothing to say,' he repeated.

Pantaleone Buzacarini came a step forward and punched him full in the face. Gerardo, already weakened by the beating-up before his arrest and from lying in the cell, dropped limply to the floor like an empty sack, bringing his hands to his face. He felt warm blood flowing from his nose through his fingers, staining his tunic that was already in a sorry state.

'Don't you understand that you've got no way out?' exclaimed Pantaleone, in an angry voice. 'Well then, we'll have to make you understand. I'm going to call the executioner and the notary. You will tell us what we want to know. I can guarantee that.'

He turned to go, but the *Podestà* raised his arm to stop. He seemed to be thinking. For a second no one moved and a silence fell in the underground room, through which they could hear, albeit from a distance, the noises of life on the upper floors of the building. Exclamations, slammed doors, bolts sliding across.

'We cannot directly challenge the Inquisitor,' said Enrico Bernadazzi, with an astute smile. 'But I've just thought of a way to find out what we want to know without colliding with the Church. Take the prisoner back to his cell.'

The Captain of the People opened the door and a second later the two massive guards came in. Gerardo was dragged out. He didn't have time to hear the *Podestà's* idea. But it didn't make much difference. In the hands of a lay executioner or a cleric the suffering would be much the same.

Straight after the midday meal, Uberto da Rimini joined the prior outside the basilica. Putting on a show of cordiality, he interested himself in the work on the new bell tower that had just started again after a month's interruption due to financial difficulties. There were unlikely to be any more problems now and the prior was confident that the bell tower would be inaugurated within a couple of years: in the Year of Our Lord, 1313.

The walls of the building were teeming with day workers and labourers dressed in sackcloth, among whom the more comfortable and elegant clothing of the master builders stood out. As did the black and white robes of some Dominicans who drifted among the stones carrying out various jobs.

'It will be magnificent,' said the prior, with an ingenuous smile. He was a vastly fat man, taller than Uberto by a head, but decidedly stupid. The only thing that interested him in life was to be remembered in the basilica registers as the origina-tor of the new bell tower. 'It was the only thing missing from our church.'

'I agree,' said Uberto. To avoid the dust, they were standing a convenient distance from the site, at the point where a low wall marked the edge of the churchyard, paved in cobble-stones, and the cemetery behind the basilica. 'I'm sure that the Archbishop will be most impressed when he sees it.'

The prior's face was instantly diffused with a guilty red. 'How did you know he was coming?' he asked, without both-ering to deny the fact.

That morning Uberto had overheard a snippet of conversa-tion between two confrères, the bursar and the cook. They had been talking about there being various guests to supper and he had worked out the rest for himself. But he didn't waste time in explanations and simply answered the question with another.

'Why wasn't I told?'

'The messenger only got here this morning,' replied the big man, without looking at him. 'And we have been caught unawares. In the rush of preparations it must have slipped my mind.'

Perhaps he was telling the truth and perhaps not. Uberto suspected that the Archbishop had meant to make him a sur-prise visit and would have specifically asked the prior not to tell him. All things considered, he couldn't have chosen a worse moment to come and upset the applecart.

He looked in the direction of St Dominic's cell, now

converted into a chapel. 'It doesn't matter,' he said, pretending indifference. 'It's only that I would have liked time to prepare myself.'

The prior nodded, excusing himself again, and went back to looking at the slow growth of what he thought of as his 'creation'. Meanwhile Uberto tried to work out how to ward off that rough stroke of destiny. He had asked the student cum arsonist to be transferred to the prison in the basilica so that he could interrogate the youth at his ease and extort a confession by his own means. He assumed that someone had immediately gone to report this development to the Archbishop. However, once the accomplished fact had been laid before him, Rinaldo wouldn't be able to do anything about it without coming up against Clement V in person. Only now Uberto discovered that the Archbishop would be arriving in Bologna that very evening. And that he would not be staying at the Episcopal palace or the Templar House where three years previously he had set the trial in motion with the archbishops of Pisa and Cremona. He would be staying at the Basilica of San Domenico. Naturally this had not seemed strange to the prior, he was simply happy to have another memorable event to note down in the registers: a visit from the Archbishop of Ravenna during his priorate.

Rinaldo would insist that the interrogation be conducted according to the law and nothing useful would come out of it at all. The only possibility seemed to be that of putting off the request for the prisoner's transfer till after the Archbishop's departure, but that too presented problems. Above all Uberto didn't know how long the visit would last. It might be a day, but it might be a week. Obviously Uberto didn't want to leave the prisoner in the hands of the *Podestà* for too long. If condemned for arson, he might end up dead or incapable of speaking again.

Fortunately no one at the monastery apart from Uberto

knew about the youth's arrest. This gave him a bit of time to reflect, but he needed to make a decision in a hurry.

He was about to take his leave of the prior when a young messenger from the *comune* turned up in the churchyard and began to walk their way. Uberto assumed that he was bringing news from the *Podestà*. Whatever it was that he had to tell Uberto, the prior must not hear. He started to get to his feet but the giant took him by the arm. With a benevolent smile, he said, 'Let him come to us, Father. I know how modest you are, but hierarchies must be respected.'

Before Uberto could reply, the messenger had reached them. He made a bow and handed a rolled parchment with the *Podestà's* seal on it to the Inquisitor, immediately retiring to a respectful distance to allow him time to read it.

'My orders are to wait for a reply,' he said. 'If you would like to go up to the monastery to write your answer, I can wait for you here.'

Uberto nodded and signed to him with a wave of his hand, grateful to have the pretext to leave. 'It will be quicker if you come with me,' he said. Then he turned to the prior. 'Please excuse me,' he added, turning away before the man had a chance to reply.

As they were walking towards the monastery, Uberto broke the seal and began to read the letter. The *Podestà* of Bologna, Enrico Bernadazzi, agreed to his request to interrogate Francesco Salimbene, but since the student under arrest was responsible for a civic crime, he could not consent to the transfer to and incarceration at the Basilica. However, the Inquisitor was welcome to come and interrogate him at the *comune* prison in the presence of the *Podestà*, the Captain of the People and a notary.

Uberto's thin lips slowly shaped themselves into a smile. The *Podestà* had certainly intended to insult him with that letter, and in normal circumstances he would have succeeded.

But just then the chance of interrogating the prisoner without the Archbishop seemed heaven sent. And perhaps it really was.

Nonetheless, everything depended on secrecy and speed. There was not a moment to lose.

'I will give my reply to the *Podestà* in person,' he said to the messenger. 'I'll come back to the *comune* with you now.'

He made a sign for the man to go on ahead and prepared to follow him. Out of the corner of his eye he saw the prior, who suddenly seemed more vigilant than usual. Could he be Rinaldo's spy, the person who kept the Archbishop informed of Uberto's every movement? It seemed impossible to him, but by now the question was losing its importance. If he managed to make the prisoner confess, Rinaldo da Concorezzo would no longer have a chance to put a spoke in the wheel.

As he walked, Uberto tore the parchment into tiny pieces and crossing one of the numerous bridges over the Savena, he threw them into the river and watched them float on the current, little white blotches covered in black ink.

A minuscule fleet of Dominicans running to the defence of the faith.

Hearing the door open, Gerardo thought the guards had come to collect him again. He mentally prepared himself for torture. Not knowing if or for how long he would be able to stand it, he only hoped that he wouldn't collapse like a sickly child at the first hint of pain.

He had closed his eyes so as not to feel the shooting pain of sudden light in the cell. He heard a man's voice say, 'You can go in, but don't stay too long', and then he smelled the unexpected scent of clean clothes and perfumed hair. A woman's smell.

Completely thrown, he opened wide his eyes and then quickly had to shut them again. What he had seen in that brief instant didn't make any sense at all.

'Does the light hurt?' asked Fiamma. 'If you would like, I'll put out the lamp.'

She must have covered it with something because the light grew less strong. Gerardo opened his eyes again and looked at her properly. She was wearing a simple white gown with a veil over her head and was sitting on her heels on the dirty floor. She had put the lamp behind her, next to the closed door. Gerardo was mortified by his own appearance and the acidic stink that hung like a pall in the cell. He hardly noticed it any more, but Fiamma did. She was holding a linen handkerchief pressed to her mouth.

'The light is fine now, mistress, thank you,' he mumbled, through his swollen lips. 'Why are you here?'

'Aren't you pleased to see me?' she asked.

Gerardo shook his head. 'It's not that. Of course I'm pleased. But now they know you know me, they could interrogate you and extort information about me from you. I couldn't bear it if you were hurt because of me.'

In an impulsive gesture, Fiamma stretched a hand out to touch his face, and then she quickly removed it. In that tiny cell they were forced into an inappropriate closeness and despite the pain in his bones and muscles, Gerardo felt a growing sensation that filled him with embarrassment.

The girl had put a small basket down on the floor and now she took out a piece of linen and a jug of water. She dipped the cloth into the water and softly began to clean the dirt and dried blood off Gerardo's face.

'They won't harm me, don't worry,' she said. 'The Captain of the People had a large debt with Remigio and he was very happy to allow me to visit you in return for a letter certifying the remission of the due sum.'

'You shouldn't have!' exclaimed Gerardo. 'Your father—'

'Remigio is not my father!' interrupted Fiamma, vehemently. 'I've already told you. And anyhow he has disappeared, as you know. When he comes back, if he comes back, he won't be able to do anything but take note of my decision. I forged his signature so that even he couldn't tell the difference.' She paused briefly, then added, 'I would have done anything to be able to come and see you.'

Gerardo felt his heart beat faster at those words, but he said nothing. He realised with surprise that the idea of breaking his vows didn't seem so terrible now. Perhaps it was his closeness to death. Fiamma finished washing his face and took her hand away, putting the dirty cloth on the floor. Apart from when she had made the comment about Remigio, she always spoke through the handkerchief.

'I've brought you something to eat and some fresh water to drink,' she said, putting the basket down beside him. 'Please, help yourself.'

Gerardo stretched out a hand for a covered bowl of soup that was still warm. He drank it avidly, savouring the rich, salty taste. Then he took a big piece of meat from the bottom of the bowl, put it on a chunk of bread and bit into them. Fiamma watched him eat from behind her handkerchief, with an expression that reminded Gerardo of his mother. Lastly, Gerardo drank half the water in the jug, saving the rest for later.

'Thank you,' he said. 'I truly needed that.'

'Is there anything else I can do for you?'

Gerardo was about to say no, but now that he had finally had something to eat, he felt stronger and more awake and for the first time he remembered that he had left Hugues de Narbonne lashed to the bed.

'There is one thing, mistress.'

'Tell me.'

Without going into too much detail, Gerardo explained that the previous night Hugues had suffered a wound to his head. Mondino had operated on him and to keep him from moving they had had to tie him to the bed and gag him.

'Then we left him like that, for reasons that I cannot explain,' he said. 'I was counting on going back to untie him this afternoon, after speaking to your father. Then I was arrested and I forgot all about him until now.'

'Would you like me to go and see how he is?'

Gerardo hesitated. 'If no one goes, he might die. I was supposed to meet the Magister there, but he can't get in alone. As I was certain I would arrive first, I didn't tell him where I hid the key.'

'It's all right, I'll go and wait for him.'

Gerardo remembered the looks that Hugues had given the young woman when they had visited Remigio and suddenly the idea of sending her into the lion's den didn't seem such a good one, even if the Frenchman was weak and recovering from an operation.

'Remember,' he said, with a serious look. 'Wait for Mondino to get there before you untie the cords. We have reason to believe that Hugues de Narbonne is not who he says he is.'

'Don't worry, I'll be careful,' she reassured him. 'My father's two servants will accompany me as the bank is closed for the time being anyway.'

So Gerardo told her where the house was and where he had hidden the key. 'I thank you for your kindness with all my heart, mistress,' he said, smiling. 'God knows I need it right now.'

Fiamma nodded, but she didn't return his smile. She seemed to have something else on her mind. She waited a moment in silence, as though she were deliberating with herself. 'That's not the only reason that I came,' she said, and then after a pause, 'I must speak to you.'

'What about?'

'About me.'

Surprised, Gerardo only managed to say, 'I'm listening.'

Fiamma was quiet for a long while, then she took a deep

breath. 'This wasn't done by a physician trying to treat a cataract,' she said, removing the handkerchief from her mouth and showing him the left side of her face. In the trembling light of the oil lamp, the scar seemed to flash like a little white snake from her eye almost down to her chin. Gerardo was confused. What did the scar have to do with it? The young woman seemed too shaken to speak coherently.

'That was what I told everyone, even Remigio,' continued Fiamma. Curled up, with her hands around her knees, she almost seemed a child. 'I needed to forget.'

She shook her head, almost as if she couldn't go on, and pressed the linen handkerchief to her mouth again. It looked as though she wanted to weep, but couldn't. Her chest was rising and falling rapidly beneath her light gown.

'Mistress, please calm yourself,' said Gerardo, and on an impulse he moved over and tried to take her in his arms.

Fiamma cried out as though he had bitten her. She moved quickly backwards and put her hand to the sash that she wore round her waist, while Gerardo stared at her aghast, thinking that she was about to pull out a knife. But the girl took out a little embroidered bag. It contained three things: some folded cotton paper, a piece of parchment and a minuscule notebook, the like of which Gerardo had never seen before. She was about to put them in his hands but thought again and laid them on the filthy floor between them.

'The first is a letter for you,' she said. 'The notebook is a diary that I wrote many years ago and the piece of parchment is a useless thing, but I know you are looking for it. Please read the letter and the diary. I would like you to understand me, if not forgive me.'

Then she called the guard to open the door, took up the basket with the crockery and went out without turning back or saying goodbye. She was visibly agitated.

Gerardo found himself alone. All the well-being he had felt

after finally being able to eat and drink had vanished and he felt his stomach clench like a vice. He took the letter, which was very short, and had only just had time to read it when he heard the sound of footsteps in the corridor. He hurriedly wet his fingers and pinched the flame to put it out. Then he hid everything in the only possible place: under the pile of dirty straw.

'Come out, so we don't have to come in and get you,' said one of the guards, running the bolt across. 'The Inquisitor's waiting.'

Gerardo crawled out of the cell on all fours and then slowly got to his feet. This time the two giants let him walk between them without dragging him along.

Opening his eyes in the dark, Hugues de Narbonne began to feel afraid. When he had come round, he remembered everything, although in a slightly bleary fashion as though in a dream. Gerardo had brought him home and then left him alone and come back with the physician. Hugues recalled a terrible pain in his head and then a strange feeling, as if air had entered his skull. The physician must have trepanned his cranium, and he had lost consciousness.

Given that he was now lucid, the operation had been successful despite the constant throbbing pain in his head. But why didn't they untie him before they left? Was it possible that they had discovered his secret?

In his mind's eye, Hugues ran over every corner of the house in search of clues that Gerardo and Mondino might have found, but he was certain that there was nothing. Nothing at all. Books, documents and objects that might have compromised him had all been well hidden in Toledo, where he had moved after leaving the Templar House at Tortosa.

Unfortunately he had succumbed to nature's call and the smell coming from his own excrement made him nauseous.

From the change in the light filtering through the shutters he thought it must already be afternoon. Why did no one come? Could they have left him there to die of hunger and thirst? No, it didn't make any sense. They had no reason to kill him and if they had wanted to, they would have found a quicker way. And they wouldn't have wasted time operating on his head. No, they were obviously coming back, but something must have happened.

Again he tried to loosen the cords that held him to the bedposts in the sitting position. There was nothing he could do, the knots were too tight. The gag was also well tied around his head, tight enough to force his lips open. Hugues had already tried shouting with all his might, but he'd only managed to produce a low and indistinct growl that it would be difficult to hear outside because of the closed shutters.

Besides, every time he struggled and tried to shout, the pain in his head became intolerable.

He flopped back against the bedhead, exhausted. He tried to sleep in order to build up his strength, but in that position it was almost impossible. As well as the continuous sharp pain above the nape of his neck, he also felt pain in his wrists, ankles and shoulders. As soon as his head began to nod, he would wake up, only to fall back into a light and agitated sleep and then wake again.

At one point when he was slipping between sleep and wakefulness, he thought he heard a sound. Suddenly he was awake and alert, with all his senses straining.

Another sound. A door closed.

Someone had come into the house. Gerardo or Mondino, or perhaps both of them. It was the moment that Hugues had been waiting for, and yet he wasn't ready to tell them the truth. First of all he had to convince them to untie him. Perhaps, if they found him asleep, they would undo the knots, at least so he hoped. And until he knew their intentions, he

279

would continue to pretend to be unconscious. Hearing the sound of steps, he closed his eyes and dropped his head on to his chest.

'Good morning, sir,' said a woman.

Surprised, Hugues forgot his plan and looked up sharply. Standing before him, with a candle in one hand and a cloth bag in the other, was Fiamma, the banker's daughter. They had sent her to help him. At last Hugues de Narbonne felt relief flood through his veins.

'When I heard you were hurt I came as quickly as I could,' said the girl. 'It's lucky that you are still alive.'

It was kind of her to take such trouble over him. Looking at her closely, Hugues had the feeling that she reminded him of someone. Who knows, perhaps he had known her mother in Tortosa. He had had dozens of amorous adventures in the lands of Aragon. Although he would surely have remembered a beautiful woman as Fiamma's mother certainly would have been.

The young woman took the candle over to another in an earthenware stick on the chest and lit the wick. Then she spilt some drops of wax on to the wood and pressed the candle into it, so that the two candles stood side by side. Finally she pushed the chest over to the bed.

'Better to see well,' she explained. 'I wouldn't want to cut in the wrong places.'

Now that it was lighter, Hugues felt a mortifying shame at the stains of excrement on the mattress. It certainly wasn't the ideal situation in which to meet a woman. As soon as she freed him, he would open the window to get rid of the smell and go and wash.

Fiamma took a knife out of her cloth bag and came towards him. Hugues felt a second of panic seeing her point it at his chest and not at the stout cords binding his wrists, but he relaxed when she began to cut his tunic. She obviously wouldn't want to touch his clothes as they were dirtied by blood and shit. She'd cut them and leave them on the bed. In that way she would see him naked, but if it didn't matter to her, Hugues had no objection either. Despite his age, his body was still firm and muscular; nothing to be ashamed of. It was a pity about the bed being reduced to a pigsty and the piercing pain in his head. Otherwise as soon as he was free, he would have pulled her towards him. But then again he might have waited until he had washed and eaten, he thought with a slight smile.

Fiamma bared his solid chest to reveal a coat of blond hair sprinkled with white. Then she carried on down, opening the whole tunic, without touching his breeches. As she moved his clothes, the smell got stronger, but she didn't seem to notice. She was concentrating hard, careful only to cut the material and not to nick his skin. Hugues was thinking that she really was very beautiful, with her silky tallow-coloured hair, intense expression and breasts straining against her white tunic. Even the scar that disfigured her cheek couldn't diminish her beauty.

The girl moved away from him and emptied her cloth bag on to the chest. Some metal objects rattled on to its wooden lid. Why didn't she cut the cords at his wrist? Hugues tried to speak, but the gag transformed his words into an incomprehensible mumble.

Fiamma turned and looked him long in the eyes without speaking. Then she said, 'I had to knock the others out and then immobilise them with a potion that paralyses the limbs. You have had the decency to be waiting for me already bound and gagged.'

Hugues finally understood. With the clarity of mind that often precedes death, a memory came to him of the little girl with the slashed face. He hadn't recognised her until then because he had thought her dead and because the woman before him retained very little of the delicate appearance of the child. Now, however, he had no doubts. She was the one who had killed Angelo da Piczano and Wilhelm von Trier and now it was his turn.

As Fiamma came back towards him with the knife and started to cut his skin, he yelled with all the breath he had in his lungs, but through the gag there only came a pathetic whine.

When she had finished her job, Fiamma went into the kitchen, took off her bloody clothes and washed carefully in the basin that she had prepared on her arrival. Her revenge was almost complete and yet she felt no satisfaction. She was tired and much sadder than she had thought she would be over the years in which she had planned it all.

She dried herself with a piece of hemp hanging from a hook above the fire. Then she took her clean clothes out of the bag and put them on. A dark brown shirt and gown and a white cap; anonymous clothes that would allow her to blend into the crowd, once she had given the alarm. Before she left, she went back to the door of the bedroom and stood for a moment contemplating her handiwork. Hugues de Narbonne had been the leader without whom the other two might not have gone so far. He deserved to suffer the most. Before she had killed him, she had told him who she was and his eyes had filled with terror as she made her incisions in his skin, marking the edges of the cuts that she would then sever with the saw. She had even shown him the worms that she would put in his brain. Hugues was still tied to the bed in the same position in which she had found him. The room was crimson with blood. The heart of iron stuck out of his chest like a malignant flower, and his skullcap – with what remained of his blond curly hair – lay on his genitals. The head had been opened, sawn just above his eyebrows, and was full of whitish larvae, of the type that form in the scavenged morsels found by stray dogs.

Fiamma had spent years planning how she would kill them.

All three knights had their heart turned into iron to signify the absence of mercy and compassion, as well as a symbol for each one's specific crime. Angelo, who had wanted to stop the violence but hadn't, would have his hands amputated as a sign of a lack of action. Wilhelm, the old man who had cut her face, would be paid back in kind with a cross carved into his face. And Hugues, whose rotten brain had been behind the massacre, now had a head full of worms.

In her mind she had nicknamed them Pilate, Longinus and Caiaphas, after Christ's killers. The first had washed his hands of the Redeemer's blood. The second had pierced His side with a lance, and the third had been the principal schemer for His death. And, though well aware that she could hardly liken herself to the Son of God, she didn't think she was so dissimilar in her violated innocence; a sacrificial lamb who was powerless to escape her fate.

Without further ado, she turned away from the cadaver and walked out of the house, leaving the door open. The street was full of people and the afternoon sun flooded everything in a warm golden colour. She took a deep breath and let out a terrified cry. Then she began to run, shouting that there was a dead man lying there dismembered with his heart turned into a block of iron. In an instant there was mayhem and the street turned into an ant's nest disturbed with a stick. People were running all over the place. Many tore into their houses, the shopkeepers began to shut their shops; the paper-makers tried to put away their piles of paper and notebooks before the crowd trampled them, the women screamed and shouted, passing on the horrifying news.

Fiamma walked away undisturbed with her bag over her shoulder. She still had one more person to kill, but she had done enough for one day.

XIV

Uberto da Rimini looked at the young man in front of him with ill-concealed satisfaction. First he had found the missing corpse and now the person who had stolen it, after committing murder and setting fire to the house. Soon the Archbishop would have all the proof he needed.

But there still had to be a confession.

With a flash of irritation, Uberto imagined Rinaldo da Concorezzo's ascetic face as he said, '*We have a corpse and we have an arsonist. But where is the proof that the corpse was really in that house and that the arsonist is also an assassin?*'

Rinaldo's obsession with respecting the law was bordering on ingenuity, to say the least. Who would spontaneously admit to being the author of a crime that would take them straight to meet the executioner?

'So you are Francesco Salimbene,' said Uberto, in a placid tone. 'The Templar monk who lived in the lodgings in the parish of Sant'Antonino that burned down two weeks ago. Do you admit that?'

'I admit that I lived in those rooms, Father, but I am a medical student, not a Templar monk.'

'And yet the person who was staying with you, Angelo da Piczano, was. To whom would a Templar wanted by the Inquisition go for hospitality, if not his confrère?'

'He would go to a friend. I knew Angelo and his predicament, and I did not think I was breaking the law by inviting him to stay with me for a few days. I committed no crime according to secular justice.'

'The Knights Templar have no friends among ordinary people.'

'I don't know about that, but if you say so, it must be true. I only know that he and I were friends and I had no reason to deny him help.'

Silence fell, broken only by the scratching of the notary's pen. He was sitting to the left of Gerardo, transcribing the questions and answers on to a sheet of parchment laid out on the slanting surface of a writing bench and held down with two iron paperweights in the shape of cubes. Uberto reflected that if they carried on like that, they would never get anywhere. He had hoped to draw the young man into making a series of small admissions that could gradually be constructed to form a solid cage around him. This was why he hadn't immediately charged him with using a false name. However, Francesco Salimbene was showing himself to be more astute than he'd thought, despite his youth. There was only one way to make the Templar confess his crimes quickly, but at the *comune* Uberto's hands were tied.

'Could you tell us exactly what you think this young man is guilty of, Father?'

This was said in the aspirate Luccan accents of Enrico Bernadazzi, the *Podestà*. Uberto spun round to find him standing at the door, elegant as ever, accompanied by the sinister-looking Pantaleone Buzacarini, Captain of the People.

'This was not part of our agreement, Excellency,' protested the Dominican. 'I only agreed to come here to interrogate the prisoner because I was assured that I would have full liberty of movement.'

'You agreed because you had no alternative,' intervened the Captain of the People. 'However, the conditions of our agreement have changed. Do you really believe that telling us what you think the prisoner to be guilty of is a limitation of your movements?'

Pantaleone Buzacarini was a noted Ghibelline who held that position due to the new Guelph policy to include their rivals in the government of the city, while nonetheless keeping them in a minority. Uberto would have to be doubly cautious with him.

'It is not that,' replied the Dominican, choosing the path of prudence. 'It is only that I would prefer not to talk about it until I have something tangible in hand. I do not like accusing people without proof.'

'I would have said the opposite,' murmured Pantaleone, almost inaudibly, bringing a smile to the face of the *Podestà*, although he was a diehard Guelph.

'What did you say?' asked Uberto, who had heard Pantaleone perfectly.

'Nothing of any importance. But if you don't even tell the prisoner what crime you are accusing him of, how is he going to be able to confess that he's guilty?'

Uberto would have happily subjected the Captain of the People to torture on the wheel. His disrespectful attitude was the direct result of the weakness of prelates such as the Archbishop of Ravenna.

Da Rimini crossed his arms over the white tunic he wore beneath his order's black cloak and hood; a stance that usually struck terror into those subjected to his investigations.

'How and when I decide to communicate it to him is my

affair, Captain. Now, if you will allow me, I would like to go on with the interrogation.'

The notary had stopped writing and was watching the three of them from his bench, scratching his ear with the quill.

Francesco Salimbene, for his part, did not lose a word of what was being said and the look on his face alternated between hope and despair like a game of light and shade played by the sun filtering through the leaves of a tree.

'Please go on,' said the *Podestà*, going to sit down behind the notary, followed immediately by Pantaleone. 'We won't be any bother.'

The young man's face grew definitively morose, but Uberto was too cross to derive any satisfaction from that. Alas, that insolent Captain of the People was right. To interrogate the prisoner on their conditions was the only alternative left to him, given the circumstances. And he needed to get a result pretty fast.

But perhaps there was a way of resolving the situation to his advantage.

'As far as I know,' he said to the *Podestà*, ignoring the Captain of the People, 'serious circumstantial evidence points to this man being an arsonist, and yet he maintains that he wasn't there when the fire broke out.'

'That is true, but this is a crime that must be assessed by the *comune*.'

'And how will you assess it, given that the accused will not confess?'

The *Podestà* gave Uberto a perplexed look. 'The evidence against him is serious enough to justify the use of torture. But you know that quite well.'

'So please go on.'

'Do you mean to say that rather than reveal what you intend to accuse him of, you will relinquish interrogating him altogether?'

'Not at all,' replied Uberto. 'I'll be straight with you. The crime that I intend to accuse him of is the murder, with recourse to the dark arts, of a Templar, whose name I do not yet know, who died after the fire in the parish of Sant'Antonino ...' He noticed that the Captain of the People was about to interrupt him and he silenced Pantaleone with a look. 'I know that it was murder,' he said, anticipating the man's objection, 'because I've found the corpse. Now may I go on?'

'Yes, you may,' intervened the *Podestà*.

'Furthermore, I mean to accuse this young man, who in all probability is not called Francesco Salimbene at all, of the murder of Wilhelm von Trier, the German Templar found dead in an inn near the Basilica of Santo Stefano with his heart turned into a block of iron. But to be able to prove my accusations, I need the prisoner to declare that he was guilty of starting the fire. Now, if you consider it opportune, I will stand aside while you interrogate him on that subject and when he has confessed to the crime, I will proceed with the other accusations.'

The Captain of the People began to clap slowly, a vulgar habit that the populace usually used to show its appreciation of spectacles such as acrobats and ballad singers. Uberto, the *Podestà*, the notary and even the prisoner all turned to stare at him.

'My compliments, Inquisitor,' said Pantaleone. 'I didn't think you were so astute.'

'What do you mean by that? Explain yourself,' intervened the *Podestà*, assuming a severe tone.

'Everyone knows that Archbishop Rinaldo da Concorezzo abhors the use of torture,' the Captain went on. 'And as you know, an Inquisitor needs permission from the Archbishop to torture an accused man. Now, since the prisoner has not confessed *cospectu tormentorum*, the Inquisitor, seeing the instruments of torture, thought he could leave us the job of torturing him and take advantage of the results.'

'So?' replied Uberto, forcefully. 'It was you who invited me to conduct my interrogation here instead of handing over the prisoner. Now I am proposing a collaboration that could turn out to the benefit of both Church and *comune*. What reason could you have to refuse?'

The Captain of the People was about to say something, but the *Podestà* stopped him with a wave of his hand. 'That's enough, Pantaleone. Don't let your Ghibelline spirit get in the way of reason. If this young man is really guilty of crimes against the city and the Church, the best thing, in everybody's interests, is to forget our differences and combine forces. Call the executioner, please.'

This time it was Uberto who had to stop himself applauding. 'Well said!' he exclaimed, while the Captain walked out of the room.

His words were followed by a fraught silence that continued until Pantaleone Buzacarini returned with the executioner. Uberto went to stand next to the *Podestà* and left the Captain the job of interrogating the prisoner. Gerardo merely repeated his version of events and so was immediately subjected to the pendulum. The executioner bound his hands behind his back with a rope attached to the wooden frame fixed to the ceiling. Then, rotating the other end of the rope round a spool, he slowly began to lift the Templar off the ground by his arms. They left him the time to feel the intense pain of his shoulders being stretched in that unnatural manner. Then, at a sign from the Captain, the executioner let go of the rope so that the prisoner dropped and then the executioner immediately grabbed it again, stopping Gerardo fall with a jolt. Gerardo let out a yell of pain as his arms jerked upwards behind his back, almost coming out of their sockets.

'This is only the first stage,' explained Pantaleone Buzacarini.

'If you confess immediately, you will be spared the second. At the third almost everyone confesses.'

'No ... I didn't start the fire, believe me,' replied Gerardo, in a strangled voice. 'When I got back to the house it was in flames. I was afraid they would blame me for it so I ran away.'

The notary took down the question and answer. The Captain turned to look at the *Podestà* and receiving a nod of the head, he ordered the executioner to winch the prisoner up again. This time when the ropes lifted Gerardo off the floor, the pain brought a few tears and a forlorn groan.

'You've still got time to save yourself from agony,' admonished the Captain. 'Will you confess?'

'It wasn't me,' the young man managed to say, through his teeth. 'I beg of you, I'm innocent.'

The executioner let the rope go again. This time the prisoner's cry finished in a sob.

'Did you start the fire in that house in the parish of Sant'Antonino two weeks ago?' asked the Captain in a monotonous voice.

Uberto, standing at the *Podestà's* side, didn't take his eyes off the young man's face, even for a second. He was noting the signs of surrender that were beginning to appear. The youth would soon confess. Then, weakened by the pulling of the ropes, he wouldn't have the strength to oppose the interrogation about the double killing. And even if he did, he would only be tortured again until he confessed. After that it wouldn't be difficult to convince him to repeat his admissions *sponte non vi*, that is, without the use of torture. Uberto knew from experience that when a prisoner yielded once, he never recovered strength enough to resist after that and ended up doing everything they asked of him.

'I am innocent,' insisted Gerardo, showing uncommon obstinacy. 'Of this accusation and of the others that the Inquisitor wants to charge me with.'

The Captain nodded in the direction of the executioner, who began to pull on the ropes again. At that moment voices were heard coming from along the corridor. A guard entered the room and said that two people were demanding to see the Captain of the People and the Inquisitor.

'Who are they?' asked Uberto.

'A Dominican friar and a paper-maker. The Dominican says that he has a message from the Archbishop and the artisan wants to speak to Messer Pantaleone to report a monstrous crime.'

Exchanging hostile glances, Uberto and Pantaleone Buzacarini left the room and followed the guard. The two men waiting for them were showing signs of great anxiety. The first to speak was the paper-maker. When they were still a few yards away, he couldn't stop himself shouting, 'Captain, in the paper-maker's borough a man has been found tied to his bed with his head full of worms and a piece of iron where his heart should be!'

Hearing those words, Uberto stopped in his tracks. Another person killed in that extraordinary way! This automatically cleared Mondino's student, who couldn't be the perpetrator given that he'd been in jail at the time. The whole edifice of accusations that he had prepared was in danger of collapsing miserably.

But he didn't have time to think about that before his assistant, Friar Antonio, came up. The young priest, who was even shorter than him, must have been running because he was out of breath and red in the face. But he bowed with the usual propriety. 'Forgive my disturbing you, Father,' he said, in a low voice. 'The Archbishop has arrived and is asking for you urgently.'

'Did he use the word "urgently"?'

The friar nodded. 'He is already sitting at your desk going through all the trial papers to make certain there are no irregularities.'

Uberto da Rimini had never sworn in his life and didn't even do it now. But he had to exercise every ounce of self-control not to ask God why He insisted on frustrating every effort he made. Less than an hour would have been enough to get a confession out of the bogus student, but he didn't dare go any further now. The most important thing was to maintain secrecy; he wouldn't even mention the arrest to Friar Antonio. God willing, he could come back the next day and go on with the interrogation.

'As you heard, a matter of great urgency requires me to return to the monastery,' he said to the Captain of the People, who had been speaking to the paper-maker in a hushed voice. 'I would ask that the interrogation be stopped and continued only in my presence, in the name of the collaboration that unites us in this cause.'

'Agreed,' replied the *Podestà*, coming up from behind him. 'But we will only wait until noon tomorrow. Then we will proceed with or without you.' He turned back towards the interrogation room, where the notary and the executioner had remained, and shouted, 'Untie the prisoner and take him back to his cell. We'll carry on tomorrow.'

Uberto made him a brief bow and hurried away, preceded by the friar.

'There's one more thing,' said the young Dominican, quietly. They had left the *comune* and were navigating their way through the confusion of shops that filled most of the space beneath the huge arches, leaving only the narrowest gaps for people and handcarts to pass. 'I didn't want to mention it in front of strangers.'

'What is it?'

'The ex-priest, Guido Arlotti. He came looking for you at the monastery, saying that he had some important news. He was covered in bruises and his clothes were ripped. Since you weren't there, he went home to change and deal with his injuries, but he said he'd be back later.'

Uberto nodded, with a sigh. Too many things all at the same time. He had to take a moment to think clearly and decide on his plan of campaign. But to do that he had to be free of constraints. He only hoped that the Archbishop would go back to where he'd come from as soon as possible.

The trip to the port of Corticella was straightforward and enjoyable. They followed the bank of the Navile by land, surrounded by the shouts of the muleteers urging on the mules pulling the barges and the whistles of the boatmen telling each other to watch out when they passed each other. All that coming and going was in itself protection enough from Guido Arlotti and his henchmen if they had been thinking of getting their own back. But Adia doubted whether they would feel like trying anything in their current sorry state, and Mondino agreed with her.

They walked along in line: first the donkey, weighed down with bags held in strong cord nets. Then Adia and Mondino, who took turns in spurring the donkey with a slap on his rear when he came to a halt, and then the dogs constantly running back and forth, panting with their tongues hanging out, but aware of every movement around them.

They were still talking about the death of the German Templar and Adia asked if the corpse had by chance had the mark of a wound like that of an awl in the chest.

Mondino looked at her with a combination of amazement and suspicion. 'How did you know that?'

While general information about the state of the corpse was by now in the public domain, that particular had not leaked out. In fact, Mondino might have been the only one to have noticed it, and only because Angelo da Piczano had an identical wound.

Adia smiled enigmatically. 'Thanks to my sorceress's gifts, naturally. Didn't the people who told you about me say that I can also read the past and the future?'

293

'Don't joke, please, just answer my question.'

Adia smacked her hand against the donkey's rump, clicking her tongue at the same time, and the animal, which had stopped for a second to stare at the canal, obediently walked on.

'It's only a guess, Messer physician,' she said, with a twinkle in her eye. 'If that man was killed with a powder that transforms blood into iron, it's unlikely that he drank it dissolved in a liquid, don't you think?'

'I've already thought of that,' said Mondino. 'If it did, all the blood vessels in the poison's passage would be transformed into metal too. Whereas the transmutation only took place in the heart and surrounding veins.'

This was the question that most flummoxed him from a scientific point of view. And the one that he hadn't known how to answer when Gerardo and Hugues de Narbonne had put it to him.

'That means,' continued Adia, 'that the poison, as you call it, was injected directly into the heart. Through a hollow stiletto or something similar.'

'But such an instrument doesn't exist!' exclaimed Mondino. 'I keep myself up to date with the most modern scientific discoveries and I've never heard of a thin, hollow blade that is strong enough to puncture the heart of a man without bending.'

A costermonger came out of a turning to their left, pulling a cart heavy with vegetables. His dog, a great big half-breed with drooping ears, started snarling and barking at the two Molossers and Mondino was afraid that a dogfight would break out. Adia issued a brief command in Arabic and the mastiffs stood stock still on the verge, without showing the slightest animosity towards the costermonger's dog, which went on snarling and drooling, but didn't come any closer. The man, having yelled at his hound without response, dropped the handlebars of his cart and went to give the dog a decent kick up the road. As they walked on, Mondino noticed that he made a superstitious sign to ward off evil with his left hand.

'People hereabouts believe that my dogs are possessed by the Devil because they behave in a reasonable manner,' Adia commented, with a shrug of her shoulders.

'Their obedience to your commands surprised me too,' replied Mondino.

'In my country the training of dogs, horses and falcons is an age-old tradition,' she said. 'My people discovered centuries ago that to make yourself obeyed you need to use gentleness rather than violence.'

Mondino stopped himself from making a stinging comment about the Muslims who infested the Holy Land, and their remorseless manner of fighting. They used anything but gentleness.

'You were talking about the instrument,' he said instead, going back to the subject he had most at heart.

'There's nothing more to be said,' answered Adia, her mood suddenly darker. The peasant's sign to ward off evil must have hurt her more than she liked to admit. 'A thing doesn't exist until someone finds a need for it. When there's a need, sooner or later, it will be invented.'

Mondino reflected a moment and thought to himself that she might be right. No physician had ever needed to inject medicine directly into the blood, but the idea was fascinating. Certainly, in that way the medicine would have a much faster effect. But again, to be able to do that, you would have to clarify exactly how the circulation of the blood functioned. That took him back to all his current problems and reduced him to silence too.

They went on a fair distance without speaking, and only when they were in sight of Corticella, a small but very lively and noisy hamlet, did they renew their conversation. Mondino wanted to take the first barge to Bologna, but he felt a strange reluctance at saying goodbye to the woman with the amber skin and the throaty voice. And not even the thought of the Inquisitor and his ultimatum stopped Mondino from accompanying Adia to the friends with whom she was staying.

The port was congested with boats of every type, from basic punts, which moved with agility even in very shallow waters and were used to transport small merchandise about, to the more imposing merchant ships with trapezoid sails that navigated the wide Po river, as well as the open sea. Mondino was fascinated by the spectacle of the boats and the haggling that was going on practically everywhere: on the embankment, on improvised benches dotted around, and in the few stone-built shops that had grown up around the port. One of the shops attracted his attention because it had its own little harbour and the smaller boats, passing under a high arch, could sail straight into the building to unload their goods. The sight made him think of the descriptions he had heard of life in Venice, and suddenly, perhaps because of his closeness to all the boats, he was seized by a longing to travel, to see new places and not to limit his life to one city.

Adia seemed to know a lot about the boats and sails and as they walked she explained their various functions. Mondino asked if she had travelled much and she replied that she could talk for hours about all the places she'd been to.

They finally arrived at the inn she was heading for, a building that seemed too big for the hamlet, with a tavern on the ground floor and several bedrooms on the two upper storeys. The innkeeper made a great fuss of Adia, telling her that she could stay for as long as she wanted, and he wouldn't hear of payment.

'I healed his daughter of a nasty form of herpes pox,' explained Adia, while she settled the animals in the courtyard behind the house.

'What did you give her?' asked Mondino, curious.

'Elder leaves, in a decoction and compresses. But if I'm honest,' she added with a smile, 'I had the impression that the illness went away of its own accord, once it had run its course.'

When they had both freshened up, Adia in her room and Mondino at the well in the courtyard, she suggested they ate together before he went on his way.

'With all the excitement that followed your arrival at my house, I have only just remembered that I haven't eaten yet. And they serve a delicious rabbit in wine here,' she said.

Mondino accepted immediately, showing an enthusiasm that was perhaps more than the circumstances called for, and they went into the tavern. It was full of people. The innkeeper said that there were no free tables just then and asked if they'd mind eating in a room upstairs, assuring them that the food would be brought as soon as possible. Mondino realised that the man had mistaken them for a couple and began to protest, but Adia pulled his sleeve and signalled to him to be quiet.

As they walked upstairs, she explained: 'He's too nice to say so, but many people here recognise me and he doesn't want his customers to be uncomfortable, seeing a witch in the room.'

They ate their meal in a small private room adjoining Adia's bedroom, decorated with a low table and two small sofas upholstered in red velvet. In fact, given the late hour, they were nearer the evening than the midday meal, and the sun, already in its descent towards the horizon in the direction of Modena, lit the room with a warm reddish light.

While they ate the rabbit, dipping pieces of bread in the sauce and drinking a fresh and deceptively light Trebbiano, they carried on talking of alchemy and Adia told him about all the places that her thirst for knowledge had taken her. She had been to Greece, where she'd seen the ruins of the Parthenon and the rock of Athens. Then she'd travelled to Sicily, from where she had sailed to Barcelona and continued on foot to the Basilica of Santiago di Compostela, and from there she had crossed the Pyrenees and then on to Bologna.

Now she was planning to go to Venice, where she wanted to meet a Hebrew sage about whom she'd heard a great deal, then she would travel on to France.

Mondino said that one day he wanted to visit the School of Medicine in Montpellier, but he knew that he would find it difficult to make time for such a long trip, at his age and with all the responsibilities tied to his family and profession.

'Our responsibilities are where we want them to be,' replied Adia, looking at him keenly. 'As for your age, I don't know what you mean.'

'Don't make a fool of me, Mistress Adia,' said Mondino, somewhat offended that she wanted to take him up on that point. 'I'm quite aware that I am no longer in the first flush of youth, and—'

'Don't be ridiculous, please,' she interrupted him. 'Can't you see that for every one of your desires, you immediately find an excuse not to carry it out? Don't you see that everything depends on you?'

'No, I don't, and I would ask you to let it be, so as not to ruin this nice moment with an argument. Let's just say that perhaps I am simply too weak and lazy to take on the journey to Montpellier.'

'Weak?' she laughed. 'To judge from the way you fought those cut-throats, I would have felt safe with you even without my mastiffs.'

At those words, Mondino felt the blood rise to his face, but he did his best to appear indifferent and said nothing.

Adia looked at him and burst out laughing. 'You really are funny right now, do you know that? You force yourself to sit there looking as inscrutable as a statue, but you're not really like that.'

'You seem to know a great deal about how I am and what I want.'

'That's right,' she answered, with a cheek that Mondino didn't have the time to find irritating, because of what she added immediately afterwards. She looked him straight in the eye and with her lips slightly apart, she said, 'And I also know what I want.'

In the headiness that the wine had brought on, Mondino didn't know how they found themselves in one another's arms, while their mouths searched eagerly for each other. Murmuring in his ear, Adia told him to carry her into the bedroom and he obeyed immediately, lifting her up in his arms without ceasing to kiss her and feeling vaguely sacrilegious as he crossed the threshold with her in the manner reserved for spouses.

He didn't waste time looking for a candle; the beam of light that filtered underneath the shutter was enough. Gently he laid Adia down on the mattress, which was makeshift but covered in a clean sheet. Quickly and expertly she helped him take off his tunic and breeches, provoking a passing fit of jealousy in him, then she too was naked, kneeling at his feet.

For a moment they just stared at one another, motionless and in silence. Their desire was speaking for them, and what Adia did next didn't seem vulgar to Mondino, but an act of love, tender and terribly exciting. He ruffled her dark hair, muttering words that made no sense at all. Twice he tried to pull away from that avid mouth to unite himself with her, and twice Adia dissuaded him with her hand, while Mondino adapted to being guided and not taking control of their lovemaking.

At a certain point Adia lay backwards on the mattress with languid movements, never losing eye contact with him. Mondino overcame the impulse to jump on her like an animal, and stood there contemplating her body in the half-light, guessing at what she wanted him to do.

'Come here,' said Adia, in a hoarse voice, beckoning to him.

Mondino knelt on the mattress and began to caress her slowly, starting at her knees and moving up towards her breasts. Adia let out a soft groan and tried to pull him to her, but this time it was he who resisted. Her every look and gesture gave him a pleasure that until then he would not have thought possible.

'You learn quickly,' she laughed, softly.

She pulled him by his wrist and this time Mondino was on top of her with the impetus of a river in spate, holding nothing back.

They made love with eagerness the first time, then, after a brief rest in which there was no need for them to speak, they did it again more slowly, but with equal relish. Mondino fell asleep thinking that he had missed the last boat to Bologna. He had confused dreams in which all the events of the long day seemed to swirl in a vortex: the operation on Hugues de Narbonne's brain, the three armed men who had burst into Adia's house, her sad dogs and her warm smell.

Uberto da Rimini tried to hide his fury without much success. He couldn't explode in a fit of rage in front of the Archbishop of Ravenna. And yet Rinaldo da Concorezzo seemed created for the very purpose of making him lose his calm. As soon as Rinaldo arrived he had installed himself in Uberto's study, called for all the papers relating to the Templar trial, and only then had called for the Inquisitor. Now, after a frugal supper, he was subjecting Uberto to an out and out interrogation. Uberto only prayed that he hadn't left any compromising notes among the papers by mistake.

But what seemed to interest Rinaldo the most was the death of the German.

'Monsignor,' said Uberto, trying not to give his words too

challenging a tone, 'I am convinced that the murder of the Templar, Wilhelm von Trier, found dead in Santo Stefano, is the second murder of that type here in Bologna. The first, as I have told you before, was not discovered, but only because the cadaver had disappeared, as well as the assassin.'

'I am in no doubt that you are convinced,' replied the Archbishop. 'And I am also prepared to believe that it really did happen just as you say it did, Father Uberto.' He paused, looking at the papers and parchments strewn across the table as though searching for inspiration. 'The point on which we continue to misunderstand one another is that, to be relevant to the trial, personal convictions must be supported by proof.'

Uberto would have liked to reply that there was plenty of proof. A corpse with an empty hole in place of the heart and a man who, after killing him, had paid two gravediggers to throw the body in a nameless grave. But if he gave in to the temptation of revealing the truth, Rinaldo da Concorezzo would scupper everything, with his mania for absolute legality and his obstinate refusal to use torture to obtain confessions. He would even be capable of formally reprimanding Uberto if he found out about da Rimini blackmailing Mondino de Liuzzi to stand witness at the trial.

'I agree with you, Monsignor,' Uberto said, simply. 'I am doing my best to get hold of the necessary evidence.'

He felt strange, sitting on an uncomfortable chair on the wrong side of his desk, in his own study. He wanted to get to his feet and put his papers in order, but etiquette demanded that he do nothing until invited to.

'How exactly are you going about it?' asked Rinaldo.

The moment had arrived. Until now Uberto had got by with half-truths and omissions. Now it was a case of taking the plunge and knowingly telling a lie to his own Archbishop. A lie in the name of faith was not a true sin, but Rinaldo certainly wouldn't see it like that. If he found out, he would dismiss Uberto. As he looked up at the ceiling in search of ideas, Uberto felt something akin to hate. Why on earth hadn't the Archbishop stayed a few more days in his castle at Argenta, in the middle of the Ferrarese swamps? Once he had the confession from the young prisoner in the *comune* and a statement from Mondino de Liuzzi, the manner in which they were obtained would take second place and what would count was the result. Should he then have any problems, Uberto would even be able to bypass the Archbishop, sending a message straight to the Pope.

But Rinaldo had chosen precisely that moment to come and cause trouble, and he had to put a good face on it.

Just as Uberto was getting ready to unleash a stream of untruths, a novice knocked and put his head round the door. After bowing deeply to the Archbishop, he announced, red in the face, that there was a certain Guido Arlotti waiting for Father Uberto downstairs. Arlotti said it was urgent and they had not managed to make him understand that the Inquisitor could not be disturbed. What was the novice to do?

If Guido dared to insist on seeing him at a time like this, thought Uberto, it must be something serious. But however much he burned with the desire to know what it was, he could not interrupt his meeting with the Archbishop.

'Tell him to come back later,' he said to the novice. 'I'm busy now.'

'Why does this person want to see you so urgently?' intervened Rinaldo da Concorezzo.

'He is an ex-confrère who for years now has been on the path to perdition,' said Uberto, again embarking down the road of the half-truth. 'Recently he has been returning to the faith, but his crises of conscience can very well wait until the end of our meeting.'

'Allow me to correct you, Father,' said Rinaldo. 'Nothing is more important than the return of the prodigal son. Please go, I will wait for you here.'

Uberto swallowed the rebuke, thanked the Archbishop for his magnanimity and hurried after the novice down to the floor below, worried about the news but pleased by this unexpected piece of good fortune.

Guido Arlotti was standing in the atrium. He was wearing a clean tunic, faded green breeches and a floppy cap that hid his ears, but not enough to hide a face covered in grazes and bruises. His lips were swollen and cut and he had a black eye. Uberto led him to a little room with a crucifix painted on the wall and sparse furniture where the friar who guarded the street door received the postulants. The room was dimly lit by a candle at the foot of the crucifix, but the Inquisitor didn't bother to light the oil lamp on the cupboard next to the small table. Nor did he invite Guido to sit down on one of the two benches. He indicated to him that he should speak quietly and asked what had happened. The ex-friar told him about the misadventure with Mondino, Adia and the mastiffs.

'And what did you do when the woman sent you away?'

'All three of us needed a physician so we came back to the city.' Before the Inquisitor could object, Guido raised his eyes to him and added, 'The witch will pay for it sooner or later and I can find Mondino when I want. But that's not why I'm here. Do you know about the latest murder?'

Uberto let his hands drop to his sides with irritation. 'I've just found out, when I was at the *comune*. It's a serious problem, because the young man I intended to accuse of the first two can't have committed the third. He's been in prison all morning.'

'That is exactly what I wanted to talk to you about,' replied Guido, with an expression of triumph on his huge face. 'The murderers are Mondino and a young man called Gerardo. I am almost certain that it's the bogus student you were telling me about, the one who's in jail now.'

It was almost too good to be true. Now Uberto knew Francesco Salimbene's real name and the next day he would be able to use the fact to break the Templar. But it was very important to check the information. There was no room for a false step.

'Are you absolutely sure?' he asked.

'Yes,' answered Guido, without hesitation. 'The body was found at vespers, but the man was killed between lauds and daybreak. I saw everything.'

Uberto da Rimini stared at him at length before speaking. If Guido really had witnessed the murder, the case could be considered closed. And the trial against the Templars, despite all the Archbishop's nitpicking, would be concluded with an exemplary sentence. A monk disguised as a student, who killed three confrères in a devilish manner, with the help of a physician who had always been against the Church. A fact that would not fail to influence even the Franciscan Inquisitors themselves, who with their misplaced compassion represented the last obstacle to overcome before the Order of the Temple was entirely rooted out from the garden of the Church.

'If you saw everything, why didn't you call the guards immediately so that they could catch them at it?' he asked, struck by a sudden feeling of mistrust. 'And if you couldn't do it for some reason that you are about to give me, why didn't you inform me immediately? Next to a thing of the kind, all the rest takes second place.'

Guido must have understood the importance of choosing the right words, and he thought before answering. 'I didn't actually see it,' he corrected himself. 'I was hidden outside the house and I *heard* what they were doing. They were talking about an operation to the brain, but I had no idea that they were opening his head to fill it with worms. When they came out, I thought that the man was alive and decided to go and have a look later. Only when I got back to the city from Bova did I hear the news, and then I realised what had happened.'

'Did they mention the heart too?'

Again, Guido Arlotti paused slightly before replying. 'No, but if it's for the good of the Church, I could swear they did before a notary. Naturally, in exchange for the plenary indulgence I have already asked of you. Bearing false testimony is a mortal sin.'

Uberto began to pace to and fro in the narrow space between the door and the wall with the crucifix. The most important thing now was to arrest Mondino. There was no sense in making him testify against the Templars any more, given that he too was a murderer. The physician didn't know that he had been found out yet and he had to be delivered into the safe hands of the *comune* before he tried to escape.

Uberto opened the rectangular cupboard beside the table and took out some writing materials: thick paper, quill, a half-full pot of ink and a bar of red sealing wax. Without sitting down, he leaned over the table and wrote a brief letter to the *Podestà* and then waved the sheet to dry the ink. After which he folded it and took the candle that stood at the foot of the frescoed Christ and held the bar of sealing wax over it, making two large drops of wax fall on to the paper. He pressed the soft wax with his ring and handed the letter to Guido.

'This says that I request the immediate arrest of Mondino de Liuzzi, the renowned physician of the *Studium*. He is wanted with Francesco Salimbene, currently detained, for his part in a triple murder committed with recourse to the magic arts,' Uberto said. 'Take it to the *Podestà* and repeat what you have seen and heard, just as you said it to me, except for the fact that the youth's real name is Gerardo. I would prefer that information to remain secret for the present. Do you understand?'

305

'Yes, Father.'

'Then go. And come back to report to me when you can.'

Guido left the monastery and Uberto began to walk slowly back up the stairs to the Archbishop. Now he was ready to lie without hesitation. The game was coming to an end and, after Mondino's arrest, Rinaldo da Concorezzo would be able to do very little to put a spanner in the works.

He only had to keep the Archbishop in the dark about everything for another couple of days.

Dear Gerardo,

As I write this letter you are being shut in a cell. When you find out the truth, you will think me a monster, and perhaps you will be right. The scar that disfigures my face is nothing compared with the horror that I carry in my soul. I know that what I've done can never be forgiven, and I don't want anyone's forgiveness.

I will soon be lying in my grave, protected by he who protects Bologna. We met when it was too late for us to change the course of our lives. God is unjust, to some he gives with full hands, from others he takes everything.

But at least I want to make sure that you are not convicted of a crime that you did not commit.

Please read my story, I ask nothing else of you.

Fiamma

These words stuck in Gerardo's mind. The letter was the only thing that he had managed to read before the guards came to take him to the Inquisitor again. As soon as he was brought back to his cell, exhausted, in pain and with his left arm dislocated, his first thought was to read the rest.

In the darkness, he moved his hand around under the warm straw and with a sigh of relief found that the diary was still there. He found the lamp too, and then he had to rest because those simple movements had left him drained. When he had found his strength again, he went down on all fours and began to pat the walls and ceiling of the cell in search of something to use as a flintstone.

In a corner he felt a crack beneath his fingers and clawed at it with his nails until he managed to break off a fragment of brick.

His arms and shoulders hurt so much that he couldn't manage to strike the shard of brick with enough force to produce a spark. After a number of failed attempts, Gerardo gave up and instead lay slowly down until he was stretched prone on the freezing floor.

Despite the interrogation and the prospect of being tortured again the following day, his thoughts turned almost exclusively on Fiamma's letter. The fact that she had used such an intimate tone in her letter provoked an emotion that was difficult to explain. But the sense of her words had frightened him. What had she done that was so terrible that it could never be forgiven? Why was she convinced that she was about to go to her grave? When she spoke of a crime that he hadn't committed, was she referring to Angelo da Piczano? And how did she know about that? The answers to his questions must be in her notebook, but to be able to read it, he had to light the lamp.

He tried to get up, without success. His short rest and the damp air seemed to have made his limbs even more rigid. In the end he slept on the floor, curled up on his side like a dog, his head resting on his good arm.

XV

When his waking dreams filled with images of Rainerio on his deathbed, Mondino suddenly opened wide his eyes, struck by a sense of guilt. How could he have forgotten his father?

He quickly got up, dressed in silence and left the room without finding the courage to wake Adia. Perhaps they'd never see each other again and just then he didn't feel up to a distressing farewell.

It was still dark, but downstairs the innkeeper was already up and spreading clean straw over the floor with a pitchfork. As he worked, he kept up a continuous sniffing, hawking and spitting; he must have caught a cold despite the hot weather. Mondino mumbled a greeting without looking him in the face, paid for the previous evening's supper and went out into the street. At the port he got on the first barge he found and accepted the inflated price that the owner requested without wasting time bargaining. He sat impatiently through the slow journey pulled by a mule along the towpath that followed the embankment. As he arrived in Bologna, the sun was just rising, the light picking out the red bricks of the houses. He got off just past the Circla in front of the salt shops and got a ride on a cart pulled by a donkey. Soon afterwards he was letting himself into his house, furtive as a thief, ardently praying that his father hadn't died while he had been away.

Uberto rose early to receive news from Guido before the Archbishop took up his whole day re-examining the trial papers. But the prelate burst into Uberto's study just as Guido was making his report.

'What is this story about a student and a physician accused of murder and witchcraft?' Rinaldo asked, without taking any notice of Guido, who immediately got up from his chair and moved discreetly towards the door, leaving as soon as the Archbishop had taken a few steps into the room. 'And why was I not informed that the student you suspected of these murders is under arrest at the *comune*?'

'I was going to tell you this very morning, Monsignor,' lied Uberto, wondering who had told him. 'I was only waiting for you to get up. I'm amazed that someone else has got there before me.'

Rinaldo da Concorezzo gave him a cold look. 'You can give up your ham-fisted attempts to find out who my informers are. All you need to know is that in every monastery of my diocese there are trusted people who keep me in touch with everything that goes on. So don't try to keep me in the dark about anything any longer, or you will regret it.' Uberto bowed his head without replying and the Archbishop went on: 'Go and tell the *Podestà* that I would like to interrogate the young man myself.'

'But, Monsignor, what about going through the trial papers?' said Uberto, playing for time.

'The re-examination of the papers is of secondary impor-tance with respect to the murders that have shaken Bologna in these last weeks. If the Templars really are implicated in such a thing, our priority is to verify the fact. I am certain that we can count on the full cooperation of the *Podestà*.'

Uberto didn't know which way to turn. If Rinaldo turned up at the *comune*, he would find out that Uberto had already started interrogating the Templar the day before and hadn't told him. He would also find out that it had been done under torture, and it would be futile hoping to convince him that Uberto had nothing to do with it. It was even possible that the Ghibelline of a Captain of the People would openly accuse him of having manoeuvred in such a way that the *comune* took the responsibility for torturing the prisoner while the Church reaped the benefits. Pantaleone had intimated as much to the *Podestà* the previous day.

At this moment Uberto realised that if he didn't want to end up as parish priest in some isolated mountain area, he would have to act quickly, without getting bogged down in moral scruples.

'It will be done as you wish, Monsignor,' he said, bowing. 'Please be good enough to wait while I go and make the necessary arrangements.'

Guido had been waiting in the corridor outside. When they had walked far enough away not to be overheard, he said quietly, 'What should I do?'

Uberto briefly explained. He had to spread the word that a Templar by the name of Gerardo, going under the false name of Francesco Salimbene of Imola, had killed three people in an atrocious manner to respect a pact with the Devil. And incite the crowd to a good bit of hotheaded unrest.

'It won't be difficult,' Uberto said. 'The discontent about the price of bread doesn't seem to be abating, and a spark should set them off.'

Perhaps the frenzied crowd might even break into the *comune* and tear the prisoner limb from limb. Or, as had happened occasionally in the past, the *Podestà* might decide to throw him from the balcony to be pulled apart by the populace to avoid things getting any worse. In one way or another, the resulting brawls would create the diversion that Uberto needed in order to convince the Archbishop that it was too dangerous to leave the monastery. Then, even if Gerardo did survive, it would give the Inquisitor time to think of a new strategy.

'It will cost you,' said Guido. 'I've done this sort of thing before and I know that to get the right results you need at least six or seven good scandalmongers to unleash in the markets and taverns.'

Uberto couldn't use the monastery's money for that sort of operation. The bursar would notice and report him to the prior. And he couldn't even draw on the special funds that the Inquisition could make use of because Rinaldo da Concorezzo would be going through every single note of expenditure with a fine-tooth comb. He had no choice but to pay with his own money.

'Give them the necessary in advance,' he said to Guido. 'And I'll pay you back as soon as the Archbishop has left.'

The smirk that covered the defrocked priest's face made the Inquisitor's guts boil in rage. Uberto knew what he was going to say before he even opened his mouth.

'Father, unfortunately I do not possess that much money,' said Guido. 'If it were only me, I'd wait, but the agitators will need to be paid immediately. Besides, I need to send them out with their pockets full, to pay for the beer to create some agreement about what they are saying.'

Pursing his lips into a narrow line, Uberto looked at Arlotti for a long time, but Guido stared straight back at him. The fallen priest who lived off criminal earnings, in the company of murderers and prostitutes, was defying him. His instinct had told him that Uberto was in disgrace with the

Archbishop, and he was no longer disposed to run risks if he wasn't promptly paid. Uberto was overcome with a sudden desire for a quarrel, but he managed to control himself. Guido wasn't his enemy, but the others, those who were conspiring against him from above and below. They were the ones who must be stopped, and Guido was the only instrument he had to do it.

'Come with me,' he said at last, walking towards his cell.

When they got to the door, he signalled to Guido to go in. From a table by the door, Uberto picked up a soft leather bag of coins and threw it towards Arlotti contemptuously. Guido caught it in mid-air and briefly weighed it in the palm of his hand before it disappeared under his tunic.

'There are enough florins and Bolognese lira in that to pay for everything,' said Uberto. 'Make sure you do a good job.'

'You will be well pleased, Father,' replied the ex-priest, with a cunning smile. Then, in a voice that appeared almost concerned, he added, 'In these situations there is always a death or two. Women raped and killed in the alleys, children trampled, stabbings ... Once it is stirred up, the crowd is uncontrollable.'

'I know, and it is a tragic pity,' replied Uberto, shaken by an involuntary shiver at the thought of what he was about to do. 'But this is a question of defending the Christian faith from a murderer who thinks nothing of selling his soul in exchange for who knows what squalid favours, and from a prelate who is too weak for the position he holds. Unfortunately sacrifice is necessary.'

'If it is for the faith, that suits me,' said Guido. 'But when it is all over, I want the plenary indulgence you promised me without delay. I need to be absolved of all the sins I've committed to carry out your orders.'

'You will have it, don't worry,' replied Uberto. 'Now go, there's no time to lose.'

Guido Arlotti went out and Uberto was about to follow him, but caught by a sudden impulse he went down on his knees and began to pray with fervour. Guido would have his indulgence, but who would absolve the Inquisitor? Several times he asked forgiveness of God for what he was about to do, for the deaths he might cause and the lies that he would have to tell. Only the certainty of being in the right gave him the strength to go on. Of course he wanted to save himself too, but only because he knew that he could still do so much for the Church and the defence of the faith. It was up to him to fight, given that the Archbishop was a coward. And if he managed, if his actions were shown to be pivotal in the successful condemnation of the Templars, as was doubtless the wish of His Holiness Clement V, he had no fear that his loyalty would be rewarded in a higher place.

Comforted by these thoughts, Uberto left his cell and ordered the first friar he met in the corridor to go immediately to the *Podestà*, to advise of the Archbishop's imminent visit. Then he returned to his study, where he told Rinaldo da Concorezzo that he had made the arrangements and that in a few hours the *Podestà* would be ready to receive the Archbishop.

'Then we'll go on with our work,' said Rinaldo. 'We can go over to the *comune* later.'

'As you wish, Monsignor.'

If Guido did his job well, in about two or three hours the centre of the city would be impassable. Uberto armed himself with patience and docility as he went to get the trial papers from the large locked cupboard at the end of the room.

Gerardo opened his eyes in the darkness. He had no idea how much time had passed. The thought of Fiamma's diary consumed him entirely, but his tortured body was now almost frozen by the cold and prevented him from sitting up. With great patience he began to move his hands and feet a little at a time. Very slowly he rolled first on to one side and then on to the other; then he stretched his neck and lifted his shoulders. Only after interminable efforts did he manage to teach his body elementary movements again, like a dead man resuscitated from the grave. Then he managed to get on to all fours, took the lamp and struck the ground with the sliver of brick with enough strength to create a little cascade of sparks.

Nothing happened.

A spark wasn't enough to light the wick, he needed some tinder and the straw was too damp.

With his good hand, Gerardo grabbed the hem of his tunic and put it in his mouth. He began to tear at it with his teeth until he managed to rip a piece off. Then, with minute perseverance, he pulled the strip of cloth apart, gathering the threads on the floor in a small pile. On top of them he laid some wisps of straw that weren't too damp, and went back to striking the brick on the floor. At the fourth or fifth attempt, the tinder took and began to burn, although without a flame. Gerardo gently blew on it, careful not to put it out, and finally the pile of threads caught fire. Quickly, he took a piece of straw and held it to the wick and a second later the cell was filled with a trembling light. There wasn't much oil left in the lamp so Gerardo quickly began to read the diary. It was written in Latin, with the date at the top of every page.

18 January AD 1305
Today I've been in the cave for a week, or perhaps longer. The pain in my cheek has lessened a bit, but the skin feels stretched as though it weren't my own. I don't know how I got here. I walked a long way, crying and raving as if I were mad, then I slept and my

314

memory of the next few days is unclear. Whereas what happened before that is vivid in every detail, almost as though I were still there now. Initially I couldn't see anything, I could only hear, curled up in the secret hideaway under the floor where my father had told me to hide when the three men pulled up their horses outside our house.

They were three Knights of the Temple. They entered the house, tied him up and began to torture him with scalding irons, asking him to tell them the secret of the elixir. He continued to deny any knowledge of it, but they didn't believe him. They mentioned a Turkish alchemist who had been killed and found at the gates of Gharnata with his heart missing from his chest. They accused my father of killing him. My father denied that too, but I could tell he was lying. I knew because in the last year he had abandoned his alchemy experiments, had given up teaching me about medicinal herbs and had insisted that I learn how to cut bone and flesh like a surgeon. First he made me practise on the corpses of cats and dogs and then on human bodies that he got hold of who knows how.

In actual fact I didn't realise then that I had understood. It was only afterwards, when I got here, that I put it all together. Then I was trembling from fear and praying to Jesus that the men would stop making my father suffer and that they wouldn't find me.

But they did find me. I must have made a noise without meaning to, because suddenly the room fell silent, then one of the men lifted up the carpet, opened the trap door and pulled me out. I was shouting and crying, and my father was shouting too. But they were completely without pity. They tied me up and put me in

315

front of him. Then they said that if he didn't talk they would kill me. Crying, my father told them that he had no secret to reveal, that he had been trying all his life to discover how to make the elixir, but had never managed. The oldest Templar and the young one had a moment of doubt, and I turned to look at the one who seemed to be their leader. He was an imposing man, with blond curly hair and hairy arms. He pointed to the brazier with the hot irons that they had used to torture my father.

'Let's see if your secret is worth your daughter's suffering,' he said.

The young one, who by the look of him could almost have been a good man, stood in front of the brazier, saying, 'Commander, the child's got nothing to do with it! We can't have that on our consciences!'

The other, who spoke Latin with a French accent, said, 'It's too late to change your mind, Angelo. He must talk. If the pain from his own flesh is not enough, perhaps the sight of his daughter's will convince him.'

I hoped that the young man would contradict him and defend me. I wasn't guilty of anything! But he just lowered his head and moved away. Then the older Templar, the one the others called Wilhelm, took a red-hot iron from the brazier and brought it close to my face. My father yelled to them not to harm me and he would tell them all they wanted to know. The old man took his hand away and my father began to speak. He said that the secret of the elixir was too important to be kept at home so he had hidden it in a cave in the hills. In the house he only kept a map indicating where the cave was. He nodded with his head at the larger bookshelf. The three men pushed it over without

*hesitation. It came crashing down and there in the wall
behind was a niche with the map in it.*

*At that point the leader made a sign to the old man
to come back over to me.*

'But Hugues,' he said. 'He has already confessed.'

*'We haven't got much time,' the leader insisted. 'He
must understand that it is not worth his while to try
anything and send us who knows where to find the
elixir. Brand her face. If he doesn't tell us everything
immediately, we will blind her, first one eye, and then
the other.'*

*'No! I beg you!' shouted my father. 'I've told you the
truth!'*

*But this time the old man didn't hold back. I saw the
burning iron coming towards me, I cried out, I felt a
hot wind on my face just like when you open the oven
door to check the baking, then a pain that was so strong
that it went beyond all my imaginings. Then there was a
smell of burned meat. I let out a terrible scream just as
everything became muddled.*

*It is from that moment on that I can't remember very
well what happened. Suddenly I opened my eyes, and
the house was in flames.*

Gerardo looked up, he was breathing heavily. It couldn't be
true. Knights Templar, people who had sworn to rescue the
Holy Land from the infidels and to keep Christ's true faith at
any cost. They couldn't besmirch themselves with such infamy.
Torture, murder, violence to a child ... And yet the diary was
evidence of the opposite. The scar on Fiamma's cheek had
been produced in that brutal manner.

And the names of the three Templars who were responsible
for the abomination were all too familiar to him.

He looked back down at the page and read on.

317

6 February AD 1305

I've killed a man, and all for nothing.

He was a goatherd who had five goats. I attracted his attention by calling for help and then smashed his head with a stone. I killed a goat as well, to eat, and I've kept another alive. I let the rest of the flock go.

Then I cut the goatherd's sternum as my father taught me and took out his heart by carefully cutting the veins and arteries. Then, step by step, I followed the instructions that I found in the cave, putting the ingredients to macerate together under a bed of manure made from my own excrement.

After only three days I went to check the compost and saw that it had turned into a grey and uniform matter, instead of red as it said in the instructions. I followed the next steps, adding the other ingredients and grinding it all until I had a very fine powder. Then, with a prayer for God's forgiveness for what I had done, I wet a piece of cloth and applied some of the powder to my scar.

Nothing happened.

Consumed by an indescribable anxiety, I tried to make the live goat drink the elixir dissolved in water, to see what happened before taking the risk of drinking it myself.

Nothing happened.

Distraught, I decided to kill myself. I had done all this in the hope of being able to heal the wound that had ruined my face by making one cheek swollen like a piece of cord soaked in water. But my father must have made a mistake when he copied down the secret he'd extorted from the Turkish alchemist. Or else the secret was false from the beginning. When I found the little book with the secret instructions, I understood

318

*why the man who had turned up at our house had
been found at the gates of Gharnata without his heart.
My father had killed him to make the elixir. But he
can't have succeeded either. Otherwise he would no
doubt have told the three Templars who had tortured
him. Above all when they turned their wickedness on
me.*

*I cannot believe that he would have wanted to
protect the secret at the cost of his life. And mine.*

*When I realised that I had killed a human being for
nothing, I knew I was no better than the three men who
had killed my father. And I decided to kill myself.*

*But before cutting my own throat with the knife, I
wanted to practise. I didn't want my hand to tremble so
that I would suffer for hours before dying. I dragged the
goat into the cave and butchered it with one strike, but
in the process it struggled and managed to bite my
hand. As it bit me I made an involuntary movement,
knocking over the bowl that contained the fake elixir,
and some of the powder fell on to the goat's throat, as it
lay there juddering in the spasms of death.*

*Then something happened that is beyond
comprehension: before my eyes the goat's blood began
to turn into a metal similar to iron. I saw its veins swell
and break the skin, as they became filaments of metal.
The transmutation went on until the poor animal was
dead and then it stopped because the blood was no
longer carrying the granules of grey powder around the
organism.*

*It was in that precise moment that the bittersweet
idea of revenge began to germinate inside me. I did not
yet know how or when, but I realised that I could never
kill myself without relieving the world of my father's
murderers and the architects of my ugliness.*

319

Sitting on the floor of his prison cell, Gerardo's mind was somewhere else entirely. It seemed to him that he could almost see the little girl's horror. She had just escaped from a house in flames, wounded and pained in body and soul, and then, more by instinct than conscious decision, she got herself to her father's secret hiding place in the mountains above the city of Granada. It must have been the place shown on the map that Mondino had taken off the German's corpse. But how was it that the three Templars who had taken the map from her father under torture hadn't found her?

Perhaps the answer was in the following pages, but there was no time left to read on. It was clear that Fiamma was the murderer they were looking for, and something should be done to stop her as soon as possible. She would definitely have killed Hugues de Narbonne by now. And despite the Frenchman's guilt, Gerardo felt his heart contract at the thought that it was he who had delivered Hugues tied and gagged into the girl's hands.

Suddenly the words of Fiamma's letter came back to him: *I will soon be lying in my grave.* Without thinking, Gerardo began to pummel his fists on the door of the cell, shouting to the guard as loud as he could.

Mondino awoke with a jump and a muffled shout. Only when his breathing had calmed down did he realise that he was in fact back in his own bed, and not snared in a muddy swamp, being chased by thugs armed with sharp-ended pikes.

He sat up and the contact of his bare feet with the cold floor woke him properly. He had got home when everybody was in bed, had checked that his father was asleep and gone upstairs to his own room. He had just had time to take off his shoes before he collapsed on to his bed and fell asleep fully dressed.

From the light coming through the window, he realised that

it was already late morning. Another long day awaited him. He would have to go and find Gerardo to tell him to leave. Mondino would give him the whole day to get out of the city and that very evening would go to the monastery at San Domenico to speak to the Inquisitor. It was pointless hoping that he would succeed in catching Angelo da Piczano and Wilhelm von Trier's killer. He was certain that Gerardo wouldn't have discovered anything useful either. Mondino didn't regret what he had done, from the evening when he had helped Gerardo to get rid of Angelo's body to his skirmish with Guido Arlotti – a fight that might have cost him his life, if it hadn't been for Adia's mastiffs. His dream of mapping the complete human vascular system was worth the risks he'd run. But that road had led to a dead end.

He pulled out the chamber pot from under his bed, went to empty it out of the window over the garden and then put it back. It was Lorenza's job, but the woman had already got far too much to do looking after his father.

He went to the chest of drawers, filled the tin basin from the jug and washed, savouring the pleasure of the fresh water on his face. Then he picked up a razor, soaped his face carefully and began to shave, looking at his reflection in the silver mirror on the wall: bloodshot eyes, stubbly chin, dirty hair. The face looking back at him certainly wasn't the portrait of a great anatomist, famous throughout Italy and France. It was more that of a petty thief of the stamp of Guido Arlotti and his thugs.

But everything would be different from the next day on. Mondino's life would go back to being an ordered sequence of study, lessons and daily tasks, with no more running away, being chased and coming to blows. With no more scrapes between life and death. He would apologise to Liuzzo and ask him to go back on the decision to break up their collaboration and throw him out of the School of Medicine. And he would try not to think about Gerardo, obliged to start a new life from scratch in some foreign land.

When he had finished shaving, he put on a clean shirt and breeches and a flame-red tunic that he kept for special occasions. He didn't want to meet the Inquisitor tired and defeated. It was important at least to keep up a sense of decorum. So before he went downstairs he put his fur-trimmed cloak on over the tunic.

Dressed in full pomp, he went into his father's room. Rainerio was awake and seemed slightly better, but instead of giving him the usual tired smile, as soon as he saw Mondino, his face took on a look of alarm, almost terror.

'Mondino! Where have you been?'

'I got in at dawn, Father. No one saw me.'

'Thank heavens. You must leave immediately.'

Mondino felt his breath fail him. 'Leave? Why?'

'Last night a judge from the *comune* came round. He's a Tuscan who's been a friend of mine for years and he wanted to warn me that the city guards are coming to arrest you today.'

'On what basis?'

Rainerio lifted his chest, trying to raise himself up on his elbows. Mondino ran to the bedside and helped him sit up. When the old man was settled again, with a great big feather cushion behind his back, he looked at Mondino long and hard. 'Mondino, you must be honest with me,' he said. 'A father understands everything. But I must know the truth.' He paused and added, in a whisper, 'Have you killed someone?'

Mondino's first thought was that Guido Arlotti had died after their fight. But it wasn't possible. Arlotti was in a bad state, but not more so than himself. So it must be the old woman. But it was impossible that it had got back to his father.

He didn't want to lie to Rainerio, but he wasn't quite ready to admit to himself that he had killed Philomena.

'Have I been accused of killing someone?' he asked, cautiously.

Rainerio nodded. 'A Frenchman, Hugues de something, I don't remember what. He was found tied to the bed in his house, with his head sawn in half and full of worms. And the heart …'

'Turned into a block of iron,' murmured Mondino, almost to himself.

He couldn't believe his ears. When his father had mentioned Hugues, he thought that the man must have died as a result of the operation and the accusation of murder referred to that. Whereas in fact the murderer had found and killed Hugues and now they were accusing him of it.

'So you know,' said Rainerio, looking at him closely. 'Was it you?'

'No, I swear it wasn't,' replied Mondino, happy to be able to tell the truth at least about that. 'But I did go into that house and someone must have seen me.'

'Can you prove your innocence?'

Mondino shook his head, dismayed. Only Gerardo would have been able to testify in his favour, if the Templar hadn't been a wanted man too.

'Then you must leave,' said his father. 'I will ask Liuzzo to engage one of his lawyer friends, and we will do all we can to stop them convicting you. If we manage, you can come back.'

'I am sure it will all be resolved,' lied Mondino, without managing to look his father in the eye. 'When you see Liuzzo, please tell him that as soon as I can, I will ask his forgiveness for my unspeakable behaviour towards him.'

Saying that made Mondino feel better. To think that he might have the chance to apologise to his uncle helped him convince himself that he really did have a future.

'I will. Now go,' Rainerio said. 'The guards will be here any moment.'

Mondino said goodbye to his father with a kiss on the

323

forehead, left the room and hurried towards the kitchen. He almost fell over Lorenza, who, as soon as she saw him, childishly tried to hide something behind her back. It was a wooden cup of milk.

'Not again!' exclaimed Mondino, furiously.

'Forgive me,' said Lorenza, shaking nervously and looking at the floor. 'I beg you ...'

In an outburst of rage, Mondino put his hand out towards the cup, which fell to the ground spilling its contents all over the floor.

'I'll clean up straight away,' murmured the woman, turning to go back into the kitchen.

The smell coming from the floor reminded Mondino of something. On an impulse, he bent down and dipped a finger into what was left of the spilt milk and tasted it. The unmistakable pungent flavour awakened confused feelings and memories that he didn't know he had.

He suddenly understood what Lorenza was trying to do and when he saw her come back with a cloth in her hand, he exploded: 'You are giving my father your mother's milk instead of cow's milk.'

The woman tried to deny it by shaking her head. She was so terrified that she could hardly speak.

'No, it's not true ...'

'Don't lie, Lorenza. Not to me.'

Lorenza was giving Rainerio her mother's milk in the conviction, widespread among the populace, that women's milk possessed miracle-working properties, capable of healing every ill.

'Please,' she said, dissolving into sobs. 'Don't send us away ... We've nowhere to go ...'

She was trembling with fear. Hers was only a superstition and yet she had denied her own daughter the milk in order to give it to Rainerio. She deserved respect for her action, certainly not rebukes. To calm her, Mondino did something that he would never have thought himself capable of. He hugged her to him, holding her tight to his chest.

'Forgive me, Lorenza,' he said, softly. 'Do whatever you think is right for my father. It will be fine.'

Then leaving her stupefied and still sobbing with the cloth in her hand, he quickly crossed the kitchen and a few seconds later opened the street door.

Just at that moment a squad of the *Podestà's* guards was coming around the corner, led by a section leader. Mondino took a step backwards so as not to be seen, closed the door and stood motionless, not knowing what to do. There was no time to get away now. The only possible place to hide was inside. He turned and ran back across the courtyard and through the kitchen.

Lorenza was on her knees in the corridor cleaning up the milk. Mondino bent down to touch her shoulder. 'The guards are coming to arrest me,' he whispered. 'Don't betray me.'

He ran upstairs, while the guards entered the house asking for him in loud voices and walked into his study to look around for a place where someone might hide. For a second Mondino thought he could get out of the window and escape over the rooftops as Gerardo had done on the night that the whole ordeal had started. But the wall was too high and he would be in danger of finding himself hanging there like a haunch of Parma ham, without being able to hoist himself up on to the roof. And the courtyard below was too far down to jump without breaking a leg. Just then he heard steps and voices on the stairs. Without stopping to think, he climbed on to the window ledge and huddled on the narrow cornice that ran round the house.

He was only just in time. A second later the door was thrown open and a voice said, 'You two look in the bedroom. I'll search in here.'

It was a voice that Mondino thought he knew. He waited motionless in his spur-of-the-moment hiding place, hardly daring to breathe and hoping that he wouldn't be seen from the neighbouring houses. He tried not to think about what would happen if he were caught. Defamatory accusations, a trial in which it would be impossible for him to prove that he was innocent, almost certainly the death sentence. While the guard walked round the room rummaging in everything, Mondino thought of his notes for the anatomy treatise. The man might open the bundle, see it contained sheets with notes and drawings on them, and decide to sequester it as proof against him. Who knows what would happen to it then.

But his thoughts froze when he heard the steps come towards the window.

The man stopped and Mondino prayed that he wouldn't look out. The physician was squatting on the cornice, crouching with his head down to keep his balance. From below he must have looked like one of those gargoyles that can be seen on the façades of churches. He could hear the man breathing and even smell him; a blend of sweat and onions, strong but not unpleasant. Suddenly Mondino realised that the smell was getting stronger, and he understood. He slowly lifted his head and looked the man in the face.

Mondino recognised him immediately, not just because of the small scar that slightly disfigured his mouth. He had come to see Mondino a year earlier, desperate because he had a tumour on his lower lip that the surgeon he had been to see wouldn't dare touch. Mondino had operated on him and he had recovered, proclaiming that he would be eternally grateful. In the few seconds in which they stared at each other in silence, Mondino remembered that the man's name was Luca, like the patron saint of physicians.

'They sent me because they know that I know you,' said the guard, in a low voice.

He went quiet. The indecision on his face was evident. Mondino dared to hope.

Then, all of a sudden, the glimmer of hope died.

'I've found him!' he shouted. 'Over here!'

He grabbed Mondino by the scruff of his neck and pulled him up, helping him climb back over the window ledge. The guard's face now seemed covered by a mask.

Resigned, Mondino gave himself up to the two guards who had meanwhile come running into the room.

'Mondino de Liuzzi' said Luca. 'You are under arrest, in the name of the *Podestà*.'

XVI

Uberto da Rimini worked with a light heart. The Archbishop had got it into his head that he wanted to read every single document concerning the trial. It was a clear sign of distrust towards Uberto and yet he didn't mind all that much. An hour earlier Guido Arlotti had come in person to tell him that the plan had worked. The crowd now amassed in the piazza was unlikely to disperse before the mob had seen the bogus student's body, and the Captain of the People had sent a squadron of guards to arrest Mondino de Liuzzi.

The friar whom Uberto had sent to inform the *Podestà* of their visit had returned with the alarming news that the piazza was full of angry people and that he had not even been able to reach the *comune*. The Archbishop said that he would not be intimidated, but according to Uberto he was only putting it on. The Inquisitor was sure that when the moment came, the Archbishop would abandon the idea of the interrogation, preferring the safety of the monastery's solid walls. And the next day it would be too late.

Everything was organised. Now he only had to wait.

'It says here, and I quote, that when accused of practising the rite of *osculum sub cauda* [erotic kissing below the tail], the prisoner lied, protesting his innocence,' said Rinaldo da Concorezzo, looking up from the interrogation transcript.

'Exactly,' confirmed Uberto, absent-mindedly. 'They do nothing but declare themselves innocent of everything.'

'That's not what I meant,' said the Archbishop, dryly. 'I wanted to draw your attention to the words you have used. You didn't say "He declared himself to be innocent", but "He lied, protesting his innocence". How can you be sure that he was lying?'

'Forgive me, Monsignor,' replied Uberto, now at the limits of his patience. 'My mistake. I was perhaps being too superficial. I simply imagined that the office of the Holy Father would not include in the list of crimes something as obscene as novices kissing the ass of their older confrères if they were not first absolutely certain that it was a well-founded accusation. So I implied that the accused's declaration of innocence was mendacious. It was a question of doubting him or the Holy Father's office.'

The Archbishop nodded to himself. 'I see that we are speaking in different languages, Father Uberto,' he said. 'For you it is a simple matter of believing or not believing in someone on the basis of the presumed reliability of the person. The question of proof is entirely alien to your way of thinking.'

'It is a failing that I have, I recognise that.' By now, after all the time spent trying to put up with Rinaldo's criticism, anger began to sneak into Uberto's words without him being able to do anything about it. 'The fact is that I am a monk, and since I was a small boy I have been taught that faith has no need for proof.'

'So it seems logical to you to apply the same system of judgement to the sins of human beings and to Christ's teaching, as though they were equal.'

329

'I didn't say that, Monsignor.'

'You didn't say it, but your actions speak for you. I'm going to be straight with you, Father Uberto. I am beginning to have grave doubts that you are the right person to carry out this mission.'

It was a low hit and one that Uberto wasn't expecting. He opened and closed his mouth twice without making a sound, then finally he managed to say, 'You want to dismiss me? But that's not possible. There are only a few weeks left before the trial ends. We are already behind the pontiff's schedule, and—'

'Calm down, I know that it is rather late now to find a substitute. I only mean that you will be assisted by two Franciscan friars whom I trust, so that, by way of a constructive collaboration, you can decide together what is for the best.'

This time Uberto was genuinely struck dumb. To be subjected to the judgement of the Franciscans in everything he did was a humiliation worse than removal from his position. It was all quite clear now: the Archbishop had declared war.

'If that is your decision, I will respect and accept it without argument,' he said, with a visible effort to remain calm. 'If, however, there is anything I can do to regain your trust, I would ask you to tell me.'

The Archbishop sighed. 'We'll see. Much depends on what the prisoner says when we interrogate him. If he turns out to be incontrovertibly guilty of the murders that he is accused of, and if the responsibility for the crime is not his alone, but involves others of his order, as you seem to think, the trial will come to a swift conclusion without the need to make any new appointments.'

'Thank you, Monsignor. I trust that things will happen as you have just described.'

Rinaldo made a sign as if to say that it was too early for thanks, then he looked out of the window and said, 'At this point, I'd say that the time has come to lay aside our work in the monastery and pay our visit to the *Podestà*.'

It was the moment that Uberto had been waiting for. He had considered trying to convince the prelate to change his mind and he was sure that, after a minimum of insistence for form's sake, Rinaldo would see sense. But just then he was altogether too cross. Let him find himself confronted with the consequences of his stubbornness, he thought.

'Certainly, Monsignor. I will go immediately and give the orders for a small cortège to accompany you.'

'No cortège and no ceremony,' replied Rinaldo. 'We'll only stir up the crowd. You and I will go alone, with two thurifers and a cross-bearer.'

Uberto bowed his head as though this idiocy was a sensible idea. 'As you wish,' he said, and left the room.

Striding down the stairs, he already knew which monks he would order to accompany them. One of them was almost certainly the spy who reported everything back to the Archbishop. In the course of the previous day he had twice caught the man speaking to Rinaldo. Uberto would make him carry the cross. It was only right that he shared the risks of a situation that had been created through his own fault. Then Uberto chose two brawny young men who would be able to defend them if they got into difficulties.

Standing in front of the prior's closed door, Uberto stopped himself just as he was about to knock, struck by a sudden thought. At such an important moment in his life, he should pray before doing anything else. He hurried away towards the little chapel made in the cell where St Dominic had passed away.

As soon as Uberto went in he fell on his knees and addressed himself to the saint, asking him to intercede with the Lord. The Inquisitor's career was now almost over and Uberto knew it. If he didn't manage to interrogate the prisoner, the Archbishop would subject him to the humiliation of having to report to two Franciscan priests, which was almost worse than being dismissed. If, on the other hand, they reached the *comune* safe and sound, Rinaldo would find out that the Templar had already been interrogated under torture in Uberto's presence and would suspend him from his job.

Only divine intervention could save him now.

Uberto examined his conscience and concluded that he had done his duty in the stamping out of heresy. Now the responsibility was no longer in his hands. If God wanted him to continue defending the faith, He would send a sign, removing the obstacles in his way.

In that precise moment an image entered Uberto's mind of the Archbishop being lynched by the hordes.

Horrified, Uberto covered his face with his hands. Was it possible that St Dominic, the preacher saint who founded his order, would suggest such a vicious action? Without admitting to himself that he would even consider the murder of a minister of the Church possible, Uberto began to examine the occurrence in a dispassionate manner, as a sort of intellectual exercise. If Rinaldo da Concorezzo was out of the way, the Church would have him instead, and his career, instead of being crushed to oblivion would take a leap forward. Without the Archbishop, Pope Clement V might well trust him to take on the full responsibility of the trial. And even if another archbishop were nominated in haste, the director *in pectore* of the trial would nonetheless be Uberto, who had followed it from the beginning and knew the ins and outs better than anyone else.

Still thinking of it as an abstract possibility, the Inquisitor considered the ways in which an eventual killer would carry out such a crime, and his face darkened. In practice he could only count on Guido Arlotti for jobs of that kind and the ex-priest would never consent to assassinate an archbishop of the

Church of Christ, or not unless he was ordered to do so by the Pope himself.

The only answer was that Uberto himself should carry out the saint's wishes. But even that made no sense. The Archbishop had to be got rid of immediately and even if he wanted to, Uberto could hardly stab the man in his study or in the middle of the street with everyone watching.

Resigned, Uberto mentally confessed to St Dominic that he was unable to decipher his message; da Rimini made the sign of the cross and opened his eyes.

In a trice everything became clear.

A beam of sunshine coming through the half-closed shutter lit up what had been the saint's bed, the very place where he had taken leave of the temporal world. The rest of the room was in darkness, but the modest mattress lying on a few boards of rough-hewn wood shone like a royal throne. Uberto knew that he had committed the sin of presumption and he hurriedly began to ask for pardon, tears welling up in his eyes at the emotion of it all.

He had thought that it was up to him to interpret the message, that it was up to him to act. In his pride he had even considered, albeit in an abstract way, the idea of committing murder, damning his soul for eternity. Whereas the vision of the Archbishop killed by the mob was only a premonition, sent by St Dominic to reassure him. God and the saints were themselves capable of removing every obstacle from his way. How could he presume to do their job for them?

Uberto promised that he would impose a heavy penance on himself, humiliating his body and his spirit, to atone for his sin of presumption. And immediately afterwards he gave thanks for what had been granted to him: the opportunity to move up a step in the Church in order to fight against heresy more readily.

As though in answer to his prayers, the ray of sunlight slowly vanished and the room returned to its former dimness.

333

Uberto got to his feet and left the chapel, full of renewed energy. He dropped in to the prior's office to ask permission to go out with three monks and the cross. When the big man objected, he explained that it was the Archbishop's explicit request and having obtained permission he went to tell his chosen monks to get ready. Then he walked back upstairs to his study. There was no doubt that Rinaldo da Concorezzo's final hour had come. Guided by the divine hand, a rock or a club would kill him that very morning.

Uberto himself wouldn't have to dirty his hands and he was pleased about that. Still, he would keep his eyes open and if he got the chance to give divine providence a helping hand, he wouldn't hold back.

The guards took the long way round when escorting Mondino to the *comune* to avoid crossing Piazza Maggiore, where more and more people were gathering. From a long way off, noise and shouting could be heard coming from the piazza, despite the fact that the market was not being held there because it was a Sunday.

'What's going on?' asked the physician of no one in particular.

They hadn't bound his hands. In order to stop him running away, two guards flanked him, while Luca, the section leader, walked a few yards ahead of them.

It was he who answered, without turning to face Mondino. 'Word's got around that they've arrested the sorcerer who killed those men and turned their hearts into a piece of iron, and since it's a Templar monk, the *Podestà* thought he'd let him go and hush it all up so as not to get into trouble with the Church. The mob want to dispense justice without having to wait for a trial.'

Mondino felt his heart miss a beat. His last hope of salvation had vanished with those words.

'What's the name of the man you've arrested?' he asked, just to be sure.

'Francesco Salimbene. But they say it's a false name. I should think you probably know him.'

'And does the *Podestà* really want to set him free?'

'Are you joking? I don't know who would suggest such a thing.'

They were passing behind the Palazzo di Accursio that had been bought by the *comune* and become the headquarters for Council of the Elders. Mass had finished and people were swarming out of the churches and then heading off in small groups towards the piazza. No one paid any attention to the party of guards.

'Keep quiet and don't do anything stupid,' said Luca, suddenly stopping and turning to look at him. 'If they find out that you're implicated in those murders too, they'll lynch you on the spot and we wouldn't be able do anything to help you.'

'I am innocent,' said Mondino, looking him in the eye.

'Well then, you must be doubly quiet,' replied Luca, with a touch of sarcasm in his voice.

They walked on and soon afterwards came out into the piazza next to the main square where the tinkers set up their stalls on feast days. The whole area between the Palazzo degli Anziani and the old town hall, which had served as prison to King Enzo, was overflowing with people. The piazza itself was as crowded as St Bartholomew's Day, during *La Porchetta,* the Suckling Pig Fair. But the rabble that had come together that day didn't have the look of joyous expectation as they did for the traditional throwing of food and money from the balcony of the *comune*. The shouting and general drone belonged to a crowd of malcontents, baying for blood.

Mondino put his head down and walked on.

The few dozen steps that separated them from the rear entrance to the *comune* seemed like leagues. To avoid being recognised, he didn't even lift his head when they passed under the cross vaults that supported the Arengo Tower. They were now behind three adjoining buildings, two belonging respectively to the *Podestà* and the Captain of the People, the third being the one everyone now called King Enzo. Apart from the soldiers, who were guarding the entrances, the two streets that crossed beneath the vault were deserted. Everything was going on in and around the main piazza on the other side.

A long time had passed since the last occasion on which Mondino had witnessed a public execution, but he remembered the unadorned ceremony of it perfectly. The condemned man appeared on the balcony among the friars, the guards and the hangman. One of the friars held panels covered in biblical illustrations in front of the accused's face so that he couldn't see the expressions of the yelling populace. Then a rope was put around his neck and the executioner threw him over the balustrade. There had been cases in which the rope had snapped, and the poor man had ended up falling into the crowd.

The idea that such an end might await him seemed unreal.

The guards let them pass and they went up the steps to a distant chorus of voices demanding the immediate handover of the guilty man. On the first floor, where the judges usually worked, the *dischi,* rooms decorated with the coat of arms of the unicorn, eagle, stag and other animals, were empty, as were the notary's *scabelli.* The building that was generally so full of life seemed dead on Sundays.

The guards stopped to talk to a man in a toga who directed them towards a high door with pointed arched pilasters. Luca knocked and waited for the invitation to go in. It didn't come so he went in anyway.

Mondino finally lifted his head. They were in the great hall, at the end of which, sitting in a corner by a long table, were Enrico Bernadazzi from Lucca and Pantaleone Buzacarini from Padua, respectively *Podestà* and Captain of the People. Standing in front of them was Gerardo, who was talking animatedly.

Mondino noted the particulars with a sort of detachment. Since he had been arrested everything had been sliding past without affecting him. Even the roar of the crowd, which wasn't dimmed by the plain linen drape that waved in the breeze at the open window, had become a background noise, like the thunder of a river in spate, which seemed to have nothing to do with him. But one thing shook him out of his state of passivity. Gerardo should have been in fetters, but he was free. One of his arms was hanging limp at his side, showing that he had been subjected to brutal treatment with ropes, but his was not the behaviour of a prisoner under interrogation. Rather, he seemed to be pleading a cause.

In any case the explanation for what was going on would arrive soon enough. At his entrance the three of them had stopped talking and turned towards the door. Mondino hoped that Gerardo would have the presence of mind to pretend indifference, but he was disappointed.

'Magister!' exclaimed the young man. 'Thank goodness you've come.'

'I didn't come, I was arrested.'

The guards stopped a few feet from the *Podestà*, and the section leader went forward to ask for his orders.

'Leave us alone,' said Enrico Bernadazzi.

The three men obeyed and when they had left, closing the door behind them, the Captain of the People greeted Mondino and explained the situation to him, raising his voice to make himself heard above the clamour. But understanding wasn't that easy: Mondino couldn't believe that the banker's young daughter and the vicious murderer whom they had been looking for could be the same person. It was as though his mind were paralysed, reacting with lumpen slowness to every new piece of information. In less than an hour he had discovered that he was wanted for murder, had been arrested and now found out that he was a free man again. All of a sudden it occurred to him that it was a trap, set up with Gerardo's complicity, to induce him to contradict himself and to admit to crimes he hadn't committed. He only became convinced when Pantaleone Buzacarini pointed to Fiamma's letter and diary lying open on the table. Mondino picked them up, flipped through them, reading a few sentences, and finally he relaxed.

'My God,' he said at last.

The Captain of the People and the *Podestà* both nodded. 'That's what we said when this young man showed us what you see there,' said Enrico Bernadazzi. 'We allowed him this interview thinking he wanted to confess. You wouldn't believe our amazement and disbelief when we found out how things really stood.'

'I can imagine,' said Mondino, still shaken. Then, when he'd calmed down, he added, 'Does this mean that I can go home?'

'First, we must stop Fiamma!' exclaimed Gerardo. 'Or she'll kill herself!'

The youth was in an obvious state of euphoria. His eyes were shining and he was trembling, as though he had continually to get the better of an impulse to jump up and run away. His left arm was the only motionless part of his body.

'Why do you think that she wants to kill herself?' asked Mondino. 'In the letter it says, "I'll soon be in my grave", but it doesn't say when or how she'll die.'

'I believe that Gerardo da Castelbretone is right,' interjected the Captain of the People. Mondino realised that Gerardo had told them his real name and the physician was pleased. One less lie to keep up. 'Now she has taken her revenge and delivered the proof of her guilt, it can only mean that she had organised her escape to avoid punishment, either in another country or in the next world.'

'Then we should let her kill herself,' said Mondino, coldly. He felt no pity for the woman who had so nearly ruined his life.

'Magister!' Gerardo exclaimed in a tone of reproach. He only seemed able to express himself with exclamations.

The *Podestà* raised a hand to silence Mondino's irritated rejoinder. 'The diary and the letter stand as strong evidence of guilt,' he said, above the racket. 'But if Fiamma Sensi were to take her own life before confessing, it would take much longer to acquit you.'

Mondino stood there speechless. From the piazza there rose three small words, chanted at regular intervals: 'Hand ... him ... over! Hand ... him ... over!'

'So go and get her,' he said then. 'I don't see what the problem is.'

'Don't you understand?' intervened the Captain of the People, walking over to the window and drawing aside the linen drape. 'This is the problem.'

Mondino glanced outside and was horror-struck. Seen from above, the scene was appalling and impressive at the same time. Some members of the city militia, lined up in battle formation in front of the *comune*, seemed somewhat pathetic with respect to the mass of people crammed into the piazza. There must already have been some injuries and perhaps even some deaths; people crushed by the throng.

'They are threatening to storm the *comune*,' said Pantaleone Buzacarini, letting the drape fall. 'I can't spare a single man to go and get that woman. Apart from the fact that we don't even know where she is.'

'And what are you going to do to disperse the crowd?' asked Mondino.

'The easiest thing, to avoid mishaps, would be to hang this young man from the balcony,' said the *Podestà*. 'Unjust, I agree, but done for the good of the city.'

'You're not serious!' protested Mondino. Gerardo had turned round fast but said nothing, as if the idea didn't strike him as such a bad one. 'Such an act would not only be a heinous injustice, but a grave step backwards in the defence of civil liberties.'

'Of course I wasn't being serious,' said Enrico Bernadazzi, with a look that contradicted his words. 'However, the problem remains. We might be attacked from one moment to the next, and we can't send anyone to catch Fiamma Sensi. Besides, right now a squad of guards would have little chance of getting through the mob uninjured.'

'We'll go!' said Gerardo.

'Where?'

'To fetch Fiamma. There's no time to lose. I think I know where to find her.'

There was a moment's silence, in which everyone weighed up his suggestion.

'As the one responsible for civic justice,' the Captain of the People then said, 'I cannot allow it. It's too risky, and besides citizens cannot make an arrest. Furthermore, although you two may have been cleared of the accusation of murder, you are still guilty, respectively, of arson and of concealing a corpse.'

Mondino had finally made up his mind. The idea of going out into that hell hole and risking his life didn't attract him one bit, but it was the quickest way to free himself from an accusation that could earn him the death sentence or, at the very least, irredeemably ruin his career. Besides, his mind was filled once more with the dream that had been at the origin of everything: once she was in the hands of the law, Fiamma would be unreachable. If he had a chance of understanding her secret, it was now. He had risked everything; it was madness to pull out at the last moment.

'They are accusations that we can get off easily with the help of a good lawyer,' he said, addressing the two notables.

340

'And you know that. I will pledge my house as a guarantee that we will not take advantage of our freedom to run away. I'll even sign a promissory note right away.'

At those words Gerardo gave Mondino a grateful look that he preferred to ignore. 'Just lend us one guard dressed in city clothes,' he added. 'He can arrest Fiamma Sensi and the formalities will be respected.'

The *Podestà* and the Captain of the People glanced at each other, undecided.

'Apart from anything else,' concluded Mondino, 'if the mob really did manage to storm the *comune*, it would be better if they didn't find us here.'

'Do you really know where she is?' the *Podestà* asked Gerardo. 'I'd be very surprised, after all that she's done, if she were sitting at home waiting for us.'

'At this point nothing matters to her any more,' replied Gerardo. 'Although you are right to think that she's not at home. I'll tell you where I mean to look for her only when you have given me your word that you will agree to send me with the guards who must arrest her. Under my guidance they'll waste less time trying to find the place.'

'Very well,' said the *Podestà*, springing into action. 'I will send three men with you, no more. Now let's write that letter.'

He had parchment, quill and ink brought, but as there wasn't a notary to be found in the building he had to draw up the deed in person and countersign it. Then he called the three guards who had been waiting just outside the door. The Captain of the People took them to his private rooms and lent them some nondescript civilian clothes that were baggy enough for them to hide the daggers that they wore at their sides fastened to a belt between shirt and tunic.

'It would be better if we were armed too,' said Mondino.

'The law is clear on that one and I'm certainly not going to be the one to break it,' responded Pantaleone. 'It is forbidden for citizens to carry arms within the confines of the city walls. You will be with my men so no harm will come to you.'

Soon afterwards, the posse left the *comune* quietly by the rear entrance. The crowd was thronging the front of the building and they passed by unnoticed. But they had only gone about fifty yards, making quick headway through the deserted stalls of the Mercato di Mezzo, when they heard a cry behind them: 'The murderer's getting away!'

They all turned round together, and with a leap of his heart Mondino recognised the stocky frame of Guido Arlotti pointing an accusatory finger at them.

The outermost part of the crowd began to undulate like a field of corn in the wind. Many of them turned towards the little group and the cry 'The murderer's getting away!' was repeated by dozens of voices. Gerardo saw that a lot of people were breaking away from the crowd and coming towards them, first slowly, as if undecided, then faster.

'Run!' yelled Mondino behind him. Gerardo followed him without delay, going as fast as his broken body allowed. Whereas the three guards, perhaps responding instinctively to their fear, made the mistake of unsheathing their daggers. An indistinct but concerted cry was discharged from the crowd, and they were on top of them in an instant. Gerardo heard the cries of pain as the guards were torn apart; he clenched his fists without turning round. He couldn't have done anything to help them even if both his arms had been working, but with the left one out of its socket, there was absolutely no chance. Mondino was running a few steps ahead of him, holding up his ankle-length red robe and taking great long paces.

Just before the bridge over the Aposa they saw two groups of richly dressed people approaching each other at a solemn pace. Gerardo realised that it was a nuptial procession. The bride came from the left, on horseback, surrounded by her family and followed by a cohort of wedding guests. The groom was approaching from the right, on foot, with a falcon on his wrist, also encircled by friends and family. They were probably getting married in St Peter's Cathedral and had decided to meet on the road to the Mercato di Mezzo to walk the rest of the way together. Gerardo noticed that the bride was a beautiful blonde, dressed in white and gold with an embroidered veil that rippled in the breeze. The decorations to the horse's harness took up the same theme as her gown.

He saw their expressions change from surprise to alarm. The groom let go of the falcon, which sailed rapidly up into the blue sky, and pulled out his ornamental sword. Then all the men in the cortège followed suit. Mondino dashed off to the right and Gerardo followed him. However, behind them the mob threw themselves on to the swords without hesitating, perhaps trusting in their numbers, perhaps simply out of a suicidal mania. The two packs bumped into each other head on with shouts and clanging of metal, a sign that many of their pursuers were armed, despite the law. Gerardo hoped that the bride would manage to turn the horse in time and get away at a gallop.

Not even in the panic of the chase had Mondino forgotten where they were heading, and twice he tried to take a turning towards Santo Stefano, but both times the masses armed with clubs barred their way. They were latecomers converging on the main piazza so as not to miss out on the spectacle. Mondino might have been able to trick them, but preferred not to take the risk. In the end they were pushed south, towards the Church of San Domenico, the last place that Gerardo wanted to find himself. Just the memory of Uberto da Rimini's shining face and wily expression brought a knot to his stomach.

All of a sudden Mondino stopped and turned to him, puffing and pressing a hand to his side.

'Are they still following us?'

Gerardo nodded, too breathless to speak. Their pursuers were fewer in number now, because the majority were still busy in the skirmish with the nuptial cortège, but the shouting was coming closer. There must be at least six or seven people: too many for two unarmed men to take on.

The streets were now full of other bands of men, yelling and armed with clubs. It seemed as though the mob had divided and instead of staying put in the piazza had begun to look for opportunities to let off steam around the city. Every so often the neighbouring streets rang with the noises of a fight or insults flung at some noble who had dared to lean out of his window. Now and again there were cries of 'Bread! Bread!' All the doors were bolted.

Gerardo and Mondino reached a high city wall with no way through. They certainly couldn't stop there. Worn out from running, they still hurried on, until they got to San Domenico's Basilica. They darted into a shadowy lane between two rows of houses and finally stopped to get their breath back. Just then Gerardo saw a strange procession emerging from the church courtyard. Two broad-framed Dominican monks, in white habits and black cloaks, walked along shaking incense burners. They were followed by another monk carrying a gold cross, and behind them came the Archbishop, in full vestment with all the paraphernalia: mitre, white dalmatica with red stripes back and front and a silver-plated staff. Bringing up the rear he saw the bald head of Uberto da Rimini, hoodless and looking disdainful as ever.

Gerardo wondered where they were going and if they knew the danger they were in. The ecclesiastics were feared and respected, but they were unpopular among the people just then, and at times of public disorder such as this the best thing for them was to be safely shut up in their churches and monasteries. He would have run the risk of telling them as much, if it weren't for the presence of the Inquisitor. Uberto da Rimini didn't know about the new developments in his situation and might react in a rash manner on seeing him free. Beside him, Mondino was also looking in amazement at the posse of priests striding towards disaster.

Perhaps he should have warned them anyway, but now there was no time. A bevy of marauders rushed out of a side street, shouting and hitting the doors of the houses with their clubs. As soon as they saw the priests they paused, intimidated by the sight of an archbishop in full pomp. But it sufficed for one of them to pick up a stone from the ground and fling it with a cry, for them all to descend on the religious group with their clubs raised.

A furious riot broke out. The two thurifers in the front line began to wield their incense burners like iron clubs, dispensing smoke and sparks around them. One managed to catch one of the aggressors on the head, sending him crashing down to lie in a heap. A piece of burning coal landed in the collar of another and he dropped his stick, shouting and jumping around to get rid of the embers. But these episodes only served to enrage the others all the more and they began to fall on the priests in a close-knit pack. The Archbishop and the Inquisitor were standing stock still as though the scene had nothing to do with them. Then one of the thurifers was hit on the head with a club and three men leaped on the Archbishop; they were now too angry to be intimidated by his sacred regalia.

A chorus of women wailing could be heard behind the closed windows of the neighbouring houses. Gerardo, who until then had merely been watching, found himself running forward without knowing he was doing it, and heedless of Mondino's shout to come back. He would happily have left Uberto da Rimini to look after himself, but he could not stand by and watch while the crowd ravaged an archbishop of the Church of Rome, above all one with the reputation for fairness of Rinaldo da Concorezzo. The image that stuck in his mind, as he raced out of his hiding place in the alleyway and threw himself into the mêlée, was the ecstatic expression on the Inquisitor's face. The man seemed to be contemplating the scene as though witnessing a miracle, not a horrific spectacle of violence. Gerardo saw two men lift their clubs to cosh the Archbishop and Uberto doing nothing whatever to defend him. On the contrary, Uberto was watching with an expression of sublime joy and at a certain point seemed even to have nudged him forward into the fray. Rinaldo da Concorezzo bent double beneath the attack, lost his mitre and fell to his knees.

The two rioters exchanged a look, in all likelihood stunned by the enormity of their actions, and in that moment Gerardo thundered in, dispensing kicks, and thumps with his good hand, to push the men away from the prelate. Out of the corner of his eye he saw Mondino, who had followed him, pick up a stick that had been dropped and begin to swing it at arms length to keep them at bay.

Gerardo helped the Archbishop get back to his feet, but just then Uberto da Rimini hurled himself at the Templar and clamped his hands around his throat. Gerardo saw a murderous intent in the dark gimlet eyes that terrified him. But the Inquisitor was smaller than him and not as strong; nor was he trained to fight. Two swift punches to the face were enough to knock him to the ground, where he lay with a stupefied expression on his face. At that moment they were joined by a swarm of monks from the monastery, unarmed but ready to use their fists. People started coming out of the surrounding houses as well, and yet the aggressors gave no sign of retreating. More rabble-rousers, attracted by the sounds of a fight, began to assail the monks from behind with a shower of stones. They were mainly men and women farmers, barefoot and dressed in sackcloth clothes with chausses wound around their calves and ankles.

'Let's go, they don't need us any more,' said Mondino, coming up beside him.

Gerardo realised that the physician was right. The fight continued, but the monks and the people who'd come out to help them were getting the upper hand. It was not the moment to waste time and risk having to give explanations that might not be believed.

The Templar felt his bad arm being grabbed, causing him a wave of intense pain, while the peevish voice of the Inquisitor bawled as loud as possible: 'Here's the sorcerer! Here's the murderer!' holding on to him with a strength that was difficult to credit in such a small pair of hands. Gerardo turned quickly round, elbowing him full in the face. Mondino, with noteworthy readiness, followed the blow with a stroke of his club to Uberto's bald head, laying the man flat out on the ground.

'Run!' he shouted, looking around for an escape route.

Fortunately the Inquisitor's shout had been lost in the general hubbub and no one took any notice of them. On impulse, Gerardo knelt down by the Archbishop and kissed his ring. 'We are innocent, Monsignor,' he said. 'The *Podestà* has set us free. Please tell the Inquisitor, when he comes round.'

Rinaldo da Concorezzo looked at him with a warm smile, giving him his complete attention, as though there weren't a pitched battle going on around them and they were alone in the piazza.

'I believe you, my son, although I don't know who you are,' he said, lifting his right hand. 'And I bless you.'

Gerardo briefly bowed his head and then leaped up again and set off after Mondino who was already a long way ahead, running in the direction of Santo Stefano.

Guido Arlotti didn't let himself be distracted by the nuptial procession, but his men had caught the contagious feeling of excitement and violence that was now pervading the city.

They had thrown themselves into the fray, lashing out at the bride's relations, jabbing the horses' hocks with daggers to make them crash to the ground, their frantic neighs joining the general babel of shouting. The bride had managed to get away, turning her horse quickly and kicking hard with the heels of her embroidered slippers. But her parents were left on the ground in a pool of blood, wounded or perhaps even dead, relieved of their purses and jewellery. The lure of loot was even stronger than that of violence and Guido had a hard time extricating five of the men that he had used to foment trouble in the crowd. Only by promising them twice the agreed money did he convince them to follow him, and they walked on, hiding what they'd stolen under their robes as they went.

They hurried towards the road that Gerardo and Mondino had taken. Although the two were out of sight, Guido was able to follow the sound of their pursuers. He couldn't let them get away. If they had been freed, it meant that the *Podestà* thought them innocent, and that was precisely why it was better for everyone if they didn't talk.

Now they had to die and Guido was quite happy to carry out their death sentences. In any case the plenary indulgence would absolve him of any blame.

But first he had to catch up with them.

He gave a shove to one of his men who was about to divert into a prostitute's lane, anxious to squander a part of the booty as soon as possible. 'No women until we've finished the job,' he said. 'Start running, we've lost too much time already.'

With their knives unsheathed to discourage any marauders in the chaotic battlefield that the centre of Bologna had become, they ran until they turned up in the area of San Domenico's Basilica, where a thick crowd of Dominicans was driving back the remaining ruffians.

Guido saw the Archbishop standing calmly with his mitre on his head and staff in his hand. Although he wasn't doing anything at all, he dominated the scene. Uberto da Rimini was just getting up off the ground, with a scarlet bloodstain on his bare crown. Guido caught his eye and the Inquisitor nodded imperiously towards a road to the right that led to Santo Stefano and St Jerusalem. Mondino and Gerardo must have gone that way.

Guido looked about him. He couldn't spot a couple of his men, they must have deserted. But the three he had left were more than enough for what had to be done. Although beginning to run out of breath, he threw himself back into the chase.

'Is this the place?' asked Mondino, looking doubtfully at the gap in the ruined house at the end of the alleyway. 'Are you sure she'll be here?'

'No, but if I had to bet on it, I'd do it without a second thought.'

The Templar seemed certain of what he was saying and yet Mondino was having difficulty imagining the banker's daughter going through the dark doorway that gaped like a toothless mouth, to descend into a subterranean ruin that, from what Gerardo said, seemed a cross between a Roman sewer and a catacomb.

Then he remembered that Fiamma was responsible for the most horrendous deaths he had ever seen. There was no saying what she would be capable of.

They walked towards the house, without taking any notice of the rocks and rubbish strewn across the road under their feet, but they had only gone a few yards when a voice behind them said, 'Commend your souls to God.'

Mondino recognised the voice instantly, and turning round felt no surprise at seeing the thuggish shape of Guido Arlotti accompanied by a man whose long hair didn't quite manage to cover his severed ears. What truly frightened Mondino was the sight of another two men blocking the other end of the lane.

Gerardo and Mondino stood back to back without saying a word, firmly set on defending themselves although it was clear that they didn't have much hope. Two unarmed men against four cut-throats with daggers. This time there hadn't even been the pretence of arresting them. It was all over.

'Let's see how you manage without a cur-loving witch to hold your hand,' continued Guido, coming towards them.

'We must disarm at least one of them,' murmured Gerardo.

Mondino shrugged his shoulders. It was pointless discussing strategy now. They would just have to die with dignity, and possibly not alone.

'At my signal, we'll both go for Severed Ears,' whispered Gerardo. 'If I manage to grab his dagger, we've got a chance.' Then, without waiting for confirmation, he yelled, 'Now!' and tore forward.

Mondino was right behind him, determined to sell his life dearly. They had both lost their caps in the struggle to save the Archbishop and Gerardo's long hair fell over his eyes, obstructing his vision for a second. That second was fatal. While the youth bounded towards the man with the lopped-off ears, dodging a thrust and deflecting its trajectory, Mondino felt an acute pain in his right shoulder and only when he crumpled on the ground, in the filth and excrement, did he realise that he'd received the blow meant for Gerardo.

In an instant his mind was filled with the thought of Adia and of what might have developed between the two of them. Then he thought of his treatise, which would never be finished now, and the secret that he hadn't been able to discover.

He saw something falling on top of him and managed to roll out of the way just in time. It was Severed Ears, clutching at a wound to his abdomen with both hands. Gerardo must have succeeded in disarming him and knifing him with his own dagger, but there were still three adversaries left and the Templar couldn't fight alone.

With an effort of will, Mondino forced himself to raise his head.

Gerardo was now armed and having a go at Guido's two other accomplices. Taking advantage of the narrow space, he concentrated on hampering their movements in turn, so that he could take them on one at a time. But Guido Arlotti was about to stab him in the back.

Mondino rolled on to his side again, so that he could stick his feet between Guido's legs, who, caught by surprise, lost his balance. Gerardo, without taking his eyes off the attackers in front of him, jabbed Guido in the face with the handle of the knife and he collapsed on to Mondino with a cry.

The strike had been a hard one, but Arlotti was a strapping man and immediately tried to get back to his feet. Mondino couldn't move his right arm, but he could kick. He leaned on his good elbow and planted a shoe in the other man's face, pushing him back down on to the ground. Then, with all the strength he could muster, he kicked out again, getting Guido in the throat.

With his senses in a kind of fog, Mondino could hear the noise of Gerardo struggling above and he dragged himself on top of Guido and began to hit the man repeatedly in the face, using the same arm and hitting in the same place until there was no more resistance. Only then did he look up, in time to see the last of their foes bolting for safety after Gerardo had stabbed his accomplice in the heart.

'Magister, are you all right?' asked the young man, leaning over him.

'No, but the wound isn't a serious one,' replied Mondino. 'Leave me here and go and find Fiamma.'

'Are you sure?' asked Gerardo, doubtfully.

'I've seen enough injuries to know that this one isn't fatal, even if the pain is bad. Help me to stop the blood, then go. There's no time to lose.'

As Guido Arlotti was still unconscious, Gerardo reached under his tunic and pulled off his linen shirt. He cut a piece with the knife and gave it to Mondino, who pressed it to the wound. Then he took off Guido's belt and used it to tie Arlotti's hands behind his back. Gerardo did the same to Severed Ears, who was just alive, but instead of his hands, he bound his legs. Finally, after handing a dagger to Mondino to keep the prisoners at bay, he went into the ruined house and disappeared among the rocks that cluttered up the interior.

At the *comune,* preparations were well under way. The crowd in Piazza Maggiore had begun to disperse soon after Gerardo and Mondino had left with the guards, but the *Podestà* and the Captain of the People knew well that this was not the prelude to a return to peace. On the contrary. Reports continued to come in of bands of citizens carrying sticks or makeshift weapons who attacked anyone they found in their path, preferably nobles and representatives of established authority. It even appeared that, by some miracle, the Archbishop had narrowly escaped death, although Enrico Bernadazzi didn't believe it. What on earth had the Archbishop been doing wandering the streets on a day like that, anyway? It had to be a rumour exaggerated by continual repetition.

In any case, a catastrophe of that sort had to be avoided.

'Are we ready yet?' he asked the Captain of the People, who was looking out of the window.

'Not long now. The men are already beginning to fall in. As soon as they're ready, I'll go down too.'

Pantaleone Buzacarini had given the order for the entire civil militia to line up outside the *comune,* as well as any volunteers that could be found. He would divide them into groups, the largest under his own command, and then begin to patrol the city to reinstate order. The groups were to keep as close together as possible and stay in contact via runners. Enrico had complete confidence in the Captain of the People, who had already directed a similar operation some months before when both of them were fresh in their posts, and it had been a success. Yet he couldn't help asking himself why a problem of the sort had to happen to him, almost at the end of his term of office. He sincerely regretted not throwing the young Templar to the crowds. The only reason he hadn't done so was because that type of action required everyone to be in agreement and Mondino hadn't assented. It had occurred to Enrico to give them both to the crowd, but that would have caused a problem. Mondino was too important a personage. There would have been an inquiry and thorny questions to answer and it all might have gone horribly wrong.

But if he had known there'd be a revolt of this sort, perhaps he would have done it after all. Now he would be called up in front of Council of the Elders, and was in danger of spending the last month of his tenure defending himself from the accusations of incompetence that would be levelled at him, at enormous cost of time and money.

The only honourable path left was to quell the disorder with a firm hand and catch the two prisoners, hoping that they had succeeded in finding Remigio Sensi's daughter. In that case all would end well and the elders would approve his decision to let them go. If, on the other hand, the pair were killed by the mob, their death would be yet another blunder for which he would be held to account.

'I'll come with you,' he said to the Captain of the People.

'We can't both go. One of us should stay here, to receive reports and coordinate the operation.'

It was true. To leave the *comune* without a leader capable of assuming command and issuing orders would be to invite disaster. Enrico nodded reluctantly. Alas, there were no guarantees that the affair would be quickly resolved. And as for finding Gerardo da Castelbretone and Mondino de Liuzzi, there was no certainty of that either. After the events of the last few days, the *Podestà* was ready to believe the strangest things, and yet the underworld that the young man had mentioned seemed more like a figment of his disturbed mind.

'Very well. But you must send me a dispatch every half hour,' he said to the Captain.

Pantaleone assured Enrico that he would and left. The *Podestà* stood four-square in the middle of the room and began to wait.

In an hour or two at the most his destiny would be decided.

As soon as he got to the underworld, Gerardo ran down the right hand tunnel. It led to the crypts of the seven churches of Santo Stefano's Basilica, near Santo Sepolcro that poor Bonaga had told him about. Fiamma couldn't be aware that Gerardo knew about the underworld, so she had thought she could allude to the place where she had chosen to die without danger of being found out. *Protected by he who protects Bologna* it had said in the letter. And the Church of Santo Sepolcro held the remains of St Petronio, one of the city's patron saints.

But knowing about the place was no guarantee of saving her. Gerardo was not sure what he really wanted. On the one hand, to fully exonerate both his order and himself from all the accusations, it was vital that Fiamma be interrogated in court. On the other, the idea that she might be tortured was insufferable to him, even if she was a murderer.

Gerardo now had personal experience of torture. The feeling of impotent terror that he had felt at the hands of the executioner made him shudder more than the memory of the physical pain itself.

Even in her madness, Fiamma was a victim.

He headed towards the light that shone dimly at the end of the tunnel and soon after entered a small room on the tips of his toes. It was decorated with frescoes that had now almost disappeared with the damp.

Fiamma had her back to him. She was dressed entirely in black and stood in front of a rectangular platform at the opposite side of the room.

By the light of the two tall candles standing on blocks of stone, Gerardo also recognised Remigio Sensi. He was lying on the platform as though on a sacrificial altar, dressed in a white linen shirt. Around him, in the half light, Gerardo could make out the remains of three or four bodies, in various states of decomposition. Each one had its sternum cut lengthways and ribs broken. They must have been the beggars that Bonaga had talked about. Fiamma had used them to practise on.

'Fiamma,' said Gerardo, under his breath, almost as though he were in a church.

She turned round slowly to stare at him, astounded. She was wearing a black gown, embroidered with gold, which went down to the ground and was pinned to her shoulder with a gold stud. Her bodice and shoes were made of black cloth too and a dark veil covered her blonde hair falling around her shoulders. Draped in all that black, her pallid face shone out like a beacon.

'Gerardo. How did you find me?'

'A crippled boy showed me the entrance to the underworld. When I read your letter, I knew this was the place you were referring to.'

Fiamma nodded. 'Bonaga. He showed it to me too, a year and a half ago. That was when I realised that the moment had come.'

In the diary there had been no mention of Bonaga and the

underworld, but the day when Fiamma had decided to begin taking her revenge was recorded. She had access to all her adoptive father's papers and had known for some time where she could find her tormentors. She had written the letters to lure them to Bologna. To convince the knights, she had put in each letter a finger transformed into iron, taken from the hands of one of the beggars she had killed. At the same time she began to send anonymous letters to the Inquisition, reporting the Templars on the run that passed through Remigio's offices.

'Don't talk like that, please,' said Gerardo. 'It's not too late to—'

'To what? To be burned alive like a witch? I've spent years preparing all this and I'll be the one to decide how it ends. Don't come any closer!'

Gerardo had taken a step towards her, but he stopped immediately. Fiamma picked up a strange-looking awl with a triangular blade that was lying on the stone platform next to a multi-coloured glass that shone in the candlelight.

'The handle of this stiletto is full of the powder that turns blood into iron,' said Fiamma. 'And the blade is hollow. It would only take a scratch, and you'll die a horrible death. Please, don't make me do it.'

Gerardo didn't move a muscle, but he was overcome by an interior turmoil. He knew what Fiamma was about to do and he wanted to stop her, but didn't know how. She moved towards the stone altar, without completely turning her back on him, and with a sudden movement she planted the stiletto first in one of Remigio's feet and then in the other. The banker hardly moved at all and didn't even whimper.

'His body is paralysed, but he is quite able to feel all the pain he deserves,' said Fiamma.

Gerardo had read the part about Remigio in the diary. He had adopted Fiamma as a little girl, but treated her as a wife, abusing her from the age of thirteen. Gerardo had been appalled and wanted to get back at the banker himself. And yet, seeing the inhuman punishment reserved for him by the girl, the Templar couldn't help feeling pity for him.

Remigio Sensi's veins were swelling and hardening visibly, breaking the skin in certain places like knotted tendrils creeping slowly up his legs. His pupils, the one part of his body that could move, were darting frenetically this way and that, but it didn't seem as though he could see, lost as he was in a sea of pain and terror.

'Pilate, Longinus and Caiaphas died quickly,' said Fiamma. 'He abused me for six long years. He deserves a slower death.'

Hearing her names for the three dead Templars, Gerardo became fully aware of her madness. Fiamma wasn't there with him at that moment, just as she had never really been living in the present at all. Her soul had remained hidden in the cave in Spain, where she had experienced the desperation of losing her family, her home and her beauty all in one go and hadn't been able to bear it. She identified herself with none other than Jesus Christ, the blameless sacrificial lamb. But unlike Christ, she had not forgiven the people who'd done her wrong. She had prepared her revenge with great patience. She had got herself taken into service and then adopted by Remigio so that through his contact with the Knights of the Temple, she would be able to trace her father's murderers; to carry out her plan she had put up with the years of violence that the banker had subjected her to. But while she'd done all this, her soul had been dead and only her body kept up the appearance of life.

Gerardo had no doubt that if he tried to disarm her, Fiamma would stab him with the poisoned stiletto. With a sense of shame, he had to admit that his courage did not stretch to risking the same ghastly death as Remigio.

The banker's legs were now as rigid as tree trunks, laced with a network of iron that stuck up under the taut skin and broke through in places. In its inexorable progress towards his heart, the poison had already reached his torso, but Remigio was still alive. Fiamma looked into his eyes, sensitive to every tiny start of his body.

'How did you convince him to follow you here?' asked Gerardo.

She replied without removing her gaze from the eyes of her adoptive father. 'I used the lure of my body, just as I did for the beggars you can see around the place.'

Gerardo looked at those poor martyred souls, callously abandoned by the walls of the room.

'You used them to practise with the saw and the knife,' he said. 'You sacrificed those innocent people in your vendetta.'

'They weren't innocent!' shouted Fiamma. 'They feared this place, but lust was stronger than fear. And they paid for their sins with death.'

'And Remigio? How did you convince him to come down here?'

Fiamma stretched her upper lip, uncovering her teeth in a grimace that had little in common with a smile.

'I meant to kill him at home, then come here just for the last part,' she said, in a thoughtful tone. 'But he made the job easier.'

In a sing song voice, perhaps more to remind the banker of his errors than to clarify the facts, she explained that Remigio had hidden and listened to the conversation between Gerardo, Mondino and Hugues de Narbonne, and had decided to take advantage of the situation by getting rid of his enemy. He had sent for a young noble who owed him a large sum of money and had offered to annul the debt in exchange for the Frenchman's death. A few days later Remigio had seen Bonaga speaking to Gerardo, and persuaded the crippled boy to tell him what they'd said in return for some money. The banker found out about the underworld and paid the boy to keep the entrance under surveillance. One evening Bonaga went to report that he'd seen Gerardo and a taller, older man going down. Remigio realised that it was Hugues de Narbonne and sent for the young nobleman, who immediately posted two archers at the entrance of the tunnel. But the intended victims had managed to kill their ambushers, and when Remigio heard about the outcome of the skirmish, he became afraid.

'He feared that the young man's father would come looking for him to avenge his son's death,' said Fiamma. 'He was terrified. I advised him to hide in the underworld for a few days, in a secret place where no one would ever find him; and in the meantime, I would go and speak to the dead man's father and try to put things right. The idiot even thanked me.'

Gerardo shook his head. 'But once he got here and saw the corpses, he must have realised his error.'

Fiamma shrugged. 'At that point it was too late,' she said, darkly.

A heavy silence fell in the subterranean room, broken only by the murmur of the underground stream and Remigio's agonised breathing, as his body became more and more like a statue. Gerardo had nothing more to say. What he didn't know, he could imagine. Somehow Fiamma had imprisoned her adoptive father in the small room with the frescoes and gone home, telling everyone that he had disappeared. Then Gerardo had been arrested and she had come to visit him in jail, either to save an innocent man from being condemned or to make public her account of what she'd done. She must have planned Hugues de Narbonne's death, but with his revelations, Gerardo had made her task all the easier.

He was dumbfounded by what the woman was capable of. And yet the attraction he felt for her won over his horror. Fiamma was guilty of letting herself be overpowered by her thirst for revenge, but how much she must have suffered before falling victim to her lunacy! Watching her upright figure, her pale face framed by the blonde hair and the scar that heightened her charm instead of diminishing it, the young man felt more like taking her in his arms and covering her in kisses than immobilising her and dragging her in front of the *Podestà*, as was his duty.

It was the girl who solved his dilemma for him. In the same instant that Remigio let out his last breath, with a strangled wail and a convulsion that screwed his mouth into a smirk despite the paralysing potion, Fiamma pushed him off the altar. His body fell with a heavy thump. Then the young woman grabbed the coloured glass with her free hand, drank the contents in one gulp and lay down on the stone slab.

The meaning of her action was very clear. Gerardo ran to her, heedless of the knife that she still held in her hand. He lifted up her head, with the intention of getting her to her feet and making her be sick to get rid of the poison, but the girl murmured, in a sad voice that clutched at his heart, 'It's too late. Kiss me, please.'

They stared deep into each other's eyes, and then Gerardo slowly leaned over her and placed his lips on hers.

He told himself that he did it out of compassion for a dying woman, and he was expecting to feel disgust at kissing a murderer guilty of such bloody crimes. But the kiss set free all the love there was between them and that was waiting to come out. For a time that seemed infinite, their lips were joined, their tongues touched and their hands moved madly in an explosion of the senses at the imminence of death. Then Fiamma's breath became more irregular, her hands fell to her sides and the stiletto dropped to the ground. Gerardo pulled away from her, crying and muttering incoherently, but she opened her lips with a tired smile. 'Thank you,' she murmured, looking into his eyes.

She coughed and her mouth filled with a yellowish foam. Then, suddenly, she began shuddering with tremors as her body retched, but she forced herself not to be sick. Her body was covered in a cold sweat as Gerardo inundated her face with tears. Soon life left her and she lay there inert in her black gown. The youth held her tight for a long time, crying despairingly. Then he straightened her body on the ancient altar she had chosen for a tomb, and with the sleeve of his tunic he wiped her mouth of the fluids that her body had produced to try and combat the poison. Only when he had given her back at least some of the beauty she'd had when living did he take her in his arms and walk out, to go and help Mondino. He could have asked the Captain of the People to send some men down to fetch both corpses, but his action wasn't dictated by reason.

Mondino was concentrating on pressing the piece of cloth to his shoulder to stop the blood, ignoring the threats and protests of Guido Arlotti, who sat on the ground with his hands and feet bound. Severed Ears only had his legs tied up, but couldn't free himself because he needed his hands to stop the blood and guts from pouring out of his stomach, as they were in danger of doing with every movement he made.

'My friend's going to die and you will too if you don't let me go and call for help,' said Guido all of a sudden. Exhausted by his efforts to intimidate Mondino, he was now trying to persuade the physician through compassion and fear.

'I'd prefer to die of a loss of blood than set you free,' said Mondino. 'So don't waste your breath. And anyway,' he added jutting his chin up the lane, 'here are the *Podestà's* men.'

A pair of city guards in battledress had appeared at the corner of the lane, followed by Pantaleone Buzacarini, in military tunic and coat of mail, with more armed men behind him. The street was so narrow that they had to walk two by two, almost touching one another. Mondino told the Captain all that had happened, and Pantaleone immediately began to take command.

He took one look at Severed Ears' wound and, with a blow of his sword, ended the man's suffering. 'He would have died on the way back anyway,' he said, shrugging his shoulders. Then he stood in front of Guido Arlotti.

'You heard what the physician said,' Pantaleone remarked, in a practical tone. 'He claims it was you who spread the groundless rumours that caused the uprising and I have every reason to believe him.' Guido began to protest, but the Captain interrupted him with a brusque wave of the hand. 'I'm not interested in your excuses. You'd better confess immediately, because it is only on account of whoever is behind all this that you'll be taken to prison in one piece. Otherwise, before I have my men take you away, I'll cut off your hands.'

Without waiting for a reply, he lifted his sword and made a sign to a guard, who grabbed Guido's shoulders, pushing him flat on to the ground.

'Wait!' cried Guido Arlotti. It was the first time that Mondino had seen him look genuinely frightened. 'I am in the service of the Inquisitor, Uberto da Rimini. Don't touch me or you'll pay dearly for it.'

Before the Captain could reply, the soldiers suddenly turned and went silent. Mondino followed their gaze and saw Gerardo emerging from the ruined house, with the same slightly mad expression that he'd worn on the night he'd knocked on the door of the *Studium*. And, as on that night, he was carrying a dead body.

Gerardo approached in silence, holding Fiamma Sensi in his arms as if she were his bride. The girl's blonde head was resting on his chest, her scar was hidden and her black robe hung down to the ground in soft folds. In those squalid surroundings, her beauty was even more striking.

'Is this the murderer we've been looking for?' murmured a soldier, incredulous.

'Yes,' confirmed Gerardo, in a tired voice. 'In the under-world behind me, you'll find her last victim, Remigio Sensi, her adoptive father.'

The Captain of the People lowered his sword and shaking himself out of the enchantment that seemed to have descended on everybody present, he began to bark orders. Three men were to take Guido Arlotti to the *comune*, after he had been gagged to stop him crying for help or trying to incite the crowd. Pantaleone looked each of the soldiers in the eye and told them that if the prisoner escaped, he would pay for it with his life. Then the Captain gently took the girl's body from Gerardo and passed it to two more guards, sending them to the *comune* as well. Finally he left two men to guard the ruined house and got ready to go down into the underworld, after asking Gerardo to tell him the way. Only then did the young Templar turn to Mondino.

'Master, how are you feeling?'

'Not too good. I need Liuzzo.'

'Would you like me to fetch him and bring him here?'

'No, the streets are still dangerous,' replied Mondino. 'Let's go to his house. I can walk if you give me a hand.'

Gerardo stood at his side and Mondino put his good arm around his shoulders, still holding the cloth pressed to his wound, and they set off slowly. Gerardo didn't speak and was moving as though his mind were detached from his body. Mondino sensed that he had felt something much deeper than mere sympathy for Fiamma Sensi and didn't want to interrupt him in his pain. But when they came out into Piazza di Santo Stefano, now deserted and silent, Mondino couldn't hold back any longer.

'And the secret of the iron?' he asked.

'Lost,' replied Gerardo, in a distant voice. 'Fiamma injected the preparation into her victims' hearts with a hollow stiletto. When she drank the poison herself, the knife fell out of her hand and the powder went all over the floor.'

Mondino absorbed the information with genuine suffering, like another stab of the knife. Adia had been right about the stiletto, but in the end the secret was lost and it had all been for nothing.

'Fiamma injected the poison into Remigio's feet,' Gerardo went on, after a pause. 'The banker's blood was turned into iron before my very eyes. If you think a horror of that kind could be of use to science, you could examine his body.'

Mondino heard what he said, but couldn't manage a reply. He felt himself grow weak, and concentrated on the massive job of putting one foot in front of the other, in a series of small steps that would get him to safety. He'd worry about the rest later.

They hobbled towards Via San Vitale, draped over each other like two drunks after a night of revelry.

Epilogue

The port of Corticella, lit by the June sun, was a hive of activity. Mondino got slowly out of the boat, careful not to make any sudden movements with his right arm. The injury to his shoulder was healing well and he'd soon make a complete recovery, but Liuzzo had told him to take it easy for another month.

He opened the purse that he carried at his belt, pulled out a coin and paid the boatman. Then he made his way to the inn where Adia was staying, forcing himself not to walk too fast.

He couldn't wait to hold her in his arms again. During the trial of the heart of iron murders, as people had begun to call them, he had put her completely out of his mind in order not to betray her. He and Gerardo had agreed just to mention a sorceress who had not been able to help them and who, after Guido Arlotti and his accomplices' attack, had moved away. No one had contested their statements. A mystery had been unveiled. What might have been a stain on the competence of the *Podestà* and the Captain of the People turned out to be the greatest success of their careers and neither were interested in digging any deeper. So much so that the trial for Fiamma Sensi's crimes was overshadowed by a much more important one: that of the Templars of the province of Ravenna, concluded on 21 June with the recognition of their basic non-involvement with respect to the charges. Rinaldo da Concorezzo had ordered the knights to undergo a simple purgation. In practice, they had to report to their archbishops and declare their orthodoxy, supported by at least seven witnesses of proven faith. Then they would be free again.

No one yet knew how Philip the Fair and Pope Clement V would react to the sentence, but the news had spread rapidly all over Europe. Mondino wasn't really that interested in the fate of the Templars and from what he understood, even Gerardo meant to renounce his vows. The young Templar had seen with his own eyes the deviations that could occur in even the purest and most devout monastic order, and he had decided to serve God as a layman.

The result that both had appreciated was Uberto da Rimini's demotion from the position of Inquisitor.

Once he had been informed of the Dominican Inquisitor's impropriety, machinations and use of blackmail, the Archbishop had ordered Uberto to make a pilgrimage to Rome on foot, without escort or money, providing for himself along the way by asking for charity. After which he would be sent to occupy himself with the saving of souls in an obscure mountain parish on the Via Francigena.

In all that time, which only lasted a few weeks but seemed an eternity, Mondino had seen Adia only once. Having heard he was injured, she had paid him a visit. It was a couple of days after Rainerio's funeral and the sadness that weighed down on the house had meant that they met as strangers. But now that the horizon was clear once again, Mondino couldn't wait to see her. As he walked along he could already smell her scent and feel the warmth of her amber skin.

He had thought about waiting until he was completely recovered before going to see her, but Adia had sent for him the previous day, saying that she had something important to tell him. As he slowly made his way among the carts, piles of goods, boatmen and farmers, Mondino couldn't stop wondering what she wanted to tell him. Perhaps she had finally found a passage to Venice, on a boat big enough to take her books, dogs and donkey, and she wanted to say goodbye to him before leaving. But he hoped and, at the same time, feared that the news was something else, to which he didn't know how he'd react.

He found her in the garden behind the inn, busy feeding her mastiffs, which were both tied to the same chain. She was wearing a white sleeveless gown, a pale green brocade bodice and a pair of leather sandals. On her head she had a simple young girl's linen cap from which her dark curls were escaping.

As soon as she saw him, she put down the bucket full of entrails and bits of stale bread and ran to fling her arms round him.

Mondino wanted to kiss her on the mouth, but she moved away, stiffening slightly.

'What's wrong?' he asked, alarmed. 'Aren't you pleased to see me?'

'It's not that,' replied Adia.

The dogs, at the sight of their food, had begun to drool and pull at the chain, but without barking or yelping, as other dogs might have done. Mondino took a step backwards.

'Well, at least tell me what you wanted to say to me. I didn't sleep at all last night for worrying.'

Adia took a step backwards, dropping her eyes. Her joy as she had run towards him had seemed spontaneous, but now she was nervous. Confused, Mondino could no longer keep silent about what had been tormenting him since the night before.

'Are you with child? Is that what you wanted to tell me? If you are, don't worry, I—'

He was interrupted by Adia's crystalline laugh and stood there stupefied and offended.

'You're such a gentleman, and I'd expect nothing less of you,' she said, laughing again with her eyes. 'But that's not it.'

'What is it, then?' Mondino was relieved not to have to take care of an illegitimate child and yet he couldn't quite hide his disappointment.

'Wait. First, I'll deal with the dogs.'

She walked over to the mastiffs, picked up the bucket and poured the contents on to the ground. The two animals slavered copiously, but waited for her to give the order before they began to wolf down the food with grunts of satisfaction.

'Let's go to my room,' said Adia. 'I want to show you something.'

They went up to the first floor. She took him into her room and offered him the only chair. It was pulled up to the table on which there was a large open book and an unlit candle in an earthenware stick. Mondino only needed a glance to recognise the text.

'How do you manage to convince people that you are a country sorceress,' he joked, 'if you have Averroes' *Destructio Destructionis Philosophorum* on your desk?'

'It wouldn't make any difference what it was,' she answered, picking up her blackened kettle from the brazier and pouring a cup of *atay*. 'None of my customers know how to read.'

While Mondino sipped the amber liquid, Adia pulled a cloth bag out of the enormous sack of straw that did for a bed. She went up to the table, closed the book and laid out the two maps with the directions to the secret cave in Spain in front of Mondino.

'So, it's about these parchments?' asked Mondino. 'But now it's obvious that they're fake.'

When Adia had come to his house, he had given her the second map that Fiamma had given to Gerardo in prison. But since Fiamma herself had said that it was useless, he hadn't expected any great revelations.

'They say that two wrongs don't make a right,' replied Adia. 'But it's not always true.'

'What do you mean?'

She leaned over and pointed at the red circle on the first parchment.

'This is not the point of departure as I thought, but the point of arrival,' she said. 'Fiamma's father hid his secret well.'

She explained that the words *al-hamrā* didn't mean the Alhambra in this case, the red fortress in the Arab city of Granada, but the final phase of an alchemical transformation, called 'the red one'.

'I don't understand,' said Mondino. 'What does it mean?'

'That the journey indicated on here is not to be travelled on foot or horseback, it describes the stages to obtain alchemical gold.'

'How can you be certain of that?'

'Because the two maps go together. Each is incomprehensible unless it is put next to the other. Do you remember the incomplete verses on the first parchment? Well, the missing words are on the second. What is confusing is that the information is so well disguised that studying the maps one has the impression that they describe real places.'

'So,' cut in Mondino, 'you are telling me that you've discovered the secret of alchemical gold that so many scholars have spent centuries searching for?'

'I'm telling you that, studying these parchments carefully, I've discovered *one* way of obtaining it.'

Remembering the parable of the mountain that she had told him before, Mondino nodded. 'And not the right one, I imagine.'

'No.'

'But nonetheless, the result is the same.'

'Yes. If you were to scrupulously follow the process, you could, without too much trouble, make alchemical gold, which, as you know, is quite different from normal gold.'

'If it really does exist,' murmured Mondino, 'it would be infinitely more precious than normal gold: an elixir capable of healing any injury, any illness, and of prolonging life for hundreds of years ... It can't be true. It must be legend.'

Adia shook her head silently. She was remarkably beautiful, but just then Mondino could think only of the secret, the main reason for which he had been running after a murderer and had risked both life and career. In her diary, Fiamma didn't mention how she had made the powder used to transform veins and blood into iron, and by now Mondino had abandoned the dream of making a complete map of the human vascular system. No one had wanted to touch Remigio Sensi's body – fearing who knows what evil spell – and the banker had been left where he died. The civic authorities had ordered that access to the underworld be closed and, after chasing out all the beggars who lived there, they had flattened the ruined house, concealing the entrance to it and filling in the gap with tons of bricks and stones. Mondino, relieved to have escaped death and renewed his collaboration at the *Studium* with Liuzzo, had not wanted to push his luck by asking for permission to study Remigio's body. He had made himself stop thinking about anything other than work and family responsibilities, particularly since his father had died.

And now Adia had come back to stimulate that part of his soul that was best left dormant.

'Have you tried it?' he asked, with a tremor in his voice.

He was almost pleased when she answered no.

'So you don't know if it really works.'

'No. And I don't want to know. There's been too much blood spilled for this secret.'

'However, I do want to know.'

Adia stared at him, horrified. 'You don't know what you are saying.'

'You're wrong. I understand your speeches about the importance of the manner in which things are done, but think of what a great gift to humanity the elixir would be.'

While he was speaking, Adia had not stopped shaking her head for a second. 'Think hard about it, please,' she said then, in a sorrowful tone. 'Fiamma's father killed the man who passed the secret on to him, the Turk who was found in the port of Gharnata without a heart. Then he in turn was killed and his daughter left scarred in mind and body, all because of that secret. The Templars who wanted to get hold of it have committed unspeakable vileness and then ended badly. Fiamma killed them and herself after a life of suffering. Do you really want to end up like them?'

'No, but—'

'But what? Don't you understand what you would be setting in motion? You would be killed as well. Powerful and greedy men slaughter one another to possess the secret by taking it off others, because for the greedy, power only exists if it is possessed by the few. And if the news got around that the elixir had been found, the deaths would increase. Perhaps there would even be a war, in which the Church would participate, make no mistake. Do you seriously want all this?'

Adia looked at him with an intensity that was almost frightening. Mondino sensed that she would judge his worth as a human being by the reply that he gave her. He wanted to please her at all costs. And yet his scientific mind wouldn't let him. Her tale of the mountain was suggestive, but not very credible. When a physician operated on a patient, what mattered was how the operation turned out. If it went well, the patient got better even if the physician were a murderer and a contemptible creature.

'What would you do, then?' he said, finally, preferring to answer the question with another question.

'I would destroy these maps,' she said. 'But they are not mine to destroy. I need your permission.'

Mondino was silent for a long time, aware of the implications of what he was about to say, but incapable of holding his tongue.

'I would like to see alchemical gold, at least once,' he said, in a low voice. 'If you don't want to help me, tell me what I must do. I'll try it on my own.'

Adia stared at him with an indefinable expression. 'Only you can decide your fate,' she said, pointing to the pen and ink on the table. 'Write.'

Mondino could hear the hostility in her voice, but nonetheless he picked up the quill, dipped it in the ink and began to note down on the back of one of the maps all the steps that Adia was dictating to him. When there was no room left he wrote on the second map, filling half the page.

'That's it?' he asked.

'There's something else. The most important thing.'

'What?'

Adia turned to the brazier, where the embers could just be seen glowing red beneath a layer of ash. She sighed, and when she turned back towards him she held in her hand a small knife with an inlaid wooden handle that she must have taken out from beneath her gown. Mondino looked at her in amazement, too surprised even to react. Adia came towards him with the knife in her hand, and held it out with the handle facing him. Her eyes were moist with tears, but she wore a decided expression.

'Show me,' she said.

'What?'

'That you are prepared to do it alone.'

Stupor twisted Mondino's lips into a nervous laugh. 'Please, put that knife away.'

'If you want to obtain the elixir following the system I dictated to you,' said Adia, deeply serious, 'you need a human heart that is still palpitating. Take mine.'

Mondino didn't know what to think. He was convinced it was a joke and was trying to work it out, but couldn't. She continued to gaze at him holding out the knife by its blade.

'Adia, I could never hurt you—'

'Whereas you could hurt someone else?' she broke in, aggressively. 'If an unknown woman was standing in front of you now, would you kill her to make your dream come true?'

'You mean that you can't obtain the elixir without murder?'

'To obtain it in *this* way, no,' said Adia, without dropping her gaze. 'That's what I've been trying to tell you from the beginning, but you don't want to listen.'

'I didn't understand,' said Mondino, softly.

'Liar.' Adia's expression was implacable. 'You understood perfectly, but you didn't want to think about it. That's how the worst atrocities are committed: without thinking. Now make up your mind.'

Mondino bent his head. It was pointless to reply. Now there was only room for decisive action. He would show Adia, but above all he would show himself what stuff he was made of. How much he really was prepared to risk in the name of science.

Without hesitating, he took the knife she was holding out to him and put it on the table, next to the book by Averroes.

Then he put an arm round her shoulders and with his free hand threw the maps on to the glowing embers.

Turning to kiss her, while the parchments with the secret of immortality curled at their edges and became ash without producing a single lick of flame, Mondino was stunned by how all the rest counted for nothing at all.

Acknowledgements

I would like to thank all those who have helped me in the various phases of drafting this novel. My friends, the writers Silvia Torrealta and Matteo Bortolotti for being patient readers and giving their advice. Piero P. Giorgi, Adjunct Professor at the University of Queensland, for details concerning the life and work of Mondino; Professor Rolando Dondarini, medievalist in the Department of History at the University of Bologna, for reading the book from the point of view of historical and urban reconstruction. All the staff at Piemme, who have the gift of making every working discussion feel like an enjoyable chat, and in particular the editorial director Maria Giulia Castagnone, for believing in this story from its first synopsis, and my editor Francesca Lang. My thanks also go to my agent Roberta Oliva, and to Giancarlo Narciso, without whom I might not have become a writer.

Deepest thanks go to my wife Ana Luz for believing in my work from the very beginning, and often more than I have myself.